PRAISE FOR CHARITY NORMAN'S *REMEMBER ME*
WINNER OF THE NGAIO MARSH PRIZE FOR BEST NOVEL

'Beautifully observed . . . a moving and memorable read.'
—*The Sydney Morning Herald*

'A stunning mystery; an astounding piece of work.'
—Ngaio Marsh Awards Judges

'Charity Norman establishes herself as an author in control, aware of her audience and adept at her craft. Compelling . . . a nuanced page-turner.'   —Fay Helfenbaum, *Books+Publishing*

'Sensitive . . . beautifully written.'   —Adele Parks, *Platinum*

'Count me as a huge fan of Kiwi author Charity Norman. Her books are gritty, gripping, suspenseful and heartfelt, and always total page-turners . . . get your hands on a copy of *Remember Me*.'
—Nicky Pellegrino, *New Zealand Woman's Weekly*

'Norman continues to explore humanity, confront large issues and find new ways to tell a great story.'
—Craig Sisterson, *New Zealand Listener*

'Clear-eyed and compassionate . . . Like all Norman's books *Remember Me* is also a compulsive read . . . extraordinarily moving.'   —Catherine Woulfe, *The Spinoff*

'An atmospheric and emotional tale of family, mystery and love . . . an extraordinarily talented storyteller.'   —Kelly Rimmer

'A suspenseful page-turner.'   —*Bella*

'A riveting tale of betrayal, love and deception . . . The added pleasure of reading Norman lies in the humanity she packs into her novels; there are no false notes, no sentimentality . . . just an incisive look into what makes humans tick. The result is a wonderful and heartbreaking novel that will stay with readers long after the final page is turned. Highly recommended.'
—Greg Fleming, Kete Books

'Powerful and heartbreaking.' —*Better Reading*

'A superb piece of mystery fiction, imbued with compassion and insight into the human condition, an absorbing and well-crafted novel from an assured writer.' —Living Arts Canberra

'An emotionally charged story full of compassion and warmth . . . incredible storytelling.' —Compulsive Readers

'Charity Norman writes the sort of stories that are difficult to discuss without giving away their endings . . . Norman gets it right.'
—*North & South*

'Powerful, intense, conflicting and deeply atmospheric, *Remember Me* is an extraordinary tale that I rate very highly . . . Magnetic, mysterious, thought provoking and stirring.'
—Mrs B's Book Reviews

'A phenomenal story . . . stunning.' —1Girl2manybooks

'In *Remember Me*, Norman deftly weaves together two time-lines to create an engrossing, slow-burn mystery that builds to a devastating and unexpected end.' —*The Weekend Australian*

'highly recommended.' —Mrs G's Bookshelf

'Crisp, compelling writing that's not just enjoyable to read, but a lesson in how to write.' —Maya Linnell

'beautifully executed with humour, heartbreak and absolute connection between the reader, the storyline and the potential consequences for everyone.' —*Newtown Review of Books*

'engaging and thoughtful, an absorbing read.' —Book'd Out

'With an all-consuming plot and characters that feel vibrantly real, this is an engaging and eloquent novel . . . even as it dances through memories with devastating results.'
—Liz Robinson, LoveReading

CHARITY NORMAN was born in Uganda and brought up in successive draughty vicarages in Yorkshire and Birmingham. After several years' travel she became a barrister, specialising in crime and family law in the northeast of England. Also a mediator and telephone crisis line listener, she's passionate about the power of communication to slice through the knots. In 2002, realising that her three children had barely met her, she took a break from the law and moved with her family to New Zealand. Her first novel, *Freeing Grace*, was published in 2010. *Second Chances* (*After the Fall*) was a Richard and Judy Book Club choice and World Book Night title. *The Secrets of Strangers* was a BBC Radio 2 Book Club choice for 2020, shortlisted for Best Crime Novel in the Ngaio Marsh Awards for Crime Fiction, and for best International Crime Fiction in the Ned Kelly Awards. *Remember Me* won the 2023 Ngaio Marsh Award for Best Novel.

Also by Charity Norman

HOME TRUTHS

CHARITY NORMAN

ALLEN&UNWIN
SYDNEY • MELBOURNE • AUCKLAND • LONDON

First published in 2024

Allen & Unwin
Cammeraygal Country
83 Alexander Street
Crows Nest NSW 2065
Australia
Phone: (61 2) 8425 0100
Email: info@allenandunwin.com
Web: www.allenandunwin.com

*Allen & Unwin acknowledges the Traditional Owners of the Country
on which we live and work. We pay our respects to all Aboriginal and
Torres Strait Islander Elders, past and present.*

A catalogue record for this book is available from the National Library of Australia

ISBN 978 1 99100 690 5

Set in 11.5/16.5 pt Sabon LT Pro by Midland Typesetters, Australia
Printed and bound in Australia by the Opus Group

10 9 8 7 6 5 4 3 2 1

For Hetta
And for Sebbie, her little black dog

Being in a minority, even in a minority of one, did not make you mad. There was truth and there was untruth, and if you clung to the truth even against the whole world, you were not mad.

George Orwell, 1984

February 2022

They're coming back. Single file, sombre, poker-faced. The most powerful people in the world.

They seem burdened by the weight of their verdict. Day after day they've sat in their two rows, following every turn of the story—watched the anxious parade of witnesses, winced at exhibits, listened to a cacophony of voices. They're old hands now. A couple of them cast fleeting glances around the courtroom, but most stare dead ahead as they take their seats for the last time.

People reckon if a jury won't meet your eye, you're going down the pan.

The silence screams with tension, thrums with it. The defence barrister pours a glass of water, cracks his knuckles, as though he hasn't noticed that the jury are just feet away. His opposite number is frowning determinedly at her open laptop. People sitting behind them keep their heads down, pretending to be engrossed in random documents. A uniformed police sergeant slips in through the doors from the lobby, taking a seat in the public gallery between those who loathe the defendant, and those who love her.

The judge is the only one who openly watches the twelve as they find their places. She nods her thanks to the bailiff, who shuts the door behind them. She has warned that there must be calm in this room, whatever happens now. She runs a tight ship.

The victim—sorry, the *complainant*—isn't in court to hear the verdict. He turned up for just one morning, gave his evidence from behind a screen and was escorted out by minders immediately afterwards. He's not been back. By his own account, his life was shattered by what the defendant did to him. He's a broken man, physically and mentally. He'll never recover from the cold-blooded cruelty of that attack.

His supporters are here, though, craning their necks for a better view of the person in the dock, who represents everything they most hate and fear. On the first day they planned to yell abuse from the public seats, but the judge put paid to that. *Behave or leave*, she said, and they weren't going to leave. They've watched every second of the trial. They want to make sure justice is done. More of them shiver in the blustery wind outside the building: a small but passionate mob, waving slogan-covered signs. They too have been warned by the judge. And every day she's reminded the jury: 'You must decide this case *only* on the evidence presented to you in this courtroom. Ignore everything else. Ignore everyone else. Ignore what you've read on placards, or on social media, or anywhere else at all.'

But how can they possibly tune out the noise? Everyone in the country is an expert on this case. Everyone knows what That Woman did. That Unwomanly Woman. That woman who tortured a man.

The defendant sees everything from the dock. She's come to know them well, these twelve who hold her future in their hands—or at least to know the people she imagines them to be. The scowling, surly figure in the back row, for instance. *Mr Darcy*. The handsome boy with the beard and man bun, who always looks as though he's suppressing laughter, or possibly tears. The motherly woman in the dove-grey hijab; the older one wearing cornflower-blue glasses, who uses a walking stick but moves gracefully, ramrod-straight, head high. *The Dancer*. Five men, seven women. All ages, all stages. From eyebrow piercings to pearls, dreadlocks to short back and sides. And this common purpose, this civic duty. This power.

Until today, they've been mute. Now they will speak, and their words will define the rest of her life.

If a jury won't meet your eye, you're going down the pan.

Her thoughts shriek and flutter, a bird in a forest fire. When the clerk asks her to stand, her shaking legs threaten to give way. She grips the rail of the dock, suspended over a yawning abyss.

You're going down the pan.

Fifteen hellish seconds. The clerk leafs through papers, clearing his throat. 'Would the foreperson please stand?'

It's The Dancer. She gets to her feet neatly, without fuss. She's been taking notes throughout the trial, especially during the summing-up. No surprise that they've chosen her.

'Has the jury reached verdicts upon which you are all agreed?'

'We have.'

The judge's pen is poised. The entire room seems to stop breathing.

'On count one,' begins the clerk, 'attempted murder, do you find the defendant guilty or not guilty?'

ONE

August 2019

Livia

It began so beautifully, the day that destroyed us. Soft moorland air billowing our bedroom curtains, Scott singing in the shower while I plumped up my pillows and luxuriated, humming along with his Elvis Presley imitation, 'Can't Help Falling in Love'.

Two sets of feet racing along the floorboards of the landing. Heidi appeared first, copper hair a wild halo around her face, falling almost to her waist. Thirteen today. She wasn't as sophisticated as her friends, with their crop tops and phone-scrolling and world-weary air. She still thought it was fun to bounce on her parents' bed, and her smiling eyes looked like crescent moons.

'Happy birthday!' I cried, holding out my arms.

'Thanks, Mum.'

Noah clambered up beside us, still in his dinosaur pyjamas, handing me his greatest treasure.

'Bernard wants a cuddle.'

'Good morning, Bernard.' I pressed the soft bundle against my shoulder: a sloth with a goofy grin, whose charm lay in his relentless state of bliss. According to his label, Bernard was made of one hundred percent recycled plastic bottles. Every school day, before setting out, Noah propped him on the windowsill in the hall—'to watch for me coming home'.

My bed became a less peaceful place as both children began to use it as a trampoline. Up, down, up, springs creaking, Heidi's hair flying.

'*Happy birthday to you, squashed tomatoes and stew,*' warbled Noah, wheezing with the effort of jumping and singing. '*You look like a monkey . . . and you act like one too!*'

He was repeating this hilarious punchline when Scott appeared from the bathroom in jeans and a sweatshirt, rubbing his hair with a towel, grinning as he joined in the song. Without missing a beat, Noah launched himself right off the bed and into his arms. Such trust. He was five years old, and never doubted that his father would catch him. Not back then.

Heidi was still bouncing. 'What time's our bike ride, Dad?'

'I reckon . . .' Scott kissed Noah's head before setting him down. 'Let's say ten thirty. That'll easily put us in Thorgill by lunchtime.'

'Promise you don't have a meeting or a pile of marking or something?'

'Nope! This is your day. Ten thirty on the dot.'

When asked what she'd like to do on her birthday—a trip to the cinema, tenpin bowling, a sleepover with friends?—Heidi didn't hesitate: pancakes for the four of us, followed by a bike ride with Scott. They planned to stop for lunch at the tiny pub at Thorgill, a hamlet on the roof of the world.

'Not that I don't love you and Noah, Mum,' Heidi assured me now, sliding an arm around my neck. 'But it's a long way and all uphill and you don't like biking.'

'I certainly don't. Noah and I will have a happy morning in the library.'

'And I *always* have to share Dad with half of Yorkshire.'

We clattered down our lethally steep staircase. For some reason best known to himself, Noah always hopped the whole way on one foot—*thud, thud*. Left foot on the way up, right foot on the way down.

The Forge was cramped and very old, as were many houses in Gilderdale. Visitors exclaimed rapturously at the sloping ceilings and wobbly floorboards, but its rooms felt increasingly small as our family grew. The narrow stairwell led through a wooden-plank door, straight into the kitchen. Stone flags, peeling shelves. Previous owners had added an extension, a sitting room adjoining the kitchen. The cottage's ancient plumbing gurgled like an elephant's stomach, the roof leaked more every winter. But it was our home, the only home our children had ever known, and we loved it.

Heidi opened birthday cards at the kitchen table while I snuck a glance through my work emails. Even on a weekend there were always more, more, more.

'From Uncle Nicky,' said Scott, producing a giant envelope, at least a foot square.

'Aw, Nicky!' Heidi slid out a card covered in cartoon kittens— thirteen of them, each with a coloured bow. Playing with balls of wool, washing their paws. Two miniature tigers were engaged in fluffy battle.

'He read every single birthday card in the shop,' Scott said with a groan. 'Hundreds of 'em. We were in there for an hour.'

Heidi picked up Scott's phone from the dresser. 'I'll ring him now. I bet he's waiting.'

I listened as she chatted to her uncle. *Thanks, Nicky! I love my card!* Life had dealt my brother-in-law a tough hand: type 1 diabetes along with an intellectual disability. He was getting on for fifty, and middle age had brought anxiety. He seemed to have a new worry every day. Sometimes—when his little dog, Ozzy, had fleas, or his washing machine was broken—he kept Scott talking for hours, fretting.

By the time Heidi's call was over, Scott had tied a spotty apron over his jeans and was mixing pancakes, giving a running commentary in his 'French chef' accent. His hair was still wet, tousled from the shower.

''Ere we have zee—how you say?—zee flour? And zee shoogar, and a leedle *pinch* of baking powder.'

He'd barely begun before his phone rang: that perky Nokia tune.

'Don't answer it, Dad,' begged Heidi. 'Voicemail is your friend.'

But he did. Of course he did. Scott had time for everyone. He was head of the English department at Barmoors High School, year eleven dean and picked up every stray project along the way—drama club, poetry society, school trips. I could hear the caller's strident voice from across the kitchen: Jane Jameson, chair of the board and dragon mother of an entitled little blighter called Dylan. Instead of reminding her that she was bothering him in the summer holidays, Scott listened politely, grimacing as he forced down one of his cowpat-coloured superfood shots.

'Yes . . . no,' he murmured. 'Mm. I really understand your concern, Jane, but Hazel's already done a lot of work on that risk assessment.'

Heidi rolled her eyes at me. 'See? Half of Yorkshire.'

The green muck in his glass was the latest potion he'd bought from our local holistic retreat. Megan and Marcos Espinoza—nice people, at the wacky end of the alternative health spectrum—guaranteed the potency of their herbal anti-inflammation remedy. Scott, who swore by all their stuff, reckoned it was miraculous. The knee he'd sprained last month became pain-free overnight, apparently. I suspected the placebo effect.

At last, he managed to extricate himself from Janet's call. He was about to ladle a batch of pancake batter into the frying pan when the jolly ringtone sang out again. Someone from his mum's care home, letting him know about a minor change in medication.

'They never stop,' Heidi whispered. 'I don't believe this bike ride is going to happen.'

The first pancake was sizzling when the inevitable happened. That bloody ringtone.

Sighing, Heidi picked up the phone and looked at the screen. 'It's Uncle Nicky again. That's that, then.'

She seemed defeated as she handed the phone to Scott. She and I took over at the stove while he reassured his brother.

'We're not going to see Mum today, mate.' Endlessly patient. 'You're quite right: we normally do on Saturday. Yes, and normally we go to Tesco as well. But it's Heidi's birthday, remember? You just talked to her. So we'll do Mum and Tesco tomorrow instead. Look on your calendar, you've written it there . . . can you see that? Great! Okay, Nicky. I'll pick you up tomorrow morning.'

He ruffled his hair, listening.

'*Who* came round? Not again! Don't talk to those people, they're scammers. You didn't give them your credit card details, did you? What company are they from? Okay, I'll tell them to get lost.'

'Double-glazing people again,' Scott huffed, once he'd rung off. 'They got him to sign a contract this time. He doesn't even own his home!'

'Sharks.' I took Scott's phone out of his hand, setting it onto vibrate mode and putting it back on the dresser. 'That's been three calls in twenty minutes. It's Saturday, it's your daughter's birthday—the rest of the world can manage without you for a while.'

I kissed him. Then I kissed him again, and once again for good measure.

'Ew,' said Heidi.

That was such a happy time: pancakes, coffee, presents, and no more Nokia tune. Heidi kindly went into raptures over her present from Noah: a velvet choker with a green butterfly hanging from it. He'd wrapped it all by himself, albeit rather haphazardly. She put it on, said she'd wear it forever. My parents had sent a hardback copy of *Anne of Green Gables*. Finally Scott winked at me, slipped out and returned wheeling a new bike, far bigger than the old one which Heidi had long outgrown, with a lightweight frame and tyres wide enough to tackle moorland tracks. Our neighbour had let us hide it in his garage for a fortnight.

Heidi seemed overwhelmed, silently touching the smooth red of the handlebars before whirling around to hug us both.

'Try it out,' said Scott. 'We can adjust the seat, or drive down to York and change it, if the size isn't right for you.'

She was already wobbling her careful way around the table and into the sitting room, navigating Noah's scooter and chain of toppled dominoes, her crescent-moon eyes gleaming.

'I can't believe you got me this. Can I ride it today?'

'You bet,' Scott replied, pouring us both more coffee. 'It's an outdoor bike, not a kitchen one.'

Everything took longer than we'd planned. It always does, doesn't it? Half past ten came around, and the cycling party wasn't ready to leave. Scott turned on the garage lights and lifted his own bike down from the wall, only to discover a puncture.

Heidi was horrified.

'Dad! We'll miss the pub. They close their kitchen.'

'Plenty of time,' he assured her calmly, flipping his bike upside down. 'If you scoot inside and fill up our water bottles, I'll throw on a spare tube.'

Meanwhile, I went to search the car for a lost library book. Noah was lying flat on his stomach by our pond, his long fringe flopping over his face as he fed the goldfish. He was a real Doctor Doolittle, that boy. His fish recognised him. They'd swim right into his cupped hands—something they wouldn't do with anyone else. Random cats in the street wound around his ankles. When we visited friends with dogs, he always ended up throwing balls for them. He loved all animals, which made it extra tragic that we couldn't keep pets ourselves because of his severe asthma. Only goldfish, and Bernard the Sloth.

Scott's mother reckoned he was an old soul.

'Look at his *eyes*,' she whispered, when he was barely old enough to sit up. 'Grey as smoke, with that dark blue ring. Those long, long lashes. The knowing way he stares at you.'

'That serious expression on his face right now? Wind.'

She tutted at my levity, reaching out to touch Noah's bald head. 'You've been here before, haven't you, darling?'

She was a loving mother-in-law, Geraldine, and she hadn't had it easy: a son with complex health needs, a husband whose heart gave out long before he reached retirement. We were close, but we'd never see eye to eye when it came to karmic reincarnation.

'He's just a chubby baby,' I said. 'The cutest baby in the world, I'll grant you, but that's genetics. He's the spitting image of Scott at the same age. I've seen the photos.'

'This child has lived many lives, I'm telling you. His spirit has wisdom. His *spirit*.'

Remembering her words now, I smiled as I watched Noah, in his red shorts and Superman T-shirt and little sandals, talking amiable nonsense to a shoal of fish.

•

Why am I obsessing over the details of that day? Why am I trying so desperately to describe where everyone was, what everyone was doing, at precisely ten forty-four on one particular Saturday morning? I do it all the time. I replay the scene at night, lying alone in the darkness as I dread the light of another day. Because this is the moment that changed everything.

If, if, if.

If I could go back in time.

If I could change just one small thing.

If I could save us.

In my imagination it is exactly ten forty-four. We're frozen in our various places around the house, the garage, the garden. Two bright-eyed blackbirds pause their hopping and pecking on the lawn. Even the fish stop flitting among Noah's fingers.

And then we're in motion again.

•

Noah sat up; the birds took flight into the apple tree. Heidi came dancing outside, a water bottle in each hand, exclaiming at how quickly Scott had mended his tyre. 'You're a legend, Dad!' Father and daughter high-fived.

'Just gotta grab my phone,' Scott called, heading indoors.

He returned a couple of minutes later.

'Can't find it,' he said to me. 'I could have sworn it was on the dresser.'

'Pockets?' I suggested. 'Backpack?'

But it wasn't in his pockets, or in the backpack he always took cycling. It wasn't on the kitchen dresser where I'd last seen it, or in the garage, or by the soap in the downstairs toilet. He and I stood in the kitchen while I called his number from my own phone. We listened for the buzz-buzz of its vibration. Nothing.

'Sorry,' I said. 'My fault for putting it on silent.'

Heidi appeared in the doorway, clutching their bike helmets.

'No luck? Never mind, Dad. I've got mine if we have an emergency.'

Scott hated to be separated from his phone. He worried about Nicky, whose diabetes wasn't well controlled despite the best efforts of both Scott and the health services. He worried about Noah, whose asthma could flare with terrifying swiftness. He worried about his mum, who'd been struck by dementia and lived in a care home. He always patted his pockets before walking out of the front door, just to check.

But Heidi was hopping up and down. The Thorgill Arms had one small bar with smoke-blackened beams, a log fire in winter. They closed their kitchen early if there were no customers wanting lunch.

'Sod all phone signal on the moors anyway,' I reminded him. 'Might as well leave it behind.'

His gaze ran along the dresser one last time before he accepted defeat.

He and Heidi swung onto their bikes—the whirr of chains, the crunch of wheels on the gravel, Heidi waving to me as she turned off the drive and headed with her dad towards the moorland road, both of them bent over their handlebars.

I caught the first, gentle scent of heather flowers drifting from the moors. Sunlight shimmered on the ripples of our pond, on Noah's dark blond hair, on the sumptuous foliage of the lime and ash trees along Back Lane, the square tower of Gilderdale Church. I found the missing book under the passenger seat. All seemed well.

But it was already happening. The first domino had already fallen.

If Scott hadn't needed to fix a puncture, if I hadn't been looking for a picture book, if Heidi hadn't been so desperate to get started on that bike ride.

If, if, if.

TWO

Heidi

Dad and I cycled across the moors in all that clean wind and sunshine. To reward ourselves for pedalling up the steepest hill, we stopped to have a drink of water and admire the view. The heather was just starting to bloom, waves of pink and purple stretching away for miles. I could smell it, and the peaty bracken unfurling alongside the dry-stone walls. I swear it's the most beautiful place in the world.

The Thorgill Arms was still serving lunch. We sat at a picnic table in the garden watching the world go by, with sheep grazing nearby. I took a selfie of us making faces at the camera. Dad didn't have his phone, so for once it was just him and me. I complained about my friends, Maia and Keren, who'd fallen out and weren't talking.

'Literally not speaking,' I said, as I soaked my Yorkshire pudding in gravy. 'They both bitch to me about the other one. So that's awkward.'

Dad agreed that it must be. 'Communication is vital,' he said. 'Never stop talking to people, no matter what they do.'

'Have you ever stopped talking to anyone?'

'I've tried. Can't shut up long enough.'

The ride home was mainly downhill, which was lots of fun. But as we came freewheeling along Back Lane, I spotted Anthony's grey car parked outside our house. My heart sank into my trainers. Now I'd have to share Dad again.

Imagine a lumbering bear from Teesside, with a try-hard American accent. That's Anthony Tait. He and Dad were flatmates at university, but that was years ago; they'd only met up again recently. He and Mum appeared from the house while we were pushing our bikes into the garage. She looked delicate beside him, wearing the ankle-length skirt and baggy cardigan she'd thrown on that morning, long hair all twisted up and spraying out of a butterfly clip on the back of her head—ginger, the same colour as mine, though she insisted on calling it 'copper'.

But something had changed. There was something broken about her. She was gripping her elbows, hugging herself.

'Tait! Look what the cat dragged in!' cried Dad, as he lifted his bike onto its holder in the garage.

'I've been trying to call you on Heidi's phone,' said Mum. 'No signal.'

Dad turned away from the bike, dusting off his hands, smiling. In that second, he was still a happy person. 'Sorry! Something important?'

Then he took a look at Mum's face, and his smile faded. It was only about four o'clock, on a bright and sunny afternoon. But I felt the world get darker. I did. The light dimmed.

'Nicky,' she whispered.

'What about him?' Dad looked from her to Anthony. 'Hypo?'

Neither answered.

Dad was already moving towards his car. 'Where is he? Home or hospital?'

'They found him unconscious in his garden,' said Mum. 'A courier delivering a parcel. Someone called an ambulance and they took him to York, but . . .' She laid her hands on Dad's arm, resting her forehead against his shoulder.

Dad's whole body sagged, as though someone had hit him over the head with a hammer. A weird quietness filled the garage. It felt like a bomb about to go off. I didn't know sadness could sound like that: complete silence, on the verge of an explosion.

'No,' he said, with a hopeful, twisted smile. 'Can't be. They've got the wrong person. I spoke to him this morning. So did Heidi— didn't you?'

'The police were here,' said Mum.

'I talked to him.' Dad sounded desperate now. 'He was fine.'

Anxious, kind Uncle Nicky. He'd got up this morning without any idea of what was coming. I imagined him brushing his teeth, maybe humming—he had a lovely mellow singing voice, like Dad. It took him a long time to dress himself but he always looked smart. I'd phoned him about my birthday card and we had a cheerful chat. He called Dad about the double-glazing people. But then he must have slid into one of those scary episodes in which he was like another person. Confused and strange, sometimes angry. He only needed a cup of sweet tea or a glucose tablet.

He only needed . . .

That was when I understood what I'd done. It hit me full in the stomach, like a football kicked by a giant, knocking the air out of me.

'C'mon, man,' said Anthony, dropping his big hand onto Dad's shoulder. 'Let's get you a drink.'

I trailed after them as they trooped inside. Dad sat bolt upright at the kitchen table. He didn't want any alcohol, so Anthony put the kettle on. Mum went to check on Noah who was watching telly in the sitting room. I heard her trying to be breezy, pretending everything was normal. 'Okay, Captain Noah? What are you watching?'

I was curled up in the rocking chair in the corner of the kitchen, by the low windowsill with its trailing pot plants. I felt as though I'd never breathe again. My birthday cards were propped up along the sill. The biggest and brightest by far was Nicky's kittens. He'd written inside, in his tidy handwriting: *Happy 13th Birthday to my favourite niece! Nicky and Ozzy XOXO*

Mum reappeared in the archway, holding up Dad's phone in its black case. 'Look what Noah found,' she said.

Dad shrugged as if he didn't care, but my heart broke into a headlong gallop. I knew *exactly* where Noah had found that phone.

'Way down the back of the armchair,' added Mum. 'He was making a fort with the cushions. God knows how it ended up down there. Maybe it fell out of your pocket when you were doing up your cycling shoes.'

She put it on the table and began to rub Dad's back, talking about practical things. The police had given her a number to call; they wanted Dad to go to the hospital to identify Nicky's body.

Dad was sighing, reaching for his phone. There was nothing I could do to stop him. I watched in despair as he swiped the screen.

'Missed calls,' he said. 'Some from you, when we couldn't find the phone. Five from Pam at the Malt Shovel. She'll have seen the ambulance in the road. And . . .' He stared at the screen. 'Nicky. Nicky tried to ring at ten forty-four. He's left me a voicemail.'

The football whacked into my stomach again, and this time I doubled up in the rocking chair.

Dad was tapping the screen frantically, navigating through to voicemail. He turned on speakerphone.

'*You have one new message. To listen, press one.*'

We all leaned closer. Then Nicky spoke to us.

'*Hi, Scott? You there, Scott?*'

It was obvious he wasn't well. His voice sounded flat, like he was stunned. I'd seen him in this kind of a state.

'*Scott? Um, I've been out in the garden, I can't get back in. Can't get my door open. You there, Scott?*'

He began breathing heavily, muttering to himself.

'*You there, Scott? Come on, say something!*'

Anger now. I loved my uncle. He could be a massive fusspot, but he was *never* angry—except when his blood sugar dropped too low.

A series of loud thuds, which must be Nicky trying to get back into his house, maybe hitting or kicking his front door. More muttering. Then—and this was the worst thing—we heard long, high-pitched cries.

'*I've lost my cat. Cat's run away. Come and help me. Scott? You there, Scott? I've lost my cat.*'

For at least a minute, the four of us listened to the terrible sound of Nicky crying like a little boy. When he spoke again, he could hardly get the words out.

'*Please, Scott? Please?*'

He kept on trying to talk, but after that his words slurred into one another and made no sense. Finally he drifted into silence.

Dad pressed the palm of his hand over the phone, as though to shush a crying child, or perhaps a dying brother.

'He doesn't have a cat,' said Mum.

'Ten forty-four,' Dad whispered. 'We were still here at ten forty-four. I'd have driven straight over. I should never have gone out without my phone. Why didn't I . . . why didn't I . . .'

And then he made a noise, a cross between a yell and a wail. He didn't even sound like a human being, let alone my cheerful dad. People talk about someone being 'a broken man'; now I knew what that meant.

I rushed up the stairs to my bedroom, where I jammed a pillow over my head. The tears made it wet. I felt as though sadness was ripping my heart out of my body.

Please, Scott? Please?

While Dad and I cycled on the moors, poor Nicky was falling over in his garden. While we were taking our selfie and eating Yorkshire pudding among the hollyhocks and bumble bees, he was in an ambulance with lights and sirens. And at some moment on this sunshiny day, Uncle Nicky had left us forever.

Mum came to find me. She took the pillow off my head and sat on the bed, stroking my hair.

'It's so stupid,' I moaned. 'All he needed was a cup of sweet tea.'

'I know what you mean. It does seem senseless.'

But she didn't know what I meant. And she must never find out.

THREE

Livia

I was in a family room at the hospital when my mother rang. Scott had been led away somewhere to identify Nicky's body. He'd wanted to go alone.

'I've just phoned Heidi to wish her many happy returns,' said Mum, 'and she told me the awful news. Poor child! For the rest of her life, her birthday will have a double meaning.'

'We're all in shock. We just can't believe it.'

'Where's his little dog?'

'The landlady at the Malt Shovel has taken him for now.'

We talked for a time, going over and over what had happened.

'Heidi and Scott both spoke to him this morning,' I said. 'Maybe he gave himself too much insulin? I used to wonder whether it was safe for him to manage that by himself. Maybe he's not been eating properly. Maybe he knew he was in trouble but couldn't get to food because he was shut outside. Maybe he was never going to have a long life.' On I went, maybe after maybe.

'Dear Lord,' sighed Mum. 'That lovely man.'

I ended the call as the door to the family room opened, and Scott stumbled in.

20

'It's Nicky,' he said, as if there'd been any doubt.

He was with a woman who introduced herself as Emma, one of the doctors—youngish, medical scrubs, rubber clogs on her feet. It was she who met the ambulance when Nicky arrived, she who pronounced him dead at twenty past one that afternoon.

Scott sat on the sofa, holding his head in his hands as Emma answered our questions. There would be an autopsy, she explained, but all the signs were that Nicky's death was the result of hypoglycaemia. He arrested in the ambulance.

'Would he have been aware?' I asked. 'Did he suffer?'

'Not at the end. Of course, we don't know for sure what level of awareness people have, but he was unresponsive when the ambulance crew arrived. His systems would already have been shutting down.'

'Was everything possible done for him?' asked Scott.

'Everything.' She looked him in the eye. 'But it was too late.'

•

The sun had set, leaving sullen fire along the western horizon. Scott seemed absent as I turned out of the car park, the shadows of street lighting flowing in a silent waterfall down his face. I glanced at him from time to time, but I couldn't begin to reach him.

Once we'd crossed over the York ring road, he dragged his phone out of his pocket.

'I keep expecting him to call,' he murmured, looking at the screen. 'Drove us nuts, didn't he, phoning all the time? Huh. I'd give my right arm to have him ring me now. C'mon, Nicky. C'mon.'

Scott and I were thirty-odd when we met, weekend guests of mutual friends. Stephen and Belinda were blatant matchmakers and they hit the jackpot with us. I felt irresistibly drawn to this teacher called Scott Denby, with smoke-grey eyes and a hint of a Yorkshire accent, charmed by his combination of physical confidence and slight social awkwardness. Our hosts' tiny children hurled themselves at him; he'd stagger along with a giggling child holding on to each leg. And he was terrific at reading aloud, throwing himself into all the voices without a shred of self-consciousness. Even the cat seemed to single him out for smooches.

He and I sloped off for long walks together on that first weekend. We talked, and talked, and talked some more, putting the world to rights through the hay-scented summer evenings, knocking back whisky and listening to jazz long after our hosts had turned in. He spent the second night in my bedroom. By the time I dropped him at the station on the Sunday evening, we both sensed that our lives might be about to change significantly.

I phoned him the following morning.

'I've got two tickets for *The Mousetrap* on Saturday,' I said, 'and a friend has just cried off.'

The first part of this statement was true; the second was a shameless lie. But here we were, flirting over pre-theatre drinks in a West End bar: a probation officer and an English teacher, both of us on the rebound.

'There's something you need to know about me,' he said.

He looked so serious that I leaned closer, preparing myself for a confession of heroin addiction or bigamy or some scandalous sexual proclivity. Instead, he began to describe his older sibling.

'Nicky's a wonderful brother,' he insisted. 'He understands people. He understands *me*. It's just that he needs support with day-to-day things, otherwise he wouldn't be able to live independently.'

'I see,' I said. But I didn't. I *really* didn't.

Scott turned over an imaginary poker hand.

'Cards on the table. The reason I went back to live in North Yorkshire, work there, and plan to stay there for the foreseeable, is because of Nicky. He can't handle change. He's got his little rented cottage, the locals all know him. Mum drops by every day, but she's not so well herself now. Whatever happens, whoever else is in my life, Nicky will be a priority.'

'So, applicants for the job of soulmate are buying two guys for the price of one?'

'That's about it.'

I downed the last of my drink, thinking about what all this might mean in practice. I was impressed by his devotion to his brother; not so sure about being tied to one part of the country.

'My mum is a firm believer in soulmates,' added Scott, smiling affectionately. 'And reincarnation. Dad only made it to sixty. She thinks he'll be reborn one day and so will she, and they'll be together again.'

'Maybe they will.'

'Hope so.'

I caught myself thinking that his eyes really were extraordinary. Battleship grey, with startling indigo rings around the iris.

Get a grip, I scolded myself. *Stop swooning over a pretty face.*

'She'd approve of you,' he said.

'Me? Why?'

'Because you're a Gemini and I'm Aquarius and we met at the summer solstice. That makes us a dream team.'

'Nice to know that!' I laughed, though I wasn't sure he was joking. 'You're not into astrology, are you, Scott? And horoscopes, and fortune-telling? Because—cards on the table—I'm definitely *not*.'

'No! No. But I mean . . .' He was fidgeting, tapping his glass with a teaspoon. 'You never know, do you?'

'Yes, you do. It's pseudo-science.'

'I try to keep an open mind. *There are more things in heaven and earth, Horatio.*'

'The stars of the zodiac aren't even on the same plane,' I protested. 'They're hundreds of light years apart. Put five thousand random dots in the sky and people are bound to join them up, bound to imagine patterns and gods and whole mythologies. That's what the human mind does: it looks for patterns. Always has, always will. It's in our psyche.'

Scott shrugged, still tapping his glass. 'It's a nice idea, though, isn't it?' He looked up at the ceiling of the pub, as though the night sky were scattered across it. 'That there's some kind of guidance up there. That it isn't just random chaos.'

'A celestial road map?'

'*Any* kind of road map.'

I couldn't help but smile. Each to their own, I thought. And there was something arresting in his honesty.

'Was it through random chaos that we met last weekend?' he asked. 'Or was it all part of a plan?'

It was on the tip of my tongue to point out that our getting together jolly well *was* part of a plan—Belinda and Stephen's plan. There was nothing random about it; our friends had set us up, laying on candles and booze and tinkling jazz.

But I didn't want to spoil the moment, so I leaned across to kiss him. We left the bar and strolled in blissful harmony, our arms around one another and our steps in sync, through gilded evening sunshine to St Martin's Theatre.

The Mousetrap. Scott guessed whodunnit before the last act, but I didn't see it coming at all.

And now here we were—a marriage, a mortgage and two kids later. Still in harmony. Stephen and Belinda, meanwhile, were messily divorced and had drifted out of our lives.

But Nicky had died today. We'd failed him.

I was concentrating on the road. It was narrow just here, and unlit, and some jerk in a van was driving about two feet behind us with their headlights on full. When Nicky's voice came blasting through the car's speaker, I practically swerved into the ditch.

'*Hi, Scott? You there, Scott?*'

I pulled into a gateway and slammed on the brakes, letting the aggressive van driver roar past.

'For goodness' sake!' I protested. 'Not again. Not now.'

Scott often bluetoothed his phone to the speaker, playing music or talking books for the children. It connected automatically. Now it amplified Nicky's voice, made every breath as painful as if this man we loved was dying on the back seat of our car. I already knew the ending of the story. I pictured him confused, trying to get into his house. I saw him reaching for his phone, his lifeline, calling his brother and waiting in vain for an answer.

We sat in our car in the darkness and cried, all the way through to Nicky's final words.

'*Please, Scott? Please?*'

Neither of us moved. Winded, wordless. The dashboard was a faint outline in the glow of Scott's phone.

'You didn't know,' I said at last. 'You couldn't be available for him every second of every day.'

'I could have been there for him *this* time.'

I started the engine again, pulled out onto the empty road. We had to get home. We'd left a pair of very upset children with Anthony, and that was a big ask. Noah might have an asthma attack. Stress tended to trigger them.

As the car gathered speed, Scott put his earbuds back in.

'Don't listen to him again,' I begged. 'Delete that message. I know it's your last link with Nicky, but it's unbearable.'

'I owe it to him to listen.'

I gave up. Perhaps it didn't matter. He might delete the message from his phone, but he'd never be able to wipe it from his memory. Neither would I.

FOUR

Scott

He'd lived ten doors down from this church. Less than two weeks ago, he lay dying in a pile of leaves, within spitting distance of where I stood right now. I knew the squeak of his gate, the loose bricks on his garden path, the blue paint of the front door. He'd light up when I walked in, greeting me with the same joke every single time: *Scotty! Beam me up, Scotty!*

Anthony kept me company while we waited for the hearse. I'd rather have been alone, but it was kind of him.

The thing is, when a person dies, you can't hibernate. You're hurled into a storm of bureaucracy and organisation, and everything has to be done quickly. Closing accounts, cancelling benefits, talking to the solicitor. Emptying a lifelong home, with all its treasures and echoes and shadows. The toothbrush on his basin, the clothes that smelled of him, the half-eaten pie in his fridge, the newspaper open on the table, the crossword book with his handwriting. Do I bin the scarf he always wore, the photos by his bed, his *I Love Ozzy* mug? Ferrying clothes and bric-a-brac to the Salvation Army shop. Organising a funeral, the final chance to celebrate a man who lived almost fifty years and meant the world to me. Erasing a human existence. All in a few days.

Anthony got it. He couldn't do enough for us. He was growing a fledgling business, but again and again he made the thirty-mile drive south from his flat in Guisborough, while Livia was heading in the opposite direction towards the Probation Service office in Middlesbrough. And here he was again, on the worst day of all, right beside me.

Yorkshire was wilting in a heat wave. I regretted my dark suit. Anthony tied back his mane of hair and took off his jacket. Livia, Heidi and my mother had already gone into the church, Livia pushing Mum's wheelchair. Noah was at a friend's house for the afternoon. I envied him. I'd much rather be splashing in a giant paddling pool.

I greeted well-wishers through a fog of unreality. Random figures drifted up to me through an underwater world, like in a dream. The district nurse who'd made such a difference to Nicky. Childminder Chloë, who'd been in our lives since Heidi was a toddler—a grandmother herself now, opinionated but kind. A group from Nicky's day centre, piling out of their van. Regulars at the Malt Shovel. Neighbours. They all told me how they valued their chats with Nicky, missed the familiar sight of him and Ozzy in his garden. My brother made the world a better place and he should still be in it.

Pam crossed the road from the Malt Shovel with Ozzy at her side. We couldn't adopt him because of Noah's asthma, so she'd offered to take him in. The dog's tail was down, his steps slow. I knelt to stroke his ears, his glossy black head.

'He's pining for his dad,' said Pam.

'A lost phone, for God's sake,' I muttered to Anthony, once Pam and Ozzy had moved on. 'A lost phone. Why?'

My friend shook his head, laying his hand on my shoulder. Seconds later I found myself wrapped in the arms of the Espinozas, owners of Rosedale Retreat, a health spa on the moors. Everyone liked Megan and Marcos. They were in their sixties, successful but community-minded, their annual New Year's bonfire party a local fixture. They kept an impressive herb garden from which they made their own products—they'd once shown me round it. Livia was sceptical, but I wasn't. Not at all. They had a wealth of knowledge, and their remedies worked.

I introduced them to Anthony, who was immediately included in their hugs.

'Nicky was a beautiful, beautiful soul,' said Megan. 'It's always the angels we lose.'

Marcos seemed quite agitated, unusual for him. 'He could have been cured. This should never have happened. He should have lived a long, healthy life.'

'It's wicked,' added Megan. '*Wicked.*'

I was taken aback. 'You mean his diabetes could have been cured?'

'We wish we'd talked with you about it before now,' said Marcus. 'There's a lot behind all this. We're only just learning ourselves.' He patted my arm. 'I'm sorry—now's not the time.'

Megan pressed a brown paper bag into my hand.

'Use it as you would tea. Every day. Don't let them give you sleeping pills or antidepressants.'

The bag was labelled *Loss Plants, for Healing and Grieving.* I thanked Megan as I tucked it into my pocket.

'I hope I haven't just received Class A drugs,' I said to Anthony, as we watched the Espinozas wander off through the graveyard hand in hand.

We both chuckled. It's what we do, isn't it? We laugh. We make weak jokes. We pretend the world is still bright.

●

I was five the first time I first witnessed one of Nicky's episodes—the same age as Noah was now. Nicky would have been about ten.

We were on our way to Coniston Water in the Lake District. We used to go every summer, staying in the same static caravan in a holiday park. It was still dark when we left home, and our parents had promised us breakfast at the Happy Eater on the way. Dad was driving, towing what he called 'the *other* love of my life', an eighteen-foot trailer sailer named *Geraldine* in honour of Mum. I have a vivid memory of his ears under his tartan flat cap—his holiday hat—my trainers scuffing the back of his seat.

The sun was up when Mum turned around, peering at Nicky. *You okay? D'you want a biscuit? ... Nicky?* I remember him screaming, *I can't see! I can't see!* and Dad swerving onto the hard shoulder, Mum sprinting around to yank open my brother's door. They gave him jam on a spoon straight out of the jar, and the bottle of Lucozade they always kept handy.

The next thing I remembered was sitting cross-legged on a bed in a hospital A&E department. Apparently I sulked because we hadn't gone to the Happy Eater. I must have been a selfish wee tyke.

We made it to the Lakes in the end. Dad took a whole roll of holiday snaps, which ended up in an album: *Coniston, 1980*. Mum and Nicky shelling peas outside our caravan; Dad looking ecstatic as he hoisted *Geraldine*'s sails; Nicky and I in midair, holding hands, as we leaped off the bow into the lake.

I had only the haziest memories of the holiday itself. What I did remember—much too vividly—was the suffocating terror that filled the car that day. I inhaled the fear. I never forgot it.

All Nicky needed was a spoonful of jam. All Nicky needed was for me to answer my phone.

All I needed was to understand why it happened.

•

The black car was gliding down the village street, sunlight reflecting off its gleaming surfaces. Anthony and I stood back as it pulled in between the traffic cones at the kerb. And there was the coffin, with its spray of mauve heather flowers.

The funeral director shook my hand before opening the back of his hearse. The man was a model of professional mourning: solemn but competent, like a profoundly depressed sergeant major. He marshalled us pallbearers—Anthony, two men from the day centre, a couple of friends from the village and me—and paced ahead of us in his black top hat as we carried Nicky into the church. Ozzy trailed along behind. He didn't need to be on a lead. I swear that little dog knew we were bearing his master.

For one of the few times in his life, my brother was the main event. Nobody was patronising him, he wasn't a problem or a patient. Death gave Nicky a new dignity.

'We have come here today,' said the vicar, 'to remember our brother Nicholas.'

I'd finished writing my tribute at four o'clock that morning. I'm an English teacher, for crying out loud; I ought to have been able to think of something erudite and poetic to say. But it was impossible to condense a whole person into four minutes. Nicky had been there all my life—literally *all* my life. I had photos of six-year-old Nicky making me giggle with his funny faces, as I sat grinning toothlessly in my baby chair. On pocket money days, he bought chocolate buttons which we ate in our den at the bottom of the garden. He sat beside me on the school bus, trying to help me with my very first homework, though by the time I was eight it was beyond him. He rejoiced when my children were born, sobbed with me when our dad was taken from us. He was my oldest, closest friend. And now I was expected to sum him up in a few words.

'Nicky was my best man, here, in this very church. I can see him now, sitting beside me in the front pew: grey silk ties, carnations in our buttonholes. My carnation came askew but he put it right for me. Thank you, Nicky. When the organ stopped playing and everyone fell silent, I knew Livia had arrived. That's when Nicky nudged me and said loudly, *If you're gonna beam up, Scotty, now would be a good time!'*

A ripple of laughter among the mourners. Same church. Same time of day, same time of year. And Nicky was wearing the same suit.

I talked about the chocolate buttons, the den in the garden, the easy friendship Nicky offered to everyone he met. I described how I gradually began to notice he was different from other kids his age. But by different I didn't mean that he couldn't keep up with their conversations. I meant he was kinder, wiser, less of a show-off.

'Sometimes, Nicky,' I said, reaching out to touch the coffin, 'you needed my help. But far more often I needed your wisdom. Sometimes I worried about having to look after you my whole life, but more often I worried about how I'd ever manage without you. I relied on you. You relied on me too, and I'm so infinitely sorry that . . .'

Empty words. I could see Mum in her wheelchair, tears glinting on her creased cheeks. As the organ struck up for a hymn, I crouched beside the coffin on its trestles. I laid my palms on the polished wood, my face on it. I didn't care if I looked unhinged; Nicky was inches away, in his best man suit.

You there, Scott?

You there, Scott?

'I'm *always* here,' I used to promise him. 'I might be busy, I might be teaching or in a meeting—it doesn't matter. Leave a message if I don't answer. I will ring you back straight away. Okay?'

'Okay.'

'Promise?'

Eyes wide, he nodded. 'Promise.'

Come and help me. Scott? You there, Scott?

He kept his promise. I didn't keep mine. All he needed was a cup of sweet tea. All he needed was for me to do my bloody job. *Sorry, sorry, sorry.*

Anthony and the other pallbearers had joined me. I was carrying my brother out of church. Tomorrow the sun would rise on a world without him in it.

Livia

Ozzy lay by Nicky's empty chair in the Malt Shovel, his nose between his front paws. Heidi sat beside him on the floor and tried to cuddle him, but the most he could manage was a despondent wave of his tail. The sight of that sad little dog undid me. He was our last link with Nicky.

I'd been back at work that week. We were chronically understaffed at the Probation Service, never enough hours in the day, but Scott had somehow managed the bleak practicalities on his own. I'd suggested booking a weekend getaway for all of us after the funeral. Maybe an Airbnb on the Northumberland coast.

The pub was airless. People drooped in the heat, fanning themselves with their funeral service sheets. Some drank too much. Scott drank *far* too much, but everyone understood, and Anthony—his faithful bodyguard—kept plying him with sandwiches. It's never the people you expect, is it? The ones who have your back when the chips are down. Anthony was a mansplainer, the sort who tells a female probationer officer all about how the criminal justice system works, and the Californian twang didn't quite ring true. But the man had a heart of gold. He'd been a godsend.

I'd noticed a couple sitting at the back of the church and assumed they were former pupils of Scott's, but afterwards, in the Malt Shovel, Anthony turned up with them in tow. They were both tall and lanky, wearing dark clothes. Maybe still in their teens. They looked embarrassed.

'Scott, I know you'll want to meet Lawrence,' said Anthony. 'He's the courier. And this is Sophie.'

It took me a second. The courier. *Of course.* The police had told us about this young hero, and we'd asked them to pass on our thanks. He'd heard a dog barking and looked over the hedge to see Ozzy trotting in anxious circles around the body of a man half buried in a pile of leaves. Poor Nicky must have flailed about, because the autopsy found leaf litter in his airways.

'Sorry to intrude, Mr and Mrs Denby,' Lawrence said. 'Sophie and I just wanted to pay our respects to Nicholas.'

Scott reached out to shake Lawrence's hand, clasping it in both of his.

'You called the ambulance. You put your own jacket over him. You held his hand. Thank you. Thank you.'

Lawrence, blushing, bent to pat Ozzy. 'Wish I could have done more,' he said gruffly.

Sophie had jet-black hair, a gold stud in her nose. 'We were just telling your friend,' she said, with a glance at Anthony, 'that they sent the ambulance from Thirsk! God knows why, when Malton's so much closer. Lawrence reckons it took forty-five minutes.'

'I wasn't timing it though,' said Lawrence.

'And you felt they weren't great when they did turn up,' prompted Anthony.

Lawrence shrugged unhappily. 'They just didn't seem to be in much of a hurry. The landlady—Pam—she told them he's diabetic, and they saw his special bracelet, but they didn't seem to get it. He was still alive when they arrived, still breathing. I honestly thought he was going to be okay. To my mind they faffed about. I think they'd lost him by the time they got him in the ambulance.'

Scott had turned pale. 'Weren't they trying to save him?'

It was time to shut this speculation down. Finding Nicky had obviously been a dramatic and disturbing experience for this very young man. He and Sophie must have talked about it endlessly. People naturally look for someone to blame.

'I'm sure they did everything they could,' I said firmly. 'And maybe the wait felt like longer than it really was.'

'Yeah.' Lawrence scratched his nose. 'It's just . . . it seemed to take forever, just sitting with him in that pile of leaves, feeling useless. The emergency operator had me get him into the recovery position and check his breathing, so I did that. I was talking to him the whole time, don't know if he could hear me. I was listening for the sirens. I just wanted to hear a siren! I kept telling him to hold on, hold on. I said, *The ambulance will be here soon, they'll have you back on your feet in no time.* I kept promising him it would be okay, but . . .' His voice gave out.

Sophie put her arm around him. 'But it wasn't,' she said. 'And they didn't.'

●

We'd left the curtains open. I woke to the silver light of dawn, the cool of the morning. A blackbird stirred, warbling peaceably in the apple tree beyond our bedroom window.

Scott lay on his side, facing away from me. I knew him so well. I sensed his wakefulness, the angry misery as he rubbed his face with both hands. I moved closer, resting my cheek against his back.

'The funeral was perfect yesterday,' I told him. 'So much love and affection for Nicky. And your tribute did him proud, you had that whole church laughing and crying. Everyone was telling me how much it meant to them.'

'My brother died among strangers. All the fine words in the world won't undo that.'

I tried a different tack.

'People are kind, though, aren't they? Pam adopting Ozzy and taking all the catering off our hands. Lawrence caring so much. And Anthony—what a star.'

Scott sat up, reaching for his clothes.

'Don't,' I whispered. 'Don't listen to Nicky anymore. Delete his message.'

'And then what?'

'We get on with our lives.'

'Done and dusted.' A brief, bitter laugh. 'Brush him under the carpet.'

'You have to let him go.'

'What's the point of getting on with our lives if they can be taken away just like that? If a lovely, healthy man can die in his garden, just because of a lost phone. What's the point of any of it?'

'It's four in the morning,' I said, as the door closed behind him.

I have a degree in psychology, for God's sake. A master's in criminology. I've worked with hundreds of people during the darkest, most disastrous phases of their lives. It's what I *do*. But when it came to my own husband refusing to sleep, listening over and over again to his brother's cries for help, I had nothing to offer.

Best to let him work through his grief, I thought, as I closed my eyes. *Early days. This will pass.*

FIVE

Livia

We never did take that weekend getaway. Scott was in no mood for sandcastles on a Northumbrian beach. He claimed to be swamped with curriculum planning before term began, and I didn't press him. It would have been tricky for me to take more leave, anyway.

Ten days after the funeral, a flight of swallows flowed and swelled over the church tower. The neighbours' tabby—Tabitha—came to wind around my legs as I hung washing on the line.

'Hi, Tabs,' I murmured, sitting down on the edge of the terrace.

The cat purred, butting her head against my hand, her fur warm and dusty in the sunshine. Butterflies flickered among the buddleia flowers along our hedge. Noah was making *brrm-brrm* noises as he steered the pedal car we'd recently inherited from my sister's children. He was wheezy this morning, out of sorts, but he was loving that car.

'It's heaven, Tabs,' I sighed, as I stood up again, steeling myself to walk inside. 'This right here. Heaven. No need to go traipsing off to Northumberland.'

It wasn't at all heavenly indoors. Heidi had barely emerged from her bedroom since Nicky died—for some reason, she seemed determined to blame herself. Scott slumped at the kitchen table, watching a YouTube video on his laptop, looking like death warmed up in a microwave. His eyes drooped at the corners. I prattled desperately about the swallows, the butterflies— perhaps he'd like to get out for a bike ride? In the end I gave up, sick of the sound of my own false positivity. I was tired of being the chirpy one. My fingers were itching to shut his laptop and tell him to snap out of it.

'You were awake all night again,' I said. 'Is it time to see the quack, maybe ask for melatonin or something?'

'I don't want sleeping pills. I've got Megan's tea.'

He replaced his earbuds and went back to his video. I began making coffee, resisting the urge to comment on his grubby T-shirt and bed hair and the fact that he hadn't shaved in days. I had another stressful week at work ahead of me. The house was a mess, washing was piling up, we had nothing in the fridge for lunch. Scott wasn't pulling his weight.

'We've run out of milk,' I announced, hurling mugs onto the table. 'D'you feel like walking up to the shop, at least? Scott? *Scott?* What are you watching?'

'Mm?'

'What are you watching?'

'This Canadian professor. Megan and Marcos put me on to him. They think it might shed some light on what happened to Nicky, and I agree.'

I was instantly suspicious. I liked the Espinozas—it would have been churlish not to appreciate their kindness and generosity—but I didn't trust their judgement. The brochure for Rosedale Retreat boasted *immersive wellness* and *naturally medicinal fare* and a *deep-cleansing mind, body and spirit regime to reverse the ravages of conventional medicine.* Scott's knee-sprain remedy was relatively conventional. Staying guests were offered crystal healing, geranium oil enemas and *joyous dancing with tambourines*, alongside ice baths and saunas. Fair enough, each to their own—no doubt many of their customers came away feeling lighter in mind as well as in pocket. But I'd not be taking any medical advice from *them*, thank you very much.

'D'you know how much those charming charlatans charge for a weekend of crystals and geranium oil up your bum?' I asked Scott. ''Cos I do. Eye-watering.'

He patted the chair beside him. 'I'll start this video again and you can see for yourself. Watch it with an open mind.'

'Black coffee it is, then,' I muttered, fumbling among the Lego castles on the table for my reading specs.

The film featured an elderly man in a cable-knit jersey, delivering a lecture at some kind of conference.

'Professor Brian Tabard,' said Scott, turning up the volume. 'He's a pharmaceutical scientist, been in medical research all his life. He got sacked for whistleblowing.'

'*You will all recognise what I'm about to describe,*' Tabard was saying. '*Many of you will have come across it in your professional lives. You'll know that those we trust to look after our health are not working for us at all. No. Whether they know it or not, they're the servants of monsters: multinational pharmaceutical companies. Those entities are both powerful and amoral, a lethal combination. A corporation has no soul. It is, by definition, psychopathic: fixated on maximising profits for shareholders, at any cost.*' The professor smiled—a shy, sad smile—took off his rimless glasses, polished the lenses. '*Any. Cost.*'

It sounded intriguing, but I could see this lecture was fifty minutes long, and I didn't have fifty minutes to spare.

'Could you just précis it for me?' I asked Scott.

He paused the video.

'Okay. In a nutshell: the pharmaceutical industry is monstrous. Side effects get hushed up. Cures are actively suppressed.'

'Why on earth would cures be suppressed?'

'Simple. Every year, these companies make billions of dollars out of the most common chronic diseases. A cure would bring the gravy train to a halt. So researchers who come anywhere near one find themselves defunded and discredited. They're written off as cranks. They're struck off. Or worse.'

I raised one eyebrow. 'Worse?'

Scott was nodding rapidly. 'Professor Tabard knew a scientist who had a breakthrough with type 1 diabetes. Cheap and simple, an absolute game-changer. It would have cured Nicky. She was close to announcing her findings when her car ran into a tree. She was killed instantly. No witnesses.'

'Surely her work would have been published anyway.'

'No! Her team disbanded. Their data disappeared from the system. None of them will talk about this cure.'

'Come on,' I said. 'He's not seriously suggesting she was murdered, is he, and all her work magically erased? Sounds like the plot of a really bad movie.'

'He's just giving us the facts.'

'Hm.' My bullshit detector was bleeping at full volume. 'What kind of a professor is Tabard, anyway? Professor of what, at which university? And how come this tale about the car crash and a miracle cure for diabetes wasn't on the news? The media would be all over it!'

Out in the garden, Noah coughed a couple of times. Scott and I both fell silent, listening for more, but all was quiet.

'Anything can be hushed up,' said Scott, 'if you've got the clout. Doesn't it strike you as odd that diabetes is still destroying lives? And asthma. And arthritis, epilepsy, cancer. We landed a man on the moon in 1969 but we can't seem to fix these illnesses.'

I put down my mug and blinked at the frozen screen. Nice Grandpa Tabard gazed earnestly back at me through his rimless spectacles. I thought he was probably a nut job. Then again, if it distracted Scott from his guilt over Nicky—gave him an hour of respite—well, better for him to blame some nebulous corporate villain instead of loathing himself.

Scott was already restarting his video when Noah coughed again. And again. And again. This time, I heard trouble. The breathlessness, the wheeze. I charged through the back door to find him coughing in his pedal car. One wheel had run into a flowerbed.

'Hey, hey,' I exclaimed, dropping to my knees beside him. 'What's happening?'

'I'm trying to—' A gasp for air, nostrils flaring. 'It won't—' Another gasp. 'I keep getting stuck. I can't get out of the flowers. I've got a tummy ache.'

'Can I have a listen?' I asked, pressing my ear to his chest. There it was: the dreaded *woosh-swash, woosh-swash.*

'Let's find your reliever,' I said, as I scooped him out of the car.

It came on fast. By the time I got him into the house he was scared, his breathing fast and shallow. I ran to grab his flare-up kit from the pantry—peak flow meter, blue inhaler, spacer, Prednisone.

Scott had been staring at his laptop, apparently mesmerised by Professor Tabard, but as soon as he spotted me fetching Noah's kit he leaped to his feet. It was a relief to see him back in the game.

'Noah?' he asked, tugging out his earbuds. 'How bad?'

We were like a military unit when it came to these asthma episodes. We knew our action plan all too well, and worked efficiently together. No need to use the peak flow meter. Noah's high-pitched wheezing, his hunched little body told their own story. He was trying to lie on the sofa, but Scott helped him to sit up while I gave him his inhaler through the spacer. One puff, six breaths. One puff, six breaths.

It wasn't working.

Scott and I kept up a determined show of calm, but there was panicked paddling under the surface. He measured out oral steroids while I tore upstairs to grab Noah's overnight bag, always packed and ready to go, along with Bernard the Sloth. It was a scene that had played out horribly often in our son's short life, no matter how vigilant we tried to be. Every time, we knew that his tiny airways might close completely, and mucus might stop life-saving medicine from opening them again. Every time, we knew he might die. Every time, we were petrified. I'd lost count of how often I'd followed the flashing lights of an ambulance, fearing what was happening in there, praying he'd be okay.

Gilderdale was a forty-minute dash from York District Hospital. As I watched Noah's stomach sucking in under his ribs, I wished fervently that we lived closer.

'Ambulance,' I muttered, reaching for my phone.

'I'll drive him. You call ahead.' Scott was already lifting Noah into his arms. 'I'm not waiting for them to send an ambulance from bloody Mars.'

•

Twenty seconds later I stood in the road, watching the brake lights of Scott's car flash on—off—on as he charged down Back Lane. A postal van was forced to swerve. Scott wasn't stopping for anyone.

After Heidi was born, we imagined ourselves with three or perhaps four children, all evenly spaced, as though human beings could be made to order. But the months and years passed, and no sibling for Heidi came along. We saw doctors, researched, learned all about secondary infertility. We'd resigned ourselves to being a one-child family when Noah burst into our lives—a miracle, with his steady gaze and constant smile. We were afraid that Heidi might be jealous after having us all to herself for the first seven years of her life, but the opposite was true. She seemed besotted as soon as she met her newborn brother, six hours old and fast asleep. She used to have long conversations with the baby, her face close to his, delighting in his laughter and gurgles. When he learned to crawl, she crawled along beside him. And he adored her too—her name was his first real word. They had a wonderful bond.

But his priceless life was fragile. He was still a toddler when he had his first flare-up, which eventually led to a diagnosis of severe asthma. By the time he was four, Heidi knew all about his long-term and rescue medicines. She learned how to use an EpiPen, *just in case*. She read bedtime stories to him, slept in his room when he was wheezy—sometimes she was first to notice and alert us to a change in his breathing. It worried me, that she was so in tune with her brother's health needs. She was only a child herself.

Scott's car had turned out of sight. I was still standing in the lane when Heidi appeared from the house. She was barefoot, in shorts and a T-shirt.

'What's going on?'

'Noah. Bit of a—'

'Not again.' One hand pressed against her open mouth. 'Is he going to die this time?'

'Of course he isn't.'

'You're just saying that. You don't have a clue. Nicky died.'

'That was very different.'

'My stupid bike ride. My stupid, *stupid* bike ride.'

I thought I understood. I carried it too, that gnawing guilt about Nicky, about how we dropped the ball. I knew it was eating away at Scott.

'It's okay,' I murmured. Hollow, minimising words. 'I'll phone ahead to warn the hospital. He'll be okay.'

'It's going to get him one day,' she said. 'One day we won't be here for him. We'll be stuck in traffic or something, and he'll be all by himself. Like Nicky. I'll be carrying my own brother into church, like Dad did.'

'It's not that bad,' I said, trying to reassure her. 'Most people with asthma live totally normal lives.'

She turned on me. 'Why the fuck does everyone around here pretend things are just dandy?'

'Heidi Denby! Wash your mouth out.'

'Seriously?' She was looking at me as if amazed by my stupidity. 'You're griping about me saying the word *fuck* when my brother's being rushed to hospital for the zillionth time? When my uncle's a pile of ashes in a box? Things aren't dandy, Mum. Things are fucking disastrous. People die.'

Funny how you can hear the unspoken distress signals from total strangers and yet be utterly useless when it comes to your own child. I gibbered a stream of platitudes—*We're lucky, we have each other, at least we're not in a Syrian city being bombed*—while she ran into the garage and emerged pushing her new bike.

'Please don't storm off,' I said. 'Where are you going?'

'Anywhere that isn't this house.'

'It wasn't your fault Nicky died. In *no way* was it your fault. It's not your fault that Noah has asthma.' I pulled a fiver out of my pocket. 'Get yourself an ice cream. And while you're in the shop, could you pick up a bottle of milk?'

She snatched the note out of my hand as she shot past me.

'It wasn't your fault,' I called after her as she pedalled away.

Heidi

'It wasn't your fault,' yelled Mum, loud enough for the whole of Back Lane to hear.

She had no idea. I was no longer the stupid little kid who jumped on her parents' bed. I'd left my childhood behind in ten seconds flat. Sometimes I woke up almost happy—until thoughts came screaming down the track like express trains, one after the other, slamming into me. I'd shut my eyes and try to stop thinking, but the more you try to dodge those thoughts, the harder they hit you.

I rode at top speed up onto the moors, trying to get myself lost among the tracks. But I didn't get lost, and I didn't feel any better. I ended up leaning my bike against the humpbacked bridge in Gilderdale, sitting among the feathers and daisies by the beck. Nicky and I used to come here on Sundays with porridge oats for the ducks. We had our favourites—that bossy one with the bright orange beak, this little guy with a limp. We gave them names like Bigfoot and Quacker. In spring we'd coo over the tiny ducklings.

A text from Mum came in on my phone: *Dad says Noah's already on the mend!*

Until the next time, I thought. *Or the one after that.*

Just a few days ago I was sitting next to Nicky's coffin. *I am the Alpha and the Omega*, the vicar said, standing at the altar with medieval dead people lying nearby, their stone hands pressed together. I had this wild urge to get up in front of everyone, in front of Nicky, and confess to what I did. But I was too much of a coward.

The ducks came quacking and gabbling, hoping I had something for them. They knew me. Quacker even pecked my foot. *Cheeky bugger*, Nicky would have said.

'Sorry, guys,' I said sadly. 'I've no porridge oats today. And Nicky died.'

They shook their tails in disgust and moved off along the grass, pecking for worms and whatever else ducks ate. That was when I remembered Mum's fiver. She'd wanted to buy me an ice cream because *she* felt guilty.

'Hang on,' I said to the ducks.

The village shop was a tiny Spar supermarket across the road from the market square. The bell rang as I went in. Mrs Ponder, the owner, was stacking shelves. A couple of customers were chatting in the wine aisle.

No ice cream for me. I didn't deserve one. I grabbed porridge oats and milk, but I didn't leave. People in here were normal, they hadn't killed anybody. I felt angry with them for being smug and guilt-free.

The aisles were cluttered. The one furthest from the door was always stacked with random hardware: string, scissors, candles, those blue blocks people put in the toilet. A pair of gardening gloves caught my eye. I took them off their peg board and turned them over, admiring their softness, their decoration of red and orange poppies. I'd never liked gardening and avoided it like the plague. When I was small, Dad and I sometimes went out to plant seedlings, but he did all the work while I played on the swing. There was zero chance I'd ever wear these gloves.

But I wanted them. I *really* wanted them.

I had almost forty pounds in a jar at home. I'd been saving up my pocket money and doing odd jobs for extra, and my aunt Bethany sent cash for my birthday. I could easily have paid for those gloves. But I knew I wasn't going to. I hung them up again and walked away, gripping my basket in both hands, jumpy and super-alert—*like a cat on a hot tin roof*, Dad would have said. More people came in, talking about the fine spell we'd been having. I felt as though I was being stalked up and down the aisles by a serial killer. I pretended to look at ice creams and cake mixes, but no matter which way I turned, I always ended up back in the hardware aisle, obsessed by those gloves: so bright, so soft.

Later, I couldn't understand how they came to be hidden under my T-shirt. I mean, I *did* know—I grabbed them off their hook and stuffed them into the waistband of my shorts. But

I didn't remember deciding to do it. It was as though my body had acted without my mind giving it the go-ahead.

I plonked milk, porridge oats and Mum's five-pound note on the counter, leaning forward so my T-shirt hid the shape of the gloves. I was terrified but electrified too. I had this crazy idea that the world had screwed me over and I was taking something back. I even chatted with Mrs Ponder, telling her the porridge was for the ducks. She said a fox had got one of them last night, feathers everywhere, poor thing, but then again, even foxes had to eat, didn't they? She counted the change into my hand. *Three, four and that's your five.* As I thanked her, I could feel the rubbery fingers of the gloves I was stealing pressing against my stomach.

The most nerve-racking part came as I walked towards the door. Past the cereals, past the bread. I felt Mrs Ponder's gaze on me, making my back prickle—but when I snuck a look over my shoulder, I saw she'd gone back to stacking her shelves.

'Bye,' I called out, taking hold of the doorhandle.

'Bye, love.'

The bell tinkled. I burst into the sunshine, feeling like Superwoman, like I could fly. Easy! I grabbed my bike and tore off across the square, laughing with an out-of-control kind of excitement. It was the first time I'd laughed since Nicky.

The ducks were snoozing with their beaks laid across their backs. I spotted a sad patch of feathers under the bridge, some of them joined together as part of what had once been a wing. The fox. I wondered how the other ducks felt about that. Did they hear her screams? Did they see these feathers and cry for her?

'I'm back!' I called to them, fumbling to tear open the box. 'Lunch is on me.'

Porridge oats scattered across the grass as I spun around and around like a whirligig. By the time I rode away, my feathered friends were tucking into their feast. I stuck my legs out sideways and whizzed down the slope of the humpbacked bridge with my hair streaming.

I hoped that brilliant, flying feeling could last forever, but I wasn't even home before I fell to earth with a thud that made my teeth rattle. I was made of lead. I hurt.

Oh my God, Heidi, I whispered to myself as I put my bike away and crept into the house. *What have you done?*

Mum was in the office, working at her laptop. She heard me coming in.

'Dad phoned again,' she called. 'Noah's much better. They'll be back tonight.'

'Great,' I said, heading for the stairs.

Part of me was hoping she'd call me back. Mum had superpowers when it came to knowing her children were up to something. It used to make me feel safe when I was Noah's age, but now my secrets were far more shameful.

I shut my bedroom door before pulling the gloves out of my waistband and chucking them away across the floor. I didn't want to touch them ever again. What was wrong with me? *Stupid, stupid,* I muttered, kicking them under the wardrobe.

I wanted to kick myself under there too. I wasn't Superwoman. I was a thief, as well as the selfish brat who let her uncle die.

Livia

The late-summer day was at an end by the time Scott carried a sleepy child into the kitchen.

'We went to the hospital,' mumbled Noah, without lifting his head from his dad's shoulder. His hair was rumpled, eyelashes long and dark against his soft cheek.

'I know,' I whispered, as I kissed him. The smell of disinfectant clung to his clothes.

'They gave me a dinosaur sticker.'

'Lucky you.'

Once he was tucked into bed, Scott and I sat at the rickety table on the terrace, debriefing over a glass of whisky. Scott's dash to the hospital sounded like all the others: triage, treatment, observation. Fear, helplessness, exhaustion.

'It never gets any less awful, does it?' I asked.

'Never does.' His face was indistinct, a pale smudge in the dark. 'They're going to contact the respiratory team, review the plan yet again. But . . .' He shrugged. 'You know.'

'I do know.'

'I never stop worrying. I worry that next time he won't make it. I worry about what kind of a life he'll have, assuming he *has* a life. How's he going to cope at secondary school? Will he be able to hold down a job, fall in love, go travelling? If he keeps taking steroids, will he end up with osteoporosis? It's so monstrously unfair.'

I agreed with him as I struck a match, lighting the citronella candle on the table. The evening was warm and scented, but we were in no mood to enjoy it.

'We do everything,' Scott said. 'Hardly any carpets, no pets, following the treatment plan to the letter. We do *everything* right, and still we live in terror of losing him.'

Noah was breathing normally now, safe in his own bed. For tonight, that was enough. The whole family was worn out. I just wanted to sleep.

Scott didn't. He was sparking with nervous energy.

'Have a listen to this,' he said, propping his phone against my glass.

I smothered a yawn. 'Really? Now?'

'I think it explains a lot.'

Moths fluttered to the light, crawling across the screen. It took a moment for my eyes to adjust to the brightness, but I recognised Professor Tabard's voice. He was in earnest conversation with two companions: one a woman with prickly hair and a silk scarf, the other a tall, black man with a London accent. According to the caption underneath the video, both were medical doctors with strings of letters after their names.

The trio sat around a table with mugs and an untouched plate of biscuits. The lighting, film and sound seemed professional, the room unnaturally sparse.

'*This is the dark secret,*' the woman was saying. I thought she might be Dutch, or German. '*Hidden in plain sight. Conventional medicine is absolutely* not *evidence based. It's not interested in cures or the alleviation of suffering. People don't want to hear this, do they? Like the children in "The Pied Piper of Hamelin", they only want to follow the nice man with the soothing music, sleep-dancing to their deaths.*'

'*So true, Birgit!*' cried the Londoner. '*Society is addicted to the reassuring myths of the* caring *doctor, the* caring *scientist.*'

Tabard held up a hand. '*The caring scientist and doctor do exist, of course.*'

'*They exist, but they work for big pharma, whether they know it or not. Like both of you, I was drummed out of mainstream medicine because of my interest in alternative therapies—drummed out and silenced, just for asking questions, for helping patients with chronic conditions. Big pharma hates cures. Curing millions quickly and cheaply is not a sustainable business model! Sickness means profit.*'

Enthusiastic agreement from the other two.

'*So how do we wake the sleepers?*' asked Tabard. '*Birgit?*'

The woman sighed. '*Big pharma has unimaginable resources. But we must unite, we must get our message into the mainstream. Our music must be more hypnotic than the Piper's.*'

Tabard wrapped up the discussion, thanking his guests before asking us to '*hit the like button*' and subscribe to his channel. Oh, and buy his book through the Amazon link. Next time, he said, he'd be discussing vaccines.

Scott took his phone back.

'You see? Noah could have been cured by now. Nicky could have had a completely different life.'

This sounded like wishful thinking to me, but now was not the moment for an argument.

'Shall we turn in?' I suggested, standing up. I leaned down to wrap my arms around his neck. 'Come on. You must be shattered.'

'I'll be up soon.'

'If you were Heidi, I'd confiscate that phone.'

He was already scrolling, moving on to the next fix. 'Lucky I'm not, then.'

On the way to bed, I stopped to check on Noah. His room was a scruffy, happy place: toys on the floor, a sheepskin rug, shelves crammed with picture books. Heidi had painted a rainbow across one wall, and stencilled silhouettes of wheeling birds among the colours. I felt proud of her every time I looked at it.

The darkness was filled with sleep. Noah's mouth was open, his cheek resting on the back of his hands. No wheezing.

I picked up Bernard the Sloth, who'd tumbled out of bed.

'Night night,' murmured Noah, as I tucked his smiling friend in beside him.

'Night night,' I whispered.

He was safe. Both our children were safe at home—and no harm could come to them here. That's what I promised myself.

SIX

September 2019

Livia

I had such high hopes for the new school year. I imagined Scott throwing himself back into work mode—he was a teacher to his core, always flat out during term time. He would forget about listening to Nicky's last message, and Professor Tabard, and all the other self-professed experts on YouTube. He'd get things back into perspective.

The first morning of term was chaos in our house. Par for the course. We'd run out of milk again. Noah couldn't find his shoes. Heidi put on her school skirt and discovered that the hem was coming down.

'They're doing band auditions, and I look like a bag lady,' she moaned.

Scott produced a box of safety pins.

'Thank God for this very advanced, state-of-the-art technology,' he said, sitting on the bottom step of the stairs while he pinned up her hem. 'Better not go through any metal detectors.'

Father and daughter set out early to drive the five miles to Barmoors High, Heidi clutching her guitar and audition music. Half an hour later I dropped Noah at Gilderdale Primary. He flew off with a flock of small friends, while I stopped in at the office to make sure his asthma kit was up-to-date and the new school secretary had all the emergency numbers to call.

Finally I headed out of town, up the steep and narrow road with dry-stone walls on either side before rumbling over the cattle grid and onto the moors. Mine must be one of the most beautiful commutes in the world. Today it felt unearthly, as rock-strewn uplands rose like islands out of a sea of mist. I switched on my fog lights, watching out for sheep, steering in and out of the clouds. I found myself thinking about Anthony, who'd driven in the opposite direction so often since Nicky died, just to support us. I'd never even heard of the man until last Christmas, when he tracked Scott down via Facebook Messenger: *Long time no see, old friend! How's life, Scotty? I'm back from the US for good. Marriage went tits-up. Got time for a pint?*

'Who is this blast from the past?' I asked, when Scott showed me the message. 'A close friend?'

'Wouldn't call him a *close* friend. We used to share a revolting student flat in Newcastle with about six others. He dropped out after the second year, failed his exams and didn't bother to resit them because he thought the lecturers were useless. I've not heard from him since.'

'What's he like?'

'Twenty-five years ago?' Scott shrugged. 'Nice enough guy. I'm not sure he liked me. Bit competitive, bit of a know-all, spent half his life down at the gym. He pissed people off by hitting on their girlfriends—my girlfriend Carrie included. She couldn't stand him.'

'Did anyone challenge him about it?'

'Carrie certainly did! He denied it point-blank.'

I was intrigued by this glimpse of my husband's past.

'Invite him here for dinner,' I suggested. 'He's probably lonely. He can dish the dirt about your psychedelic drug-taking and wild student orgies.'

Scott put his arms around me, nuzzling my hair. 'You're going to be very, *very* disappointed.'

So Anthony came for dinner, bringing the ingredients for mulled wine, which he proceeded to make on our stove, giving me step-by-step instructions in his Californian accent. *Bit of a know-all.* Our low-ceilinged kitchen seemed to shrink in his affable, shambling presence: six foot tall, maybe sixteen stone, some of which was unruly beard and hair. After the meal he showed us photos of life in California: his wife Martina, their blue-eyed husky dogs, a swimming pool and sprawling home. The couple had employed ten people in a thriving tech business until the marriage ended. Martina kept the house, the business, even the huskies. Anthony landed back in the UK with a couple of suitcases.

'Nightmare employing all those people anyway,' he said, putting away his phone. 'I'd rather keep it small. Less aggravation.'

'But you lost so much,' I said.

'Martina was an alcoholic; she had a *lot* of problems. I couldn't help her anymore. It was time to move on.'

I got out mugs and filled the kettle, wondering what Martina's side of the story might be.

Anthony's parents still lived in Teesside—*though we've never seen eye to eye*—and he was setting up an importing business out of a warehouse in Guisborough.

'What d'you import?' I asked.

'Metal fittings and fastenings. Mainly from the States. Exclusively online.'

'Metal fastenings.' I couldn't resist. 'Riveting.'

Scott laughed. Anthony didn't seem to get the pun, or perhaps he didn't find it funny.

'I'd never have picked Scotty to be the one to have it all,' he told me, as I poured his coffee.

'Really?'

'Hell, no!' He grinned at Scott across the table. 'Our boy was quite the spindly little nerd. Lived in the library like a cave troll. Those godawful specs, Jesus Christ, remember those, Scotty? Where have they gone? And look at him now! Sporty as all hell. A beautiful wife and kids, gorgeous home, job he loves. The man who has everything. Unbelievable.'

I glanced at Scott, wondering how he'd take this backhanded compliment. He was helping himself to another mince pie, with Noah snuggled contentedly on his knee. He looked completely unruffled.

'*Spindly little nerd.* Yup, I'll cop to that,' he said amiably, talking around a mouthful of pastry. 'And you were a super-ripped bodybuilder with dreams of earning your first million by the age of thirty. Whatever happened to us, eh?'

Ouch. For a second, Anthony's smile froze and a flush—anger or embarrassment, probably both—spread under his beard. Or perhaps I imagined it, because the next moment he was chortling away, asking Scott if he remembered the time Greg fell asleep in the shower and flooded the bathroom. By the end of the evening, the two men seemed to have picked up where they left off all those years ago.

And just a few months later, when tragedy struck our family, we saw the real quality of Anthony. While other friends disappeared into the shadows or sent kind texts—*Thinking of you, let me know if I can help*—Scott's old flat mate was one hundred percent there for him. We owed him so much.

Must have him over again soon, I thought, as I found a space in the car park of Holme House Prison. *Say thank you properly.*

I flicked into work mode while navigating the prison's security system. I knew the drill. I'd long ago grown used to the depressing clang of steel gates and doors behind me, the pervasive smell of a thousand captive human beings: sweat and hopelessness, stale nicotine, urine, cabbage. Disinfectant swilled all over the floors. I was used to the determinedly breezy banter of prison officers with radios, handcuffs and bundles of keys at their belts. *Come to see Shepherd again? Got his parole board coming up, hasn't he?* I was well-acquainted with the plastic chairs in the meeting room, the crazed web of graffiti on the table. These things were as familiar to me as the classroom was to Scott. I could have applied for a management role by now, but this was where I wanted to be.

Footsteps outside the open door. A reedy voice singing 'Roll Out the Barrel' had me smiling before a slender figure was shown in. I'd known Charles Shepherd for about a year, since he was moved into Holme House. I'm five foot six; he was slightly shorter, and I'll bet he weighed a whole lot less. His defining characteristic was an air of peace, the sense that he was happy in his own skin. Charles had spent most of his adult life locked up in one kind of institution or another, but I'd never heard him complain of his lot. If you met him in the street, you'd put him in the twinkly grandfather category, maybe a retired choirmaster. I mean, why not? Choirmasters can be murderers too. It's a free country.

'Livia! Thanks for dropping by to see me. How have you been? Kids okay?' He spoke quietly, each word precise.

I gave him a stock reply: 'They're fine, back at school today.' Charles knew nothing of my personal life, beyond the fact that I had two children. It was a lesson I'd learned early: protect your boundaries.

By contrast, I knew almost everything there was to know about this man, at least on paper. Over his sixty-seven years he'd amassed hundreds of court documents and reports from probation officers, mental health professionals and prison staff. Charles Mervyn Shepherd had been partially deaf since babyhood, the

result of his father repeatedly 'boxing his ears'—a chirpy euphem-
ism for violent abuse. Nobody noticed. Perhaps nobody cared.
Teachers, social workers, foster carers, children's home workers:
for years everyone thought the boy stupid and rude, commenting
on the unsettling way he stared fixedly at their faces. I'll bet some
of them boxed his ears too. But the truth was that young Charles
was very, very far from stupid. He looked at people's mouths
when they spoke, because he'd taught himself to lip-read.

His criminal career began with shoplifting sweets, and later
cigarettes, for older children. He soon graduated to swiping slates
from roofs, and thence to commercial burglaries. In his thirties
he tried to settle down: worked as a plasterer, married the girl
next door. They had a baby daughter, Jess. But the marriage blew
apart, and so did he.

That was when he fell in with a crime syndicate up in
Newcastle and really hit his stride. He carved out a niche as a
notoriously efficient enforcer, collecting debts and information
while 'discouraging' rivals. He hadn't only learned to lip-read, he
read people too, and soon earned quite the reputation for himself,
perfecting a method of persuasion that didn't call for strength,
height or sophisticated weapons.

His heyday ended abruptly when the body of a man called
Jarrod Jeffries was discovered on a park bench in Gateshead.
Charles was immediately arrested. While assessing him for
parole, I'd read extracts from hours of his police interviews. I'd
learned all I needed to know about the crime for which he was
now serving life.

DI Campbell: *Okay, so, Charles, we've established that
you assaulted Jarrod Jeffries in the early hours of Friday
morning, after he left the Big Cat nightclub. I've just
shown you some CCTV footage. Do you agree that's you
on the film?*

Shepherd: *That's me. And the big guy in the film is Jarrod.*

DI Campbell: *How well did you know Jeffries?*

Shepherd: *I've only met him a couple of times. There was nothing personal. My job was just to persuade him to settle his debts.*

DI Campbell: *Why did he owe your boss money? What was that all about?*

Shepherd: *I have no idea. I never deal with the money side of things.*

DI Campbell: *I think you do. We know Jarrod Jeffries was dealing crack. Was that on behalf of your boss?*

Shepherd: *No comment.*

DI Campbell: *It would be a big help if you'd give us a bit more, Charles. You're looking at a murder charge here. Why should you be the only one to carry the can?* [10-second pause] *Okay, Charles. You have a think about that.*

Shepherd: *It was just me. You can see on the silver screen there.*

DI Campbell: *All right. Can you tell us exactly what happened?*

Shepherd: *You've got the film, starring yours truly. You can see for yourself. I never meant to kill him, though. That's not what I do.*

DI Campbell: *We need to hear it in your own words.*

Shepherd: *My own words.* [Sighs] *Okay. I was waiting for him outside the Big Cat. I knew he was in there, I'd been told by people who I'm not going to name. I saw him leave and started following him. He was in a heck of a mess. I bet you found crack in his bloodstream, did you? Shouting at shadows. I followed him for about fifteen, twenty minutes until he sat down on that bench. I waited in a shop doorway—you can see me, on the film. He was fumbling in his pockets, lighting up a ciggy. That was when I came up behind him, chucked my belt over his head and across the front of his neck—like this—and just gave it a good tug. Like this, see?'*

DI Campbell: *For the tape ... you're demonstrating holding a belt in both hands and pulling it forcefully towards you.*

Shepherd: *That's right. Ninety-nine percent of the time, that's all it takes. Cut off their windpipe, people very rapidly change their priorities. They give you their bank PIN numbers or safe combination or whatever. Anyway, Jarrod. I kept it tight for about ten seconds, then I slackened off to let him talk. He told me to eff off. So I tightened it again, he's waving his arms and legs. I was explaining to him that I just wanted his card and PIN number. Next moment he's gone limp. Sometimes people have a bit of a nap, just for a few seconds. I didn't panic at first. I didn't panic until it dawned on me that he wasn't waking up.*

DI Campbell: *How did you react once it dawned on you?*

Shepherd: *My first thought was shit, shit, shit, this is bad. I gave him a shake, tried to wake him up—you can see me doing that. Ran to a phone box, called an ambulance. Made myself scarce. I bet you've got my voice on the call recording.*

DI Campbell: *You've done this before, haven't you? Obviously you've a right to remain silent, Charles. I've reminded you of that, haven't I, at the start of this interview? But come on, let's get some of these other offences cleared up while we're at it. We've had a few people turn up in hospital with exactly the same ligature injuries on their throats. They're all telling*

the same story about being attacked from behind by
someone they never even saw. You've got a nickname,
haven't you?

Shepherd: *Have I?*

DI Campbell: *You're smiling. You know exactly what I'm*
talking about.

Shepherd: *No comment.*

DI Campbell: *Everyone knows you've got a nickname.*
You're called the Garrotter. Why do they call you that?

Shepherd: *You tell me.*

DI Campbell: *Because garrotting people is your speciality.*

Shepherd: *It's hardly a new method, is it? The chokehold*
is old as the hills. Guards on the prison ships used it
to control the poor sods they were transporting. Even
little kids did it back in Victorian times.

DI Campbell: *Did they? You learn a new thing every day,*
in this job.

Shepherd: *The point is, I never meant to kill anyone. I've*
never in my life carried a knife or a gun. Nobody's ever
died until now.

DI Campbell: *Yeah, but if you pull on a belt around some-*
one's neck, and their windpipe's cut off, you're quite
likely to kill them, aren't you?

Shepherd: *No, no. I didn't set out to hurt Jarrod Jeffries,*
let alone kill him. I never saw that coming at all. I wish
it never happened. I wish I'd never met him.

But the jury at Newcastle Crown Court didn't believe Jeffries'
death was an accident. Charles was convicted of murder and
handed the mandatory life sentence, along with several concur-
rent terms for similar attacks and other offences. With his record,
'life' meant a very long time.

Charles was always neatly turned out, economical in his movements; I sensed a delicacy about him, as though a puff of wind might knock him down. His gentle courtesy put me on my guard when we first met. This was the first rule in my line of work, especially with lifers who had little to lose: be alert to manipulation, watch out for attempts to share confidences, to build a close friendship. Watch out for too much interest in your personal life or your appearance. I'd seen colleagues get themselves into career-ending trouble by allowing themselves to be manipulated. One of them ended up in prison himself.

But Charles didn't seem the sort to set me up for a sting. He had no need to, because after nineteen years and two applications, he was almost certain to be granted parole this time. He hadn't put a foot wrong, had steered clear of prison power games and been assessed as a low risk of reoffending. The underworld had changed in the new millennium, and so had Charles.

He used hearing aids as well as lip-reading, but I was careful to speak clearly as we ran through the plan. Release into the community was a critical period for any long-term prisoner. Many found themselves lost in a society that had changed beyond recognition. Often they had no family or friends remaining on the outside, which left them vulnerable and lonely. Charles was in touch with his adult daughter, Jess, and I'd arranged for him to live in a probation-managed address. He hadn't completed his sentence and he never would—he'd be on licence for the rest of his life.

'I see you passed your computer course with flying colours,' I said.

A modest dip of his head. 'Even the oldest dog can learn new tricks.'

'You're probably a lot more tech-savvy than I am. I've never really got into social media. I'm a dinosaur.'

He smiled. 'I bet it's safer that way. In your line of work.'

'Too true. Best to stay under the radar.'

His smile faded. 'Everything's changed, Livia. The whole world has moved on and left me behind. Telephones aren't even for phone calls anymore. Jess talks about buying rail tickets on her phone, and calling taxis. People don't even go into the bank. Is that true?'

'Partly,' I said. 'But it's easier than it sounds. You're going to be okay.'

'I have to be. I wasn't there for Jess when she was growing up. I want to do better for my grandchildren.'

'She's looking forward to having you around.'

'I just want to be normal. A boring, regular old geezer. That's my big ambition.'

For a long moment he was quiet, blinking at me. The single bulb above our heads was reflected in his glasses.

'That's enough about me. What's been happening in your life, Livia? You never say a word about it.'

'That's because it's my job to talk about you.' I was scribbling a note of our meeting, getting ready to wrap up. 'The usual. School. Work.'

'I've learned a lot in here. I've noticed that people who moan the least often have the biggest troubles. You've got a bit of a worried look about you today. I'm just wondering whether all's well in your world.'

'I'm fine. You focus on your future.'

He stood up, pushing his chair under the table. 'Sorry. I'll mind my own beeswax.'

I felt as though I'd just snubbed a friend. Since the moment a pair of solemn police officers knocked on our door to break the news about Nicky, I'd been in crisis mode: supporting Scott, fretting about the children, teetering along the tightrope between mourning and crass jollity. Until now, nobody—not one person— had asked how I was doing.

'You're right, Charles,' I admitted. 'All's *not* well in my world. Thank you for asking.'

I felt a tightness ease in my chest, just enough for me to take a deeper breath than I had in days. And then I broke my own rule. I told Charles all about Nicky dying in his garden, the mislaid phone, the harrowing message.

'So your husband is blaming himself,' he said.

'Exactly.'

'For a tragedy that could have happened any time, might have happened years ago if he hadn't been around to help.'

'Yes. And Heidi too. It was her birthday and they were out for a bike ride, but that doesn't make it her fault. Maybe it's because she's a big sister to a little boy with health problems; she's grown up taking on too much responsibility.'

'Mm.' Charles considered this, his head tilted. I heard the squeak of trainers outside, the rattle of keys in a lock. 'You blaming yourself as well, Livia?'

'I wish I'd found that phone earlier. I wish I'd dropped in on Nicky myself that morning. I wish . . .' I shrugged. 'Magic wand.'

It was high time I called a halt to the conversation. I had other meetings, phone calls to make, emails to answer, reports to write. And I'd strayed way, *way* beyond the boundaries I guarded so carefully.

'Still,' I said brightly, getting to my feet, 'no point in wishing things hadn't happened, is there? Keep moving forward. Starting with your parole hearing.'

I opened the door to let the officer know we'd finished our meeting.

'If you were my daughter, I'd give you a hug,' said Charles, as we parted. 'You look after yourself, all right?'

•

Charles's kindness buoyed me on my drive home, with Classic FM for company—music up and windows down, the sky clear now, the moorland plateau a haze of purple ling heather.

On my way through Gilderdale I collected Noah from his beloved childminder, Chloë, who managed all the practical gaps in our care. We arrived home to the melodic twang of Heidi's guitar upstairs, the smell of shepherd's pie in the oven. Scott was emptying the dishwasher. I heard Professor Tabard's voice coming from his phone before he shut it off.

'Tell me one thing that happened in your new classroom at school,' he said to Noah. 'Did you meet someone interesting?'

Noah grinned and said he'd met someone called Miss Gardiner. 'But she's *not* a gardener! She doesn't actually even *have* a garden.'

'Not a gardener?' echoed Scott. 'Then what is she?'

'Guess!'

'Is she a pirate?'

'No!'

'Um . . . maybe a zookeeper? An astronaut?'

'No.' Noah's grey eyes were alight. 'D'you give up? She's my teacher!'

'Lucky Miss Gardiner,' said Scott, hugging his son. 'She gets to hang out with you all day.'

I left them chatting while I went up to tap on Heidi's door.

'How was your first day in year nine?' I asked.

She was tuning her guitar, a folder of sheet music on the stand in front of her.

'I got into the school band.'

I did a little dance. 'Hurrah! Congrats, you genius!'

'There's only two of us playing guitar, me and Flynn Thomas.'

'Is Flynn new too?'

'Flynn? No! He's in year eleven, he's literally ten times better than me. He's doing grade seven guitar *and* piano. Mr Butterworth has to adapt the music for us, because you don't normally have classical guitars in bands like ours. I hope I'm going to be able to keep up.'

'I'm so proud of you,' I said.

She seemed to shrink into herself.

'Thanks. I'm not.'

•

Close one eye and squint, you'd think everything was hunky-dory. Even when I woke at three in the morning to find Scott's side of the bed empty, and knew he'd be staring at a screen, watching something weird—even then, I was determined to believe that this was all normal grief. Tragedies happen, life goes on. We were on the mend.

I was too hopeful, too distracted. Too desperate for everything to be fine. I didn't hear the relentless rattle of the falling dominoes, *flack-flack-flack*. But they were gathering speed now. Their trail was laid all the way to this dock, to the prison transport van waiting for me beyond the cells. I came into this building through one door, but I'll be going out through another. I've packed my bag. It's here, by my feet.

If a jury won't meet your eye, you're going down the pan.

They won't look at me.

'Would the foreperson please stand?'

SEVEN

October 2019

Livia

'Fifty shades of black,' said my mother, when Heidi came downstairs in a faded black hoodie and leggings, her long hair tangled.

Mum was making one of her royal visits. She'd nip up from Hertfordshire and stay a couple of nights, enveloping everyone in hugs and throaty laughter. Then she'd be on the train back to Dad again, leaving pillar-box red lipstick on cups and traces of her scent on the cushions. Sometimes Dad came too, but more often not. He managed a haulage company, and they could never spare him; he seemed to have no intention of ever retiring. My parents didn't live in one another's pockets.

Heidi glanced down at herself. 'So?'

I shot Mum a warning glare, willing her not to say anything tactless. Heidi seemed to have morphed overnight from smiley childhood into moody adolescence. She'd dumped her giraffe nightie and bright T-shirts with jolly slogans. Nowadays it was all gloomy, shapeless stuff from the Salvation Army shop. It was as though she wanted to erase herself.

By contrast, Mum was vibrantly turned out in a billowing shirt and lapis lazuli earrings, which set off her eyes. Silver hair with a hint of smoky violet. She'd always been plus-sized and she rocked it. She outdid my sister Bethany and me in the fashion stakes when we were teenagers; she still outdid us in her seventies.

'I love black,' she declared, grasping in the nick of time that her granddaughter was a grenade waiting to explode. 'Very chic. Can't wear it myself, washes me out, but you're so lucky with your fabulous Titian hair.'

Heidi muttered, 'Thanks, Grandma. It's ginger. I think I might have it all cut off, though; it's a pain to keep it clean.'

'No!'

Heidi pulled up the hood of her sweatshirt before announcing that she was off to get a Diet Coke from the shop.

'Oops,' Mum whispered, once the front door had slammed. 'Sorry! Foot in mouth.'

'I liked your screeching U-turn.'

'What's up with that girl? Got a face like a slapped arse. It can't still be about poor Nicky?'

She and I were sharing a pot of tea at the kitchen table before I drove her down to York station. The days were shorter now, the light thinner. I'd lit the fire in the sitting room.

'And Scott seems to be in a bad place,' she added.

'He's just sad. Nicky was a massive part of his life.'

'You two okay?'

'Of course we're okay.'

She looked pitying. 'He's never home, Liv. He's not home now.'

'Visiting Geraldine! You can't bag the poor man for spending time with his bereaved mother.'

'And last night, and the night before? He missed Noah's bedtime for no good reason. That's not *like* him! He was always such a hands-on parent. Even when he does put in an appearance he's glued to his computer. He looks exhausted. What's going on with him?'

'It's just that he's more productive in the staffroom,' I insisted. 'Access to resources. Faster internet. No interruptions. He gets stuff done.'

'Oh well, if he's getting *stuff* done . . .' Mum let the sentence hang as she poured herself more tea. 'Another drop for you?'

'Grief deconstructs people.'

She arched an eyebrow, pushing my refilled mug across the table just as I heard Scott's car turn into the drive. I knew the engine note, the slight scraping sound as the wheels crossed the gutter. That sound used to be a micro-happiness, one of those small, familiar things that gild our daily lives. I used to meet him at the front door, just to snatch a few moments alone with him.

'He's not having an affair,' I said, getting up.

'Never suggested he was.'

By the time I opened the door, Scott had left his car and joined Noah by the pond, among drifts of dried-up leaves and waspy windfalls from the apple tree. I stood rapt and motionless, like a wildlife photographer. The two figures—one tall and rangy, one tiny and gangly—lay side by side on their fronts, heads and shoulders cantilevered over the water, matching hair lifting in the breeze. 'No doubt about that child's paternity,' my mother once said. 'Dirty-blond hair. Eyes like a wolf.'

Clouds soared in fast motion across the sun, giving the autumn day a dappled quality. Father and son chatted earnestly as they peered into the green gloom below a patch of water-lilies. Noah was fascinated by the idea that these creatures, his friends, couldn't breathe at all when out of the water, while he couldn't breathe when he was in it. The surface of the pond was the meeting of their two universes. Noah loved to imagine what it was like down there. Were the waterlilies like clouds to the fish? Were the water boatmen that skimmed across the surface like birds?

'They come up to say hi to me,' he said. 'They swim through this tunnel I make with my hands. Look, Dad! See?'

'They're having fun,' said Scott.

'Big Red just nibbled my finger—it tickles!'

'And here's Piglet,' said Scott. 'Hello, Piglet. You're looking very perky today.'

Something made him glance towards where I stood at the front door, and on seeing me his face lit up. For five wonderful seconds, the love of my life wasn't grieving or tortured by guilt, he wasn't obsessing about new and strange ideas. I smiled back at him, and felt the old blaze of longing.

'Hurrah, here's your mum!' he cried. He got to his feet and hurried over to take me in his arms. His kiss was longer and fiercer than usual. I returned it. *Don't let go. Don't let go.*

'How was Geraldine?' I asked.

'Confused today. Upset. *Where's Nicky? Have you brought Nicky?*'

I hugged him tighter. 'What did you tell her?'

'I told her Nicky's busy today, I'll bring him next time. There's no point in breaking her heart all over again, is there? That would be cruel.'

Inside, Mum had made another brew.

'Perfecting timing,' she said, as she poured a mug for Scott.

We were cracking open the chocolate biscuits when her phone rang.

'It's John,' she said. 'He'll be wanting to know what train I'm on. I've told him a million times.'

She was right on every count. I imagined my father standing in their tidy, plant-strewn conservatory: still handsome, fresh-faced, with his thinning grey hair. Mum put him on speakerphone so we could have one of those awkward four-way conversations. Dad never was good on the phone, but he did his level best.

'Are you looking after any notorious murderers, Livia?' he asked me. He was an avid reader of crime fiction and had been asking the same question since I took this job. Confidentiality rules meant that I couldn't talk much about work, but the details of Charles Shepherd's murder trial had been all over the newspapers at the time.

'Actually, yes,' I said. 'Do you remember the Garrotter? Teesside gangland enforcer, back in the early 2000s?'

'The Garrotter ... Rings a bell. This was all about drug money, was it?'

'Drugs, protection racket. He used a belt as—'

I swiftly changed the subject when Noah pottered into the kitchen. He was keen to talk to his grandfather, but since he was even more awkward on the phone than Dad, their conversation was short-lived. Dad rang off. Mum got Noah to sit on her lap, produced a small comb and began to tease his luxurious locks into miniature braids. He sat absolutely still, entranced, eyes drooping.

'I've just caught up on some horrifying research,' said Scott.

My heart sank. *Not now. Please not now.*

He took another biscuit and dunked it in his tea. That was a habit he'd formed long before he met me.

'They reckon mobile phones cause brain cancer. So does wi-fi. And guess what? Surprise, surprise, not one mainstream news channel wants to report it.'

'Perhaps because it's complete bollocks?' suggested Mum.

'Let's talk about this later,' I said.

But Scott wasn't to be deflected.

'Thing is, Polly, it isn't bollocks. Turns out the whistle was first blown way back in the 1990s. And this isn't some crackpot theory on the fringes of the internet—the WHO classified wireless radiation as a possible human carcinogen. I'll find it for you, hang on . . .' He had his phone out, apparently oblivious to the irony.

I was glaring at him, willing him to receive my telepathic message—*shut up, shut up*—but he was in no state to pick up subtle clues. It was as though he *couldn't* stop.

'Radiofrequency fields,' he said. 'Our nearest tower is a long way off, so there's a lot of energy being put out by our phones to make the connection. Then we've got dangerous 5G technology coming on stream . . .'

Mum had begun to chuckle. 'Please tell me you're joking,' she said. 'Come on, Scott. You're an intelligent man.'

While they argued, I was rummaging feverishly through my memory banks in search of some useful fact from A-Level physics, almost three decades earlier. *Radio waves*. They were low frequency, weren't they? Harmless end of the spectrum . . . but maybe constant exposure could have a cumulative effect? I once had a work colleague whose brush with breast cancer nearly killed her. 'I'd got into the habit of shoving my phone down my bra,' she told me, when I visited after her surgery. 'On the same boob that got the cancer. The doctors say it's a coincidence. Still. Never doing that again.'

I'd never done it again either. Just in case.

Mum was shaking her head. 'Even if there's a small risk—which I doubt—I'm certainly not going back to the Dark Ages. Neither are you, Scott; neither is anyone else. The world would grind to a halt. Imagine the travel chaos! You'd have a global financial crash. There'd be no food in the shops, no electricity in our homes, there'd be riots. People would die. It's never going to happen. So what on God's green earth is the point of this discussion?'

'You're right,' Scott agreed. 'Big tech has got us addicted. So we turn a blind eye to a cover-up that threatens the health of the human race?'

'They wouldn't sell billions of phones if they gave everyone brain tumours,' reasoned Mum.

'Ha! Wouldn't they?'

'I saw some tinfoil in the pantry,' said Mum, with a pert little smile. 'You could make yourself a very dapper hat. Ward off those death rays.'

I looked at my watch. 'Gosh! Time flies. You all packed, Mum? Train to catch.'

•

'Poor Scott. He's in a hell of a state.'

Mum was in the passenger seat of my car as we headed for York. She'd said an affectionate farewell to Scott, but began to gossip about him as soon as we were out of earshot.

'Shh! Big ears is right behind you.' Changing gear, I glanced over my shoulder. Noah had asked to come with us, and his enormous eyes were fixed on his grandmother. He still sported a forest of tiny braids in his hair. For some reason best known to himself, he'd balanced Bernard the Sloth on top of his head.

Mum lowered her voice. 'Admit it, Livia. You must be worried. You say this began when his brother died?'

'I think that's been the catalyst. He's eaten up with guilt because of losing his bloody phone, not even knowing Nicky was in trouble. He can't seem to accept that Nicky dying was a random event. He started questioning everything. And of course he immediately found people on the internet with answers. To him, they're the only ones talking sense. It's become a . . . a . . .' I searched for a non-judgemental word. 'Well, it's taken over. It's his new hobby.'

'Hobby! I'd call it an addiction.'

She had a point. I'd met scores of addicts in my time—alcohol, drugs, gambling, porn. I ran through a mental checklist and found myself ticking every box. *Giving up activities that used to bring pleasure. Denial, secrecy, obsession. Excessive consumption. Isolating himself.*

'I have to keep an open mind, though,' I said.

'Don't you dare follow him down the rabbit hole. Scott isn't himself, and you know it. He's lost his mojo, he's crying out for help—so for God's sake find him some help. Isn't there a friend you could call on? Someone he'll listen to?'

'He's fine.'

'And I'm the Queen of Sheba.'

'He's *fine*.'

'None so blind as them that won't see.'

'I spy,' I said loudly, speaking to Noah, 'with my little eye, something beginning with ... um ... *P*.'

I heard Noah's giggle before he yelled, 'Poo!'

'Nope.'

More giggling. 'Pants!'

'Nope.'

'Piddle!'

I was regretting my choice of letter.

'Plaits,' I said. 'It's plaits. On your head.'

Mum looked sideways at me, chewing her lower lip. 'Or paranoia,' she muttered. 'In your father's.'

•

After leaving the station, I took Noah to one of those family-friendly burger joints as a reward for Being So Good While Grandma Was Staying. While he dived around like a dolphin in the ball pit, I thought about what Mum had said. She had a point. We were all sharing Scott's head space with whatever demon had taken up residence in there, and I was failing to exorcise it. Sometimes you've got to have the humility to ask for help. Scott had loads of friends, didn't he? His cycling buddies, for instance. But they seemed so competitive—lots of tight lycra and silly helmets, sharing their statistics on Instagram. I wasn't about to give them any ammunition. There was always Anthony, but he'd done so much for us already, I didn't want to ask another favour. Who else then? Who the heck *were* all these friends? Scott worked long hours, ran after-school clubs, cycled, was devoted to his family. That left little time for friendships outside work. I couldn't think of anyone in our local community who really knew him.

Okay, then: what about his colleagues? But again, I drew a blank. People liked Scott. Staff and parents were always phoning to ask for help or grizzle about the job. A couple of times a term, he and I put on our glad rags and fronted up at fundraising quiz nights or dinner parties. We had a lot of fun. But the teachers were a gossipy bunch, they loved a scandal. Going behind Scott's back to any one of them would be a betrayal.

There had to be someone. But as reluctant as I was to call on him again, I couldn't think of anyone other than Anthony.

He answered immediately, bless him. I'd never expected to be so pleased to hear his Californian drawl.

'Livia. Everything okay?'

'Not really,' I said.

EIGHT

Scott

Livia reckoned everything would be peachy if I'd just delete Nicky's message and 'move on'. She was a master at the art of downplaying negatives. Sometimes she minimised them into non-existence.

'That's how she handles things,' I told Anthony, when he phoned out of the blue and dragged me out for a pint at the Fattened Goose in Gilderdale, 'by Not Making a Fuss. The Show Must Go On.'

'Is she wrong?'

'There's too much cover-up in the world.'

I massaged my face with my knuckles, trying to de-zombify. Sleep. I'd always taken it for granted—until my life shattered like a glass on a concrete floor. I dreaded the screaming silence when there was nothing between me and the voice of Nicky begging for help, and Lawrence the courier saying, *He was still alive . . . they faffed about*, and Professor Tabard asking, *How do we wake the sleepers?* No matter how tired my body became, my brain would not stop firing. It wouldn't shut down, it kept on trying to make sense of the chaos.

Anthony said I looked knackered and wanted to know if I was doing okay. Nice of him. People didn't ask, not even colleagues who'd known me for years and saw me every day. Nicky's death had pulled back the curtain on a cowardly side of human nature: people don't want to be reminded about death or grief. Those things are taboo. As the bereaved, your duty is to reassure everyone else. There's a script. *I'm fine, I'm fine. It was for the best. Life goes on.*

'Do you ever have this sneaking suspicion that we're living in a fake world?' I asked Anthony.

'How so?'

I was taking out my phone, opening YouTube. 'Hang on, let me find it . . . Here we go. Watch this guy. The Espinozas put me on to him.'

'I bumped into those two last week.' Anthony propped up my phone, getting ready to watch. 'They greeted me like a long-lost nephew. Next thing I knew, I'd agreed to help with their broadband connection and overhaul their website.'

'At Rosedale Retreat? You'll enjoy that. It's very swish.'

I went to the pub's bathroom, leaving Anthony with a bowl of wedges and Professor Tabard. On the way back I was flagged down by a couple, both of whom I used to teach. They wanted me to meet their new baby, a snoozing sweetheart in a car seat. I said I was honoured, and I truly was. Made me feel old, though.

'Sorry, got held up,' I explained, as I rejoined Anthony.

'Perfect timing. Prof Tabard's just signed off.'

Another video was automatically beginning. Anthony paused it before sliding my phone back to me across the table. The paused video showed a frozen image: a cartoon doctor in a white coat. The description beneath it read: *A lethal scam: how adolescent girls are paying the price.* This wasn't one of Tabard's; YouTube was constantly offering something new based on what I'd watched before.

'What did you think?' I asked, grabbing a handful of wedges.

'Well . . . Tabard's a great communicator. I can see why you find his message so disturbing.' Anthony himself didn't sound too disturbed. He began to construct a tower with beer mats.

'If he's right, then Nicky was a victim,' I said. 'He could have been cured. I'm wondering about trying to get affected families together to start a class action. Sue the pharmaceutical giants. Maybe the hospital as well.'

'You might as well put your money in a brazier and set light to it.' Anthony added another floor to his House of Mats. 'Medics are a bit of a cult. They circle the wagons. I saw stuff when I was working as a hospital porter that would make your hair stand on end.'

I'd forgotten about that chapter in my friend's history. I topped up my miserable student allowance with bar work while he did night shifts at the hospital. I imagine he was pretty useful when it came to moving heavy equipment and people.

With surprising delicacy, he laid the final mat on his tower. We both admired his handiwork.

'There are some absolute bastards in this world, that's for sure,' he said. 'Ever heard of the Tuskegee Study, in Alabama? In the 1930s, the public health service decided to study what happened when syphilis went untreated among African Americans.'

'*Untreated?*'

'You heard me right. They tricked hundreds of men, promising them treatment—only it wasn't treatment, it was observation. Blood tests, X-rays, even spinal taps. Those men didn't know they had syphilis. Penicillin might have saved their lives, but they were never given any. They were left to die, to infect their wives and children.'

I stared at him, horrified. 'I don't believe it. Nobody could be that barbaric.'

He flicked the bottom rung of his tower, making the whole thing collapse.

'Yeah—not to mention racist. But they were, right up to the 1970s, when someone blew the whistle. Look it up; Bill Clinton even apologised for it. Tuskegee was a real conspiracy, a cover-up. And not just one rogue doctor, it was generations of 'em.'

His final words were almost drowned by a vivacious group of women who'd just arrived in the bar. A hens' night—laughing, banter, downing of shots. The bride wore a net veil, a red lace garter on her thigh. They looked so young. I had a feeling I'd taught most of them. For the second time in half an hour, I felt as old as Methuselah.

'Some unsuspecting sod's about to put on a ball and chain,' said Anthony, wiping froth from his moustache.

I think he meant to be funny, but I heard bitterness.

We left soon after that; Anthony had to get back to his office to call suppliers on US time zones. A knife-sharp wind had us sprinting to our cars, parked in the market square.

'You need to get some sleep, mate,' said Anthony. 'You've been through the mill.'

'I'm fine. Life goes on.'

He raised his eyebrows. 'Go easy on yourself, okay?'

It doesn't mean anything, does it? *Go easy on yourself.* But it meant something to me at that moment. I thought Anthony a bit of a joke when we were students, but we'd both matured since then, both been knocked about by life. He had my back.

I stood and watched as he reversed out of his parking space and turned north.

Once he was out of sight I got into my own car and slammed the door against the wind, reaching for my phone. Whenever I was alone, I felt this irresistible urge to trawl for new knowledge. I had to understand. I had to get to the truth.

The video Anthony had paused was still on the screen. Its creator described himself as a *whistle-blowing doctor, working in a major UK hospital*. The circular icon showed a cartoon doctor wearing scrubs and a white coat, a stethoscope around his neck. Heavy-rimmed glasses, shiny brown hair, friendly smile. I understood the need to remain anonymous. Whistleblowers lost their jobs. They sometimes lost their lives.

This one's name was Dr Jack.

•

It was nearly midnight by the time I arrived home. The lights were all out. Livia wasn't going to be happy with me. I'd promised to be back after one drink, promised I'd do Noah's bedtime, find an hour to hang out with Heidi. But after Anthony drove off, I couldn't resist taking a brief look at Dr Jack's video, just to get an idea of his message. Why would an NHS doctor be warning about a scam involving adolescent girls?

The first thing I saw when I pressed play was a montage of photographs: children in school uniforms, glinting hypodermic needles. A small human under a shroud on a gurney, being wheeled into a morgue.

'*Trigger warning: what I'm going to talk about today involves the deaths of children*,' said the voiceover. '*It keeps me awake at night. But that's why I run this channel. I can't stand by any longer.*'

The market square was too public. Sooner or later some cheerful acquaintance was bound to rap on my windscreen and catch me watching YouTube. So I drove out of town. My first encounter with Dr Jack was in a pitch-black layby on the North York Moors, while blasts of wind rocked the car.

Dr Jack's style looked and felt very different from Tabard's. He'd brought the endearing cartoon doctor in his icon to life, explaining that it was an avatar of himself. He spoke unhurriedly, using what he admitted was text-to-speech audio—though, as he wrote in his blurb, he'd used his own voice to set up the sound bank, so really it *was* him. '*Text-to-speech suits me. I'm no public speaker.*' I found the robotic steadiness of it reassuring, with a Scottish burr that reminded me of Sean Connery, my mum's pin-up. Like all good teachers, he used everyday language, very little jargon.

'*This video is about the HPV vaccine. That's the cervical cancer one.*'

Like most parents of teenagers, I knew about this vaccine. Livia and I were all in favour—her sister Bethany was diagnosed with cervical cancer after a routine smear and needed treatment. Heidi had already had her first shot.

The Dr Jack avatar held up his cartoon hand. '*Now, in the interests of fairness, let me remind you of the propaganda around the HPV vaccine, and its positive aspects. If you've watched my content before, you'll know that I just provide the facts and statistics. Then it's up to you to decide. There is certainly evidence that this vaccine can prevent infection by the human papillomavirus, which can cause cancer, most often of the cervix. Many millions of doses have gone into arms since it became available in 2006. We're assured that it's perfectly safe. Countless lives will be saved, countless people will avoid invasive surgery. Future generations will thank us. Cause to celebrate!*'

The cartoon doctor raised a cynical eyebrow, while a celebratory firework flared across the screen.

'*Right,*' he said. '*Okay. So . . . you might be asking, if all that's true, why are so many of us ringing alarm bells? Why am I even making this video?*'

The screen filled with slow-motion footage, accompanied by sombre music: a blurred figure on a trolley being rushed along a corridor—people in scrubs, someone holding up an IV drip bag, someone else holding back distraught parents.

'Let me tell you about Jenny. That's not her real name. Jenny would have been fifteen now, but she was thirteen when she had the HPV vaccine.'

Family snaps and selfies: a cheerful girl with a mass of ginger hair, very like Heidi's. She was running a race, holding a puppy, blowing out birthday candles. She really *did* look like Heidi.

'Jenny was happy, sporty, loved swimming. They gave her the vaccine at school. Hours later she collapsed with a TIA, a mini-stroke, and was brought by ambulance to my hospital. I got to know her and her family well. Over the next month she suffered complications and, tragically, she died. You'd think Jenny's case would set off alarm bells about the HPV, wouldn't you? Think again. The neurologist, pathologist, coroner—they closed ranks. According to them, Jenny's death had nothing to do with the vaccine. It was a complete coincidence! Her parents have never accepted that coincidence, and neither have I.'

Video of a printer, working in fast motion with documents pouring from it.

'After I mentioned this vaccine in an earlier video, I received hundreds of messages from health professionals around the world, all worried about extreme adverse reports and deaths. Like me, they're being silenced. Our social media is being watched, and we're at risk of losing our jobs. I'll share just a few extracts.'

He read out graphic descriptions of seizures, of brain damage and deaths.

'Many doctors won't allow their own kids near the vaccine,' said Dr Jack. 'My own daughter hasn't had it. Yet schools and parents still coerce children into rolling up their sleeves.'

A cartoon hand used a cartoon whiteboard, drawing a graph to show the statistics on cervical cancer in the UK. The case numbers seemed vanishingly low, especially compared with his projections of adverse reactions to the vaccine.

'*Why would we be pushing a dangerous substance into the arms of our children, if it isn't even necessary? Who stands to gain? Give you one guess.*'

Banknotes showered from the sky, swirling like leaves, while ABBA sang 'Money, Money, Money'.

'*Follow the money. Big pharma and their enablers are making billions off the back of this scam. Billions. Do your own research; it's all out there. Watch the stories of parents who're speaking out against the vaccine, of children who have lost everything—children like Jenny. All to line the pockets of billionaires.*'

The final piece of footage was from the point of view of someone approaching a hospital morgue, pushing the doors open and passing through. The camera focused on one of the dead. A cascade of ginger hair showed from beneath the shroud, slim little feet with painted toenails. It could have been Heidi. It really could.

'*Jenny had her whole life ahead of her. She and her parents trusted this vaccine. She paid with her life. And the worst part? All this is only scratching the surface—we'll talk about the big picture another time. Please go ahead and join the conversation in the comment section below. And always remember that you're—*'

I paused him as I fumbled for the doorhandle, needing to pee. In three steps I was crashing through soaking bracken, almost on top of a sheep who burst out of a hollow and trotted away from the terrifying human.

Two minutes of freezing wind cleared my mind. What the hell was I doing up here while Livia waited for me back home? Anthony was right: I needed to get some sleep. Nobody was going to deliberately harm children. How could they pull off a conspiracy on that kind of scale? The medical profession, watchdogs and parents would be screaming from the rooftops. The scandal would bring down governments.

'Get on home, you daft twit,' I said aloud, zipping up my fly.

My eyelids felt heavy as I headed home, steering down a treacherously steep and winding stretch of road. I tried to put Dr Jack's video out of my mind, but I was haunted by Jenny, the girl who might be Heidi. *Nobody's going to deliberately harm children.*

Swinging around the next bend, I got a hell of a fright: a swarm of laser-point eyes, right in the middle of the road. My first thought was of aliens, landed on this lonely moor. I swore and braked, tyres screeching, fighting to avoid flying down the bank as I skidded to a halt on the verge. The glowing eyes stared at me for another moment before melting away. *Sheep. Bloody sheep.*

I cut the engine and sat gasping, my heart racing. The urban sprawl of Teesside smouldered dully to the north, and to the south lay the Vale of York, but in the vast expanse around me there was nothing. No stars, no life. I felt irretrievably lost.

Nobody's going to harm children? Tell that to the ones who contracted syphilis in Tuskegee.

Once my pulse had settled, I reached for my phone. My hands were still shaking.

'*Always remember that you're not alone,*' said Dr Jack.

I listened to his voice in the darkness as I'd once listened to Nicky's. The gentle Scottish accent, the robotic calmness. I'd never felt so disorientated, but I'd found a guide.

'*You're* not *alone,*' he repeated. '*You're not the only one who's beginning to wonder. There are thousands of us. Look beyond the end of your nose. Ask questions. Check things out for yourself. All of a sudden, you'll see that nothing—nothing—is as it seems. Once you've seen the truth, you can't unsee it.*'

NINE

Livia

I was in bed by the time I heard Scott's car purring into the garage, more or less asleep by the time he tiptoed upstairs. He'd been in the Fattened Goose with Anthony, I knew, and it was now long after chucking-out time. Good. I hoped they'd had a happy blokes' evening, talking about whatever the hell it is men talk about in the pub.

I'd taken the opportunity to work late, trying to catch up on the backlog of record-keeping that followed every interaction, decision or report. The system was already groaning, and a colleague had gone on leave with stress. I didn't blame him—there but for the grace of God—but we all shouldered his caseload, and the system groaned still louder.

One bright spot, though: Charles had been granted parole and arrived at the probation hostel I'd arranged. Willow House was nondescript, the kind of red-brick building you could walk past every day and never notice. The team there knew what to expect: a man in his late sixties, partially deaf, institutionalised after almost twenty years inside. Visiting him was first on my to-do list for tomorrow.

Heidi had arrived home around eight. She'd been into York for late-night shopping with her friends, driven by Maia's mother.

'Claire didn't want to come in?' I asked, looking past her towards the lane.

'I got her to drop me off in the square.' Heidi was already heading towards the stairs. 'She hates turning around in Back Lane 'cos her car is massive. She says hi.'

Thank the good Lord for the narrowness of Back Lane. Maia's mother depressed me. Fabulously privileged, endlessly complaining. Give me an honest-to-goodness, straight-up criminal every time.

'Fun evening?' I called as Heidi stomped up the stairs.

'Yup.'

'Have you eaten? Would you like some—'

Her door shut.

A little later, I tapped on that firmly closed door. I'd brought her a mug of hot chocolate, thinking perhaps we could sit on her bed and chat, like we used to before Nicky died. I wanted to know she was okay.

No answering voice, no light. I hoped she was asleep.

Heidi

Mum was being so sweet. *Heidi? Heidi? Want some hot chocolate?* But there was no way I could let her in. She'd have found me crying and got it out of me. The whole story.

Nicky's birthday card was pinned to my cork board. I kept it there to remind me. The ridiculous gardening gloves were still lurking underneath my cupboard. I never wanted to see them or think about them again, but they had other ideas. It was like having a dead rat in my bedroom; I could almost smell them. And it wasn't just the gloves anymore. Other rats had joined them: a biro, a packet of birthday cake candles and a puzzle magazine.

My stealing was out of hand, and now it had lost me my friends. If nothing else, I'd learned my lesson. I'd never do it again.

Mum gave up in the end. I heard her footsteps on the wooden stairs. I was sitting on the carpet with my back against the door, longing to call her back and tell her everything. It felt as though my life was finally over, after what had happened this evening.

Maia and Keren had been my best friends for two years. But since Nicky died, I felt like I came from another planet. They'd banned me from mentioning his name because I should have 'got over' him by now. Once, when I told them how he used to say, *Beam me up, Scotty*, Maia rolled her eyes at Keren. That hurt.

Still, it was fun to go late-night shopping in York. Maia's mother, Claire, went off to do her own thing. Most of the shops were decked out for Halloween: webs with monster spiders, luminous skulls, sexy witch outfits. Maia and Keren tried on berets and earrings in the artisan market. We sheltered from the wind, eating baked potatoes from a stall. When I casually dropped the information that I sat next to Flynn Thomas in the school band, my friends almost choked on their potatoes.

'Does he talk to you?' asked Maia. 'Can you introduce me?'

Flynn could easily be in a boy band: dark brown eyes, loads of curly hair and a lopsided smile. He could play any style on the guitar—classical, blues, country, flamenco, you name it—*and* he played the piano, *and* he could sing. On top of that, he was friendly and funny but not a loudmouth.

'D'you fancy him?' asked Keren.

Of course I did.

'Nah.' I wrinkled my nose. 'He's a really nice person, but not my type.'

'You're mad,' said Maia.

If only we'd never gone into that toyshop in The Shambles. The shelves were overflowing: teddy bears and doll's houses, remote-controlled helicopters and ride-on cars, kites and board games. Maia and Keren were looking for a soft toy for Keren's stepsister. I thought it would be safe to have a browse, since it was only in the Gilderdale Spar that I had the urge to swipe things. I'd just discovered that glow-in-the-dark dominoes were a thing and thought that would be perfect for Noah's birthday in December.

I found some dominoes but they were normal-sized, not the big ones that Noah liked. Not luminous either. I tried a snazzy yo-yo. The next box on the shelf was full of little wind-up dinosaurs. I picked out a purple T-Rex, just small enough to fit in the palm of my hand. I wound him up. Watched him walk. Wound him up again. It would be so easy to . . .

The urge clobbered me with no warning at all: the thudding in my chest, the strange excitement. I'd flown straight to the top of the high-diving board. I knew I was going to jump off.

Maia and Keren were going nuts over a cuddly koala with a baby in her pouch. The assistant, a bald man in red braces, climbed a ladder to fetch something for an American lady who seemed to be buying half the shop. Nobody was paying attention to me.

It was a crazy risk, but I was good at this. I was a pro. Keeping my eyes on the man up his ladder, I dropped the purple dinosaur into the pocket of my anorak. *Job done.* Off that diving board and flying through the air! Superwoman rides again.

But when I turned around, my two best friends were staring at me with open mouths.

They stood side by side, watching every move as I walked to the counter and paid for the dinosaur. My whole face was on fire. Why had I done it? *Why?* If I could have waved a magic wand and disappeared to Timbuktu to start a new life there, I'd have been gone in an instant.

Once I'd paid, the others walked out of the shop without a word. I had to run to catch up with them.

'We saw you shoplifting, Heidi,' said Maia.

'That was weird,' said Keren.

I tried to bluff it out. I told them I wasn't shoplifting, I'd always planned to pay and was only putting the dinosaur in my pocket while I looked at other toys. Maia said, 'Oh, right,' and smirked at Keren. They didn't speak to me again.

When we got to the car, Maia made me sit in the front next to her mum, while she and Keren piled into the back together. All the way to Gilderdale, while Claire was chatting to someone on her hands-free phone, I had to listen to the giggles and whispers of my ex-best friends. They made it very obvious that they were talking about me: *she, she, she.* I was terrified they were going to tell my parents, tell everyone at school.

Either way, the message was loud and clear. I was an outcast. There was no coming back from this.

TEN

Livia

'Nice time with Anthony?' I asked Scott the next morning, as I stuffed pots of yoghurt into lunchboxes.

'Not bad. Sorry to be so late.'

He looked haggard. A hangover, perhaps. I hoped he hadn't been drinking and driving but I didn't ask. I was his wife, not his mother.

'No problem! But can you be home after school today? I've got a team meeting this afternoon. It could take a while.'

'I'll do my secret-recipe mince and pasta,' he suggested, opening the lid of the chest freezer and rootling through it for mince. 'Here we go.' He seemed keen to make up for his non-appearance last night.

'Dad's mince and pasta!' cried Noah, doing a happy dance around the kitchen table.

I had no idea why everyone thought Scott's pasta bolognaise was the best in the world. You'd think he was head chef at a Michelin-starred restaurant. He cheated too; while I fussed about with garlic and herbs and fresh penne, he just boiled a bag of the dried stuff and tipped in a jar of ready-made sauce. That was his famous secret recipe.

'Heidi?' I called. 'C'mon! Dad's leaving soon.'

When there was still no sign of her, I took the stairs two at a time and burst into her room.

'You've got three minutes, chop chop,' I told her, striding across to open the curtains. 'Heidi? You okay?'

She was fully dressed in her school uniform, sitting on her bed, and she wasn't okay. She was a mess of tears and running nose. Something caught my eye, clutched in her hands. A giant birthday card. Thirteen cartoon kittens, each with a coloured bow.

●

I pulled up outside Willow House with ten minutes to spare. Sat tapping the steering wheel. Checked my watch, and dug my phone out of my bag.

Bethany answered on the fourth ring, sounding—as always—as though a call from me was the best thing to happen to her all day.

'Livia! Favourite sister! How's tricks?'

We lived at opposite ends of the country, both keeping work and family plates spinning in the air. She'd married a Cornish widower—think Captain Von Trapp, except James was a gentle agricultural contractor who wore yellow corduroys. Family in Bethany's case meant four girls: two teenagers of her own, plus two almost-adult stepdaughters. Work was their Airbnb business, barn conversions in glorious *Poldark* country.

'You busy?' I asked.

'Carrying a mountain of linen upstairs. But that's okay, the guests aren't due until three. How's the clan?'

I pictured my older sister: hennaed hair cut into a sensible bob; jeans and a jersey, endless energy. She'd be working as she talked, spreading sheets with her phone tucked under her chin. Her guests would find sprigs of lavender on their lace pillows, scones in a basket on their scrubbed kitchen table. Bethany did wholesome with a capital W.

'I'm after your wisdom on adolescent girls,' I said. 'Since you've brought up so many of them yourself.'

'Fire away.'

I explained that Heidi had taken Nicky's death terribly hard, that she seemed to have lost all her joy in life. I described how I'd found her crying that morning.

'She wouldn't tell me what was wrong. She just kept sobbing that she never wants to go to school again.'

'So, to recap,' said Bethany, 'our darling Heidi is thirteen. She's taken to wearing black, dumped her Hello Kitty. She's staying out with friends, uncommunicative, doesn't want you in her bedroom. She's grumpy. She's no longer the sweet, happy child she was a few months ago.'

'Pretty much.'

'And today you found her in tears over the birthday card Nicky gave her on the *actual day* he died, with kittens and the last message he ever wrote. Which is—objectively, by any metric— really sad.'

'Yep.'

'Sounds to me . . .' From the unevenness of her breathing, I guessed Bethany was coming to a tricky part of the bed-making process. I'd often marvelled at her immaculate hospital corners. I had no idea how she did them. No idea *why* either. 'Sounds to me as though what you have there is the Common Spotted Teenager, displaying the typical insanity of the species.'

'You think it's normal?' I wasn't convinced. 'But it's been so sudden.'

'So was Nicky's death. That must have been traumatic for poor Heidi. None of us like coming face to face with mortality, do we? My stepdaughters lost part of their childhoods when their mum died. You'll remember they were pretty hard work when I first met them, and now they're my best friends. Anyway, that's my diagnosis, for what it's worth. A combination of grief and being thirteen. Let's face it, we were all completely nuts at that age.'

'I didn't think Heidi would ever turn into one of those monosyllabic adolescents.'

'What makes you think yours should be perfect?'

'Fair point.'

'She'll come right,' Bethany assured me. 'Give her about ten years! But, Livia, what's all this I hear about Scott? Mum tells me he gave her an earful about mobile phones and death rays. She reckons he's in a terrible place.'

My hackles rose. It hurt to think of my mother and sister gossiping about my husband.

'He's fine,' I said curtly. 'Mum's exaggerating.'

'Good to hear.' Bethany had deployed her soothing voice. 'You've always been such a golden couple. But you know where I am—and you're welcome here, you know that. All of you.'

My time was up. Charles was expecting me. Bethany had lavender to scatter, guests to greet. It's all go, being an earth mother with business acumen. *Speak soon*, we said. *Hugs to everyone.*

•

One minute I was in a Cornish converted barn, the next a Teesside probation hostel.

I found Charles in the communal kitchen, up to his elbows in a deep double sink. He lit up when he spotted me. I lit up too.

'Livia!' he cried, waving pink-gloved hands, spraying soap suds. 'I've found my calling.'

Later today I had to see a woman who'd once tried to persuade me to falsify my records of her attendance at a drug dependency unit—spoiler alert, she never darkened their door—and threatened to smash me up with a chair when I refused. After her, a young guy who'd let ketamine get the better of him and desperately needed more help than the system was equipped to give. Charles was a welcome interlude.

'You wash, I'll dry,' I suggested, picking up a tea towel.

I stood on the side of his better ear while we chatted. He'd been out of prison for just twenty-four hours, said goodbye to old friends and enemies, met new ones. He had been shown around the hostel, learned its rules and routines, slept in a properly dark room for the first time in years.

'I can walk out the front door whenever I want to,' he said.

'How does that feel?'

'Lovely. Also quite nerve-racking.'

'I bet.'

'Jess gave me a mobile phone so I can ring her any time. She's been showing me how to use it. I look at this thing and I'm asking, *Where the heck are the buttons?* She says, *Dad, this is a smartphone.* I said, *What's smart about it?*'

His most pressing needs were to fix a hiccup with his state pension and set up a bank account. He even talked about finding casual work.

'Not good for much, but there's always pot washing!' He brandished a saucepan. 'Anyhow, how about you? How's your bloke doing?'

On my way to Willow House, I'd sworn that I wouldn't allow myself to be drawn into another conversation about my family; but the road to hell is paved with good intentions. I was tired and stressed and sick to the back teeth of being bloody Tigger to everyone else's Eeyore.

'He's in a state,' I admitted. 'He's got caught up in all these bizarre theories on the internet. He spends every spare second doing what he calls "research". It started with how drug companies are wicked—okay, sometimes they probably are—but now it's all kinds of other stuff. Like mobile phones giving you cancer.'

'Do they?'

I shrugged. 'Hope not. He seems to think everything's part of a massive plot, involving corporations and hospitals and I don't know what else. His ideas are evolving so fast, I can't keep up. It's making him ill. He doesn't sleep or—'

I broke off mid-sentence, mentally slapping my own wrist. What was wrong with me? I should *not* be having this conversation. I wasn't prepared to be honest with my own sister, so why with a man on licence from a life sentence for murder?

'Quality control reject,' I said, sliding a porridge-streaked saucepan back into the water.

'I know a bit about feeling guilty when someone's died,' said Charles, scrubbing the porridge. 'Course, in my case I actually *was* guilty. Even if it's a stranger like Jarrod Jeffries, it eats away at you. The dead haunt you. Jeffries was just a daft kid, really, wasn't he? A daft kid who got in way over his head.' He stood with the saucepan in one hand, dripping. 'I was like that myself, once. Messing about on the edges of organised crime, just like Jarrod Jeffries.'

I let him talk without interruption; I was meant to be his support, not the other way around.

'I'd lost my wife, my daughter. Fallen back in with old friends. Not good people, not the right kind of friends, but they gave me work. That's the usual story with me, has been since I was seven years old: running the wrong kinds of errands for the wrong kinds of people. Anyway, I picked up a magazine someone had left on a bus, and there was this story about how Londoners in Victorian times lived in fear of being choked and robbed. The garrotting panic, they called it. Even children were doing it— poor little sods, it was that or starve. I thought if kids could do it, so could I. All you need is a belt and a lot of determination.

And patience, because you have to catch people totally unawares.'
He shook his head. 'Wish I'd never opened that magazine. Wish
I'd never done any of it.'

Among many reports on Charles, I'd read one by a forensic
psychologist who worked with him when he was on remand. She'd
taken the time to listen to all the things he wasn't saying out loud.
Her impression was that he was a bright man who, from early
childhood, had been exploited and bullied. It happened because he
was deaf, because he was small, because he was adrift. Becoming
an enforcer for the crime syndicate gave him a place in the world.

I took the saucepan out of his hand. He seemed to have forgotten he was holding it.

'Wish, wish, wish,' he sighed. 'If wishes were horses,
beggars would ride. I kept thinking: *Jarrod won't be getting up
tomorrow, he won't see his mum again. Never have his favourite dinner. Never have a family of his own.* My barrister thought
it might be worth appealing my conviction, try to get it down to
manslaughter—I'd have pleaded guilty to that in the first place.
I said no. That was *my* belt that killed Jarrod, these two hands
that put it around his neck. It was time to accept what a nasty
ratbag I'd become.'

He reached into the suds to pull the plug, and we both watched
the water spinning down the drain.

Charles peeled off his gloves. 'I've met blokes who picked up
some very strange ideas off the internet,' he said.

'Really?'

'I had a cellmate, a guy from Wales. He'd got himself recruited
into one of those terrorist groups. These people wormed their
way right into his head. Ooh, but they were clever. The amazing
thing to me was that they managed it while he was sat in his
bedroom—it's almost like they reached in and grabbed him
through his computer screen. He ended up so deep into all their
hate that he was off to Syria to join ISIS.'

'Did he actually make it?'

'Nearly. He and another kid got stopped from boarding a plane at Heathrow. They'd made the mistake of talking to an undercover policeman. Saved their lives. They'd never have lasted five minutes over there.'

I knew the kind of thing Charles was talking about. Those cases always set off a wild frenzy of media interest. Not so long ago I'd provided a report on someone who lobbed Molotov cocktails through the doors of a mosque after he was recruited online by right-wing extremists. The recruiters had done a devastating job of brainwashing him. His only regret was that he hadn't managed to kill anyone. *A disturbing mindset*, I wrote in my report. *At extremely high risk of reoffending.*

The defence produced a report from Dr Isaac Katz, a social psychologist and expert on online grooming. I knew him a little. I'd been to a seminar he ran on deradicalisation programs in prisons and had commissioned reports from him myself. Dr Katz looked about fifteen years old—okay, maybe thirty— as he strolled into the witness box, wearing jeans and a black hoodie. *Hip and trendy*, my mother would have said. But he was a brilliant witness. Erudite, unflappable, completely across his subject. He kept us all spellbound.

'Online recruiters use many of the same techniques we see in quasi-religious sects or cults,' he said. 'They know exactly what they're doing. They offer community and belonging to individuals who feel disconnected. Relevance to those who feel irrelevant. Purpose and meaning to those whose lives seem pointless. It's heady stuff.'

But that's got nothing to do with Scott, I told myself now. Nope. None. He has plenty of community and purpose.

'Not saying your husband is a jihadi!' Charles peered at me, his brow furrowed. 'No offence meant.'

'None taken.'

'I was only thinking . . . I've heard a lot of talk about the kind
of stuff people do on their computers, and how the police can
look back and see what you've been up to. People swap handy
hints about how to cover their tracks. The "history", is it called?'

'That's right. Browsing history.'

'Browsing history. I mean . . .' He shrugged, scratching his
nose. 'If I was worried, maybe I'd have a look.'

Enough. It was past time I shut this down. I really couldn't
have murderers advising me to spy on my husband.

'Nine thirty already!' I cried, glancing at the clock above the
fridge. 'C'mon. Let's sort out your bank account.'

•

In a spare moment between meetings, I sent Heidi a text. Phones
weren't allowed out in the classroom, but she might see it at
lunchtime.

*Hope your day's going okay. Things will get better I promise.
Think of something nice we can do together at the weekend. Love
you so so so much! Mum XXX*

I'd been reluctant to give her a phone last Christmas, but I had
to admit it was useful. It was very basic, though she'd managed to
rig up a *Moonlight Sonata* ringtone.

I also found time to call Anthony.

'Thanks for getting Scott to come for a drink with you last
night,' I said.

'My pleasure. Just a pint with an old mate.'

'I'm not asking you to breach any confidences, but did you . . .'
I petered out. That very morning I'd been shocked at Charles's
suggestion that I spy on Scott, yet here I was.

'Did we talk about those theories?' asked Anthony. 'Yeah. He
showed me the Canadian professor on YouTube. I didn't challenge
him too much. Didn't want an argument. Better to listen, try at
least to respect what he's got to say, then add some perspective.'

'Maybe.'

'And some of it makes sense.'

I groaned. 'Not you too.'

'No, no. Not at all. But the world's a fucked-up place. Politicians lie, corporations can be evil. Terrible things happen. Right?'

I'd forgotten how annoying Anthony could be. He always had to know better. And that word—*Right?*—in that clever-dick tone. It set my teeth on edge. Still, I invited him for lunch next Sunday because I felt I owed him, and because Scott needed all the friends he could get. He accepted enthusiastically; he'd be in our neck of the woods already, doing some IT work for the Espinozas.

'They pay cash,' he said. 'I like cash.'

'Thanks again for last night,' I said. 'Five hours in a cheerful pub with a good friend instead of an online echo chamber with a load of wackos—you can't put a price on that.'

'Five hours . . .'

I caught the slightest hesitation, a glitch in Anthony's super-confident tone.

'You must have been last men standing in the Fattened Goose,' I persisted. 'Scott wasn't home till about midnight.'

He laughed—too easily, too loudly. 'Yeah, it was a good night. They had to chuck us out.'

'You'll have been late driving home across the moors, and in those strong winds.'

The confidence was back. The bluff assurance.

'No worries, Livia. Genuine pleasure. Took my mind off these goddamned tax returns. That's the only problem with running a successful business: you get to pay a whole lot back to the government.'

After ending the call, I stood at my office window, a mug in one hand, staring at the row of cars below. A paunchy pigeon flapped across from the chestnut tree by the gate, made a hard landing on the roof of my car, and began to swagger up and down like he owned it. A ruff ringed his neck, iridescent purple and green. He reminded me of Anthony.

I heard a lot of lies in my job. Every day. I had an ear for it.

Five hours . . .

The man had been taken by surprise, but he'd seen the lay of the land and recovered swiftly. Anthony Tait wasn't all clumsy bear and what-you-see-is-what-you-get, after all. He'd lied easily—lied to provide an alibi for his mate, and done it like a pro. *Yeah, it was a good night. They had to chuck us out.*

They'd met at about seven, for what was meant to be one drink. That might take an hour. So what the hell was Scott doing between eight and midnight? He wasn't the type to have an affair; he just wasn't wired that way. Above all, he'd never risk hurting his children.

The Anthony pigeon was joined by another, and another, all pecking about, bobbing their heads. A committee meeting.

So where had Scott been? Who was he with?

I had a sick feeling that I knew the answer. He'd spent those lost hours alone, probably sitting in his car, indulging his addiction. He was being lured away—but not into the arms of another woman. His obsession was with a different kind of siren voice. More elusive, perhaps more dangerous.

I was losing him to an enemy I couldn't even see.

ELEVEN

Livia

The moors put on a spectacular show as I drove home that evening. Granite thunderheads gathered and grumbled along the horizon, outlined in brilliance as the sun sank behind them. Swathes of woodland flamed in the storm light. Beautiful. Unsettling. And the nights were drawing in.

Stepping into the house, I was greeted by the cheery smells of bolognaise sauce and wood smoke, The Beatles belting out 'A Hard Day's Night'. I'd just dropped my bag and car keys in the hall when Scott appeared from the kitchen, crooning along. He wound his arms around my waist, lifting me right off my feet as he kissed me.

'You're an idiot,' I said.

He took both my hands in his, and we began to dance.

'But I somehow persuaded you to marry me,' he said, 'so I'm not a *total* idiot.'

We spun and jived for the rest of the song, laughing at every misstep. We used to go to rock'n'roll classes long ago, before Heidi arrived. We both loved it—and we were good at it: one of those annoying, exhibitionist couples who hog the dance floor at weddings. It's like riding a bike, you never forget the steps and the rhythms, the way the two of you move almost as one.

'Where's Noah?' I asked, when the song had ended and Scott was pouring me a glass of merlot.

'In the bath. Heidi should be back from band practice any minute. There's a group of them catching the bus.'

'Was she any happier once you two set off this morning?'

'I think so. We talked about Nicky.'

He began to lay the table, complaining about problems with the timetable and the thirty essays he had to mark tonight. I made sympathetic noises while I sifted through a pile of letters on the dresser.

'By the way,' he said casually, 'I checked with the school office. The HPV booster's due to be rolled out in January.'

'Uh-huh.' Junk, junk, bill. Invitation to a fiftieth.

'Heidi can't have it,' he added.

I looked up. 'Why can't Heidi have it?'

'Because it's killed thousands of children. I'll show you the statistics about adverse reactions—the real ones, not the ones big pharma want you to see.'

I gazed at him in despair, feeling my spirits plummet. Our family life had been normal for all of ten minutes. I couldn't raise the energy to argue at that moment—and anyway, Heidi was home, I could hear her kicking off her shoes in the hall.

'Hello there! Dinner's nearly ready,' said Scott, as she passed through the kitchen.

'Thanks, Dad, but they gave us pizza at band practice. Sorry.' Heidi was heading up the stairs already, guitar case in hand. She hadn't even taken off her schoolbag.

'Join us anyway?' I called after her.

'Too much homework. I've got a French vocab test tomorrow.'

Her door shut with a determined clunk.

Scott met my eye as we both took a slug of wine.

'She'll be okay,' he said.

●

The remaining three of us ate at the kitchen table while thunder seemed to crack the sky right open. Scott played I Spy with Noah at toothbrushing time—*Tap! Tummy! Toilet!*—before taking refuge in our shared office, anxious to tackle his pile of marking. As I kissed Noah goodnight, the first drops of rain began to pelt against the window.

'Bernard's a bit scared,' murmured Noah.

'Don't worry, Bernard. Noah will keep you snug and warm.'

I was reassured to catch the sound of Heidi's guitar on my way to the stairs. She was singing too. At least she was still taking pleasure in her music. I'd be really worried if she lost that.

I made two mugs of tea and took one to Scott. He seemed to be hard at work, with exercise books stacked up in front of him. But as I lowered his mug onto a coaster, I caught sight of an image on his open laptop: a human corpse, lying under a shroud. Delicate feet. Bright pink toenails. Long hair, just like Heidi's.

'Please, *please* tell me that's not a dead child,' I said.

'Her name was Jenny. She was killed by the HPV vaccine.'

I picked up an exercise book, waving it at him. 'I thought you were completely snowed under.'

'I am.'

'So why on earth are you wasting time on this nonsense? And—since we're having this conversation—were you really with Anthony until chucking-out time last night? Or were you sitting in your car, scaring yourself silly, watching homemade videos made by pseudoscientists?'

Judging by his sheepish look, I knew I'd hit the bullseye.

'Heidi can't have that booster,' he said flatly.

'You've never been for a smear test,' I retorted. 'Believe me, women wouldn't put themselves through that if we didn't need to. I for one am truly grateful that a vaccine is changing the land-scape. Heidi *will* be having the booster.'

'No!'

'She will. End of story. You're not dragging our children into your obsessions.'

He seemed distraught. This was a version of my husband that I'd never known existed until recently. He looked like Scott, he spoke in Scott's voice. But this wasn't Scott.

'Who're you going to trust?' he demanded. 'Big pharma, or people who *know* what's happening and who've got nothing to gain by revealing it?'

'Governments make them do years of testing. Double-blind trials and—'

'Governments are puppets. Democracy is a fiction, a shiny toy we're given to trick us into doing as we're told.'

'Go on then.' I crossed my arms. 'Surprise me! Who d'you reckon is pulling the puppet strings?'

'That's what I'm trying to find out. The deeper I dig, the more I find. It's much, much bigger than you can imagine . . .'

He was off. I couldn't break into the flood of words, the steamroller intensity, the nervous energy. He kept switching and twisting from big pharma to big tech to a 'much bigger' picture. If I hadn't known better, I'd have thought he was on some kind of street drug. I felt a tightness in my chest, as though I were being physically smothered.

'Scott, please,' I begged, interrupting him. 'Stop.'

'You have to think about who benefits from endless vaccines, all of them causing inflammation and long-term, chronic—'

'Stop talking.'

'You've got to listen, Livia. It's not only about money, it's about power. It's about who lives, who dies, who—'

'Just shut up, for one second!'

As I yelled those words, I slapped my hand over his mouth. I just wanted to make him stop, but his head jerked backwards.

After a moment of horrified silence, I threw my arms around him. I was appalled at myself—never in all our years of marriage had either of us laid a finger on the other. We both began apologising at the same time. *Sorry, sorry—no, I'm sorry.*

A thud shook the ceiling. Noah was jumping out of bed. 'Mummy?'

'Do you remember our first date?' Scott asked me.

I nodded. '*The Mousetrap.*'

'You scoffed at astrology.'

'Mm. And you thought it would be nice if there were a celestial road map. You hoped the universe isn't random chaos.' I hugged him again. 'But it *is* random, Scott. There's no evil master plan.'

He gripped my hand. Drowning man. Straws.

'I wish you'd listen,' he whispered, as Noah burst into the room.

Heidi

Mum never shouted. It's not that she never got angry—she totally did, she was always shutting her eyes and counting to ten. But she didn't raise her voice. She said she'd met too many people who used anger to communicate.

'It's all they know,' she said. 'As children, the only human voices they heard were screaming fights. I don't want any of that in your childhood.'

So I was shocked to hear her scream at Dad, followed by the sound of poor Noah galloping down the stairs. I assumed I was the cause of whatever was going on. Maybe Keren or Maia had ratted on me about the dinosaur, and their parents phoned mine: *Just thought you'd like to know . . .* I abandoned my guitar and sat listening, dreading the sound of adult feet marching upstairs, the knock on my door. I'd have to tell the truth and show them everything I'd stolen.

But they didn't come. Just Dad and Noah on their way back to Noah's room. Dad was using his fake-cheery voice, making a superhuman effort. I sat looking out at the rain, listening to him reading *Farmer Duck* and *The Gruffalo* next door.

Maia and Keren had blanked me all day, as I'd feared they would, except when Maia asked how my dinosaur was doing. I spent the lunch break hiding in one of the music practice rooms, making up a new song about bitchy friends. Better than sitting alone in the quad.

I wished I could be five again, snuggled in bed with stories. I wished I could be innocent again. More than anything else, I wished I could turn back time, to ten forty-four on my birthday.

Livia

I hung back in the office, listening to the tramp of my husband's and son's feet on the narrow stair treads. Noah was hopping, as usual.

Scott and I had rallied fast to present a united front. *Everything's fine, Mummy wasn't shouting crossly, she just forgot to use her inside voice.* Noah was easily reassured; we so rarely fought.

Scott had shut down YouTube on his laptop. The dead Heidi look-alike in the morgue was gone, thank God. In her place was his screensaver, an image full of life: Heidi and Noah blowing bubbles on a sunny day, the sprinkler scattering diamonds. I stared at that summer scene, thinking about my conversation with Charles Shepherd and wrestling with my conscience. Scott's browser history was just a click away.

If I was worried, maybe I'd have a look.

'It's cultic,' Isaac Katz had said, as he stood in the witness box in his jeans and hoodie. 'These groomers are experts. It's heady stuff.'

Ooh, but they were clever. It's almost like they reached in and grabbed him through his computer screen.

My conscience lost.

Scott was signed into Google, so the history showed where he'd been on both his phone and laptop. I skimmed the list, starting with yesterday morning. Some of it was work-related: Barmoors High website, teacher and student noticeboards. Gmail.

Scott's voice resonated loud and clear through the wooden ceiling above my head. He was reading *Farmer Duck*.

A search to do with *The Great Gatsby*, which was a set text. Visits to Professor Tabard and various other influencers I already knew about. Much as I expected.

Upstairs, Noah was laughing uproariously as Scott quacked in the voice of the downtrodden duck.

But last night, he hadn't been sitting on Noah's bed reading stories; he'd been alone in his car. And he'd been watching some-one new: a YouTuber calling himself 'Dr Jack'. He'd visited Dr Jack again first thing this morning, and many times today, right up until I'd walked into the study just now. Scott never had five minutes to eat at lunchtime, worked through all non-contact hours and still brought work home. But he'd made time for Dr Jack.

The sound of hop-hopping down the stairs made me leap like a burglar caught in the act. I closed everything just as Noah came scampering back into the office.

'Dad forgot his tea! It's hot, can you carry it for me? He's doing *The Gruffalo* next.'

I felt ashamed as I followed my son upstairs and sat on the sheepskin rug by his bed. No matter how I framed it, I'd just been spying on Scott. Never, ever again. Trust is everything in a marriage. What was I expecting to uncover, with all my sleuthing?

The Gruffalo was met by sleepy chortles from Noah. Scott did the voices of the mouse, and the fox, and the owl, and the snake, and the . . .

Dr Jack, though. Dr Jack. Who the hell is Dr Jack?

TWELVE

November 2019

Heidi

Mum went into cheer-everyone-up overdrive: family movie nights, talking about what we'd do at Christmas, booking a camping trip in France next spring. She'd been playing this game ever since Nicky died. She didn't believe in ghosts or ouija boards or crystal healing; she called that kind of thing 'woo-woo'. But in a way she believed in her own kind of woo-woo: put a smile on your dial, pretend everything's fine, and all your troubles will melt away. It was all an act. I noticed a crease on her forehead that had never been there before.

A couple of weeks after the dinosaur disaster, she asked me to help with the weekly supermarket shop. I had a nasty feeling this was going to lead to a heart-to-heart, but I couldn't think of an excuse to get out of it. Dad had a lot of work on. Noah had a tummy bug and had been sick in the night. The washing machine was rumbling away, stuffed full of his sheets.

Dad was peering at his computer screen when we left. No surprise there.

'We're off now, Scott,' Mum said, looking around the office door. 'Scott? Are you working?' I heard the snark in her voice. I bet she was counting to ten. 'It's not fair just to park Noah in front of the TV.'

The air was full of fine, clinging drizzle, like the clouds had come to earth. A column of white smoke drifted over the fence from our neighbours' place, with an earthy bonfire smell. That would be Pete, burning piles of wet leaves. He was a retired farmer, always busy in his garden.

Mum turned up the car heating and chatted on and on about things that didn't matter. We were driving past Nicky's house. Someone else lived there now. Someone else went in and out through the blue front door which Nicky was kicking when he tried to call.

'Dad's not okay, is he?' I said loudly, interrupting Mum as she twittered about what we could do for Noah's birthday.

'What makes you say that?'

'Come on, Mum. He's always online. He's driving you nuts. I heard you two having a massive fight a while ago; I heard you screaming at him.'

'I didn't scream at him.'

I sighed. 'Whatever.'

'He *is* okay.'

'Crap.'

I knew she hated that word. I wanted to shock her into being real. No chance.

'It's absolutely normal for people to go through stages of grief,' she said. 'To lose themselves for a while. He'll soon be his old self again, I promise.'

•

I offered to push the trolley around the supermarket. Things were beckoning to me: packets of balloons and hair ties. I stayed close to Mum, keeping both hands very firmly on the trolley handle. *Not one single solitary thing more.* Mum stopped at the make-up section and insisted on buying me mascara and eyeliner, since she'd once noticed me wearing Maia's. It melted my heart. She was trying so hard to make things happy again.

I was relieved when we made it to the checkout without me pinching anything. We'd loaded everything onto the moving belt when Mum did a last check of her shopping list.

'Damn,' she muttered. 'Stock cubes. Heidi, could you run back and grab some? Vegetable, any brand. They're next to the herbs and spices.'

Stock cubes, stock cubes, nothing but stock cubes, I whispered to myself as I shot along to the aisle and grabbed a box.

On my way back I passed a dumpbin full of matchbox-sized vehicles, three for the price of two. Noah already had a box full of cars and trucks, he didn't need any more, but I stopped to look. Mum reckoned they put toys and sweets near the checkout to make it difficult for parents to say no when their children begged them. She called it the 'nag factor', a cruel trick because so many people can't afford those things. Well, this time it backfired on whoever owned Tesco, because I walked out of the shop on a high, with a stolen ambulance in my pocket.

The buzz lasted about five minutes. By the time we'd left the car park, I wanted to wind down the window and chuck it into the ditch. Why had I taken it? *Why?*

As she drove, Mum kept glancing my way and asking questions. Were things okay at school? Why had I fallen out with my best friends?

I mumbled the shortest answers possible, hoping she'd give up.

'It can be a difficult time, being thirteen,' she said. 'All those changes. You know.'

Oh God, no. Please. She was about to launch into one of those squirmy conversations about bras and sex and tampons. I turned on the radio, cranking up the volume. She had it tuned to Classic FM as usual, so we got a blast of opera. For a while this seemed to work. We drove in silence until we were nearly home. The stolen ambulance was digging into my hip.

'I think something's up with you, Heidi,' she said suddenly. 'Something more than sadness about Nicky. It's okay, though; you don't have to share it with me.'

'Nothing's up.'

She reached across, gave my hand a squeeze and held on to it. 'Just . . . whatever it is, just remember that you can tell me. You always can. No matter what.'

I took my hand away, because it made me want to cry that she was being so kind. And because I could never, ever tell her.

•

Ten forty-four. My birthday. I was filling up our water bottles at the kitchen tap, in a stupid panic about leaving too late and missing out on lunch at the Thorgill Arms. As if it mattered.

I'd just screwed the lids back on the bottles when I heard that dreaded sound from the dresser. Dad's phone, buzzing away. I took a look at who was calling and saw it was Nicky again. I loved my uncle to bits, I really did. I knew how much he worried about things. But this was his third call today. He'd only be fussing about when he and Dad were going to Tesco. He hated any change to his routine.

The phone was vibrating in my hand. I was going to answer it, I swear. My finger was on the screen, ready to swipe.

But then I changed my mind.

All year long I shared Dad with Mum and Noah, and Nicky, and Granny Denby, and hundreds of kids at school and their parents, and the other teachers, and his annoying cycling buddies.

He was public property. But today was *my* day with him, and I'd been looking forward to it so much.

So instead of answering Nicky's call, I ran into the sitting room and shoved the phone down the back of the armchair. *We'll call him later,* I told myself, as I smothered the buzzing with a cushion. *He'll be fine.*

I'd give anything to be able to turn back time.

THIRTEEN

Scott

'*Hello again*,' said Dr Jack. '*Today's story begins in the 1930s. I wish I could say it ends there.*'

I was meant to be out cycling, battling across the hills on a damp and chilly November morning, alongside five other masochists. I'd cried off. 'Noah's not well, I'd rather stay close to home,' I said, though I knew Livia would have been only too happy for me to go with them. It wasn't a fib. Noah had a bug. He was on the sofa under a blanket, watching Saturday morning TV.

I had great intentions. Knock out some urgent lesson planning, fix the leaking cistern in the downstairs toilet, play with Noah. But Livia and Heidi had only just set off for the supermarket when I got a notification from YouTube. Dr Jack had posted a new video: *Genocide in Plain Sight*. The title sounded interesting, so I had a look. I only planned to watch the first couple of minutes.

There he was: the avatar doctor with his heavy-rimmed glasses and white coat, stethoscope around his neck.

'*Before we get underway,*' he began, '*I've got to warn you that what I'm going to be talking about today is disturbing.*

Please don't be surprised if you find you're struggling with the implications. Feel free to make contact if you want to discuss any of this a bit more. Okay?'

The avatar shrank to miniature size as it flew into a corner of the screen, to be replaced by footage of Adolf Hitler among a group of men, walking with the high-speed, jerky movements of old newsreels. Evil, yet grotesquely comical.

'To see the pattern here, we're going back to Germany just before and during the war. You might already know this nightmarish piece of history, but please bear with me because the details matter. Adolf Hitler was building his power base when he ordered what came to be known as the T4 Euthanasia Program, or sometimes the T4 Program, named after the Berlin address from which it was all directed: Tiergartenstrasse 4.'

Black-and-white photographs of a stone building: shadowy, gothic, profoundly grim.

'This wasn't about the Jews. That came later. T4 targeted another innocent demographic—one which would have included many of us, many of those we love, wonderful folk I work with every day: people with disabilities or chronic illness. Propaganda labelled them "useless eaters" and "life unworthy of life". Think about that. Life unworthy of life.'

I almost stopped watching. I'd rather be fixing the cistern. I knew of the existence of the T4 program, but few details. I wasn't sure I wanted to know. But that was the point, wasn't it? People *didn't want* to know.

'This was about eugenics,' continued Dr Jack. *'Also about economics. A secret bureaucracy was set up to "euthanise" these people in purpose-built gas chambers. One of the most chilling aspects is that victims were allegedly being taken away for hospital treatment. The SS officers in charge used to put on white coats, to seem more trustworthy. Later, families would hear that their loved one had died of some made-up cause. They'd get a letter*

of condolence, a fake death certificate. Ashes in an urn. In this way, up to a quarter of a million children and adults were murdered.'

I was looking at a photo of a 1940s-style ambulance with its back doors open, a ramp lowered. Men in white coats, patients on stretchers, families standing nearby. A baby was being handed into the arms of someone dressed as a nurse.

'I want you to think about that,' said Dr Jack, *'because it's vital that we understand the power of these symbols. White coats. Studies show that people will do as they're told if the instruction comes from someone in a white coat. Or—the modern equivalent—medical scrubs, a stethoscope around the neck. We will walk into that ambulance, lie down on that operating table. We will deliver up our child or our parent, our sister or brother.'*

Something icy breathed on me, as I glimpsed where Dr Jack was going with all this. *He was still alive . . . they faffed about.*

'How could doctors become systematic killers of the most vulnerable? Doctors, whose whole purpose is to do the opposite! I think the answer is that there are always a few truly evil individuals willing to kickstart the whole thing, and others who get dragged into these ideologies through propaganda, coercion and the subtle use of euphemisms. This wasn't "murder", it was euthanasia, it was kindness. And there is dehumanisation: the monstrous idea that some lives are not worth living.'

Wistful harp music accompanied one image after another: an old woman in an apron; a man with a kind smile, who reminded me of Nicky. An anxious girl, her hair neatly brushed to each side of her face. A toddler with wide eyes. Captions gave names and ages.

'There was resistance,' said Dr Jack. *'Brave doctors tried to hide patients, smuggled them to safety. As a doctor myself I can only begin to imagine how hideous it must have been. The growing realisation of the truth. Horror, denial—no, no, no, this*

just cannot *be happening. Then a terrible choice: collude and survive, or resist and die.'*

Dr Jack's avatar returned to its full size.

'Why am I talking about something that happened eighty years ago? Because the ideology was driven underground, and there it quietly thrived, biding its time . . . until now. Many of us believe it is awakening. Right now, in 2019, forces are gathering. As the world dissolves into factionalism and hatred of "the other", those with the real power—and by that I don't *mean governments—flex their muscles. End-of-life choices are made every day. The foot is already in the door, and that door's being pushed open. Once again, doctors are turning a blind eye because this just* cannot *be happening.'*

The slideshow paused on a stock photo of the entrance to a modern hospital, with a yellow-and-green ambulance parked outside.

'I heard a story in a discussion forum this week from a nurse in a British hospital. They were dealing with a motorway pile-up: ambulances lining up, everyone being paged, theatres under pressure. One of the vehicles was a minibus carrying four residents from a home for people with intellectual disabilities. They'd been out on a day trip. All four had serious injuries, but none were life-threatening. The youngest was eighteen years old. She was conscious, she gripped the nurse's hand, they had quite a chat. Before going home he promised he'd see her tomorrow. So he was devastated, when his next shift began, to learn that all four had died during the night. Now, of course, people sometimes die unexpectedly in hospital. But four *of them?'*

Dr Jack's avatar blinked, disbelieving.

'This nurse asked a lot of questions. But very soon it became clear that if he wanted to keep his job, he had to let this go. He was given a warning, accused of "undermining morale" and "spreading misinformation". His social media was watched, his

phone stolen from his locker. So he came to the forum—blowing the whistle in the only way he could. Were those four people smothered, was something slipped into their IV? He'd never know the answer. A month later, he was sacked on a trumped-up charge.'

My rational mind was rebelling. *Fake story! Four people? That could never be swept under the carpet.* I was on the verge of exiting the page.

But.

Nicky was fine when I spoke to him that morning. He was *fine.* Yet by two o'clock he was dead. It didn't make sense.

'*Think the T4 program could never happen here?*' asked Dr Jack. '*Think again. Because it already is.*'

FOURTEEN

Heidi

'What on earth do you mean?'

I'd never heard Mum's voice like that before. It was quiet, but there was more anger in it than if she'd screamed. A kind of flatness. The opposite of love. Not hate.

We were just back from the supermarket. I'd already run upstairs and chucked the stolen ambulance under my cupboard with the rest of my hoard. Mum was zipping around the kitchen—not easy with Noah pushing a train across the floor, tripping everyone up—as we put away a whole week's groceries. Dad helped us carry bags in from the car, but his mind wasn't on the job. He kept talking and talking, telling us about a hospital where four people died in one night.

'None of them had life-threatening injuries,' he said.

Mum was rearranging the fridge, but for a moment she looked over and met my eye, like she was trying to share something with me. I got the feeling she wanted me to take sides. I didn't want to do that.

'Let me get this straight,' she said, slamming the fridge door. 'Your only evidence of mass murder is some anonymous "doctor"'—she drew sarcastic bunny ears in the air—'with a channel on YouTube, quoting an anonymous "nurse"'—more bunny ears—'from an online chatroom full of conspiracy theorists.'

'That nurse has been fired for asking too many questions.'

'I bet he has!'

'Because he's a whistleblower.'

Mum was laughing. 'Nope, because he's a malicious liar—if he exists. A motorway pile-up, four people dead from one residential community! Did you check it even happened?'

She grabbed her phone and started googling. Thirty seconds later, she was holding up the search results to show Dad.

'Nothing. Nix. Nada. This nurse is fictional.'

'Of course it's not in the mainstream news,' Dad protested. 'That's the point. These things get hushed up.'

Noah gave up on his train and wandered up to Mum, burying his face in her jersey. He was getting big now, nearly six, but when he wasn't feeling well he became quite a baby again. She sat down in the rocking chair and lifted him onto her lap, stroking his hair back from his face.

'Real conspiracies happen,' Dad insisted. 'What was Watergate? What was the Tuskegee experiment?'

'Yes, Watergate and Tuskegee were real. But they've got nothing to do—'

'How about MK-Ultra and those mind control experiments back in the sixties and seventies? That was the CIA! It was horrible—*horrible*—and the state colluded in it.'

'I know about that. Also real. I don't see how it's relevant.'

'It's relevant because the people asking questions were ridiculed or silenced. Cases like those are the tip of the iceberg. They lie to us. They never *stop* lying to us.'

Mum hugged Noah closer as she made the chair rock.

'Scott . . . I know you're looking for answers, but these are *not* answers. None of this will bring Nicky back. The world is not being run by shadowy monsters. Hospitals aren't teeming with murderers.'

'You think I'm deluded.'

'I think you're grieving. I think you need help with that.'

He stood with his arms folded, just staring at her. It was awful, the anger and coldness between them. I kept quiet, just watching.

'I knew you'd do this,' he said.

'Knew I'd do what? Use logic?'

'Mock. You *always* ridicule things you don't understand. Anything that frightens you. You close your mind.'

Noah said he was thirsty, so I filled a glass for him at the tap. When I next looked around, Dad had left the room.

I was pissed off on his behalf. I gave Noah his water and Mum a telling-off.

'Dad's been researching this stuff for weeks and you haven't,' I said. 'He's not stupid.'

She sighed. 'You think it's me who's delusional? Maybe I am.'

'I think you didn't need to laugh in his face. You say it's all rubbish, but you don't know anything about it. You might at least watch that video.'

She set Noah down and went to stash the reusable shopping bags in the pantry. When she came out, she was rubbing her eyes like you do when hay fever makes them itch. They looked red and sore.

'Let's get the kettle on,' she said. 'Cup of tea.'

It was her answer to everything. She got that from her own mum.

'No, thanks,' I said, and went to find Dad.

He was back at the desk in the office with his face cupped between the palms of his hands, but he looked around and smiled as I sat down on the futon. On his screen, a cartoon doctor was pointing at a graph.

'What's he saying?' I asked.

'He's explaining some statistics.' Dad paused the video and turned around in his chair, resting his arm on the back. 'What proportion of people get well after being admitted to hospital needing emergency care. He's explaining that if you've got a chronic condition, or if you have a disability, you're much less likely to come out alive. It's all here. The stats don't lie.'

'Nicky had both. A chronic condition and a disability.'

'He did.'

He started the video again. The graph was replaced by an operating theatre with bright lights. People in masks and gloves and gowns, stooping over a patient. You couldn't see their faces. They might not even have been human beings. There was blood. A *lot* of blood.

The avatar doctor spoke with a Scottish accent.

'*Imagine the power of a megalithic health system turned against a blindly trusting population. Imagine that power weaponised and malevolent. It can section troublemakers, it can restrain and imprison. Don't believe me? Ever been in a dementia unit or psychiatric ward?*'

It was like a horror film. The photos flicked between modern-day hospital scenes and old-fashioned ones. The last picture was of a modern yellow ambulance shown side by side with a black-and-white photo: a kind of van with a ramp at the back, patients on stretchers, nurses with white headdresses. Something about it made me feel shivery.

'*The system has the power to sedate, paralyse, sterilise, anaesthetise. Morphine, propanol, fentanyl, withdrawal of life support . . . so many ways to subdue. It can inject mind-altering or life-ending drugs. It can remove organs, plant devices in people's bodies. All under the guise of care and cure. And of course, it can kill.*'

Mum's voice made me jump. She'd come in quietly and was standing close behind me.

'Turn it off, Scott. Right now.'

FIFTEEN

Livia

'No more,' I said that night, once we were alone.

Scott was stoking the fire.

'I didn't encourage her to watch.'

'You didn't stop her. No more, okay? Promise me.'

He poured us both a finger of whisky and sank into his usual seat at one end of the sofa. I lay along it, leaning against him, with Noah's patchwork blanket across my knees. This was a time-honoured ritual for us, a small luxury on a wintry evening. A dram of whisky, the fire lit, time alone together. But tonight everything was wrong.

'It isn't real, Scott,' I said. 'Dr Jack isn't real. He—or she, or them—could be in Brazil, or China, or anywhere at all. You're allowing yourself to be manipulated by a ghost.'

'He's male. He's a junior doctor in the emergency department of a Scottish hospital. He used his own voice to program the text-to-speech software.'

'How do you know?'

'I've talked to him. Exchanged messages.'

'What?' I twisted around to look at Scott's face. 'How?'

'I got in contact with him through Twitter. He replied. We had a chat.'

I was gawking at him. 'Why the hell would you do that?'

'To check he was real. And he is. I told him about Nicky.'

'You shared personal details about our family?'

'He's a nice guy. It's very easy to be cynical, Liv, but why would he lie? Why would any of them bother to lie?'

It was my turn to feel paranoid. This Dr Jack, this manipulator—a person, or people—knew we existed. He knew things about us.

'He suggested I write to the hospital board and the coroner to demand an inquiry into Nicky's death,' said Scott. 'And now I've seen this latest video, I understand what he was driving at. I want to know exactly how long the ambulance took to arrive, and why the paramedics didn't hurry. I want to know what happened in that ambulance on the way to the hospital— and whether Nicky really was dead on arrival in York, or whether someone decided he was a "useless eater" and left him on a gurney until he'd gone.'

'Scott! You talked to that doctor—Emma—in her clogs and scrubs. You're not seriously suggesting she's a cold-blooded killer?'

'Scrubs are just the modern version of a white coat. We're programmed to trust these symbols.'

Perhaps Heidi was right. I needed to watch some of this stuff. I needed to understand my enemy.

I reached backwards, giving a gentle tug to Scott's mop of hair. 'Show me. Just for this evening, I'll keep an open mind.'

•

I stepped through the looking glass, and into a parallel world.

For hours I was swept along with Scott and his community of Truthers, sampling a bewildering smorgasbord of beliefs. There was one unifying factor: the fundamental certainty that we're all being lied to on a colossal scale.

I watched videos, listened to podcasts, waded through forums, blogs and Facebook discussions. I immersed myself in complicated ideas about terrorist attacks, drugs and vaccines, HIV, 5G, chemtrails, disappearing airliners, the deaths of famous people—there seemed to be no event that hadn't attracted an offbeat theory. Scott was undecided on chemtrails and the moon landings, but he drew the line at believing the earth was flat or the Queen a lizard. Small mercies.

I noticed a theme in the way they operated, these influencers, or whatever the hell they called themselves. They all portrayed themselves as experts, light years more brilliant and capable of blue-sky thinking than anyone else. 'Do your own research,' they told their followers. 'Follow the breadcrumbs.' The breadcrumbs were grains of truth—statistics about vaccine injuries, for instance, or what a witness said about the 7/7 bombings in London. They exploited random facts, twisting them, making patterns that didn't exist.

'These people don't understand random chance!' I protested. 'Shake two dice a million times, and you'll get long runs of double six. It'll seem impossible, but it's actually inevitable. That's how statistics work.'

Scott had just brought in cups of coffee. 'You said you'd keep an open mind. Hang on . . . here we go. This one blew my mind. The Twin Towers.'

The video was fronted by a man called Gary Tey, an intense Texan with bug eyes and a porn star moustache. He claimed to be an ex-CIA agent who'd kept the receipts and could *prove* that 9/11 was an inside job. Why was the US Air Force stood down in the hours before the attack? How could burning jet fuel melt steel? Spoiler alert—it can't! He gave us a running commentary over slow-motion footage of the attacks.

I checked a couple of Tey's facts and found myself thinking, *Interesting, I never knew that.* I even wondered briefly whether he could be on to something. But when I dug deeper, the whole thing fell apart. An ice-thin veneer of truth, concealing a lake of misinformation and fantasy.

'This is how they hook people,' I said to Scott, as I muted the advert between videos. 'Start with a few verifiable facts as a gateway drug. Everything seems legit. Then little by little mix in the hard stuff. The hallucinogens. That's how they mess with people's heads.'

'They're not drug pushers. They're *truth* pushers.'

Dr Jack was next up. Reluctantly, I found myself liking the cute little avatar, the pleasant Scottish voice. I had to admire his blending of script, graphics and atmospheric music—a fast, subliminal way to unsettle his viewers. His earliest work investigated real-life scandals involving medical negligence. So far, so good. A grain of truth, you see? The gateway drug.

Then the hallucinogens. Dr Jack plunged us into darker territory. His video about the T4 euthanasia program was over-produced, but boy, was it chilling. I sat wide-eyed through to his warning that history was repeating itself, that the healthcare system had once again fallen into eugenicist hands.

By now my mind was turning to mush. I'd begun to think longingly of my bed when Dr Jack himself appeared on our screen: not the avatar, the human being. He sat in shadow, blue scrubs, stethoscope in his top pocket. His face and head were hidden by a blank rubber mask—a sinister contrast to his cuddly avatar. His backdrop was a wall, painted in that depressing shade of pale green you find in prisons, hospitals and schools.

His voice was still text-to-speech, presumably edited in afterwards.

'*For years I've been asking myself: Why, and How, and Who? The world isn't controlled by governments or corporations.*

Those entities think they're in control, but they're deluded. The real puppeteers have them dancing on their strings.'

He was sitting right up against that green wall. Behind him, a Z-shaped crack in the plasterwork zigzagged from top to bottom. Leaning close to the speakers, I caught faint sounds: a female voice, distinctly Scottish: *Jonty, have you seen the patient in three yet?* Trolley wheels, a ringing telephone, a screaming baby.

'How come he's got an office, in a casualty department?' I asked.

'It's for the senior registrar on duty. They hot-desk.'

'*We need to talk about this expression "conspiracy theorist",'* Dr Jack said. '*It's used to discredit us. So let's get it out there: Yes, I am a conspiracy theorist—someone who uses critical thought, who researches independently and doesn't believe every lie that's peddled by the mainstream media. What a shame the Trojans didn't listen to their conspiracy theorists! There were folk like me in Troy saying, "Hold on a minute, guys, this massive gift horse seems a bit too good to be true. Shall we have a quick gander inside before we drag it into our city?" And everyone fell about laughing. "Call in the men in white coats—poor old Laocoön has gone waaay down the rabbit hole."'*

That had both Scott and me chuckling, despite the weirdness of the figure in the featureless mask.

'*Don't be like the Trojans,'* said Dr Jack. '*Listen to the warnings. You'll find thousands of us fighting for freedom, in all walks of life. We are the twenty-first-century resistance. Hear the alarms going off. Wake up.'*

It was after two in the morning. I'd spent too long in Conspiracy World. I felt as though I'd been crawling in a roof space: no daylight, no air, nothing but cobwebs and rat bait. I couldn't see the edges of reality anymore.

'I think that's me for tonight,' I said. 'It's been a lot to take in.'

Scott sat beside me at the desk, fiddling with a biro. 'But can you see it now?' he asked.

SIXTEEN

December 2019

Livia

'So who does your man reckon is behind all this?' asked Charles, when I next saw him. 'Illuminati? Aliens? Secret society of spaghetti people?'

The Garrotter and I were sitting opposite one another under Christmas tinsel at the formica-topped table of Carol's, a high street cafe two blocks down from Willow House. The little place was always warm and fuggy and smelled of frying chips—a brightly lit oasis when the skies lowered like angry eyebrows as they did today. Carol herself was a doughty pillar of competence. She served strong tea in giant mugs, and her cheese-and-onion toasties were one of my guilty pleasures in life.

'I've no clue,' I mumbled. The melted cheese was scalding, impossible to eat elegantly, but I was beyond caring. Comfort food. 'Don't think *he* knows yet. The Big Reveal is still to come.'

'What did you tell him?'

'I said I wasn't convinced, but I'd do some more research of my own. I've been playing for time ever since. Mind you, it did make me feel a bit peculiar. Like Alice in Wonderland. You wonder if you're the one who's dreaming.'

My brain was firing on less than half a cylinder. Noah had turned six the day before, which involved a sugar-fest for a pack of wildly overexcited children. Heidi blew up fifty balloons, Scott ran nonstop party games, I was caterer, and Noah dashed around grinning all day. Parents arrived to collect their offspring and stayed to chat—which of course turned into a grown-up party in the kitchen, with wine and leftover crisps. Possibly I'd had a little too much of the wine. It was a good day, until I caught Scott pushing a Dr Jack video on some very startled parents.

'I mean, why?' Charles glanced around the crowded cafe, as though expecting to see a spaghetti person. '*Why* would doctors suddenly start bumping off patients?'

The toastie, the tea, Charles's sanity—they were all so welcome. I'd dropped by Willow House for a meeting with the manager, arranging for Charles to spend Christmas with his family. Then I'd glanced at my watch, calculated how many hours of urgent work I had waiting for me in the office, and suggested we drop into Carol's for a cuppa. I truly didn't intend to pour out my troubles to Charles. Or . . . no, actually I did.

'This is the thing,' I said. 'There *are* doctors and nurses who've murdered vulnerable patients.'

'Don't tell me, don't tell me, tip of my tongue.' Charles screwed up one side of his face. 'Harold . . .'

'Shipman. And others, over the years. A grain of truth. Always a grain of truth.'

'That's how they do it.'

'Exactly,' I said. 'In Scott's mind, everything suddenly makes sense. Nicky's death wasn't random bad luck and a missed phone call.'

'Part of a dastardly plan.'

'That's right.'

'Just to be clear, Livia,' Charles said, as he polished his steamed-up glasses on a paper napkin. 'You *do* know this is a load of rubbish?'

'I do. But it's nice to have that confirmed. Sometimes I don't know which way is up anymore. I feel like I'm going nuts.'

'You're not going nuts.'

'Thank you. Scott believes he's taken the red pill and can see everything as it really is. He wants me to take it too.' I remembered how long Charles had been inside. 'Sorry! You won't know what I'm on about. The red pill is—'

'I know.' Charles replaced his glasses on his nose. '*The Matrix* was the very last film I saw before I got arrested. Watched it at the Odeon.'

Outside, the heavens had opened. Umbrellas blossomed like peonies, shoppers ran to huddle in bus shelters and doorways. Several surged into the cafe, shaking out dripping anoraks, complaining that it was cats and dogs out there.

Charles poured us both more tea from the metal pot. 'So, what's your plan of action?'

I held up a finger. 'Option one: I pretend I've taken the red pill too. Pretend to see it all, believe it all. Maybe I can live that lie until Scott's himself again.'

'Hm.'

'Okay, not great.' A second finger. 'I say, "Scott, this is madness." I beg him to see a counsellor, which we can't afford and he would never do anyway. He'd probably think the counsellor was in on the conspiracy. So it all ends up in a massive row. He gets hurt, I get hurt. And . . . I don't know what happens next. Maybe we separate. I lose him, the children lose him. We love him so much, Charles. He's a wonderful father, he's my best friend, he's everything. I really, *really* don't want to lose him.'

'And three?'

'I carry on, learn more about my enemy. Find some way to fight back.'

Charles's expression changed subtly. There was someone else back there, someone more complex than the twinkly grandfather figure. The network of creases around his eyes deepened. Such sadness.

'You can't fight an invisible enemy,' he said.

'I can bloody well try.'

•

We stuck to practicalities as we walked back to Willow House. Charles let me know that he'd enrolled for a peer support group called ReStart and would be going along in the New Year. We talked about his seeing an audiologist, since his hearing aid was giving trouble.

'You're doing so well,' I told him. 'I'm proud of you.'

'Thanks for helping me. The people at Willow House are great. And Carol, she's been kind. She knows what I did. She knows who I am.'

When we reached my car, I dumped my bag on the passenger seat before turning back to him.

'Happy Christmas, Charles.' I couldn't resist giving him an unprofessionally emotional hug. 'Your first with your family. Jess and the kids will be so excited! Good luck.'

'Don't worry, I won't garrotte anyone.'

'Please don't.'

He hummed 'The Blue Danube' as he waltzed along the pavement, twirling with an imaginary partner.

'Merry Christmas to you too, Livia. Let's see what 2020 brings, eh?'

•

On my way home, I stopped to grab a couple of things from the Gilderdale Spar. Mrs Ponder pursed her lips as I paid.

'Is it your lass,' she asked, 'who comes in a lot? Long red hair, about thirteen, fourteen, rides a bike?'

'That sounds like Heidi,' I said, smiling.

I was waiting for her to gush: *What a lovely girl, credit to you,* or *If she'd like a Saturday job, tell her to let me know.* People liked Heidi.

Sour baggage. She just grunted, heavy tramlines of disapproval around her mouth.

'Night then,' I called cheerily, as the door ting-tinged.

I didn't give it much thought. Some people have resting bitch faces, don't they? My immediate boss, for one. Heart of gold, though.

As I turned into Back Lane, a rainbow appeared out of the leaden light, arching from the moors to the church tower. It was vivid and radiant and—had I believed in such things—I'd have hailed it as a message of hope.

SEVENTEEN

Heidi

It wasn't the best Christmas.

We did the tree thing, and the presents thing. We did the mince pies and angel chimes, and church because Mum liked the music. We decorated our front hedge with fairy lights, another of our traditions. I heard Dad talking anxiously from the top of the ladder about how the coroner had refused to investigate Nicky's death, which proved he'd been 'got at'. Mum tutted and said what a disgrace it was.

They didn't fight once. They were polite. Much too polite.

On Christmas morning Dad and I drove down to York to collect Granny Denby. She wouldn't let him bring her wheelchair, insisting on using her walker. I admired her feistiness but it was painfully slow. We all stood around with awkward smiles as she inched her way from the car into the house—Dad and I took an arm each to help her up the steps—then through the kitchen and into the sitting room, where she fell into the armchair. Dad arranged cushions around her while Mum brought mince pies and a cup of tea.

Noah was setting up a trail of his big dominoes around the floor, crooning some made-up song to himself as he balanced each one. He was good with his hands and had ten times my patience. I'd seen him spend hours setting up a long trail like this before happily knocking it over again.

'Nicky here yet?' asked Granny, all hopeful.

Dad squatted down beside her and took her hands in both of his. Granny's fingers were like gnarled twigs.

'He had other things on today, Mum.' He glanced at me. 'Would you like Heidi to play her guitar? She's been learning Hungarian folk carols. They're beautiful.'

Granny's gaze wandered from his face to mine. She didn't answer his question, but I fetched my guitar and sat on the stool by the fire to play to her. Poor Granny. Tears were dripping down onto her cardigan. I just kept playing. I didn't know what else to do.

'Where is Nicky?' she asked nobody in particular, when I was halfway through the third carol.

'Nicky died,' said Noah, without looking up from his dominoes. People think my brother's such a kind, gentle little boy because goldfish swim into his hands and he always shares his toys. And he *is* kind and gentle. But sometimes I wonder if he isn't a psychopath.

'Noah!' I hissed. 'Shush.'

'But he did. He got hype . . .' Noah frowned as he looked for the word. 'Hype . . . not enough sugar, and then he fell over in his garden and then he was deaded.'

'I expect he'll be coming soon,' I said to Granny.

'Ready?' Noah lifted his forefinger, ready to topple the first domino. 'Hey, Heidi! Ready?'

'Ready,' I said.

'Steady!' His finger was moving closer and closer to its target. I stuck a smile on my dial. It's catching, that habit. 'Steady.'

'Go!'

Just a touch of his grubby little finger and the dominoes were off, like a colourful line of dancers, all around Granny's chair.

Like I say, it wasn't the best Christmas. Actually, it was the worst I could ever remember.

EIGHTEEN

Scott

On New Year's Eve I took my mother out for lunch at a cafe. It was a good visit. She seemed brighter, and only asked for Nicky once. Her long-term memory was as clear as a bell. We reminisced about our holidays on Coniston Water: how Dad loved to take us sailing in *Geraldine*; how he and Mum would sit in deckchairs outside the caravan with an evening drink, watching us boys swimming.

I'd said goodbye to her and was driving through the gates of her nursing home when my phone pinged with a notification. Dr Jack had just posted a new video: *MUST WATCH! The Big Picture: Circles within Circles.*

Our family was going out later, to the New Year's bash at Rosedale Retreat. But I had a bit of time now, and I was alone; I could watch this video without feeling judged. Livia pretended to keep an open mind but she was resolutely blind. No matter how much evidence I showed her, she refused to see what was right in front of her nose.

I parked up in a quiet side street.

'*Happy New Year!*' began the avatar doctor. '*Time to talk about the fundamental questions: How, Why and Who. Who are these puppeteers, with the world dancing on their strings? I used to ask those same questions. The answer is so simple that, when you see it, you'll realise you knew all along. Let me show you something that happens in the natural world.'*

The voiceover blended with his signature harp music. The melody was reflective, played at a peaceful walking pace, each note reverberating.

'*Meet* Plesiometa argyra. *This orb-weaving spider, who lives in Costa Rica, is the nice guy in all of this. The unsuspecting victim.'*

The spider was a photogenic creature with delicate legs and silver-green markings, like a tiny piece of modern art. The web was subtly lit, glittering in the gloom of the forest.

'*He's about to meet an enemy he doesn't even know exists. A parasitic wasp with the snappy scientific name of* Hymeno-epimecis argyraphaga. *She already has him in her sights.'*

And there it was: a long, yellowish insect darting in like a helicopter, landing on the spider, grasping hold of him.

'*She has a use for him. She injects him with a venom that paralyses him for a while, long enough for her to glue her egg to his abdomen. Then off she flies: her work is done.'*

I already knew where this clip was going. Nicky used to love David Attenborough wildlife documentaries. He had all the boxed sets. He and I sat on his battered sofa, mouths hanging open when it came to this wasp and this spider. It was the stuff of nightmares.

'*At first her eight-legged victim appears to recover,'* Dr Jack continued. '*He seems fine. Goes back to spinning his webs, catching and eating his prey, the usual spider stuff. For two weeks he carries on pretty much as normal. But all this time the larval wasp is riding around on him, feeding on him. His body has become a nursery for the creature that will eventually destroy him.'*

The music became menacing. The larva was huge now, clinging to its poor host.

'*One night, everything changes. The parasite makes its presence known. It releases chemicals that have an extraordinary effect on the behaviour of its host. Chemicals that control its host. The spider is now a zombie slave. He works only for his parasitic master, creating something alien: a strong bed for the pupating larva to cocoon itself. Once that is finished he's no longer useful. So—you've guessed it—he's killed, eaten and what's left of him is chucked off the web.*'

The video froze on an image of a platform woven by a murdered spider, now home to a pupating larva. The music stopped dead.

'*A secret movement,*' said Dr Jack, in the silence. '*Growing steadily. Waiting for the perfect opportunity. Quietly taking control. Destroying the host.*'

The Costa Rican forest scene dissolved, re-forming as an oil painting. A man of the Victorian era: portly, with a heavy moustache and stick-up collar.

'*Let's talk about Cecil Rhodes, best known for his role in colonising southern Africa. Rhodes was one of the richest and most powerful men on earth. He was also an imperialist, obsessed with his dream of a one-world government. To that end he founded the Society of the Elect, an underground network of influential people whose life's work was to pursue his dream. Don't believe me? Look it up—this is no secret. Rhodes knew that it would take generations to achieve his goal, so he left vast riches in his will to enable his underground network to further his aim. That unimaginable wealth is still sloshing around today, still luring elite recruits into his secret society. And all of this in plain sight. The Rhodes Trust, the Rhodes Scholarship. Take a look at the roll call of past scholars, and you'll understand that this cult goes all the way to the top.*'

Scrolling names were accompanied by photos of famous people, including heads of government. Bill Clinton was on there.

'*The Society of the Elect still strives to rule the world, but the centre of gravity shifted long, long ago. Rhodes' vision has been hijacked; he created and nurtured a monstrous cabal that would horrify him now. For more than a century, the Elect has started wars, toppled governments, crashed currencies, spread its tentacles into every major institution: NATO, the UN, the European Union, the IMF. Military, police and intelligence services. Justice and health systems, banks and corporations. Religions and universities. Mainstream media, fringe media, social media. And all governments—left, right, democracy, dictatorship—it doesn't matter. I repeat: It doesn't matter. Why? Because they're all controlled by the same cabal. And what is so brilliant is that they do not know they're being controlled. They're all still going about their business as usual, spinning their webs.*'

Dr Jack's avatar appeared in the top corner, standing with his arms folded. The rest of the screen became a whiteboard with a cartoon hand holding a crayon. I wondered whether he had help with these videos. He was a family man as well as a doctor working long shifts. It must take hours to find all the elements, research and write the scripts and blend everything together so seamlessly.

'*So how is it done?*' he asked, as the hand began to draw a small circle in the middle of the screen. '*Like this. Circles within circles. In the innermost circle are the Elect: two or three individuals with unimaginable power. They are the puppeteers.*'

The hand scribbled *Elect* by the central ring before drawing another around it.

'*Beyond the Elect, a larger Circle of the Elite: around a hundred individuals, who know much of the agenda and work towards it within their fields of influence. They hide in plain sight. You've probably heard of the Bilderberg group.*'

I had indeed. Bill Clinton had been involved in that too. And Bill Gates. I remembered seeing on the news earlier this year that the group was meeting in Switzerland, picketed by angry protestors who insisted this jolly get-together of the world's most powerful people was really . . .

Oh. Oh, now I saw it.

Was really the prelude to a global coup.

'Billionaires,' said Dr Jack. 'Politicians, financiers, academics, military and security experts, CEOs of immense multinationals. When they're summoned to a meeting, they drop everything, clear their diaries, fly across the world in their private jets. No minutes are taken, no records kept, no outsiders or media whatsoever allowed. Security is unbelievably tight. Look it up—check for yourself—you'll see that all of this is true.'

The cartoon hand sped up, drawing and writing in fast motion.

'In their turn, this Circle of the Elite controls the next circle, who are high-ups in . . . well, basically everything. This one contains thousands of people. Most of them have no idea that the inner circles exist. All these VIPs are acting on a need-to-know basis, unwittingly advancing an agenda many of them would loathe. And beyond them, we find more concentric circles'—the hand drew three more rings—'each impacting the next. Millions of ordinary people working to further a totalitarian agenda without ever knowing there is an agenda. Teachers, public servants, health workers, soldiers, lawyers, police officers . . . every walk of life. This is the classic pyramid structure used by cult leaders, but on a global scale. These circles within circles have a name. This is the New World Order.'

The cartoon hand wrote three words beneath the concentric circles, as a title: NEW WORLD ORDER.

'There's no relevance to questions about who the NWO is, or where it's based. Because it's everywhere. It is all of us.

Like Plesiometa argyra, *we're building a web for our oppressors without even knowing they exist. Like the spider, we will one day outlive our usefulness. And when that day comes, we'll be destroyed.'*

NINETEEN

Heidi

I was looking forward to the fireworks at Rosedale Retreat. The Espinozas threw a party every New Year's Eve and invited lots of local people, all of us rugged up in scarves and woolly hats as we held hands to sing 'Auld Lang Syne'.

'Please, Scott,' Mum begged Dad, while we were getting ready to leave, 'promise you won't . . . you know. Talk about things. Not tonight.'

Dad froze in the act of zipping up Noah's anorak. 'Things?'

'You know what I mean.'

'I'm sorry if I embarrass you.'

She was brushing her hair in the hall mirror. I had to admit she looked great tonight, in jeans and black boots, hair flowing over the blue-and-gold pashmina Aunt Bethany gave her for Christmas. Mum could be spectacular when she scrubbed up. She brushed faster and more furiously, and I had the feeling she'd quite like to turn around and wallop Dad with the hairbrush, but instead she found a fake grin in her store cupboard and stuck it on her face. I spotted her perfecting it in the mirror.

'I'm never anything but proud of you,' she fibbed. 'But it's New Year's Eve. People don't want to talk politics. It isn't fair to Megan and Marcos. So please, check your theories at the door.'

I knew exactly what she meant. She didn't want him going into Internet Dad mode, like he had at Noah's birthday party. I was pretty sure he *was* an embarrassment to her when he did that. He'd embarrassed me too. A lot.

'Okay,' said Dad, helping Noah into his wellies. 'I promise to try. But the Espinozas put me on to Professor Tabard in the first place.'

'Tabard! Gosh, those were the days. You've come a long way since then, Scott. Megan and Marcos run an alternative health spa; it stands to reason they'd be interested in natural cures. But Tabard was mild compared to . . . wherever you are now. Which is hardcore.'

'So you're issuing a gagging order.'

Mum slammed the brush down on the hall table before picking up her fedora hat.

'Just not tonight,' she said.

•

Megan and Marcos knew how to throw a party. Each year their wild garden became a wonderland, like Narnia. Fairy lights and hundreds of candles in glass lanterns hung from branches, lighting the paths. Their bonfire was an inferno, and they must have spent a fortune on fireworks. When the little kids got tired of making themselves sick on toffee apples and rushing around with sparklers, they could snuggle down on the heated timber floor of the yoga studio. There were always blankets and beanbags, cartoons on a big screen.

Anthony was just getting out of his car when we parked next to him in the field. He'd been helping the Espinozas with some technical stuff, so they'd invited him to the party.

'Rosedale guests pay an arm and a leg to detox from modern life,' he said, with his rumbling laugh. 'They expect speedy wi-fi with their ice baths.'

'Got to be able to check the share prices,' said Mum.

As we walked towards the house, she and Anthony had a chuckle about geranium oil enemas. Meanwhile, I was salivating over the smells of roasting horse chestnuts and barbecuing sausages. According to Anthony, they were special sausages from the posh organic butcher in Gilderdale. There was mulled wine too, served in handmade clay cups. Mum took one sip and started gushing about how it was exquisite. She dived straight in when we arrived and didn't let up all night. I grabbed a cup myself when she wasn't looking. It tasted like cough mixture, but it grew on me.

I was getting a sausage in a bun for Noah when I heard someone calling me from the other side of the bonfire.

'Hey, Heidi! *Heidi!*'

I recognised that voice, felt myself blushing. Flynn Thomas, my music friend. He was wearing an overcoat and scarf, an old-fashioned flat cap on his curly hair. I'd never seen him out of school uniform before. He was with a group of teenagers sitting on logs and tree stumps. I knew some of them, though they were mostly older than me. Nice people.

'Come and sit with us,' he called, beckoning. 'We've got a stash of sparklers.'

Noah grabbed his hot dog and zoomed off with a little mate from school. As I joined the group on the logs, Flynn made room for me to sit by him.

'Good Christmas?' he asked. 'Here, have a bite of my toffee apple.'

We sat around, toasting marshmallows and drawing patterns in the darkness with sparklers, sometimes dancing to music from our phones. I tried a puff of someone's vape but it was disgusting.

Flynn and I took a selfie and I sent it to Maia, just to spoil her night. She'd have given her right arm to be in my shoes.

'You should have brought your guitar, Flynn,' said one of the girls.

I jumped up, delighted to be able to help. 'Mine's in the car. I'll get it.'

Flynn said he'd come too, and walked along with me. He pointed out his parents on the way, comfy-looking people in goose down jackets. It was a starry night. So, so cold. It seemed as though every crackly leaf, every blade of grass had turned to ice. As we crossed the field our breath came out in white clouds. I wondered what on earth I'd do if Flynn suddenly did something romantic—like took hold of my hand or tried to kiss me—but he was his usual self, chatting all the way to the car and back, clapping his gloved hands together to keep them warm. He told me about his cat, Dorothy, and how she loved to fetch things just like a dog. I was almost disappointed.

We took it in turns to play my guitar. In Flynn's hands it sounded like a different instrument. It was magical to sit in the firelight, watching his fingers fly up and down the fingerboard. It felt like being in a poem. He played some flamenco, and a bit of blues. When he began playing Ed Sheeran songs that everyone knew, we all started swaying and singing.

I was happy. I was really happy. I shouldn't have been, after all the unforgivable things I'd done in 2019. But it was New Year's Eve in a Narnian wonderland, with music and Flynn. My mulled wine was tasting better with every sip. And you can't go on feeling guilty forever, for every second of every day.

My first inkling that things were going wrong was when Mum dashed up. I hid the wine behind my guitar, but I needn't have bothered. It wasn't *my* behaviour she was stressed about.

'Have you seen Dad?' she asked.

Livia

The year had less than half an hour left of life when I got a tip-off from Katie Pryor, the head's secretary at Barmoors High. She was carrying her baby in a sling on her front, an enormous shawl keeping out the freezing air, a mug in one hand.

'Is Scott okay, Livia?' she asked.

'As far as I know.'

'Right.' She hesitated, stroking the baby's head, and my heart sank. 'Um . . . I've just had a very unusual conversation with him.'

'Where is he?

She jerked her chin towards the house.

'Holding court in the kitchen. I didn't know he had such strong political views. He's always seemed so easygoing.'

The baby was grizzling. Katie rocked from foot to foot, patting the little bundle. I knew she was hoping I'd dish some dirt on Scott, but she was plumb out of luck. I was furious, I was embarrassed, but I wasn't going to be disloyal. Not tonight, among colleagues and neighbours.

'Ben looks happy as a clam in there,' I said, giving the baby's bobble cap a tweak.

'He's like that plant in *Little Shop of Horrors*. "Feed me, Seymour!" Okay, okay. Keep your hair on, mister.'

She set off to the yoga studio to feed him, leaving me to seethe.

My first instinct was to find Scott. Damage limitation. My route took me past a group of young people lounging around near the bonfire. I stopped when I spotted Heidi among them, playing her guitar to a young man in a newsboy cap. They were both singing. He seemed to be sitting rather close.

'Have you seen Dad?' I asked her.

'You lost him?'

'He's . . .' I threw out my hands.

Heidi caught on immediately, bless her.

'Shall I go and look for him?' she asked, jumping up.

But I shook my head and moved on. This wasn't Heidi's problem. It was wonderful to see her having fun, flirting with that boy, playing her music.

Nearer the house, Anthony was roasting chestnuts over a brazier. The hood of his sweatshirt hung from underneath a bulky Nepalese jacket, like a monk's cowl.

'All right, Livia?' he called.

'So-so.'

'Have a couple of these.' He handed me a brown paper bag with salted chestnuts in them. 'Delectable on a cold winter's night. Rest of the year, inedible.'

I bit into one, taking a moment to appreciate its sweet smokiness and creamy texture.

'Where's our lad?' asked Anthony.

'Last seen in the kitchen, standing on his soapbox. I imagine he's preaching that hospitals are full of murderers and the human race is being controlled by . . . I dunno. Whatever he thinks today.'

'Hm.' Anthony was using tongs to turn the chestnuts. 'And what is it that he thinks today?'

'Couldn't tell you. He went to visit his mum this morning and came home raving about a new Dr Jack video he'd watched— crazy stuff about Cecil Rhodes and some secret society that rules the world. I didn't want to hear about it, not today. I'll tackle it later, once everyone's back at school and I'm on top of the Christmas-inspired domestic violence backlog at work.'

'Makes sense.'

'Does it, though?' I chucked my paper bag onto the red-hot charcoal. It lay inert for several seconds before bursting into flames. 'Does it make sense, or am I just a spineless enabler? He's getting deeper and deeper into this fucked-up community. Every conversation we have turns back to his obsessions.

Nobody's telling him how insane it is.' I looked towards the house. 'I feel like storming into that kitchen and dragging him out by the ear.'

Anthony grinned at me across the brazier. The shadows distorted his face, made his beard look like the lower half of a balaclava.

'You really want to see in the New Year with a public showdown?'

'I don't have the right, do I? He's not a child.' I sighed, knocking back the rest of my wine. 'But I swear to you, Anthony, if I ever get my hands on this Dr Jack character, I'm going to throttle him.'

'Now that I'd like to see.' Anthony was stashing the tongs. 'How about I go look for him instead? It's nearly midnight. He'd better not miss the fireworks.'

Heidi

Mum didn't give much away, but I could guess why she was looking for Dad.

She rushed off in the direction of the house, leaving me worried. This was the worst possible time and place for Dad to start ranting. I couldn't bear it if he made a fool of himself in front of Flynn and my new friends.

'Everything okay?' asked Flynn.

'Your turn,' I said, handing him my guitar. 'I'll be back in a minute. Just got to have a word with my dad.'

It was tricky to recognise people in the dark. Groups huddled on garden furniture, or stood warming their hands at the bonfire. Quite a few were up on the terrace, jiving to a retro playlist. Mum and Dad usually danced half the night up there. Not this year.

I stuck my head around the door of the yoga studio, hoping Dad might be in here with Noah. It was warm and cosy. Cartoons still played silently on the screen, but all the little kids were snoozing. Noah was in his sleeping bag on a sofa, clutching Bernard the Sloth.

Two women lolled on beanbags in the buttery light. One was Miss Pryor, who worked in our school office. She was feeding her baby, Ben, his little booteed feet sticking out from under her shawl. I didn't recognise her friend.

Miss Pryor seemed to be halfway between laughing and crying.

'Collared me in the kitchen!'

'Oh God,' muttered the other woman, taking a swig from her clay cup.

'Mm. I was trying to rustle up some tea while he followed me around telling me I shouldn't get Ben vaccinated because the MMR is all mercury and autism and God knows what, and he thinks his brother was the victim of a secret mass murder. I only made my escape when some other unsuspecting victims walked in.'

'Wow. Not good. Is he doing this kind of thing at school?'

'I've heard rumours. Tonight's the first time I've seen it myself. Lovely man, great teacher. So sad.'

'Does Livia know?'

'I tried to drop her a hint just now.' Miss Pryor leaned down to kiss Ben's foot. 'She didn't react at all. Poker face. I always feel that woman's putting up a front. D'you know what I mean?'

'I know exactly what you mean. She's not gone down the rabbit hole with him, has she? I hope she—'

But I never heard what the friend hoped, because Miss Pryor spotted me. 'Heidi!' she cried, with a guilty look on her face. 'Having a nice time?'

The pair of them fake-smiled at me, obviously wondering how much I'd overheard. They were like Maia and Keren, except adult. Couple of witchy gossips.

'I'm looking for Dad,' I said.

'Scott?' Miss Pryor pretended to think. She was a rubbish actor. 'Um, no, I haven't seen him.'

'Except when he collared you in the kitchen,' I said.

That flustered her. 'What? No, that wasn't Scott, that was—'

I slammed the door behind me as I left. I hoped that woke all the children up.

•

The kitchen at Rosedale Retreat was as big as our entire house, with hand-painted tiles and giant fridges. I could hear Dad's voice from way down the hall, and just by the pitch of it I knew he was in full Internet Dad mode. I hovered near the door, my face burning, psyching myself up to go in. For the second time in two minutes, I was eavesdropping.

'This expert I've been talking to,' he was saying, 'experienced NHS doctor, really switched-on guy, he says colleagues all around the world are blowing the same whistle.'

'Human beings can be bastards.' That was a woman's voice. 'We all know this. But, Scott, I think you've got this out of proportion, because—'

Dad interrupted her. 'Give someone absolute power and it will *always* corrupt, they will *always* abuse it. And nobody has more terrifying power than the person putting that drip in your arm.'

Murmurs. *Uh-huh . . . I see. Mm. Well, gosh, that's very interesting, Scott.*

Then another male voice, not Dad. He sounded offended.

'I had a triple heart bypass two years ago. Saved my life. I'm exceedingly grateful, and you're talking absolute horseshit.'

'Okay, David,' said Dad. 'That's great. But you're not seen as a drain on society, are you? If you don't believe me, look at the statistics—mortality rates among people with chronic illness are far higher than they should be. They're being culled. And it's just the beginning.'

The woman's voice again. 'Hang on! When people die unexpectedly, there's an autopsy. There's an inquest.'

'That's my point, Helen. They rubber-stamped my brother's death certificate. I've written to the hospital board, the coroner, the police. They've all shut me down. The cover-up, you see. The cover-up proves they're all working together. We're rats in a lab.'

'Whose lab?'

'The Inner Circle. It's complicated, so let me—'

'But, Scott, that sounds bonkers. What on earth do you mean?'

Dad was talking more and more intensely, like he'd drunk far too much coffee. I couldn't keep up, but I heard him mention Cecil Rhodes, powerful people going to Switzerland, circles within circles, the hidden hand through history. I had my eyes shut, my knuckle jammed into my mouth, silently hissing, *Shut up, Dad. Shut up.*

'Terrorist attacks! The Twin Towers were demolished to provide an excuse for war in the Middle East, which in turn led to a cascade of—'

People burst out laughing.

'Oh, please,' said a man. 'You haven't bought into that 9/11 conspiracy hogwash?'

'Why were hijacked airliners never intercepted by the US air defence? Because all the fighter jets were stood down in advance. Where d'you think that order came from? Physicists and demolition experts have done the maths—jet fuel can't melt steel! It was a controlled explosion that brought down the World Trade Center. Did you know there was a huge amount of trading in American and United Airlines stock the day before? Somebody knew in advance.'

'Why on earth would anyone go to so much trouble?' asked the woman.

'To destabilise the human race. To cause chaos. And it worked perfectly, didn't it? Nonstop conflict ever since. Because of the chaos we're ready to give up our freedom in return for what they tell us is "security". Once you've grasped what's going on, you see it so clearly. I know this isn't good party conversation, but it's an existential crisis, a real and present danger. Please, *please* keep an open mind. Don't be sheep, just accepting everything you're told by the mainstream media. Research this stuff for yourselves. I'm happy to send you links—'

My toes were literally curling with embarrassment. I had to stop him, right now. I marched into the room, and was mortified to find Flynn's parents and three other people standing around with drinks in their hands, all of them looking like Dad had grown two extra heads.

'Oh, Dad, here you are!' I said loudly. 'Mum's been searching everywhere for you.'

He seemed confused for a second, as if he'd never met me before.

Mrs Thomas nudged Mr Thomas with her elbow. 'It's nearly midnight, darling! Better be getting outside for the fireworks.'

Everyone else started mumbling: *Gosh, is that the time? The year's nearly over. Is there any of that splendid mulled wine left?* A crush formed in the doorway as they all escaped from my dad.

That left just him and me. I felt like howling. *Flynn's parents!*

'You promised,' I said, standing with my fists on my hips. 'You weren't going to talk about this stuff tonight.'

'I know what they think of me. I can see it on their faces. They despise me.'

He was upset. His hands were shaking so much that he nearly dropped his mug. I didn't know what to do; I couldn't just leave him alone in there.

'It's not that I don't believe you, Dad,' I said, taking the mug from his hand. 'It's just . . . people . . . they don't get it.'

That was when Anthony came striding in. I was so relieved to see him—this big, noisy guy, with his big, noisy smile—and to know that he forgave Dad for spouting strange ideas.

'How're you going, Deputy Dawg? We're being summoned to gather outside. I helped set up the fireworks yesterday. It's going to rival anything London puts on tonight.'

Outside, someone had chucked another branch on the fire. The crowd looked like a pack of goblins around the leaping flames. I thought of Rumpelstiltskin, cackling as he danced to the tune in his own head.

We joined Mum just as Megan got up on the terrace with a microphone in her hand. 'One minute to go! . . . Thirty seconds to go! . . . Twenty! . . . Fifteen!'

She began to conduct the crowd, counting down the last seconds of 2019.

'Three! Two! One . . .'

Livia

The first rocket blazed into the sky. For several seconds it hung lazily, as though asleep, before shattering into deafening, dazzling bursts of light.

That was the signal. Next moment, the sky erupted with flashes and explosions and the smell of gunpowder. It looked like a battle scene.

Happy New Year! we cried, prancing about in the firelight, pretending we had nothing to fear from the months ahead. New Year's Eve is the one night of the year when blind optimism reigns supreme. *Hello, 2020!* I hugged Heidi, then her and Scott together—though I was still bloody livid with him—before Anthony joined in a group hug.

'Thanks for running Scott to ground,' I said, giving him an extra kiss on the cheek.

He saluted me. 'You're welcome, ma'am.'

I suspected the Americanisms were an affectation: the accent, the idioms, the mountain-man hair and beard. But what the hell—he was a nice man, a good friend, and he'd found Scott and Heidi in time for us all to celebrate together.

The *1812 Overture*, played at top volume, added drama to the fireworks. Billowing plumes from the bonfire obscured the stars. When Scott saw me rubbing my cold hands together, he stood behind me and wrapped his coat around us both, resting his chin on my hair. He and I fitted so gloriously well together, and I'd downed a heck of a lot of spiced mulled wine. Maybe that's why, as we oohed and aahed at the dazzling flares and zigzagging sparks and thunder-cracking rockets, my fury lost its edge. I remember thinking that we'd still be okay. We just needed a holiday somewhere sunny. This man was the love of my life! Whatever happened, I would never let him go.

•

New Year's Eve, 2019. In our family the trail of falling dominos, set in motion as Nicky died, had taken on a life of its own. Meanwhile, on the other side of the planet, another was quietly gaining momentum—though this was of global proportions. On that same day, Chinese authorities reported a cluster of cases of viral pneumonia in the city of Wuhan. Soon afterwards the World Health Organization moved onto an emergency footing for dealing with a disease outbreak.

But these events didn't register with the world's media. The BBC showed mind-blowing firework displays in every major city on the planet—exhilarating, extravagant, tons of gunpowder flaring into the night sky, music blaring. One cheering nation after another, all of them celebrating their future as the earth turned.

The hubris of our species.

Humans plan. Fate laughs.

TWENTY

January 2020

Scott

Wake up. Take off the blindfold. All at once, the monstrous truth leaps out at you.

It's not fun, it's not easy. It turns you into a pariah. Imagine standing on the deck of the *Titanic*, spotting a vast iceberg dead ahead. You're the only person screaming, ringing the bell, begging the captain to change course—and everyone laughs at you, they carry on dancing and setting off party poppers. They think you've lost your mind. Even your own wife.

The iceberg was looming out of the mist. That's why I wouldn't stop shouting and ringing the bell. That's why I sacrificed everything. I had no choice.

•

January—the dark, dark days of winter in Yorkshire, when the sun didn't even try to appear until after eight, and even then was no more than a faint disc, smothered in fog. The temperature hadn't risen above freezing all week. Cold car engines didn't want to start, thick layers of ice on windscreens had to be scraped with credit cards. Water pipes froze. The world was pale yet lightless, cloaked in hoarfrost that never melted, only grew, glinting on ploughed fields and dead bracken.

'It's so beautiful!' Livia exclaimed, as she poured warm water over her windscreen. 'But I'd love to see a bit of sun.'

Heidi and I were in the car, creeping through the fog and ice along the road to school, when she said, 'Oops!' and started rootling around in her backpack. She pulled out a crumpled piece of paper. 'I was meant to get this signed.'

'Consent form?' I asked, with my eyes on the road.

'HPV jab.'

'Not signing that.'

I turned in at the school gates, found my usual parking spot and cut the engine. Heidi was still clutching the form.

'I don't want to get cancer,' she said.

'You won't get cancer.'

'I might when I'm older. A nurse came last term and talked to us. Far fewer people are getting ill or dying now that we're all being protected by this vaccine. Aunt Bethany can't have any more children, can she, because she had cervical cancer?'

The new term had begun three days earlier. Students in scarves and beanies milled across the gritted surface of the car park— laughing, jostling, some hurrying to get out of the cold, some sliding along layers of ice in the puddles, their breath clouding. Every one of those kids was uniquely precious, even the toerags who disrupted every class. I'd taught most of them, knew all their names. It was my job to protect them.

'You won't get cancer, Heidi,' I repeated. 'And that vaccine is dangerous.'

She shoved the form into my hand. 'Can you please just sign

this for me? They're giving jabs in the gym after break. I'll get out of hockey. Everybody's having it.'

'Everybody except you,' I said as I tore that wretched bit of paper in half, into quarters.

'Oh my God, Dad!' Heidi looked scandalised. 'Wow. I never knew you were such a rebel.'

A mittened hand tapped on her window. Flynn Thomas, whose parents had treated me like a swivel-eyed lunatic at the bonfire. Flynn was a lovely lad, though, and talented—the kind who can pick up any instrument and just play. He gave me an embarrassed wave, but he was smiling at Heidi.

'Got to go,' she breathed, grabbing her backpack and hopping out to join him. 'See ya, Dad.'

They walked off together, chatting. Any other time, I might have speculated about whether my daughter and that boy were *just* friends. Not today. I sat behind the steering wheel with the torn-up form in my hands. My mind was in freefall.

They're giving jabs in the gym after break. Everybody's having it.

If a crazed gunman were roaming around the school, I'd be expected to barricade the classroom door, hide my students, keep them safe even if it meant putting my own body between them and the bullets. But when mortal danger took the form of nurses with lanyards and syringes . . . well, suddenly my job was to collude. Welcome the enemies in, ask their victims to form an orderly queue.

The staffroom would be heaving at this time of the morning. People would be waiting to hassle me about the regional drama competition, or the library budget, or one of my year elevens swearing at a school bus driver. My car was the only place with any privacy. As students and staff streamed around me, I reached for my phone, logged into Twitter, and sent a direct message to @DrJackNHS.

Team arriving to deliver HPV vaccine in my school today. I've refused permission for Heidi. But what about all the others?

His reply arrived within seconds.

Hi, Scott. Is there any way you can stop this? You must save lives today—even if it costs you your job.

•

My first class was year nine, Heidi's contemporaries. A nice bunch. I greeted most by name as they came trooping in. Several stopped to tell me about a book they'd read, a film they'd seen, some random thought they'd had. All of them would be lining up for the HPV jab today. Boys too.

'Good morning, all!' I cried cheerily, once they'd begun to settle down. 'Now then: would you rather practise some really boring reading comprehension, or watch a really interesting video?'

Ragged cheers from some, shouts of 'Video!' from others, nothing at all from the ones who were sneaking a look at their phones.

'Okay.' I was typing rapidly into my search bar as I talked. 'This is a bit different from a normal lesson. You might say it's more science than English, but ultimately it's about critical thinking. And critical thinking is a universal skill, one that all of us need, in every part of our lives. Some of you might find the content a bit upsetting in parts, so do let me know if you need me to pause it. Put your phone away in your bag please, Josh—good lad. You need to watch properly, because afterwards we're going to talk about what we've seen. That's when we get to polish up our comprehension skills. Okay? Everybody ready? Here we go.'

Even the few still surreptitiously scrolling through TikTok seemed intrigued. All heads turned towards the smartboard as the video began.

Schoolchildren, hypodermic needles, a small figure being wheeled into a morgue.

'Trigger warning: what I'm going to talk about today involves the deaths of children.'

•

'In what universe was that appropriate?'

Bruce Jones, deputy head, a walrus with a drooping moustache. Like all deputy heads I've ever known, he held the real power in Barmoors High. He stood at his office window with the light behind him, hands in pockets, weight firmly balanced on both feet.

I'd managed to play Dr Jack's video to my first two classes, and they'd caused a sensation. It was a tribute to Dr Jack's skill as a filmmaker and teacher that everyone paid attention, everyone heard the message. Some students sat through in stunned silence, many were a lot more vocal. Two rushed out of the room, saying they felt sick.

During our discussion afterwards, I reminded them that they had a choice.

'Nobody can inject this into you today if you don't want them to,' I told them. 'That would be an assault. Your body, your choice. Say no! *Refuse to* be a guinea pig.'

By morning break, the office had been inundated with calls from angry parents. I'd expected that. Some kids were more than capable of live-tweeting an entire lesson from under their desk, so a quick text to their mum was literally child's play.

'It's appropriate in a universe where children aren't sacrificial lambs,' I told Bruce. 'They're the ones who'll live with the effects of the vaccine. Or die of them.'

'I've had parents absolutely furious, asking what the hell's going on. You ambushed their children. You made year nines watch hospital porn!'

'It's not—'

'A dead body in a morgue, Scott? A dead child? Year nines!' Bruce threw himself into his desk chair. 'You're not an idiot, man.

You *know* this is over the line. Half of them are point-blank refusing the jab now, in case they wake up dead. They're telling their friends, who will also refuse. All this hysteria is gaining traction because there were already vaccine sceptics among the parents, and you're now their hero. By lunchtime that bloody video will be the most-watched item on every phone in the school. Probably in other schools too, across the country. We'll be lucky if we're not on the national news.'

'Good.'

'It's not good! What's got into you? I ask you again: in what universe was that appropriate?'

When I didn't answer, he sighed. 'I'm in damage control mode here. I've somehow got to reassure the board, parents and staff— and the public, because this is already plastered all over social media—that Barmoors High takes our public health responsibilities seriously. I need you to apologise and admit your actions were ill-judged.'

Dr Jack had been right. I was to be silenced, just like everyone else who'd ever spoken out.

'I won't be apologising,' I said. 'Those kids were going to have poison pumped into their veins today. They had a right to know the truth. You'll hear people from all over the world on that video, bearing witness to the tragedies they've seen. You should watch it yourself. Here, I'll give you the link so you can—'

'No!' Bruce was waving his hands. 'No, I don't want the bloody link. I had a look at the video as soon as Jane Jameson phoned me, which she did because Dylan was texting her from the toilets. When the chair of the board is spitting tacks, it's a good idea to pay attention.'

'So you've watched. You know.'

'I certainly have watched. And I agree that it's disturbing— but not in the way you think. It's gibberish from start to finish. Look, Scott.' He slid his glasses off, rubbed the bridge of his nose between thumb and forefinger. 'This isn't an easy situation. It's been brewing for a long while. I know your brother's death was . . .' He replaced his glasses, blinking at me.

'Was what?' I blinked back at him. 'Murder?'

'Was very difficult for you. You're perfectly entitled to your private beliefs. But I can't have teachers pushing images of dead children and anti-vax propaganda on year nines.'

The bell was ringing. End of break. I stood up, ready to head to my next class. I hoped I'd done enough to scupper today's vaccination program, at least.

'So you want them to roll up their sleeves?' I asked curtly. 'Take one for the team?'

'What I want, Scott, is for you to go home. Right now. We'll call it stress, shall we?'

Heidi

Double science, and your dad tearing up your consent form. What a start to the day.

On the plus side, Flynn knocked on my window. I was amazed he still wanted to talk to me, after what happened with Dad and his parents. But he said Mr Denby was one of his favourite teachers—and anyway, his family were much weirder than mine. We hung about on the quad until the lesson bell, cracking a sheet of ice with our heels. Flynn was excited about his GCSE music composition. He wanted to set it for two classical guitars, and asked if I'd do the performance with him.

I was chuffed and delighted and terrified.

'If I mess it up, will you fail your GCSE?' I asked.

'No. Anyway, you won't mess it up.'

Maia walked past, and saw us tap-dancing on the ice. She looked like she wanted to kill me. Made my day.

Anyhow, fifteen minutes into double science, and we were all sitting on stools at the benches. Maia was there, but I hadn't shared a bench with her since Dinosaur-gate. I'd joined two girls called Suyin and Ruby, who got top marks in everything. They weren't best buddies of mine, but they were never bitchy. While Mr Bond droned on about kinetic and potential energy they scribbled away, taking notes, and I stared out of the window at the row of trees beside the sports field. The frost on them was so heavy, it looked like snow. I'd kept my fingerless gloves on because the radiators weren't cutting it.

That was when my phone began to go crazy in my bag. I'd left it on vibrate, so at least it wasn't playing *Moonlight Sonata* at top volume, but I heard the buzzing as notifications poured in.

Mr Bond took a hard line on phones. He confiscated them all the time. I had to wait until he went into the storeroom before I could lean down and sneak a look at my messages.

The first was from Keren: *OMG your dads showing us a fked up vid about the hpv jab☹ Feel sick*

Next, someone I barely knew: *Your dad is a LEGEND telling truth about vax! Respect!*

There were quite a few more, all of them on about Dad and some video.

Mr Bond emerged with a box full of those swinging pendulum toys. 'Newton's cradles,' he announced. 'One for each bench.' He walked around the room, distributing them. People couldn't resist playing with them. The lab was soon full of the clacking sound of metal balls hitting one another.

Once he'd passed our bench I took a final look at my phone, and just about fainted. Someone's mother was ranting on the school Facebook page:

I'm getting texts from a very distressed daughter, who's right now being made to watch a horror film about the HPV vaccine. In an English lesson!! I've told her to get up and walk out. I don't appreciate the peddling of anti-vax, anti-science rubbish in our school. I'm afraid Scott Denby has to go.

Dropping my phone back into my bag, I glanced around the lab. My two bench mates had begun the first of the experiments on the worksheet for our Newton's cradle: pulling out the ball at one end, letting it fall, watching the energy transfer itself all along the line, all the way back again. They were oblivious to the scandal my dad was causing.

But everyone else seemed to have heard the news. Giggles, nudges, whispering, phones under desks. People turning around to gawk at me. I wanted to die. Maia caught my eye and let her jaw drop dramatically, mouthing: *What. The. Fuck?* I turned my back on her, pretending to concentrate on the metal balls swinging and smashing into one another. I couldn't stop the tears, though. I was dissolving.

It was Suyin who noticed first.

'Heidi!' she whispered. 'You okay?'

I didn't speak. I'd have sobbed, and the whole class would hear me. I shrugged and tried to smile, using both my hands to wipe my face. I knew my nose was running. Not a pretty sight.

Suyin reached into her bag and pulled out a packet of paper hankies. She had a broad, kind face, with very dark hair that she always wore in a ponytail. She'd once told me that she had grandparents in China, but she only ever saw them through FaceTime.

'Don't worry,' she whispered, as I blew my nose. 'Just keep your head down. We'll fill in your worksheet for you. Nobody's going to know.'

I nodded, mouthing my thanks, squeezing my eyes shut to try to make the tears stop. Suyin whispered to Ruby, and the pair of them spent the rest of the lesson covering for me.

When the bell rang for break, I returned the pack of paper hankies to Suyin.

'You all right?' she asked.

'Yes. No. Thank you for saving me.' I gave her a grateful hug before grabbing my bag from the floor. 'I've got to go and find my dad. I think he might be in trouble.'

Scott

Heidi was waiting for me outside Bruce Jones's office. Tearful, a strand of hair stuck to her cheek. She clutched at my arm, insisting that if I was leaving, she'd be coming too.

'The whole school is staring at me like I've got three heads. The *whole* school. Even the man who rolls the sports field. I can't stay. Please don't make me stay.'

'We're going home,' I promised.

I wanted to take her—take our whole family—far away, to a safe place. But there *was* no safe place. I'd publicly signalled my resistance. From now on I'd be in the searchlights.

Katie Pryor was working in the office. When I asked for the student sign-out book, she screwed up her eyes.

'I honestly do understand where you're coming from, Scott,' she said. 'I told you at New Year's, I *hate* the idea of taking Ben for his jabs. But what about poor Heidi? Is this fair on her?'

'If you hate the idea of having Ben vaccinated,' I suggested, as I signed Heidi out for the rest of the day, 'then don't. Just don't. You have a choice.'

Heidi and I made a dash for the car as though a pack of dogs were after us. I was still on a high. For once in my life I'd made a real impact, perhaps saved lives. I'd never done anything half so radical as I had that morning. I'd chosen a side, come what may.

'I feel like a getaway driver,' I said.

'Mm.' Heidi was silent for a while, chewing the edge of her thumb. 'And Mum is going to kill you.'

TWENTY-ONE

Livia

I was on my way down to the cells when I heard the news.

The judge in Court Three had asked for a stand-down report on a woman who'd just pleaded guilty to benefit fraud. He'd remanded her in custody over lunch. I had one hour to talk to her and come up with a recommendation.

I always kept my phone on silent in the court building, but I took a quick look on my way downstairs. Missed calls from Scott and Heidi. That wasn't unusual. I'd try to ring them both once I got a free minute.

I'd rung the bell and was waiting to be let into the cells when a solicitor called Sandra Webb hurried up to join me. I liked Sandra. Only a few years off retirement, she was an old hand in the criminal and family courts. She was nobody's fool, but she cared about her clients.

'This is handy, bumping into you here,' she said cheerfully, as we waited for the custody officer to put down his cup of tea and let us in. 'Saves me a phone call. D'you remember a case called *Black and others*? Violent disorder in a pub in Darlington?'

I remembered it well. Sandra's client was the least culpable of five defendants.

'Have you seen the letter from his drug and alcohol counsellor?' she asked. 'It's really enlightening.'

She began to tell me how her boy had made good use of his time on bail to beat his alcohol addiction, qualify as a plumber and turn his life around. So when I felt the vibration of a call coming in on my phone, I wasn't thinking about Scott. I wasn't thinking about my own family at all. I was in work mode, utterly focused on other people's shattered lives.

Disorientated, I blinked at the caller's name. *Barmoors High*.

'Livia,' began a breathless voice, as soon as I answered. 'Katie Pryor.'

'Hi, Katie.' Why on earth was the school secretary calling me at work? Scott was closer to hand, if there was some query about Heidi.

'Have you heard what's happened? Bruce thought we ought to let you know before anyone else does.'

I leaned one hand against the wall, feeling the floor drop away as I imagined our car upside down in flames, a gunman bursting into a classroom. Heidi must be dead. Or Scott. Or both.

'Scott's been suspended,' said Katie.

'He's what?'

'Oh Lord. You didn't know. I'm so sorry to be the bearer of bad news.' Sympathetic tutting. 'He's already gone home, taking Heidi with him. To be honest, it was probably a good idea to get her away. We've been swamped with complaints. Scott showed a ghastly video to his year nines, fearmongering about the HPV vaccine. Graphic footage of a dead girl.'

'I very much doubt that was a real dead girl. Probably a scene from a soap opera.'

'You've seen it?' Katie sounded shocked. 'Well, it looked real to the year nines. As did the—'

Keys in the lock. The door to the cells swung open, and I was facing the inquiring face of the custody officer.

'Katie, thanks for letting me know,' I said, cutting her off in mid-gloat. 'I'm in court. I have to go.'

Suspended. Scott, who was a teacher long before I met him, who was defined by his work. *Scott, what have you done?*

Autopilot took over. I showed my Probation Service lanyard, gave the name of the woman I'd come to see. A judge was expecting a report from me at two fifteen, and I was bloody well going to deliver. Here, at least, I had some kind of control.

As we signed ourselves in, Sandra glanced sideways at me. 'Everything okay, Livia? Bad news? You look a bit sandbagged.'

'I could cheerfully murder my husband right now,' I said.

'Join the club! Mine's in the doghouse too. He's going fishing on our ruby wedding anniversary.'

The officer fetched our respective defendants. Mine had been in custody for all of twenty minutes and looked petrified out of her wits. Sometimes that was all it took: the clang of the gates, just once, and a person would never offend again. I'd be recommending a community sentence.

'Thing is,' I said to Sandra, 'I *really* feel like murdering my husband.'

•

We've all got our terrors, haven't we? *Every parent's nightmare.* Illness, accidents, violent attacks.

This, though. *This.* It had come out of left field: an enemy I couldn't see, couldn't touch, couldn't fight. This enemy had invaded my husband's mind.

I tried to call Heidi. No reply. I sent a text to say I'd heard the news, I was coming straight home and not to worry. Then I ran down to the car park and set off, clenching the wheel with white fingers. It was time I admitted I was out of my depth. We needed help from a specialist, someone who understood how a sensible man could be sucked into a kind of cult.

Halfway across the moors I stopped at a lookout. A picnic bench, upholstered in frost. A curious robin. A beck, sluggish under a layer of ice. Pockets of snow. But no breathtaking view today; just swathes of cloud, swirling across my windscreen. And one bar of signal.

Think logically. Come up with a strategy. Who can help us?

Charles Shepherd had seen it all. He understood how a human mind could be hijacked. *It's almost like they reached in and grabbed him through his computer screen.*

Of course, I thought. *Thank you, Charles.*

Pushing back the driver's seat, I logged into my work database through my phone. It didn't take long to find the contact details I was looking for: Dr Isaac Katz of Leeds University, who advised the government on deradicalisation programs, who gave expert evidence in jeans and a hoodie.

I had nothing to lose.

Hi Isaac,

You may not remember me. I work for the Probation Service based in Teesside, and our paths have crossed several times. I'd be very grateful if I could run something by you. It's about online influences affecting my own family. We're in trouble. I realise it's unprofessional of me to ask, so please feel free to ignore. I promise I will understand.

Regards,

Livia Denby

TWENTY-TWO

Scott

'Dad,' Heidi said suddenly, as we drove home from school, 'd'you really believe the people giving that vaccine would deliberately put us in danger?'

'Not on purpose. They've been brainwashed like everyone else; they're just doing what they're told. That's what evil regimes rely on—foot soldiers following orders.'

'You could get fired.'

'Sometimes you just have to do the right thing.'

She hugged her schoolbag to her chest, gazing out of her window at the frozen landscape. BBC Radio 4 was on. Chatter, chatter. An assassination by drone strike in Iraq. People disappearing in Mexico. Bushfires in Australia causing blood-red skies. An outbreak of viral pneumonia in China.

'What if Nicky hadn't died?' she asked. 'Would you be thinking these things?'

'I doubt it. I was ignorant until then. Ignorance is bliss.'

'But what if you found out it wasn't your fault, or the ambulance, or the hospital? What if it was somebody else's fault, nothing to do with any of those people?'

Such a strange question. The pitch of her voice rose to a piping treble. I reached across as I drove, tucking a lock of hair behind her ear.

'What's on your mind, Heidi?'

She pressed her face into the top of her bag, smothering sobs. I turned the car into the nearest farm gateway, yanked at the handbrake and wrapped my arms around her.

'Hey, hey, it's okay,' I said. 'Nothing bad is going to happen.'

I doubted she believed me. Why would she? I didn't believe myself.

•

As soon as we were home, Heidi changed into mufti and said she was going to feed the ducks. When I offered to join her, she said she'd rather be alone.

Minutes later, Bruce Jones called. With terse politeness, he invited me to a meeting with management and school board representatives early the next morning. Depending on how it went, a decision would be made about suspension pending a disciplinary process.

'The ball is in your court,' he warned. 'For Christ's sake back down, Scott. And say nothing to the media. Not a word, please.'

I was left alone in an accusing silence—alone, except for Bernard the Sloth with his stoner smile, waiting all day for Noah. I hung Livia's navy-blue fedora up in the hallway. A hint of her scent, a strand of her glorious hair. Doubt had begun to seep under the closed door of my mind: *What if you're wrong? What if they're right? Are you really going to risk everything you love?*

Meanwhile, messages were flooding onto my phone.

Megan Espinoza: *Just heard the news. The only thing necessary for evil to triumph is for good men to do nothing. Scott, you are a good man!* X

Anthony: *You okay? Want me to come over?*

A fellow teacher: *Can't condone what you did, but don't want to lose you over this. Have you contacted the union?*

Anthony: *I'm on my way over.*

Dr Jack: *Hi Scott. What happened today? Were you able to save those children?*

Dr Jack's was the only one I answered immediately. I filled him in on developments since we'd messaged that morning.

Thank you, he replied. *Welcome to the Resistance! Remember: you're not alone.*

•

The house shuddered at the slamming of the front door, followed by the unmistakable sound of Livia's keys being hurled into the wooden bowl.

I'd been dreading this conversation, but it had to come. I met her in the hall. She was wearing her black suede boots and an ankle-length skirt, hair rolled up and crocodile-clipped, Probation Service lanyard still around her neck. She looked exactly the same as when we'd parted this morning. But that was before I crossed the Rubicon.

Rage rose off her like steam, pulsing in every jerky movement. She wouldn't even look at me.

'Suspended,' she said flatly, as she jammed her coat onto a peg.

'Temporarily. I've got a meeting with management tomorrow.'

'Where's Heidi?'

'Went out to see the ducks. She's upset.'

'Upset! No shit, Sherlock. What the *hell* did you expect?' Livia finally looked at me. Scalding contempt. 'You've just thrown a stick of dynamite into her world.'

'I've saved her. She was going to get that jab today.'

'Oh, give it a rest. What do you think it was like for her in school this morning? Kids are merciless. This wasn't about Heidi, Scott Denby—this was all about *you*. Your obsession. Your gullibility.'

'I'm not gullible.'

'You're deluded and you need help. I'm at the end of my tether.'

She eyed me as she lifted first one foot, then the other, to unzip and remove her boots. I thought she might throw them at me, but she turned away to put them on the shoe rack.

'So what happens next? You get sacked?'

'They can't fire me for telling uncomfortable truths.'

'Oh, of course they can! They probably will.'

She stalked past me into the kitchen. 'Have you had lunch? I haven't, never do, never get time. I worked right through, and I'll be working tonight—again.' She had her hand on the open fridge door, staring at the shelves. 'You, on the other hand, seem to have all the time in the world to watch stupid videos peddled by narcissistic morons; all the time in the world to chat to your online community of fools.'

'There are more important things than—'

'No!' she snapped, kicking the fridge door shut. 'No, Scott, there are *not* more important things than the stability of your family. Don't you fucking dare give me this crusading bullshit. We have a mortgage. We have bills. We have two children to support, and what you did today was unforgivable. Jesus Christ. I can't believe you could be so selfish.'

I watched as she poured herself a glass of water. I was desperate to find the magic formula, words that would open her eyes.

'Listen to me,' I pleaded. 'I might not have long. The New World Order will be on to me now.'

'What are these monsters? Daleks? Little green men from Mars?'

'See, this is what you do,' I said. 'You scoff. You make every-thing sound ridiculous so you don't have to face the fact that you might be wrong.'

Livia sat down at the table and shut her eyes, mouthing the numbers as she counted to ten. That was her go-to, her show of anger and control. She'd weaponised it.

'Okay,' she whispered, once she'd reached ten. 'Let's stick to practicalities. Have you contacted your union? You'd better get them onside. How are you going to tackle the meeting tomorrow? What's your line?'

'That we shouldn't be offering up children on this altar,' I said, taking the seat across from her. 'That we should be teaching our students to be truth-seekers, to ask questions and see the bigger picture. That Orwell's *1984* is much closer than we think.'

'I see. So you're planning to get yourself sacked.'

'How can I carry on teaching English if I'm gagged? How do we study writers like Orwell or Huxley or Tolkien or H.G. Wells, without pointing to the fact that they could see the truth? They all knew. They *knew*. *The Matrix* and *1984* weren't just fiction; they were alarm bells being rung.'

'Scott—'

'The Elect has been the hidden hand, causing chaos through-out the twentieth century. Those writers tried to warn us.'

'This is crazy.'

'I've never felt more sane.'

She stretched both her hands across the table to grip mine, as though I was falling into a well. 'I'm begging you, Scott. When have I ever begged you for anything? Don't do this to us. Don't sacrifice the work you love. Don't sacrifice your family, who loves you.'

There was nothing left to say. After so many years together, silence *was* communication. We sat on opposite sides of the table, clutching one another's hands, knowing we couldn't hold on forever.

The clang of the doorbell seemed like an invasion.

'I'll get it,' muttered Livia, rubbing her forearm across her eyes as she left the room.

A male voice. Anthony. Of course: he'd said he was coming over. I heard murmurs. Livia would be filling him in on events, getting in first, asking him to talk some sense into me.

He looked around the kitchen door—smiling but anxious, the mane of hair and beard framing his heavy face.

'Trouble at t'mill?' he asked.

'Trouble at t'mill.'

The front door banged shut.

'Livia's gone to look for Heidi and collect Noah from the child-minder,' said Anthony. 'Your wife's not a happy bunny, is she?'

'Can't blame her.' I stood up, reaching for the kettle. Polite-ness survives, even as life falls apart. 'Coffee?'

TWENTY-THREE

Livia

I found Heidi leaning over the parapet of the humpbacked bridge, finishing a can of Coke. She was hunched against the biting drizzle, the sleeves of her anorak over her hands. She'd pulled her hood up too, hiding her hair.

'The poor little ducks must be freezing,' she said softly, as I came up to her.

I leaned over the parapet beside her. Her old friends were doing their usual thing: grazing, gabbling, launching themselves out of the muddy water with quivering tails and shakes of their wings.

'They seem perky enough,' I said.

'I bought them porridge oats from the shop. Thought it might warm them up.'

'That was nice of you.'

'It really wasn't nice of me.'

She seemed lifeless. I draped my arm around her shoulders, pressing my cheek to hers.

'Is Dad going to get sacked?' she asked.

'I don't know.'

'I'm proud of him. He stood up for his beliefs. That's what we're meant to do, isn't it? Fight for what we think is right.'

'The HPV vaccine has been tested and tested, Heidi. It's safe. I wish it existed when Bethany and I were your age.'

To my surprise, she was nodding. 'I know it's safe. I know it might have stopped Bethany from getting cancer. But that's not the point, is it? The point is, Dad *believes* it's dangerous. He honestly thought we were all about to be injected with something evil. What was he supposed to do? Just keep quiet?'

•

'Feels like snow,' said Chloë, when Heidi and I called to collect Noah. 'There's that stillness.'

She had Noah all bundled up in his scarf, hat and mittens. He coughed as soon as he stepped into the cold air, but soon recovered and chattered the whole way home. His news of the day was that he'd landed the role of innkeeper in his school nativity play.

'*No room! NO ROOM!*' he yelled, resting his fists on his hips. '*Okay then, you can have the stable. The animals will keep you warm.*'

We had cheese on toast for supper. I'd no energy for anything else. Anthony, bless him, had already dragged Scott out to the pub.

I was tucking Noah into bed when Isaac Katz got back to me. *Hi Livia, sorry to hear you're having bother. Give me a call. Any time this evening is ok.*

•

Later, once Noah was asleep and Heidi moodily playing her guitar, I slipped out to make my phone call away from listening ears. When Isaac answered, I thanked him profusely for getting back to me and apologised for ruining his evening.

'Not at all,' he assured me. 'My husband's book group is meeting at our place tonight, and I've not had time to read the book. So you've rescued me.'

He had music playing in the background. Cat Stevens.

'Now then,' he began, 'what's been happening?'

'It's about conspiracy theories. I'm not even sure if that's your field.'

'Oh, but it is! Extremism rides on the same bus as conspiratorial belief. Fire away.'

Slipping and sliding along the icy pavements, I described Scott, the determined optimist, who began to change on the day his brother died.

'Nicky's death was a catalyst,' I said. 'It was complicated grief. Lots of guilt.'

'And maybe looking for a meaning to it all?'

'That's right! He cannot, *will* not accept that it was just plain bad luck. I've tried watching these videos with him, I've pointed out the absurdities. Nothing works. He spends hours in his online echo chamber, reinforcing these ideas with people he's never met.'

'Does he still have friends in the real world?'

'Not many. People have started sidling away. He was a great teacher, a great dad. And he still is, but . . .' I hesitated. 'Actually, no, he's not. He isn't that man anymore. This morning he drove our daughter Heidi to school and then—without a word of warning to me or anyone else—he showed a gruesome anti-vax video to a load of kids who were just about to have their HPV jab.'

'Oof. Not good.'

'He's been suspended. He's refusing to back down, so he'll lose his job—and I guarantee that he will see himself as a martyr to the cause.'

'I'm sorry.' Isaac left a moment's silence. 'Is he in one-to-one contact with anyone in this online community? Any direct messaging, going to meetings?'

I paused under a streetlight. 'Yes. He's been messaging a YouTube guy who claims to be a Scottish doctor. Calls himself Dr Jack. Why isn't this stuff taken down?'

'The internet's a Hydra: cut off one head and two more grow. And there are always arguments about free speech and censorship.'

That had me chuckling bitterly. 'Free speech? Free to shout *fire* in a crowded theatre! I don't think we can go on like this, Isaac. I've run out of ideas.'

He took a few seconds to marshal his thoughts, while Cat Stevens sang about moonshadows and I walked on towards the market square.

'First,' he said, 'I think you're right about Nicky. A sudden death is often a trigger. It can be on a bigger scale: plagues, earthquakes, terrorist attacks . . . things that make people feel lost and vulnerable. Nobody's immune to these kinds of ideas—and just to complicate things, they sometimes turn out to be right. We've all got a pet theory or two. Myself, I'm a UFO guy. So many thousands of sightings! Can they really *all* be hoaxes? What's yours?'

I grimaced sheepishly, though he couldn't see me. 'Always wondered about that man on the grassy knoll.'

'Ha! Right. You might find you and Scott agree on that. The point is that these ideas are as old as time. Humanity evolved with a need to look beyond the observable, to search for simple answers to complicated, frightening questions.'

I was thinking of my very first date with Scott.

'Patterns in the stars,' I said.

'Patterns anywhere and everywhere. We're obsessed with joining the dots. We have a built-in confirmation bias. My personal view is that it's a function of feeling all alone in a boundless universe.'

Snow. Twisting, floating in the sallow light. I held out one hand, letting the tiny ice-worlds melt on my palm. We were going to see *The Mousetrap*. It all felt perfect. It all felt meant.

'Scott's beliefs don't even join the dots, though,' I said. 'Big pharma cannot simultaneously be all-powerful *and* controlled by the New World Order.'

'That's a common feature. I've met people who think Princess Diana was murdered—yet minutes later they insist she's living in Bermuda. They seem oblivious to the contradiction. The over-arching certainty is that *nothing is what it seems* and *everything is connected*. Honestly, Livia, any one of us could get tangled up if the conditions were right. Those "recommended for you" algorithms on platforms like YouTube and Facebook are pure manipulation. They act as a funnel, sucking people down the vortex.'

I was crossing the bridge where Heidi and I had stood earlier that day, past sleeping ducks with their beaks on their backs, mounds of white in the gloom.

'I should have taken this more seriously early on,' I said.

'I doubt that would have made any difference. It's self-feeding, isn't it? Everything is connected, everyone is in cahoots, every-thing is a lie. So any contrary evidence presented is just more evidence of a cover-up. The more you argue, the less good you do.'

The Gilderdale Plague Cross was a relic of the fourteenth century, a warning of disease in an era when bubonic plague raged through this part of England. Nowadays its stone steps gave our little town a meeting place. I sank onto them, drawing my knees up under my coat. The market square was deserted, though warm light spilled from the windows of the Fattened Goose.

'You're up against an age-old enemy,' Isaac was saying. 'Disinformation has caused havoc forever. Lynching, witch hunts. Pogroms. Genocides.'

'But this is 2020.'

'Which means we've got social media, which is a super-spreader. Thousands of QAnon followers truly believe the elite are cannibal paedophiles. We've seen white supremacists fixated on a "white genocide" plot—that kind of thinking was behind the Christchurch massacre in New Zealand last year. Scratch the surface, and you'll often find anti-Semitism. That's a driver that never goes away.'

'Any thoughts on what I should do next?'

Isaac hesitated. 'I'm afraid it's easier to "prebunk" than "debunk". It sounds as though Scott's already invested in these beliefs. He needs to be able to talk openly with you, a friend, a counsellor. Someone he trusts, who will listen without judging him. If you just tell him he's wrong, he'll shut down.'

'I've learned that the hard way.'

'It's the usual thing: listen, listen, listen. If you're challenging his ideas, try to ask open-ended questions. Non-judgemental questions. See if you can get him to spot the holes for himself, to approach all this more critically. I can put you in touch with someone, if you think he'll talk to them.'

'Thank you. But I'm sure he won't. He says he's never felt more sane. *Never felt more sane!* What he did today was beyond selfish. How could he do that to Heidi? I just want to shake him and scream in his face.'

'But you know that won't work. The vital thing is to keep the door open.'

•

Isaac went off to join his book group. I felt better for talking to him, even though he had no easy solution for me.

I leaned my back against the step behind me, gazing up at the Celtic cross, blurred now by snow flurries. They fell from infinity, soaring and whirling like a murmuration of birds. It must be chucking-out time at the Fattened Goose. A group emerged, exclaiming at the snow. They stood with their hands and tongues stuck out, just as Noah would have done. Adults are kids. I heard them calling to one another to drive carefully as they got into their cars and crawled away, headlights quavering, wipers batting.

I stood up, shaking ice particles from my hair, stiff from crouching so long in the cold. When the door of the pub opened again, two familiar figures stepped into the streetlight: Scott in his donkey jacket and woollen beanie, Anthony the bearded mountain man. They lingered on the pavement, deep in conversation. Anthony was doing what I couldn't—staying calm, listening without judgement, being a true friend.

Perhaps he could pull off a miracle. But I doubted it.

TWENTY-FOUR

Heidi

Everything had blown apart again. Dad had got himself suspended, the whole school was talking about us. I didn't know how I was ever going to face them all.

Once Dad and I were home, I dropped into the Spar to buy a can of Coke and a box of porridge oats for the ducks. I came out with Coke and porridge oats in my hands, and a tube of Smarties in my back pocket. Just one last thing. Always one last thing. I hardly even bothered to be clever about it this time, though Mrs Ponder kept following me around. The Smarties were still in my pocket while Mum and I stood on the bridge. Later, they joined my under-wardrobe hoard of shame.

I lay in bed that night, listening to my parents talking downstairs. When I was small, I used to love hearing the peaceful rise and fall of their voices through the floorboards. It made me feel safe. I'd snuggle down and fall asleep to the soothing sound of them chatting, sometimes laughing. They were real friends.

But their voices weren't peaceful tonight. I kept drifting off and waking again. I got up for a while and sat at my window, watching the snow settle in a mound on the sill. When I finally got back into bed it was still snowing, and Mum and Dad were still droning on. Sometimes there were long silences, sometimes their voices seemed higher and sharper and sadder. And in that whole night, not one laugh. Not one.

Later, I discovered that I'd fallen asleep to the sound of my parents splitting up.

•

They put on a good show in the morning. Getting dressed, putting out breakfast, talking about the snow and which roads would have been gritted. They were being weirdly nice to one another. Our home felt like a balloon that's about to burst.

Dad looked very smart when he set off for his big meeting. Mum moved her appointments and took the day off work.

'I've got a stomach-ache,' I told her. 'I think I might throw up.'

'Me too,' she said. 'Let's both throw a sickie, shall we?'

'Must be something going around.'

The sky was white, the air was white. A blue-white blanket glittered on the lawn, on Mum's car, on every tiny twig of every tree in the garden. It looked magical. Back Lane was completely covered, just Dad's wheel tracks squashed into the white. Next door, Pete was clearing his path with a spade.

When we set out to walk Noah to Gilderdale Primary, ours were the very first footsteps in the snow. Noah kept stopping to plunge his mittened hands deep into the drifts. He was having a bit of trouble with his asthma, probably because of the cold, so Mum dropped into the classroom to ask his teacher to keep an eye out.

All so beautiful. All so very *not* beautiful.

'Have you heard anything from Dad?' I asked, once it was just the two of us. 'The meeting must have happened by now.'

She said she hadn't, and we crunched on along the pavement. As we were turning into Back Lane, she stopped dead. She stood with her hands in her pockets, staring towards our house.

'He's decided to hand in his resignation,' she said. 'He made that decision during the night.'

My mouth fell open. 'Why? They'll have him back, won't they? He's the best teacher in the school.'

'Because he knows they'll insist he keep his beliefs out of his teaching. He says he can't do that. He says that literature is all about *truth*, and he's not going to teach *lies*.'

She sounded sarcastic. I didn't blame her.

'Are we going to be okay, though? What about money? Do you earn enough for us to live on?'

'I'm worried about that too. He says he'll do some online tutoring. It's quite well paid.'

I was still gaping at her. I couldn't believe my dad would just pack it in like that. He'd taught at Barmoors all my life. It was what he did. Who he was.

'And, um . . .' Mum swallowed. Her mouth was quivering, which frightened me. 'He's going to stay somewhere else, just for a little while. We've agreed that would be best.'

'Stay somewhere else? Where? For how long?'

She shrugged, clamping her lips tight shut, though it didn't stop them trembling. I was horrified to see a tear snaking its way out of the corner of her eye, followed by another.

'Is he having an affair?' I asked.

'No!' She almost laughed, rubbing her eyes with the back of her hand. 'No. God. That would be so much simpler. At least then I'd be able to see my enemy.'

Livia

So this was how our marriage ended: not with a bang, but in miserable incomprehension.

Scott waited until both children were in bed before dropping his bombshell. He'd talked everything through with Anthony but was still determined not to eat humble pie at tomorrow's meeting.

He was going to stick to his guns about the HPV vaccine, and all his beliefs. And he would resign.

'I'll jump before I'm pushed,' he said.

I'd seen it coming but, still, I was aghast.

'How do you expect us to manage on one income? How, exactly, d'you think we'll be meeting our mortgage payments?'

He just kept walking from one end of the kitchen to the other and back again, punching his right fist into his left palm. It was both frightening and infuriating.

'Scott,' I said. 'For Christ's sake. Aren't you even going to talk to me? Your decision will fundamentally change my life, our children's lives—you're driving a wrecking ball through everything we have—and you won't even discuss it like a rational adult?'

He stopped, stood swaying in front of me. He looked haunted. 'I'm leaving tomorrow,' he said. 'Anthony's offered me his sofa, so I'll start there.'

I felt the first tearing of my heart. 'What do you mean, you're leaving? When will you be coming back?'

He never did answer that last question.

'Dr Jack thinks I need to get out fast,' he said. 'They know I'm a dissident. Car crash, house fire. Maybe I'll be arrested and found hanging in my cell. As long as I'm still living here, you and the children could be targets too.'

'I'm prepared to take that chance.'

'Are you? I'm not.'

'Don't do this,' I begged. 'Please get professional help. You're not in your right mind. This is about Nicky—'

'This isn't about Nicky.'

'I think it is.'

'No, Livia!' He threw out his hands, eyes alight with missionary zeal. 'You're still not listening. You're still brainwashed.'

He was right there. He'd had an awakening, a Road to Emmaus experience. He saw everything through a distorting lens. And me?

Well, I was an unbeliever. I was part of the problem. Perhaps we weren't compatible anymore. I had this horrible sense that he was being dragged beyond my reach by currents that were too strong for either of us. If I let go of him now, I'd lose him forever.

Snow spilled silently past the windows. We talked, talked, talked. Raged, wept, argued furiously in hushed voices, each blaming the other for not understanding, not listening. By three in the morning we were both hoarse, both out of tears. We crawled upstairs to bed and held each other for the rest of that short night, clinging sleeplessly to what we once had. I had never watched the passing of the hours with such dread.

I still hoped for a miracle. But in the morning, Scott drove the slushy roads to school and resigned with immediate effect.

•

Generous as ever, Anthony said his sofa was at Scott's disposal for as long as he needed it. But he lived in a rented studio flat—a far cry from his palace back in California—and it was never a long-term solution.

On the fifth day, Scott stopped by The Forge to collect more of his things. I took yet another morning off work, desperate to see him.

He'd deteriorated in those five days. He looked unkempt, and his eyes seemed to have sunk deeper into their sockets.

'I'm on my way to Whitby,' he told me.

'Whitby! How come?'

'Pet-sitting for some friends of friends of the Espinozas. They're off to Australia and their usual housesitter broke her leg. Rum Keg Cottage is all mine until April.'

It sounded like a neat solution. He couldn't impose on Anthony forever, and sleeping on a two-seater sofa was giving him backache. Part of me was downright envious. I associated Whitby with fun days out: ancient pubs and cobbled streets, walks along the pier, fish and chips on the beach, a ruined abbey. It was less than an hour's drive from Gilderdale but it felt like another world. Scott would be swanning about in a charming seaside town while I juggled work and parenthood.

'But . . . when are you coming home?' I asked.

'I don't know.'

He and I sat at the kitchen table with mugs of tea, talking about practicalities like two buttoned-up idiots. We agreed to tell Noah that Scott had a new kind of job, so he was living in another house for a little while.

'I don't want this,' I said. 'I hate it.'

'I don't have any choice.'

'Of course you've got a choice! Just come home, get some help.'

Moments later, he'd gone upstairs to pack. I didn't offer to lend a hand. I took up position by his car, watching him walk backwards and forwards, lobbing bags into the boot, strapping his bike onto its carrier.

'Was this written in the stars, Scott?' I asked, as he got into the driver's seat.

He stared past me, his grey eyes bloodshot. I knew he wanted to say something, but he couldn't get the words out. I crouched down to put my arms around him. He smelled the same, felt the same as ever. We lingered for a last moment, our foreheads touching.

I didn't wait to see him drive away.

The radio was on when I went back inside. The news. Donald Trump had been tweeting extraordinary things again. Meghan and Harry were stepping back from the royal family. Updates on the Ukrainian airline shot down by missiles in Iran, killing everyone aboard. Rumours, counter-rumours, speculation.

In China, a sixty-one-year-old man had died from a new virus related to SARS.

TWENTY-FIVE

Livia

Lots of red flags here, Isaac Katz replied, when I emailed to let him know what was happening. *No job, social isolation. His online community is now his only community. Stay in constant touch, keep the open conversations going. Ask others to do the same.*

I took his advice, phoning Scott daily and putting the children on to chat to him. Twice the three of us navigated the icy lanes to Whitby, bringing Chinese takeaway which we shared in the kitchen of Rum Keg Cottage, a narrow mid-terrace with chintz furniture and fussy wallpaper. Noah loved the pets: Camilla the chunky, silver-blue cat; Cully, an elderly spaniel with floppy ginger ears. He couldn't begin to understand why his dad wasn't at home, but he saw that these animals needed somebody to care for them.

I also tried to enlist the help of Scott's friends and colleagues. Anthony and the Espinozas did their best to stay in touch with him. Everyone else was useless, half-heartedly promising to 'give him a bell' or 'flick him a text' or 'drop him a line'. I knew they'd already written him off.

186

Isaac was all too right about the red flags. With each passing day the undertow strengthened, sucking Scott further and further into the whirlpool. He seemed to have given up eating and sleeping. He told me proudly that he spent eighteen hours a day online. *Researching*, he called it. I had other words for it. Better words.

I was loading the dishwasher in our kitchen at the time, my phone in one hand.

'Change of subject,' I said brightly. 'Did Heidi tell you about her new friends at school, Suyin and Ruby? Heidi and Suyin are doing a joint science fair project about soundwaves. Heidi says they're swots, and that suits her just fine.'

'If you can't beat 'em, join 'em!' Scott sounded delighted. 'Suyin Liu has her head screwed on. I always thought the Maia–Keren combo was toxic.'

I closed the dishwasher, sat down at the table.

'What about Flynn Thomas? She sees a lot of him; apparently they practise all kinds of music at lunchtimes. Flynn's fifteen. Is that too big an age gap? She swears they're just mates, they both love music, but . . .' I wasn't sure how to put this. 'What's he like? I mean . . . is she safe?'

I could hear the smile in Scott's voice. He assured me that Flynn didn't have a predatory bone in his body.

'Probably one of the nicest young men I've ever taught. She's more likely to break his heart than the other way around.'

It was a long, lovely, normal conversation. Then—just as we were saying goodbye—he had to go and ruin it all.

'Keep Heidi and Noah close from now on.'

'Why?'

'Just keep them close. There's a lot of talk on the forums about the coming storm.'

I blinked. 'The *what* now?'

'It's coming, Livia. It's coming, whether you can see it or not.'

Breathe. Breathe. I'd resolved to follow Isaac Katz's advice: *Listen without judging, keep those open conversations going.* But a switch had been flicked. I knew Scott would be fidgeting and twitching as his brain tripped into fear mode. The warm, beloved cadences of his voice were replaced by the hectoring monotone I'd come to dread—speeding up, winding up. I hated the intensity. I hated my own panic, my sense of being smothered.

'Could be today, could be next month, we know it will be soon. The signs are all there. The World Economic Forum . . .'

I held the phone away from my ear while he dipped and dived through Conspiracy World: *The Inner Circle, the Elite, puppet governments, militaries . . . follow the breadcrumbs, Livia.*

'They're gearing up for something global. Something world changing. Bigger than bushfires. Bigger than so-called terrorist attacks like the Manchester bombing or even 9/11.'

He'd crossed a line.

'So-called? *So-called?* What the fuck, Scott?' I was strident with indignation. 'Those things happened, they're not figments of anyone's imagination. There are real victims, real atrocities, real tragedies—don't you dare suggest all those dead and maimed people were crisis actors. Don't you bloody dare.'

'Maybe they happened. But on whose orders?'

'For heaven's sake—'

He was unstoppable. 'The Elect have been engineering "tragedies" for over a century.'

'Can we please apply a bit of basic history?'

He sounded triumphant. He thought he was winning the argument. 'A *bit of basic history* proves the point. Two world wars, nuclear stand-offs, endless conflicts, genocides. Fake viruses like AIDS. Chemtrails spreading disease, seeding hurricanes and earthquakes—'

'Chemtrails seeding earthquakes!' I didn't know whether to laugh or cry. 'How the hell do they manage that? Seriously, you've not bought into that claptrap? You mean *con*trails. It's condensation. Every plane leaves a vapour trail.'

'I'm talking to people who see this stuff firsthand: pilots, air traffic controllers . . .'

I listened with my palm pressed to my forehead, scrabbling through the landslide of twisted half-facts, looking for a loose thread to pull. I remembered Isaac Katz had suggested I ask open questions, so I changed tack.

'Why?' I asked, once I could get a word in. '*Why* would anyone do all these things? It's a genuine question.'

'Because a panicking humanity is like a flock of sheep who hear wolves howling all around them on a dark night. Bunched together, bleating with terror, no idea which way to run. Those sheep are so desperate for leadership that they'll welcome the all-powerful shepherds with their dogs. They'll beg for control and surveillance on a scale we've never seen before. And they will never know that the baying wolves were a fiction.'

'Can you give me some evidence that—'

'*How* is easy too. The New World Order has infiltrated every power structure. I've just read a letter from someone's son, a kid in the US Navy. He was crying while he wrote to his parents, because they're doing top-secret training exercises on tactics to subdue civilians. It's coming. They're going to manufacture some crisis and use it to subdue us—to herd us—and we're going to be grateful for it.'

I took a long breath.

'Do you think there's any chance,' I began, making a super-human effort to sound sincere, 'that this letter from the US Navy bloke is a fake? Anyone could have written it.'

No chance, according to Scott. 'His dad was on the forum.

It's handwritten, because email isn't secure. Heartrending to read. It's gone viral.'

'I bet it has.'

•

Sunday morning. Scott was coming for lunch on his way back from visiting Geraldine. Noah had spent the night in my bed—kicking, squirming, asking what time Daddy would be here. At dawn I was standing at our bedroom window—*my* bedroom window—watching the stars go out. It was going to be a bluebird day. As the sun rose, frost gleamed on the tiled roof of the potting shed, in shadows along our fence, on miniature spiderwebs all over the lawn. How could everything be so terribly wrong in such a sparkling world?

Noah woke up grumpy. I was sure it was down to anxiety, to sadness. He laughed less and clung more since Scott left.

'Daddy will be here soon,' Heidi told him as he ate his corn-flakes. She obviously meant to cheer her brother up, but instead he burst into noisy, messy tears.

Poor Heidi looked mortified. She rushed around to his side of the table, cuddling him while he sobbed. 'Shall we play a game?' she suggested. 'D'you want to play Guess Who?'

'You are the best sister ever,' I told her.

'I'm not.'

While they played by the fire I sat outside on the terrace, lifting my face to the winter sun, and phoned Bethany. I'd caught her at a good moment.

'Whitby's very pretty,' she said, when I told her about Scott.

'But he doesn't know a soul. He reckons he spends eighteen hours a day online.'

I heard her tutting. 'Not good. Eighteen hours a day with his fellow internutters.'

This had me snorting. There was nothing funny about our disintegrating marriage, but sometimes laughter was the only comfort left.

'He's meant to be visiting us today,' I said. 'Any minute now. We just want him back the way he was, Bethany. The children want their dad back.'

'How are you managing financially?'

'Heads above water.'

But only just. I'd cancelled our camping trip to France, pared back the grocery shopping to the bare minimum, dropped Netflix and Disney and everything else we didn't need. I was dipping into our savings and investigating ways to rejig the mortgage, but there was nothing to spare. Heidi had come home happy last night, talking excitedly about being picked to go to a national music camp in the summer.

'I can't believe I got chosen. Flynn's going too.' She was poker-faced as she said his name, but I wasn't fooled.

I looked through the music camp brochure, celebrating with her while wondering how much it was going to cost.

I didn't mention a word of this to Bethany. I knew she and James would offer to help, but I had my pride.

I pricked up my ears at the rattle of a car turning onto our drive, followed by Noah shouting and whooping.

'I'd better go,' I said. 'Scott's here.'

'Love you, sis,' Bethany said. 'Take care.'

•

'You look like a junkie,' Heidi told her father.

It was a fair description. The state of him! Unshaven, wild-eyed. I could have sworn he'd lost a stone since he'd left. You could see the ruins of my beautiful man, but he looked and sounded disturbingly like some of the drug addicts I worked with every day.

'I'm awake.' He stared at Heidi with a kind of exultation. 'Awake like never before in my life, even though it's frightening to know what's out there.'

'What *is* out there?' asked Noah.

'Scott,' I hissed, 'dial it back.'

Noah had dashed out to meet his dad at the car—dragged him by the hand to show him the fish and the drift of snowdrops encircling the apple tree. Now he was sitting on Scott's knee, with Bernard the Sloth stuck up his jumper.

Scott hugged him close. 'I'll look after you, my friend. Don't you worry.'

Noah's little forehead was corrugated. 'D'you mean the ambulance men who took Nicky away? Are they out there?'

I was glaring daggers at Scott, resolving to set ground rules for future visits. I wasn't going to stand by while he terrified the children with his crackpot conspiracies.

'The only thing *out there*,' I declared cheerily, doing a fake-happy dance, 'is the bakery, with shelves full of sausage rolls, freshly baked just for Noah Denby! Which is where we're all going in a minute. Okay? Yum! You'll need to wrap up warm.'

The asthma nurse wanted Noah to step up to a new preventer. I'd booked an appointment with our GP for later in the week.

'Shall I take him?' Scott suggested, when I mentioned it. 'Save you taking time off work.'

I was considering his offer when the doorbell rang.

'Probably someone collecting for the jumble sale,' I told Heidi, as she trudged off to answer it. 'You'll find a bag of stuff by the shoe rack.'

'Honestly,' said Scott, 'I'm more than happy to drive across and take Noah to his appointment.'

Behind me, Heidi was opening the front door. A woman's voice.

'By the shoe rack, Heidi,' I called, as I shook out Noah's anorak. 'The brown paper bag. Clothes and books.'

'Livia,' said Scott.

'Thanks for offering'—I was distracted, fishing Noah's mittens out of his sleeves—'but I can't have you accusing that poor hard-working GP of being complicit in a forced euthanasia program.'

'Livia . . . *Livia.*' This time I caught the urgency. The fear.

He'd got to his feet, still cradling Noah. Father and son were staring past me into the hall, both of them looking as though the devil had materialised out there.

I swung around. Heidi was standing in the kitchen doorway, one hand over her mouth and nose, eyes brimming with tears. Behind her loomed two figures. Stab-proof vests, radios.

'They've come for me,' said Scott. 'Try to get a message to Dr Jack.'

For one ghastly second my lizard brain flared into a screaming red alert, suppressing all reason or logic. *They're going to take him away. He's going to be disappeared.*

Then Heidi managed to speak. 'It's okay, Dad,' she said. 'It isn't you they're after.'

Heidi

I almost fainted when I opened the door. Two police officers in uniform, both women, both deadly serious, as though they'd come to arrest a murderer. Their panda car was parked in the lane.

'Hi,' they said, holding up their identity cards. 'Are you Heidi? Mum or Dad at home?'

I was clutching a bag with clothes and books ready for the jumble sale collectors. My heart felt like a machine gun going off in my chest. *This is it, this is it.*

'You're here for me, aren't you?' I asked.

They didn't deny it. The older one looked over my shoulder into the house. 'Mind if we come in for a minute, just for a chat?' It wasn't a request.

I put down the bag as they followed me into the hall, somehow filling the house like a pair of giants. They had all the kit: the belts with handcuffs and batons, the radios, the heavy shoes.

It took a horrible eternity for my parents to twig that I hadn't opened the door to nice smiley jumble sale collectors. One minute Mum was wittering on about going to the bakery, the next she'd frozen, as though a tiger had just prowled into the house. Poor Dad turned white. He thought they'd come to arrest him.

The older officer, Sergeant Rani Kumar, introduced them both and did all the talking. She looked to be my parents' age, with her hair parted in the middle and rolled into a bun at the nape of her neck. The younger one was rangy, like a greyhound. Maybe she'd been brought along in case I tried to do a runner. A roaring, rushing sound was filling my ears.

'Could we sit down?' asked Sergeant Kumar, placing her hat on the table.

'What's this all about?' asked Mum.

'We've just come from the Spar supermarket. They've been having a problem for quite a while. I think Heidi can help us.'

The police officer was looking at me. She had elegantly shaped eyebrows and very dark eyes, with just the hint of a smile in them.

'I'll get everything,' I whispered, and she nodded.

'That would be great, Heidi. Thanks.'

I heard Dad freaking out as I headed for the stairs.

'Get what? You're not going anywhere! Livia, she's packing; she thinks they're taking her away.'

I was in floods of tears by the time I burst into my room. I threw myself down on the floor to reach under the cupboard, hauling everything out into the open: the stupid flowery garden-ing gloves that lured me in the very first time; the stupid biro; the candles and magazine. Smarties. Stupid toy ambulance from Tesco. A part of me was relieved to be getting rid of them.

I looked around to see Mum standing by my bed.

'How long has this been going on?' she asked, gazing at my hoard of shame.

'I'm sorry.' I could hardly get the words out because I was sobbing so much. 'I'm sorry.'

'How long?'

'These were first.' I shoved the gloves with my toe. 'After Nicky's funeral, when Noah had an asthma attack and Dad took him to hospital.'

I was expecting her to lose it. I was waiting for: *How could you? You've really let us down.* But she never said any of that. She just kept staring at everything. At last, she seemed to shake herself before tipping my new trainers out of their box.

'Is that all of it?'

I nodded. Tears were streaming down my cheeks.

'Quite sure?' She glanced around the room. 'There's nothing else at all? Have a good think, Heidi, because this is your chance to make a clean breast of everything.'

I checked under the cupboard again, but there was nothing except a lot of dust, a dead spider and a slipper with a hole in the toe.

'Right.' Mum handed me the shoebox. 'Put it all in here, bring it downstairs. You're going to have to face the music.'

TWENTY-SIX

Livia

Carol rested her tray on the edge of our table.

'Two cheese toasties, two teas,' she said, unloading her wares. 'This jug's got extra milk for you, Charles, 'cos I know that's how you like it.'

'Ooh, lovely,' I gushed, as though she'd produced some rare delicacy.

Charles pressed his palms together and dipped his head.

'This one's nothing but trouble,' she said to me, jerking her chin towards him. 'Keeps insisting on doing the washing-up.'

Pouring tea into my giant white mug, I listened to the pair of them exchanging affectionate banter. I was thinking about how priceless a familiar face can be. Close friends, family—they cost, they come with baggage. It's the steady acquaintances that get us through the day.

When Carol sailed off to serve more customers, Charles turned back to me.

'You must have had a heart attack,' he said. 'Two coppers in your house.'

'D'you know what? I dived straight into Scott's conspiracy world. My first thought was: *Oh my God, he's right, they've come to get him.*'

I didn't have a valid reason for visiting Charles today. I'd been awake half the night, got two anxious children dressed and fed and off to two different schools, driven across the wintry moors, sat down at my desk, seen scores of new emails—plus all the unresolved ones from yesterday—and very nearly fell apart. I had a vivid image of myself sweeping everything onto the floor and upending my desk.

I must have appeared normal enough, though, because Jude Hipkins bustled in without a second glance. My colleague of many years—my friend—was lovable but exhaustingly energetic, bottle-blonde hair framing round cheeks.

'Morning, Livia! My Corolla's back at the garage—can you believe it?'

She complained bitterly about her dodgy gearbox, while I fantasised about hurling my office chair through the window. It would have landed on the bonnet of Jude's courtesy car, in a shower of broken glass.

I stood up, grabbing my jacket from the back of my chair. 'Just nipping down to Willow House,' I muttered. 'Running late.'

And here I was in Carol's, scoffing cheese toasties while pouring out my troubles to the Garrotter; troubles that I wouldn't be sharing with anyone else, not even Bethany.

'A pile of things she'd swiped! Under her wardrobe, all these months. She was in pieces, kept saying sorry, confessed to every-thing. Says she *wanted* to be caught. I made her carry the whole lot downstairs and hand it over to the police.'

'Poor kid.'

'Poor kid, my foot. I was ropable. We're in enough trouble without my own daughter turning into an offender.' I caught his eye and sighed. 'You're right, Charles. Poor Heidi.'

The police had put on a show of taking the whole thing extremely seriously. After talking to Heidi, they drove back to the shop for another word with Mrs Ponder. They even phoned Tesco.

'Did they charge her?' asked Charles.

'Not this time.' I mimed mopping my brow. 'Nor a formal police caution. Mrs Ponder didn't want her life ruined, she just wants her to stop nicking stock. Heidi had to apologise. She's barred from the shop for a year. She's already donated every penny she had to the Donkey Sanctuary. It was all in a jam jar, sixty quid that she's been saving forever. Mrs Ponder likes donkeys, apparently.'

'Did she apologise in person?'

'She did, very tearfully. I went with her.'

'Bet that was awkward.'

'It wasn't much fun. I don't think I'll be showing my own face in there for a while.'

Mrs Ponder had been tight-lipped, and I didn't blame her. She gave Heidi a piece of her mind, told us how many hundreds of pounds she lost each year to shoplifting. I grovelled, thanked her, promised Heidi would never do it again. I felt such a burning shame. What were we, as a family? Over-privileged. Hypocritical. Many young offenders weren't given that chance.

'Scott and I can't get our heads around it,' I said. 'She says she started after Nicky died, which fits because she did seem to change almost overnight. People shoplift for all kinds of reasons. I don't think she's a kleptomaniac, but it certainly wasn't out of need or even greed. I think it was a kind of self-harm. When the police asked why she did it, she said it gave her a few minutes off hating herself.'

'Poor kid,' Charles said again, nodding. 'Uh-huh. That makes sense to me.'

'I don't understand all this self-loathing about Nicky, just because it happened on her birthday. And what kind of a useless mother am I? I'm a bloody probation officer, and it turns out my daughter's got a secret criminal life and I had no clue.'

'You've had plenty of other troubles to worry about.'

'What else don't I know about her?'

Charles considered this question, his head tilted to one side. 'She's not heading for a criminal career, Livia. I promise you. She'll be okay.'

'Thank you.' I smiled at him. It was oddly comforting to hear him say it, even though he'd never met Heidi. 'I thought the shock might bring Scott to his senses, make him see that he needs to start behaving like an adult again.'

'No such luck?'

'If only! As soon as the police had gone, he started asking how had they tracked us down. I pointed out that Mrs Ponder only had to take our car numberplate, or a name from a bank card. Gilderdale's just a small market town.'

Charles picked up his toastie, chuckling. 'Would have taken the police about ten seconds.'

We munched in silence. I was still stressing about Heidi, remembering the awful moment when I found her dragging stolen things out from under her wardrobe. Charles was idly watching the morning chat show on Carol's TV. Three shiny presenters sitting on a sofa, talking about how gym membership always surged in the New Year. Underneath them, a rolling news banner gave us constant updates: *Boris Johnson: UK at 'Brexit finish line'* ... *Trump impeachment trial underway* ... *US firefighters killed in Australia plane crash* ... *China virus death toll rises to eighteen. Panic as millions put into lockdown in Hubei province.*

'Imagine having that much control over your citizens,' I said, nodding at the screen.

'They're building a whole new hospital in just a few days!' Charles sounded dubious. 'Hell of a reaction for eighteen deaths. Makes you wonder.'

'What does it make you wonder?'

'What we're not being told. Jess's workmate has in-laws in China. Apparently doctors there aren't allowed to utter a single word about what's really going on.'

'Which is what?'

He glanced around the cafe before dropping his voice, as though the trio of tradesmen tucking into their full English might be secret agents. 'Biological warfare. They reckon it was the Americans.'

'Don't *you* start,' I said.

TWENTY-SEVEN

Scott

They must be nautical people, my hosts. A map of Captain Cook's voyages hung on the flowery wallpaper, alongside a barometer shaped like a ship's steering wheel and a clock that looked like a porthole.

I was grateful for my temporary hideaway, though I could scarcely move for the ships in bottles and brass telescopes. Porcelain shepherdesses too, and French lace shrouding all the windows. Oddly, the fact that it was so obviously *not* my home made me feel safer. I felt anonymous among somebody else's knick-knacks. I perched on the edge of the chintz sofa, laptop open on the coffee table in front of me. I'd allowed myself only one dim lamp, to minimise my visibility. Camilla stretched herself out at my side. Now that I'd been her servant and sachet-opener for two weeks, the imperious cat deigned to share a sofa with me.

The airwaves and forums were buzzing tonight. Everyone had the same sense: war was coming, forces were on the move. Right now I was watching Gary Tey, the ex-CIA guy. He introduced two guests, both experts in cyber-surveillance with their own channels. They were in Paris and Sydney respectively, joining

Gary via Zoom. I could almost hear Livia's cynicism, demanding to know what made any of these men experts. She still refused to join the dots, refused to remove her blindfold.

Gary opened the discussion. '*People tend to think it's only in totalitarian regimes—and dystopian novels—that the ordinary citizen is under constant surveillance. They're wrong, aren't they?*'

'*Regrettably they are,*' agreed the French guy, whose English was flawless. '*And this is the illusion of freedom. Those of us who keep a close eye on intel and security are seeing no difference between totalitarian regimes and so-called Western democracies.*'

The conversation that followed revealed an Orwellian nightmare. Big Brother really *was* watching us. Spyware and malware were embedded on our phones and computers, monitored continuously by artificial intelligence. It could turn on our cameras and microphones without our knowing. Every image we ever took was automatically checked; every word we ever typed. We were also filmed by CCTV both on the ground and from satellites. There was no escape from face- and voice-recognition software. Big Brother knew everything we were saying and doing, what we bought, what we watched or read, even how we were feeling.

Gary Tey looked grave. '*You can run, but you can never hide. So be vigilant, people. Which brings us to what's happening in China right now. I've been watching this very, very closely and I know both of you have too. Do we agree that it's concerning?*'

'*Extremely concerning!*' exclaimed the French expert. '*Eleven million people in Wuhan were made prisoners overnight, all for an alleged virus that may or may not have killed just a handful.*'

'*It's so blatant.*' The Australian seemed incredulous. '*An engineered crisis, mass alarm, panic. Citizens accepting restrictions in return for "protection"—and yes, that word is in inverted commas.*'

'So . . . *could this be it?*' Gary spread his arms. '*Is the New World Order getting ready to step out of the shadows?*'

The others were nodding.

'*Maybe*,' said the Australian. '*At the very least, the Truther community must be on a war footing.*'

Gary ended the discussion by addressing us, the audience. '*We can't be sure what's going on with this alleged virus. But it feels like the hidden hand in history could be about to reveal itself. Stay awake. Be ready for the battle of your lives.*'

The porthole clock ticked and chimed. It was three am. Old Cully raised her head from her basket by the heat pump, flapping her tail twice before sighing and curling up again. I padded to the bathroom and back, my thoughts still humming—and froze at the stutter of a car's engine outside. Rum Keg was near the top of a steep street, narrow and awkward. Very little traffic passed by, and certainly not in the early hours. Swiftly, instinctively, I reached to switch off my lamp. The lace curtains took on a luminous glow as headlights swept past.

Once the street was quiet again, I risked a look out of the window. No sign of life. Perhaps just a taxi, bringing party-goers home.

All the same, I lingered at the glass. The view from here might have been an oil painting of the old fishing port. Whitby at night: painted houses with steep roofs, jostling along the waterfront and up the hill below the watchful skeleton of the ruined abbey. A hundred points of light, mirrored and shimmering across the inner harbour with its fishing and pleasure boats. I could just make out the abbey steps—a hundred and ninety-nine of the bastards; I counted every last one a few years back while carrying six-month-old Noah. It was a scene that inspired Bram Stoker to create Count Dracula, in the shape of a vast black dog leaping from a wrecked ship in a storm. True genius.

Three fifteen. My brain was beginning to stumble. I needed sleep. Going to bed upstairs didn't feel safe, so I fetched a duvet and pillow before stretching out on the sofa. Better to be down here, dressed, car keys on the table, ready for action if threatened. Camilla stomped heavily across my chest before jumping to the floor and stalking away. Seconds later, the cat flap was swinging.

Three thirty. Four o'clock. A vampire-dog loping up the steps, eyes glowing through a sea fret. A red-haired girl in a morgue. Police bursting into our home, Noah being stretchered into an ambulance, the doors closing behind him. Livia wouldn't protect him. She didn't think she needed to.

The mysterious car was back. This time it stopped outside, its engine idling. Doors slammed. Beams passed along the back of the sofa, the wall, across the ceiling. Searchlights, diffused and shattered by French lace. I lay motionless in the dark, every nerve taut.

Circles within circles. Those in the outer rings were oblivious. I'd been one of those blind servants myself, a teacher who delivered a false version of reality. For years I'd unwittingly peddled the narrative. I'd influenced hundreds, maybe thousands of pupils.

Circles within circles. The police were part of a circle too. Why send two of them, including a sergeant, to talk to a teenager about swiping Smarties and gardening gloves? And the timing. The *timing*. I'd only been home five minutes. Hell of a coincidence.

It took a while, but my befuddled brain got there in the end. Made the connections. Joined the dots.

I sent a message to Dr Jack, explaining what had happened at The Forge—and what was happening now.

He replied that he was just handing over after a night shift, would get back to me as soon as he left the hospital.

No chance of sleep. I kept watch near the window, peering through a chink in the lace. Nothing. Nobody. Only Camilla, who came sauntering up the pavement with her tail in the air, leaping easily onto the little picket fence in front of Rum Keg.

Dr Jack's reply coincided with the first hint of dawn, the slightest dimming of the stars behind the abbey.

@DrJackNHS: *You're not being paranoid. You publicly signalled your resistance, and within days the police were harassing your family. Now you've got a car cruising around your street. I don't believe in coincidences.*

@ScottDenbyTeacher: *The police were on the doorstep within minutes of my arrival home. They must have been waiting for me.*

@DrJackNHS: *Yes. And they've been waiting for the opportune moment to use Heidi's stealing as leverage. I suspect they've been monitoring your phone, maybe tracking your car. So both are compromised.*

@ScottDenbyTeacher: *What was the point? Why turn up at my family's door?*

@DrJackNHS: *Delivering a warning. Demonstrating that it's not only you they can destroy, it's your family too.*

@ScottDenbyTeacher: *So what do I do now?*

@DrJackNHS: *Be extremely careful. You're on their radar. Get ready to run.*

•

Cully and I set out in the morning twilight, padding downhill through the now-familiar maze of streets. The sun hauled itself over the horizon, only to be smothered by sulky clouds.

Shops and cafes were opening their doors along the harbour, though it was their low season. Seagulls screamed and wheeled, tearing at fish-and-chip papers in a bin. I passed the tourist boats moored by their steps, signs advertising the trips they offered. Our family once hopped aboard a bright yellow one for a cruise upriver, under the viaduct and along the picturesque lower reaches of the Esk. I wished we could do that today. I wished they were all here with me. I was a happy man, back in the days when I was ignorant.

Further up the river, the marina smelled of saltwater and diesel. A couple were backing a motorboat on a trailer down the slipway; someone drove into the car park with a kayak on their roof. The usual fleet of opulent craft stood in proud lines along the floating pontoons with their security gates. Yachts and launches, clinker-built ketches alongside the gleaming hulls of gin palaces. Beyond them, boats of all shapes and sizes bobbed among pile moorings and buoys. Others were tied up along the banks of the Esk.

The blue boat was still there. A little day sailer, drifting with the tides around an orange buoy. She'd caught my eye the first day I arrived in Whitby, because she could have been the twin of my father's beloved *Geraldine*. She stood upstream, far beyond the security and conviviality of marina life, bobbing forlornly in the wake of the passing motorboat. The sight of her transported me back to Coniston Water: Mum with her gin and tonic in a deckchair, Dad messing about on *Geraldine*, Nicky and I playing cards on the deck, or splashing in the moss-smelling lake. They were almost all gone now, all those people.

The blue boat had possibilities.

On my phone, another message from Dr Jack: *Do you have an escape plan?*

TWENTY-EIGHT

Livia

I had to steel myself to phone Scott each day, listening miserably as the man I loved poured out an unbroken stream of paranoia. I dreaded those monologues.

'The police turning up at that precise moment was too much of a coincidence,' he told me. 'I'd just walked in and—*hello!*—they're at the door. Doesn't that seem a little unlikely to you?'

'They were probably near Gilderdale when the call came in.'

'Another coincidence?'

'So you think they're watching this house?'

'I think they're watching *me*. They cruise up and down the street outside Rum Keg Cottage. And my phone's started making a weird noise. Hear that?'

I listened, straining my ears for alien sounds. I couldn't hear a thing.

'That intermittent clicking,' Scott said. 'Dr Jack thinks it could be spyware. I might get rid of it, start using prepaid phones.'

I sighed. 'Come for dinner on Thursday?'

•

As always, Noah launched himself at Scott before he was through the front door. Heidi played him her grade five exam pieces, which I thought sounded astonishing. I had to keep intervening, though, to stop Scott from saying anything too odd. My happy-family smile made my face ache. I felt sickened by the false jollity in my own voice.

The doorbell rang after dinner. I opened it with my smile still fixed, half-expecting to find the police on my doorstep again.

But it wasn't the police. Just Anthony, cradling a jar of honey.

'Hi, Livia! I'm on my way home from Rosedale Retreat and thought I'd drop by to see how you and the kids are doing.' He held up the honey. 'This is for you; it's from the Espinozas' bees.'

It was kind of him, but my heart sank.

'Scott's here for dinner,' I said. 'He's upstairs, reading to Noah.'

'Great timing! Two Denbys for the price of one.'

I smiled weakly and invited him in for a cup of coffee, but I didn't think it was great timing at all. There were four Denbys, not two, and we were all of us struggling. Scott was here to see his children, and for them every second was precious.

'How's our boy?' Anthony asked, as he leaned against the dresser with a mug in one hand.

'He's . . .' I shrugged. 'I don't know if he'll ever be coming back.'

'Hell, Livia, I'm sorry. I keep telling him: he's such a lucky guy, he had the perfect life. He must be crazy to give this up.'

When Scott reappeared, he greeted Anthony warmly. We sat around the sitting room fire. Heidi lay on the sofa with her back against Scott, while Anthony described the highly staged, professional photos the Espinozas had commissioned for their website.

'You could stay over if you like, Dad,' wheedled Heidi, twisting around to look at his face.

He booped her nose. 'Not tonight.'

'Mum won't mind.'

'You're safer when I'm not here.'

'Safer from what?'

'Safer from people who don't like the things I've been saying. I'd rather those people stayed well away from my family.'

Here we go again, I thought. I was about to intervene when Anthony saved the day.

'Well, I'd better get on the road.' He hauled himself out of the armchair, rubbing his big hands together. 'I'm setting my alarm for four; got to talk to my supplier back in the States about the paperwork we'll need once we've left the EU.'

Scott stood up too, thanking his friend for dropping by.

'What about that goddamned virus?' said Anthony, as I opened the front door. 'The very first cases in the country, and they have to be in York!'

Scott and I both stared at him.

'First I've heard of it,' I said.

'You guys hadn't heard?' Anthony couldn't conceal his delight at knowing something we didn't. 'It's leading the national news. Visitors from China. They were whisked out of their hotel through a fire escape last night, rushed to a special unit, lights and sirens like something out of a horror movie. The paramedics were all in white hazmat outfits.'

Heidi took Scott's upper arm, resting her cheek against his shoulder. 'Are those people going to be okay?' she asked.

'They'll be fine, Heidi.' Scott sounded completely confident. 'It's a hoax. They're just trying to scare everyone with their stupid sirens and hazmat suits.'

Anthony was checking the news on his phone. 'I've set this up to give me alerts. The thing seems to be spreading exponentially now. The World Health Organization just declared a global health emergency.'

Scott gave a bark of laughter. ''Course they have! Brace yourself for a cascade of doomsday plague stories. Next step will be quarantine camps and forced vaccinations. I know people who've been predicting this for a long time. We've had dress rehearsals. This might just be opening night.'

'Not now, Scott,' I hissed urgently. 'Stop.'

It was like trying to hold back a tornado with a beach windbreak.

'Can you *really* not see what's going on? Invent a mythical deadly virus, hype it up, create panic. Perfect conditions to usher in global tyranny. By the time humanity stops running around, bumping into one another, screaming, *Help help!* it'll be too late: the coup will be complete.'

Poor Anthony stood like a stunned bear, phone in hand.

'Come on!' Scott threw out his arms. 'Come *on*. Can you really not see it? Nicky was disposed of. By the time this "emergency" is over, millions more will be dead. They'll start with the vulnerable. Noah will be top of their hit list.'

'Because of his asthma?' asked Heidi.

'Shut up, Scott,' I said. 'Just shut up. Just go. I want you to leave now.'

Anthony laid a hand on Scott's back, propelling him towards the door. 'C'mon, my friend. The Fatted Goose awaits. You can persuade me over a pint.'

TWENTY-NINE

February 2020

Livia

On 7 February, an ophthalmologist in Wuhan died of the new coronavirus. Dr Li Wenliang was a father, his wife pregnant with their second child. Back in December, he'd tried to warn colleagues about the virus which would later kill him. The police had called him in, accused him of spreading false rumours and forced him to apologise.

Fake news, true news. Whistleblowing doctors.

I'd just parked at work when I saw the news of the young doctor's death on my phone. The death toll in China was in the many hundreds now, but there was something profoundly sad about the image of the brave man in the hospital bed, his eyes still bright above his oxygen mask. It broke my heart that he'd tried to sound a warning.

Sitting in my car, I phoned Scott. I'd been kept awake by a gale in the night, and violent gusts had made my drive across the moors rather more exciting than I liked.

Scott answered, but the wind was louder than his voice.

'Can't hear you!' I shouted.

'Hang on.' I heard a door open and close before he was back. 'That better?'

'Much.'

'It's wild here, the sea's massive—waves breaking right over the pier. I've taken shelter in that little tearoom on the harbour; remember we had cream tea here last summer?'

A good sign, I thought. He'd been out and about, enjoying a bit of fresh air and reminiscing about happier times.

'Did you hear about the Chinese doctor who died?' I asked.

'Yeah . . . there was a lot of chatter on the forums through the night. Most people think the guy in the photos is a crisis actor. He's had an unrealistic amount of social media exposure for someone who was meant to be battling for his life in a Chinese hospital where they've had a news blackout. Did you notice we were told he's dead, then alive, then again that he died? They couldn't even get their story straight!'

Fury, always simmering when Scott was in conspiracy mode, seethed right over.

'For heaven's sake,' I snapped. 'A caring doctor has given his life for his patients. His loss is a tragedy. But you and all those other man-child losers *have* to know better. Arrogant morons.'

'That's not fair.'

'It bloody well is, and I'm sick to the back teeth of being nice about it. You're behaving like an idiot, Scott. For the love of God, grow up.'

I lobbed my phone into my handbag, hurled myself out of the driver's seat and slammed the door with such violence that the whole car jumped.

Poor Jude happened to be walking past. She spun around with her hand on her chest. 'Gave me a heart attack.'

'Sorry. Wind took the door out of my hand.'

We walked inside together, Jude enthusing about an upcoming family holiday in Turkey, grandchildren and all—while I quietly raged. If I'd been a cartoon character there would have been a black cloud floating over my head, with bolts of lightning shooting around in it. I suspected Isaac Katz wouldn't approve of my calling Scott and his friends morons and man-child losers.

'This China virus seems to be fizzling out,' said Jude, as she spooned powdered coffee into two mugs. 'Maybe just another storm in a teacup, like bird flu.'

'Hope so.' I was thinking about Dr Li Wenliang. He didn't think it was a storm in a teacup.

Jude handed me a mug. 'Mind you, I don't care what happens—wild horses won't keep me from getting to Turkey in April.'

●

The rest of February was cold and wet and passed in a blur. I found ways to manage as a single parent, juggling, juggling, sometimes dropping a plate. Each morning I ended up running late for work, every evening I drove home at breakneck speed. The children were tired, I was tired. But we were doing okay.

Towards the end of the month, I had to spend all day at a workshop in Newcastle, so Scott drove across to collect Noah from school. It seemed like a good opportunity for him to spend some time with the children.

It was gone seven by the time I parked outside The Forge. Scott was about to serve sausages and mash. Heidi sat cross-legged on the sofa, re-reading *Anne of Green Gables*. Noah was building a Lego castle on the hearthrug, his lower lip stuck out in concentration.

'This is so lovely,' I said to Scott, dumping my bag and sliding off my boots. 'You should marry me.'

We played Twister after supper. Noah always won because he was as small and bendy as a human pretzel; Scott and I collapsed in a giggling heap with our arms around one another. For the zillionth time, I dared to hope we might be turning a corner. Clearly I was a slow learner.

My naive optimism died at toothbrushing time, when I walked past the bathroom to hear Scott telling Noah that he mustn't ever, *ever* get into an ambulance.

'Scream, scream, scream—use your outside voice, so everyone starts looking. Make a *big* noise, okay, Noah? Promise me? Jump out and run away. Don't let them shut the doors.'

'Ambulances are good, they help people,' I protested, rushing in.

'I'll kick them!' Noah shrieked at the top of his voice, fighting for his life in his dinosaur pyjamas, toothpaste foam all around his mouth. He demonstrated what he thought were karate kicks. 'Bam, wham!'

'Good lad!' said Scott. 'Bite them if you have to.'

'Bam! Wham!' The towel holder was kicked over.

I took a firm hold of Noah's arms, trying to get him to look at me. He was still kicking and shrieking.

'You've been in an ambulance lots of times. They're kind people.'

It was all too confusing and scary for such a small boy. Breaking free of me, Noah hurled his toothbrush at the ceiling then pelted out of the room. All this anxious hyperactivity, the aggression—it was completely out of character.

I rounded on Scott. 'Your son is six years old,' I hissed. 'Six! What the hell are you doing?'

'I'm trying to save his life.'

'You're *endangering* his life. He has a chronic condition. He's always believed that medical people are his friends and will look after him. You've just destroyed that trust.' I could have cried with disappointment and frustration. 'Why?' I demanded. '*Why?*'

'Because it's coming. It's happening. And if I don't warn him, who will?'

•

Noah woke up in a blind terror that night, hysterical about *the killing truck* and *the killing man coming after me.* His screams woke Heidi, who charged out of her room, armed with a hockey stick in case Scott had been right all along and her little brother was being kidnapped.

By morning we were all crammed into my bed in a jumble of dried tears and comfort-cuddles. I hadn't slept a wink.

I sent Scott a text: *Noah had screaming nightmares about ambulances. He's frightened to go to school, he's frightened even to leave the house. The children love you, Scott. We all love you. But your problems are damaging them now. I think it's best if you stay away for a while. Please will you get help? Please. We can go private. I can find someone for you to talk to. Let me know. Love always, Livia XX*

I spent a long time composing this message, agonised before sending it, and waited on tenterhooks for a reply. For hours I heard nothing. When Scott's answer finally arrived, I wasn't sure what to make of it.

I don't want to fight with you. All that matters is to save the children from an enemy that's literally everywhere. I'm getting ready to do just that, if I have to.

I rolled my eyes as I read this. *Blah blah blah.* I didn't take him seriously. I thought it was just words.

That was my mistake.

THIRTY

March 2020

Heidi

The news presenter sounded as though she was announcing the outbreak of war. *The World Health Organization has declared the Covid-19 outbreak a pandemic.*

'What does that actually mean?' I asked Mum.

'It means the whole world has a problem to deal with.'

It began to take up more and more of the evening news: the virus that was killing people in other countries. One day they announced that somebody had died in the UK. Then it was six people. Then it was fifty-five.

We started hearing new phrases: 'social distancing' and 'flatten the curve' and 'lockdown'. I couldn't really imagine what a lockdown might be like; it seemed unreal. But each day we heard they were happening in countries across the world, all desperate to stop the virus spreading. People were told to stay at home, schools and restaurants and libraries were closed. A whole cruise ship in Japan was turned into a floating quarantine unit, which meant thousands of people trapped on board. Lots caught the virus. Some died.

'They'll *never* try that in England,' declared Chloë, when Mum and I were collecting Noah.

Mum squatted down to give Noah a big kiss on the cheek. 'Might be quite nice. A few weeks at home.'

'No chance. Can you imagine us putting up with that, all for the flu? We'll take it on the chin, like Boris Johnson said.'

'I don't want Noah to take it on the chin,' said Mum.

While human beings talked about a pandemic, all of nature seemed to celebrate. Our garden came alive with nest-building birds, twittering, darting about with grass and twigs in their beaks. Lambs played running games in the fields, just like Noah and his friends in their school playground. Fluffy ducklings paddled behind their mums in the beck. Pink blossom frothed everywhere, and all the trees were turning green.

But sitting in our living room at night, we saw patients on ventilators in hospital wards, dying people saying goodbye to their families through iPads. We watched nurses dressed up like deep-sea divers, crying in corridors or sleeping on the floors of locker rooms. There were stories of Italian doctors who didn't have enough ventilators and had to choose who got a chance to live.

'Imagine having to make that decision again and again,' Mum whispered. 'Imagine having to tell their families.'

There was an interview with one of those doctors. He reminded me a lot of Dad—caring, thin and very worried. He said it was like wartime in his hospital; wards were overflowing with patients just dying, dying. Some were young people. The staff were completely overwhelmed: they were working double shifts, but it wasn't nearly enough. He warned us to get ready for the same thing in the UK.

Adverts on bus stops and TV and Facebook kept reminding us to wash our hands properly—*Happy birthday to you,* we sang as we lathered up the soap. If Noah or I so much as sniffed, Mum would take our temperature. The government said if any of us developed coughs we should quarantine ourselves. The ill person had to stay alone in their bedroom, while their family left food outside their door and washed surfaces with disinfectant. It sounded like the Black Death.

Every room at Barmoors High reeked of bleach, and there were bottles of hand sanitiser everywhere. Assemblies were cancelled. Rory, the class joker, called the virus the 'boomer reducer' because it mainly killed older people. Everyone seemed to think this was hilarious. *Boomer reducer!* But Suyin and her parents were anxious about her grandparents and great-grandparents in Beijing. She showed me photos of them all—nice, smiling people.

Mum had barred me from going into any shops since the police came, but she and Noah went to stock up on supplies just in case we got locked down. They came back with bags full of Panadol, pasta and all kinds of tins, and the news that Tesco was running out of toilet paper.

'A loo paper crisis!' Mum cried. 'What a bizarre thing to panic buy.'

'They're going to have very clean bums,' said Noah.

We all scoffed at the toilet paper hoarders. But I couldn't help noticing that Mum had bought an awful lot of it herself.

•

In the middle of March, the government warned that soon they'd be asking everyone over the age of seventy to self-isolate in their own homes 'for a very long time'.

Dad was visiting us that day. My parents had made a deal: he could hang out with us, but he wasn't to say anything about his beliefs. This wasn't easy for him, and when the announcement about the over-seventies came on the news, he almost lost it.

'And so it begins! Are we really going to stand meekly by and let this happen? The economically less useful, the "unworthy of life" are being isolated, shut into ghettoes. Always the first step.'

'Scott . . .' Mum had a warning note in her voice. She made a lip-zipping sign.

'First they came for the elderly,' said Dad. 'And I did not speak out.'

•

Grandma Polly certainly *did* speak out. When she called, Mum had to hold the phone six inches from her ear. I could hear every furious word.

'Apparently the cunning plan is to put an entire generation under house arrest,' she fumed. 'All to protect that golden calf, the economy. All so everyone else can carry on going to bloody football matches and horse races. Did you *see* those crowds at Cheltenham?'

'They're working to develop a vaccine.'

'How long will that take? This is blatant ageism. Is my freedom worth less than anyone else's? I'm fitter and healthier and a heck of a lot sharper than most of those pasty, paunchy, smug, useless bastards in Westminster who make these decisions. Maybe they should turn themselves into hermits while us oldies swan about.'

'Better stock up on loo paper,' said Mum.

'Not funny.'

'Sorry.' Mum rubbed a hand across her face. She'd twisted her hair and shoved it into a clip, but most of it had escaped and was falling around her cheeks. She always looked tired nowadays. Even her smile was crumpled and creased.

'Why don't you and Dad come up here and stay with us for a while?' she suggested. 'Let's all be together. You can have my room. I'll turn the office into a bedroom.'

Grandma said that was a very kind thought, but they'd rather stay in their own home. She and Grandad were already planning to do lots of gardening. They were going to build a pond, a pergola and a new flowerbed to attract bees 'while we sit this wretched thing out'.

'Sounds romantic,' said Mum.

I heard Grandma's laugh. 'We'll probably have murdered one another within a week.'

•

For me, the pandemic truly became real when they announced that schools would be closing. Every school in the country. You'd think I'd be excited to get a holiday, but it wasn't as simple as that. It was weird. I knew things must be serious.

I was finally seeing the point of school. Suyin and I were putting the finishing touches to our science fair project, which Mr Bond thought might pick up a place in the regional competition. Flynn had been adapting songs from films, to be played by two guitars. We'd been practising 'My Heart Will Go On' for the end-of-term concert. It sounded so good that a teacher had even asked us to play at her wedding.

Mum and I heard the school-closing news on our car radio, after collecting Noah from a party. He was sitting on his booster seat behind me, eating sweets from the party bag and humming to himself. He had no idea.

'They suffocate to death,' I muttered, as Mum parked outside our house. 'It attacks your lungs.'

'Most people are fine.' Mum was trying to sound nonchalant. 'Nine out of ten don't even need to go to hospital.'

'But others do. Others end up on ventilators. Some die.'

'Shh.' She glanced back at Noah, but he wasn't listening. He was hopping out of the car with a lollipop stuck in his mouth. Next moment he'd flung himself down by the pond.

'What about very small people with really, really bad asthma?' I whispered. 'Severe asthma, which flares up every time they catch even the slightest cold.'

Mum didn't answer. She was watching Noah as he played with his fish. For once she hadn't stuck a smile on her dial.

'Aren't you worried?' I prompted her.

'Chances are this pandemic won't come to anything.'

'You didn't answer my question.'

'Okay. Yes, of course I'm worried.' Sighing, she reached across the car to take my hand. 'I'm more than worried. But we've got the medicine we need for him, we've got a good hospital nearby. We know what to do, what numbers to call. This is just another challenge.'

Noah was still humming as he dabbled his hands in the water. He looked so little, and I loved him so much. I remembered the frazzled Italian doctor who said it was like wartime in his hospital.

'I'm worried too,' I said.

THIRTY-ONE

Scott

'*Boom!*' cried Dr Jack. '*We warned them! It's all in the open now.*'

He was hosting an online panel consisting of himself, Gary Tey and Sung-ho Kim, a South Korean intelligence expert living in Canada. Dr Jack was wearing his silicone mask, using voice-changing software instead of his usual text-to-speech. It sounded sci-fi, but still with undertones of the Scottish accent.

'*Classic,*' agreed Gary Tey. '*State-sponsored terrorism. And on a global scale this time.*'

The dismantling of freedom in the UK—in most nations—had been swift and inexorable. Schools and public places were closed, self-isolation and quarantine rules rammed through. Travel was being banned. Today's news was that the British police were now armed with draconian powers to detain, fine and force tests on people suspected of having Covid-19. France had gone into lockdown, and it was expected we would do the same. We were trapped like a shoal of fish, and the net of control was tightening around us.

'*So, to clarify for people watching, what we're seeing here is the problem–reaction–solution paradigm in action.*' Dr Jack put up a slide on half of the screen, a diagram to illustrate his point. '*Step one: the Elect and their Inner Circle, acting through puppets like the World Health Organization, invent or exploit a threat. Step two: humanity reacts with hysteria, crying out for guidance and leadership. Step three: the Elect comes up with the "solution" they've planned all along.* Et voilà! *The human race willingly gives up all freedom, in return for the fiction of protection.*'

Gary Tey and Sung-ho Kim were both looking shaken.

'*And it's all gone seamlessly so far, hasn't it?*' said Kim. '*You have to admire the orchestration of this fictional crisis. The production values, the little touches that lend authenticity. You can tell they have limitless funding and half of Hollywood in their ranks. The heartbreaking tweets from*'—he made inverted commas with his fingers—'"*doctors on the front line*", *the terrified actors—sorry, patients—on ventilators, medics in plastic face shields, faked photos of mass graves, videos of plucky Italians in tenement blocks all singing to keep their spirits up—hey, did you notice how they always sound like opera singers?*'

'*What are the chances?*' cried Dr Jack, to laughter from the other two.

Gary Tey was nodding. '*Kudos to the Inner Circle's publicity and comms. They're phenomenally effective at manipulating a global collective consciousness.*'

'*But the truth is trickling out,*' said Dr Jack. '*Courtesy of one of those balcony singers who came clean on a message board. Did you see that? He was part of a choir, bussed into those blocks of flats after dark. They all had to sign non-disclosure agreements.*'

'*Yep, yep. I saw that too.*' Gary Tey's computer screen was reflected on his oblong spectacles. '*Same with the intensive care units: I was talking to a guy on 4chan who used to work on the set of ER. He recognised that exact same set on the TV news, even a couple of the extras playing doctors. It wasn't a hospital, it was a studio. So phony, it's laughable.'*

'But with a deadly purpose,' said Dr Jack.

'That's right. One nation after another, locked—even welded—into their homes. Twenty-four-hour curfews, neighbours informing on neighbours who step outside. Nobody will object when the authorities come house to house, picking up the weak, the vulnerable, the dissidents, the whistleblowers—and herd them into military-run "hospitals" and "quarantine camps". Camps! We've seen this movie before, haven't we?'

A moment of grim reflection. A shift in the mood of the meeting.

'What we're seeing now,' said Sung-ho Kim, *'looks to me like the endgame. Nero, Hitler, Stalin, Pol Pot—there never was a dictator who didn't oppress their people. But we've never seen a dictatorship on the scale of the Elect, with modern surveillance and military might. It's global. There's nowhere to run, no allied powers to fight back. The cavalry is not coming. It's down to us to resist.'*

'Down to us,' agreed Gary Tey. *'Truthers will be driven underground. I predict the big social media platforms will label us cranks and try to erase us. The Elect will be the one source of "truth". But don't worry—we're already working on other channels, other platforms. They won't silence us.'*

Dr Jack thanked his guests and suggested they all check in again soon. He ended by speaking directly to his followers. *'This is not, repeat not, a drill. The NWO takeover is underway, exactly as predicted. Be ready. You are the Resistance. Protect the vulnerable however you can. They're first in line.'*

I sent the link to Livia, hoping it might finally convince her. I'd never needed her help more than I did now.

If even half of this is true, I wrote, *Nicky was one of the first. My mother and Noah will be next.*

By the time she replied, I'd left the house and was on my way to the marina.

Thanks for this. At work now. I'll watch it tonight. L x

•

Cully plodded along beside me. We took the long route through the park; I hoped a change in routine might make me less easy to track. I needed to plan every detail.

It felt unreal to be doing something so mundane as walking a dog, when dark clouds were gathering. Half of Whitby seemed to be doing the same, chucking tennis balls to bouncing labradoodles and picking up their mess with little plastic bags. A cheerful woman in green gumboots laughed and said, 'It's okay, she's just a big softie,' when her monster of a hound almost knocked poor old Cully over.

As we neared the marina, a police van rolled by. My gut tightened as the van slowed, the heads of its occupants turning in my direction. I walked faster, faster, ready to struggle and shout blue murder if they tried to pick me up. They wouldn't be expecting me to make a scene. Passers-by would gather to stare, perhaps film my arrest on their phones.

But the van slid past and disappeared around the next corner, leaving me light-headed and breathing fast. If their intention was to intimidate, to remind me that there was nowhere to hide, they'd succeeded. *You're on their radar. Get ready to run.*

The sun was out, the breeze cold and fresh. Yet everything felt watchful, the dropping of the barometer before a storm. I'd never seen the marina so quiet at this time of day. Just one yacht gliding in. No pleasure boats or dinghies, no four-wheel drives backing their motor launches down the ramp. A couple of people bustled about on their boats. One guy nodded to me as he passed through the gate from the floating pontoons, pulling a trolley loaded up with an outboard, a box of electronic gadgets and some fishing rods.

'Evening,' we both said.

He raised his eyebrows. 'Strange times we live in, eh?'

'Very.'

'Just been checking everything's secure. Removing valuables. Looks like we're heading for a lockdown.'

'You reckon?' I asked.

'My wife works for the Ministry of Health. She's fully expecting it. We should have done it days ago, in my opinion.'

I didn't try to put him right. He and his wife could be in the Inner Circle, for all I knew. We stood ten feet apart, making socially distanced conversation. I learned some useful facts about life at the marina, the boats, the tides on the river. We parted like old friends. An apocalypse does that to you, even if it is a hoax.

'Stay well now,' he said. 'Good luck.'

Cully and I left him to his preparations and set off across the car park, skirting around some industrial units and along the back of a marine supply store, emerging opposite the blue sailing boat. Rowing dinghies lay above the tideline here, attached to iron rings embedded in the ground.

I let Cully off her lead. The old dog stayed close, pottering around on a strip of grass and weeds while I brought out a small pair of binoculars borrowed from Rum Keg. They were powerful for their size. As I adjusted the lenses, I was suddenly aboard the blue boat. I could make out every detail, even a brass compass beside her cabin doors and the white-painted letters of her name: *Dixieland*. Fibreglass construction, about twenty-one feet—a bit bigger than *Geraldine*. Unlike our pride and joy, poor old *Dixieland* had obviously suffered years of neglect. Her paintwork was faded and cracking, with streaks of rust below her anchor chain and metal fittings. Still, she floated. Upended and covered in canvas, her outboard motor was waiting for action.

I was about to call Heidi on her mobile when I checked myself. *Jesus, Scott. Get rid of the phone. You might as well broadcast your plans on the radio.* Spyware. GPS tracking too, which explained how the police car came drifting past me just now. They'd probably recorded my conversation with the man in the marina; might be filming my face at this moment. I grinned at the screen. *Smile, you're on* Candid Camera.

That was when I noticed I had a text. I hoped it might be Livia, but a glance told me it was from the owners of Rum Keg Cottage.

'It's from your people, Cully,' I said.

It was an eviction notice, no matter how politely worded.

Hi Scott, we've been advised to return home urgently because of the virus. Flights are scarce but we hope to be back in Whitby on Monday afternoon. You're welcome to stay for a few days. So sorry about the change of plans. Andrew and Trudy Milner

It was the final impetus. The push. I needed to act fast.

●

That same evening, I went to see Livia and the children.

I made two stops on the way to Gilderdale. First at an ATM, where I used our joint credit card to take out £500. Livia wasn't going to be impressed, but at least I hadn't emptied the joint cheque account and left her high and dry. Once on the A170 I pulled into a fuel station. Two young people at the next pump were towing an open trailer, packed with furniture. A gangly lad of about sixteen fiddled anxiously with the tarpaulin cover while his companion went in to pay.

'Going far?' I asked, as I filled my petrol can.

'Back across to Manchester. Our mum bought this lot on eBay, asked my brother and me to collect it today in case there's a lockdown.' He tugged at the tarpaulin again. 'Better not fucking rain. No way this is watertight.'

I gave him a hand, moving the ratchet straps and tightening everything up.

'Cheers, mate,' said the brother, who reappeared with cans of energy drink.

'No problem,' I said. 'Safe travels.'

Both lads gave me a thumbs-up as they turned onto the road. They didn't know it, but they'd just done me a massive favour. And they had an extra piece of cargo.

The fuel station staff were all wearing medical masks. A pump dispenser of hand sanitiser gel for customers' use stood on the counter, and more were for sale. Nothing was normal. It felt disorientating. But then that was the point, wasn't it? Disorientation.

On my way to the counter, I picked up two identical pay-as-you-go phones from a display. Pale grey plastic, no bells or whistles. Disposable. Untraceable. Perfect.

THIRTY-TWO

Livia

'First day of spring,' Charles declared, as we took our usual seats in Carol's cafe.

'That's a happy thought.'

I no longer pretended that making time to see Charles was about supervision or support for him. He would be on licence for the rest of his life, but he was an exemplary resident at Willow House, a mentor to others. He didn't need this level of oversight. I was here out of friendship.

'I hear everyone's going to be working from home,' he said. 'Does that mean we won't be seeing you for a week or three?'

'Not in person maybe, but I'll stay in touch by phone. We're all going to have to get used to virtual meetings and court hearings. I'd better muck out the office. We lob everything in there; it's a junkyard.'

Carol's television was on, as always. They were interviewing a civil servant about the impact of school closures. She was obviously working from home, hunched over her screen with photos of her dogs in the background.

'*Every effort will be made to minimise disruption to our children's education*,' she promised earnestly. '*We'll be rolling out support for schools to put distance learning into place*.'

I snorted. 'There won't be much learning in our household.'

'No chance of your husband coming back?' asked Charles. 'He's a teacher, isn't he? Useful man to have around when you're homeschooling.'

'Honestly, Charles, it's best if he doesn't. Not until this is all over. He turned up unexpectedly last night, and he was in a terrible state.' I shuddered. 'He blows his fuse every time someone even whispers the word *pandemic*. "It's a hoax! It's the evil New World Order taking control!"'

'Aha. New World Order.' Charles looked bemused. 'Not 5G then?'

'Not this time.'

'There was a bloke in Willow House reckoned the virus is spread by radiation from all these new 5G signals, breaking down people's blood. He and his mates got caught setting fire to cell towers. He's back inside now.'

'Different tune. Same song.'

Carol brought our order, sliding everything expertly off the tray while warning us that the toasties were very hot.

'I hope you won't be closing, Carol,' said Charles, as she put down his extra milk. 'I don't know how I'd manage without my second home.'

In normal times she would have made some sassy retort before sweeping back to the kitchen. Not today. She sighed, lowering herself onto the shaped plastic seat of the table next to ours.

'Oh, Charles. This is all just . . . it's like being in a film, isn't it? You can't believe it's happening.'

The only other souls in the cafe were the young waitress and a man in yellow hi-vis reading a newspaper. It felt eerie. Fear of the virus had cleared the streets.

Charles stood up and pottered across to the counter to fetch another mug. 'Have a cuppa with us, Carol,' he said. 'I'll share mine.'

'Ooh . . . shall I?' Carol rested her cheek on her hand, contemplating the mug. 'Go on then. I've sod all customers. Who knows when we three will meet again?'

'I've just spent twenty years inside. I'm out for five minutes and now—*wham!* Still . . .' Charles poured tea into their two cups. 'I'm used to it, and I like my room. I'm planning to read loads of books. I've been to the library.'

'Who have you got at home, Carol?' I asked.

'My dad. He's ninety-two. And my daughter's talking about moving home for a while if we do get locked down. Best to be together.'

We clinked our three mugs.

'Cheers!' cried Charles. 'Good health to us all.'

Drinking tea, we talked about all the happy things we'd do *when all of this was over*. Later, I looked back on that half-hour—the warm cafe with its fuzzy neon sign, the comforting normality, the shared anxiety, the companionship—as a final staging post.

THIRTY-THREE

Heidi

I never forgot whose fault everything was. I never stopped wishing I could turn back time. Because of me, Nicky died, which broke Dad's heart and then his mind too. He lost his job, his home, his friends. He lost Mum. He ended up alone and frightened.

So when he called on the secret burner phone he'd given me and asked for my help the next day, I couldn't just say no.

'Are you sure about all this, Dad?' I asked.

Oh yes, he was very sure. He was in touch with a whole underground movement that saw exactly what was happening. We had to act immediately. He kept apologising, saying he knew he was asking too much of me.

I hated his plan. It really scared me. I was racking my brains for a way out.

'Shouldn't we ask Mum what she thinks?'

'No! You can't tell her, Heidi. She won't listen. She'd try to stop us, which would put all of us in even greater danger. She might even call the police—the very people we're running from. If she doesn't know, she can't be made to tell them anything.'

'Can't we wait a bit?' I suggested. 'See what happens?'

'We're running out of time. The lockdown's coming any day now.'

'We don't know that.'

'It's coming, all right. We *have* to do this tomorrow.'

While he talked, I turned around and around in my bedroom, feeling like I was being pulled in all directions. Dad was so convincing. He truly believed that evil monsters were planning to take control while the world was in lockdown. They had a list of people with chronic conditions like Noah, troublemakers like Dad. Those people would be taken away, never to be seen again. Our neighbours in Back Lane would lock their doors and pretend they'd heard nothing.

'I'd never ask this of you if I had a choice,' said Dad. 'But some fates are worse than death.'

Nightmares do come true. I'd read Anne Frank's diary and other books about the Holocaust. I'd leafed through a book in the school library which had stories told by child refugees from different parts of the world. In social studies we learned about the girls in Nigeria who were kidnapped by men dressed as soldiers— just marched away from their school to face terrible things. What if Dad had been right all along?

'Please will you help?' he asked. 'And promise you won't breathe a word to Mum?'

No matter how strange his ideas, Dad was still my dad, and he lost his brother because of me. The least I could do was trust him now, have his back, be his friend.

'Okay,' I said.

THIRTY-FOUR

Livia

I went into work on that final Monday before lockdown. I had things to do before I'd be ready to work from home. Schools were closed, but I arranged to drop Noah at Chloë's on my way through Gilderdale.

Heidi didn't get up to join us for breakfast. She was obviously making the most of this rare opportunity for a weekday sleep-in. She was old enough to stay home alone. I was only a phone call away, and our neighbours were friendly.

'We're just off,' I whispered, looking in on her before I left the house.

'Okay.'

She lay staring up at the ceiling, didn't move as I crossed the room and sat on her bed. Her face seemed bloodless, her hair splayed around it on the pillow. An image came to me—uninvited, stomach-lurching: Heidi was drowned, her lips blue, body water-logged, hair twining in the current like coppery waterweed.

'You okay?' I asked.

'Yup.'

'Sure?'

She sat up suddenly, almost violently, and clasped me around the waist. I hugged her back, promising that everything would be fine, I'd be home by five thirty.

'It'll be fun if there's a lockdown,' I said. 'We'll all be at home together. No school.'

But the more I tried to reassure her, the tighter she clung to me, pressing her face into my shoulder.

'Love you, Mum,' she whispered, her voice muffled. 'Love you.'

'And I love you! See you this afternoon. Call if you need me, okay?'

I hesitated before starting the car. Perhaps I should nip back upstairs, just to check Heidi was all right? Noah was lounging on his booster seat, legs swinging while he told me an animated story about Chloë's blue budgie.

'Bye, Bernard!' he cried, waving. As always, he'd propped the smiling sloth on the hall windowsill.

Glancing up at Heidi's bedroom window, I spotted a wan face gazing down at me. I waved as I backed the car onto the lane. She raised one hand and wiggled her fingers. Then she turned away.

•

Weird day. Hell of a weird day. I sent emails, made phone calls, updated records, packed things I might need into a plastic box. Everyone was pumping hand sanitiser dispensers, not touching doorknobs. It all felt so final.

In the afternoon, the team—sitting as far apart from one another as was possible in our office—held a hurried meeting to nut out logistics. We knew this could be our last get-together until ... well, until this thing was over. We talked about data protection, virtual conference software and weekly team meetings. People seemed dazed, muttering that the whole situation was *surreal* and *unbelievable* and *I thought we were going for herd immunity?*

'It'll only last a couple of weeks,' someone predicted.

'Did you see they're talking about using ice rinks as morgues?' said Jude. 'Storing the bodies on the ice. Setting up Nightingale hospitals with the army. Feels like we're at war.'

She and I left together. She, like me, was carrying her laptop and a box of tricks.

'I'm staying home, whatever the rules say,' she declared, as she lifted her car boot. 'Can't risk bringing anything back to Bill with his emphysema. He's had a message from his GP, advising him to shield himself.'

She slammed the boot shut and stood watching while I loaded up my own car. 'Seems wrong not to be giving you a hug.' She sounded tearful. 'Take care of yourself, Livia. Stay safe. Stay in touch, okay?'

'You too. See you on the other side.'

I followed my friend's blue Corolla as we crawled towards the car park entrance. She waved before turning into the traffic.

Everything looked normal.

Nothing was normal.

•

It took me over an hour to get home. I texted Heidi to say I was running a bit late. She didn't reply, but that wasn't unusual. I stopped by the supermarket on my way out of Middlesbrough, just to grab a few more supplies. Some of the shelves were empty, the queues out the door.

The sun was low by the time I pulled up outside Chloë's house, the sky blood-orange. I rang the bell, expecting the usual—excited voices, Chloë welcoming me with Noah at her side. But there were no voices, and a long time seemed to pass before the door opened. Chloë peered out, wearing a towel on her head, twisted into a turban.

'Livia, hi!' she said. 'Excuse me dripping, just got out of the shower. What has your young man forgotten *this* time?'

I was taken aback, but not anxious. Not at first.

'Isn't he here?'

'Noah? No! Scott and Heidi collected him this morning. About, um'—she glanced at the Fitbit on her wrist—'hours ago. Twelvish. Had you forgotten? They said it was your suggestion.'

'*My* suggestion?'

'Was it not? They were off for a picnic, since the schools are closed. Sorry . . . did I do the wrong thing? I had no reason to doubt Heidi.'

Poor Chloë was peering over my shoulder, as though my family might leap out of my car yelling, *Surprise!*

'Sounds like there's just been a miscommunication,' I said.

'Sounds like it.' She smiled, relieved. 'Have you been home yet? I bet they're waiting for you there, safe and sound.'

•

I was speeding down Back Lane, praying I'd find all the lights on in The Forge, music playing, Scott stirring his legendary pasta mush. Of course he'd want to be home with us at a time like this! All around the country people were rushing to be with their loved ones, in their safe places, merging households so they'd not be alone. Scott was doing the same.

But the house was in darkness. I swung onto our drive, slewed to a halt, burst inside without bothering to shut the car door. 'Heidi? Anyone here?'

Silence. Pitch-dark, apart from the dim glow of the kettle and dishwasher. No movement, no life. Flicking on lights I headed straight for the pantry, to the shelf where we kept Noah's flare-up kit. *Phew.* The box was right there, exactly where we always left it. This proved that Scott hadn't taken the children far, and they'd be back soon.

My relief evaporated when I looked upstairs. Noah's duvet and pillow had been stripped from his bed. No Bernard the Sloth. Some of his drawers were open. With a rising sense of panic I checked Heidi's room and found the same thing. No bedding, clothes missing from the wardrobe, along with her backpack. Both children's toothbrushes had disappeared from the bathroom.

He's taken them.

Roaming through the rooms, I'd already begun making phone calls: Scott first. I was ready to give him a furious earful. *What are you playing at? Bring them home right now!* But my call went straight to his voicemail. He must have turned the phone off, even knowing I'd be frantic. Selfish, crazy bastard. I'd never forgive him for this. I'd never, *never* forgive him.

I was sure Heidi would answer, though. She wouldn't let me down.

I was standing in the drive as I called her number, staring past my car with its door still flung open. I held the phone clamped to my ear, listening to it ring, muttering to myself. 'Heidi, Heidi, Heidi! Please answer. Please speak to me.'

Just before her voicemail cut in, I heard a sound that chilled my blood. I looked up towards her window, tilting my head to catch the very faint tinkle of piano music.

'*Hello, this is Heidi. Please send a text instead.*'

I called her number again while making my way back into the house, through the kitchen, up the stairs, into her bedroom. With each step, the music grew louder.

I found her phone on top of her chest of drawers, next to Nicky's birthday card, its screen alight as it played *Moonlight Sonata*.

The only place I hadn't checked was my own bedroom.

A sheet of A4 paper lay on my pillow, weighed down by one of my slippers. And on top of the note, a bunch of daffodils tied with ribbon. Heidi knew I loved daffodils.

Her handwriting was as familiar to me as my own.

Mum,

I'm SO sorry. Dad thinks he's saving us from a fate worse than death. I didn't know what to do, I think he needs us. I promise I'll look after Noah. Please keep yourself safe. I LOVE YOU. Please don't worry.

XXXX Heidi XXXX

PS I'M SORRY, MUM

•

Pete from next door flagged me down as I was sprinting out to the car.

'Prime Minister's making an address to the nation this evening,' he called over the fence. 'I think they're going to lock us down.'

I didn't care. Priorities.

'We'll cope,' I said. 'We'll pull together. I've just got to fetch the children, be back soon.'

He stood and watched as I reversed much too fast into the lane, crunching as I changed gear, accelerating away.

•

It should have taken at least fifty minutes to drive to Whitby. I made it in under forty, and felt a surge of hope on seeing lights inside Rum Keg Cottage. The big, silver cat ran ahead of me through the wicker gate and up the stone-flagged steps, plopping in through her cat flap. I glimpsed a twitch of lace curtains as I leaned on the doorbell, setting off an electronic *ding-dong* followed by a cacophony of barking.

They're here. Of course they are. He'd just wanted the children near him, to be sure they were safe. I was still spitting with rage, gearing up for a massive showdown—but at least no harm had been done, apart from scaring the life out of me.

I waited, pacing up and down the doorstep. Rang the bell a second time. Waited, paced, swore. *Stop messing about, Scott.* Leaned on the bell for the third time—this time not letting up—*ding-dong-ding-dong*.

An outside light was turned on. Bolts were drawn before the door was flung open.

A stooping man with a snow-white tonsure glared out at me, a woman halfway up the staircase behind him. Both were wearing dressing-gowns and indignant expressions.

'For heaven's sake!' the man barked. 'What the blazes d'you want?'

Acute embarrassment drowned out my rage. I stepped back, stammering abject apologies. 'I think I've got the wrong address. So sorry! I thought this was Rum Keg Cottage. The Milners' house. I've been here before, and your cat—'

'Right address,' the man said curtly. 'You looking for Scott?'

The woman had joined him by the door.

'We've been awake fifty hours,' she said. 'We've just flown all the way from Australia, more than twenty-four hours in a plane with a stop in Dubai, then we had to drive across from Manchester. So we're not at our best. You'll have to forgive us for being a bit grumpy.'

I pressed both hands to my mouth. 'I'm so sorry. I didn't expect . . . I thought you weren't due back until April.'

'We weren't. Pandemic. No need to destroy my doorbell.' Mr Milner was still in a huff, but his wife became positively chatty, now she'd got over her irritation. She told me how lucky they'd been to get a flight home; they were almost stranded. She described tearful goodbyes to their grandchildren in Sydney, how fellow passengers and even the cabin crew were sobbing as the plane took off.

'How awful,' I murmured. 'You must feel so disorientated. Um . . . do you have any idea where I might find Scott? I'm Livia, his wife.'

They glanced at one another, shaking their heads.

'He was already gone when we arrived,' said Mrs Milner. 'He left everything in good order. The animals seem very happy. We offered to let him stay on a few days if he needed to, but he left a note saying he had other plans. I've got his phone number, but I imagine you do too.'

I left the weary travellers in peace, wishing them a good night's sleep. They weren't staying up to listen to the prime minister's address to the nation. They said nothing would wake them now, not even the devil himself pounding on their door.

•

Back in our cold, silent home—phone in one hand, searching Heidi's room for any clues—I called the police non-urgent line.

'So these children are with their father?' asked the efficient-sounding woman who took my call. 'Uh-huh. And there's no court order in place? No order applied for? And he's got no history of violence at all?'

I imagined her filling in an incident report on a desktop.

'Okay . . .' I heard the click of a mouse. 'And does he have a gun licence?'

'No.'

'Any reason to think he's armed?'

'Armed.' I blinked. 'You mean with a gun? I don't think he's ever touched one. Then again, he never used to think some evil cabal was about to take over the world.'

She took Scott's vehicle details, but I knew she was fobbing me off. She sounded distinctly underwhelmed.

'Might be more a matter for the family courts,' she suggested. 'This person they're with is their father, is that right? You were sharing a home until January, there's been no family violence or personal protection issues. Without any kind of court order, he's got as much right to have the children with him as you do.'

I'd sat down on Heidi's bed, touching the bare sheet with my free hand. I imagined her watching me leave this morning before packing for herself and Noah, writing that note, picking the daffodils to say sorry. She'd forgotten Noah's flare-up kit, so she must have been in a state.

'But he lied to the childminder,' I protested. 'He's not answering his phone. I've no idea where my children are right now.'

'If one of our units spots his vehicle, they'll have a word with him.'

Ending the call, I let myself flop over sideways to lay my head on the place where Heidi's pillow ought to be. No help from the police, then.

Think, think, think.

I ran downstairs to check in the bottom drawer of the filing cabinet where we kept our passports. All four were there, so at least he wasn't planning to skip the country.

I logged into my banking app, scanning our accounts for activity that might give me a clue to where he was, where he'd been. 'Oh, Scott,' I muttered as I ran my eye down the list and saw that the last transaction was before the weekend: £500 cash withdrawn from an ATM in Whitby, shortly before his surprise visit here. Since then he hadn't bought a thing with his cards. No fuel, no groceries, nothing. He must be using cash. Clearly, he'd been planning this for days.

Where's he taken them? Where could he go? If they were staying in a hotel or Airbnb he'd soon run out of cash and be forced to use a card, and then I'd know which town he was in at least. He could be camping, I supposed. He might have driven all the way up to Scotland to find shelter with Dr Jack.

I made several phone calls in quick succession: to Geraldine's care home, to a couple of teachers, to the Espinozas, to Anthony. Nobody had seen hide nor hair of him.

'I've not heard a peep out of Scott in days,' said Anthony. 'Is he not still pet-sitting for those people in Whitby?'

'They came home. Covid. This is dire, Anthony. He's got it into his head that he and the children are on some kind of a hit list. D'you think he might do something desperate?'

'Like what?'

I didn't want to vocalise it. *Dad thinks he's saving us from a fate worse than death.* He thought there was nowhere left to run. Every nation had been infiltrated. Every police car was looking for him, every ambulance was a literal death trap, everyone he met a potential spy. He must be terrified out of his wits.

Anthony sounded maddeningly relaxed. 'He'll just be holed up somewhere, staying with friends.'

'He's *got* no friends. He's alienated everyone. You're the only one left.'

'If I hear from him, I'll let you know.'

I was about to ring off when Anthony added, 'Hang on—you near a TV? The prime minister's about to come on.'

•

I'd always found it difficult to take Boris Johnson seriously. But tonight, as he gazed into the nation's living rooms via almost every terrestrial channel and solemnly announced that we *must stay at home*, more than twenty-seven million people were listening. It felt momentous. I later learned that it was one of the most-watched broadcasts in the history of the UK.

Gatherings were banned. All non-essential shops and institutions were to shut down. Everyone was to stay indoors. Emergency laws would give the police increased powers. Listening to all this, I had a vivid glimpse of the monster under the conspiracists' bed: the priceless fragility of freedom, the ease with it could be smothered under the guise of emergency response. I lived in a modern democracy, I'd followed the course of the pandemic and understood why nations were pulling out all the stops, yet even I could imagine this broadcast to be the opening scene of a dystopian thriller.

Bethany phoned within minutes of the broadcast ending. 'Did you see the PM?'

'I did.'

'I can't believe we're doing this. I'm sure it's the right decision, we have to flatten the curve, horrific when you look at what's happening elsewhere. But . . . my God. Pretty drastic. Where does it end?'

'I don't know.' I didn't care either. Not at that moment.

'You all okay? How's Scott doing?'

'We're not okay,' I said. 'Actually, we've got a crisis.'

Bethany listened, murmuring in horror, while I put her in the picture.

'I'm sitting in an empty house,' I said. 'I don't know whether I can drive around searching for them, since the whole country just went into lockdown. PC Plod might already have roadblocks up.'

'But why would Scott do such a crazy thing?'

'He thinks they're all in terrible danger. A fate worse than death.'

'Hang on, James is with me. I'll fill him in.' I heard muffled voices before she was back on the line. 'I'm driving up to be with you, Livia. James agrees. He'll hold the fort here. If I set out now and travel through the night, I'll be in Gilderdale by four or five tomorrow morning.'

I was so tempted. I longed to know my sister was on her way, that she'd be with me by morning. But I turned down her offer.

'We've just had Boris telling us all to stay at home! You've got your own family to think about. Anyway, I'm probably over-reacting. They might walk in any moment now.'

I heard her relaying my reply to James, and his voice in the background. 'Give her my love, will you?'

When Bethany came back on the line, she sounded breathlessly anxious. 'I don't like this, Livia. It's such off-the-wall behaviour for Scott. You don't think he's deluded enough to . . . No, of course not. Ignore me.'

'Go on,' I prompted.

'I'm probably overreacting.' She hesitated again. 'But there's no way he could be thinking about murder–suicide, is there?'

THIRTY-FIVE

Livia

Nightmares reign in the darkest hours of the night. When there are two empty beds in the house, and not a whisper of news from your family, and the whole world is trying to bar its gates against a virus—well then, those nightmares become indistinguishable from reality.

You lie down fully clothed, you shut your eyes, you open them. You check your phone, you call Scott's number yet again. You run to the window every time you hear a vehicle in the distance. You tell yourself a thousand times: *He adores them, he'd give his own life for them in a heartbeat. Trust him. It's all fine.* But fearful warning lights flash in every corner of your mind. *He's gone mad, he has nowhere to run. It's not fine. Nothing is fine.*

In the darkest hour I wrapped myself in Scott's dressing-gown, which somehow still carried the spirit of better days, and made tea. Sitting in the rocking chair, I opened my laptop, steeling myself to watch Dr Jack. This was the video Scott sent me last Friday, a link I'd never bothered to open. I was hoping for some clue as to what had driven him over the edge.

Here we go. A trio of charlatans peered out of their little Zoom boxes on my screen. Dr Jack was wearing scrubs and that featureless rubber mask. He sat with the green wall behind him, the Z-shaped crack in the plasterwork. His guests were Gary Tey, the CIA man with the porn star moustache, and a nerdy bloke who claimed to be a security expert based in Canada.

Dr Jack was having the time of his life. The man was clearly high on his own sense of importance, even though he was wearing a mask that made him look like a cheap mannequin. It would have been hilarious if it weren't so dangerous. The voice-changing software was clever, though.

So, to clarify for people watching, what we're seeing here is the problem–reaction–solution paradigm . . .

'Tragic bloody losers,' I yelled. 'Doctor, CIA agent, intelligence expert—bollocks you are. I bet you're all eating pizza in your mothers' basements.'

You have to admire the orchestration of this fictional crisis.

They mocked dying people on ventilators, they scoffed at mass graves and quarantined Italians who cheered the world by singing on their balconies. I ground my teeth at the pompous pseudoscience of this panel of mansplainers, their know-all sarcasm, their pretence of expertise. I hated them. I *hated* them. As a direct result of their arrogance and ignorance, I'd lost the man I loved and our children had become pawns. The games these people played had consequences.

I watched right through to the end, snorting as the masked Dr Jack made his solemn pronouncement. What a jerk.

Be ready. You are the Resistance. Protect the vulnerable however you can. They're first in line.

The comments from viewers would also have been funny, except that they weren't.

— *When will the sheeple wake up? Just had a fight with my son about this. He won't smell the coffee. He's afraid of the truth.*

— *Anyone else heard that the US forces are on their way with
   50,000 personnel and weapons systems to put down any
   resistance in the UK? Invited by the Queen. My source is in
   the RAF. They've been grounded, told to turn a blind eye to
   troop movements etc*
— *Happening as predicted. As of 21.00 today the whole UK is
   under house arrest. IT HAS BEGUN. MOBILISE NOW!*

My fingers were itching. I too typed out a comment: *Funny
kind of hospital where doctors can slope off and put on silly
rubber masks and make videos in their tea breaks.*

But I didn't post it. There was no point in being a keyboard
warrior; I had no chance of changing the minds of these cult
followers. All that mattered was to find my children.

So instead, I deleted my comment and posted a plea.

— *Dr Jack, do you have any information about where my
   husband Scott Denby has taken our two children? He's disappeared with them since watching this video. I know he's been
   in private contact with you. Is he with you now? I'm extremely
   worried. Please, please help!*

Within minutes my polite request had begun to gather abuse,
much of it in shouty capital letters. I was a SHILL. I was the
enemy and a LIAR. I was, in fact, a man. I HAD NO children—
I was a team of secret agents working for the New World Order,
tracking down their Resistance leader.

More disturbing were comments from those who assumed my
family were victims of a purge: THE FIRST DISAPPEARANCES.
Had I checked the makeshift morgues? Checked the so-called
Nightingale 'hospitals'?

But not a word from Dr Jack himself.

THIRTY-SIX

24 March 2020

The rising sun smiled at the new day, its glittering path reaching for the sand-and-shingle beach of Topsham Cove, several miles north of Whitby. The first dawn of lockdown was a calm one. Clear sky, light winds. Two hours ago the entire beach had been underwater; now the tide was racing out, leaving smooth sands strewn with ridges of rock and salty clumps of seaweed.

A couple in their eighties picked their way down the steep path onto the sand. Later they would explain to the police that they often visited this beach at sunrise, bringing a bag for gathering any rubbish that had floated ashore. It was their favourite time of day. Recently they had another reason to be out and about so early: the cove would be deserted. They wouldn't end up on one of those ventilators.

At first they thought the dully gleaming object in the surf might be a stricken boat or even a beached whale. But as they drew closer they realised they were looking at a car, a hatchback, abandoned in the foaming water. The sea had tipped it into a nosedive and washed under its wheels. The passenger's door stood open, bent right back to the bonnet; the driver's door was nowhere to be seen, presumably ripped away by the currents.

The couple peered through the spray, dreading the worst. It looked as though the car belonged to a family. One of its back windows was covered by a sunshade decorated with cartoon giraffes, and children's things lay scattered through the shallows and up the sand. Small clothes, disintegrating school textbooks. A booster seat seemed almost alive, struggling and somersaulting in the breaking waves.

Judging by its position and condition, the car had been fully submerged at high tide. Anyone inside would have drowned, but trying to escape in darkness might have been just as lethal. This stretch of Yorkshire's coast was notorious for treacherous tides and rips. Even now, the North Sea surged and bullied under and over, charging through the open doors.

The sun crept higher as husband and wife talked quickly, deciding on the best course of action. Perhaps there were survivors in there—perhaps children? No time to waste. They removed their walking boots and socks, lit the torch on their phone and waded into the freezing water. The husband had recently had his hip replaced, but both were keen swimmers who often took a dip off one of the safer beaches down the coast.

Holding on to the roof, they made their way waist-deep through churning currents to the space where the driver's door should have been. The sound of the sea was strange now: echoing swells sloshing around inside the vehicle as though it were a cave.

They leaned down together, shining their torch into the gloom.

Livia

It was Rani Kumar who came to tell me. She placed her hat on my kitchen table, much as she had a few weeks earlier, while she delivered the news that our car had been found. Someone had driven it at speed, right off the beach and into the sea, at a place where the rips and tides were so dangerous that people never swam there. They'd found debris, including Noah's booster seat and a Barmoors High sweatshirt.

I'd been stressed yesterday, frightened all night, but that was nothing compared to my gut-wrenching terror now. I scurried around the kitchen, fiddling mindlessly with things—wiping the sink, rubbing at my face, *Oh my God, oh my God.* I felt as close to falling apart as I could ever remember.

Rani was quick to add the good news: there was no sign of my family. The police hoped whoever was in the car had got out. Still, they couldn't rule out the possibility of . . . She didn't finish the sentence. Searches were being organised, the Coastguard already involved.

'Any footprints on the beach?' I asked. 'Children's feet?'

'Apparently not. But you wouldn't expect any. High tide was about four this morning, and it *was* high. Several metres. My colleagues there tell me the entire cove will have been underwater. So there's every chance that whoever drove the car down there did it at low tide, around ten. They could have waded ashore and left on foot.'

I'd never even heard of this little cove. According to Rani it wasn't one of the popular ones, certainly not on the tourist brochures, because it wasn't safe. There was a steep drop-off with rocks, currents and those lethal tides. It was also a nesting site for a rare colony of breeding puffins, so the public—and especially their dogs—were discouraged. A four-wheel-drive track was maintained for occasional use by the local farmer and conservationists who monitored the puffins. Scott must have done his homework and known all this; he'd used cutters to remove a heavy chain and open two gates.

'Apparently it's not a track you'd want to tackle in an ordinary vehicle,' Rani said. 'Your husband was determined.'

'It didn't matter to him, did it? He was hell-bent on wrecking that car anyway.'

I imagined Scott with Noah on his shoulders, wading through the shallows towards the beach. I imagined Heidi beside him, bedraggled but safe.

But another scene flashed across my mind's eye: two children drugged and unconscious in the dark, unable to struggle as they drowned. The riptide might easily drag their bodies out to sea.

I showed Rani the note Heidi had left on my pillow. *Dad thinks he's saving us from a fate worse than death.*

'I phoned the police last night,' I said bitterly. 'I asked for help. I was fobbed off.'

'I know you did.'

She sat me down with a mug of tea and began to ask questions. Was Scott ever violent? Had he threatened to harm himself or the children? Did I think he was capable of harming them or himself? Had he expressed suicidal thoughts? Did he live with a mental illness? How had he coped with our separation? Had he ever done anything like this before?

'Scott loves his children more than anything in his world,' I told her. 'Actually, that's what frightens me: his obsession with keeping them safe from the monsters in his head. I caught him coaching Noah to fight anyone who tries to put him in an ambulance. Remember when you sat at this table the last time? He was convinced you'd been sent as a direct warning to him.'

The sergeant's eyebrows shot up. 'A warning from who?'

I did my best to explain Scott's belief system. 'Nothing is random, everything is significant. Two coppers turning up at your door, when you've just been sacked for spreading an anti-vaccination message, can only be a warning from the shadowy overlords.'

I'd begun to recover from the initial shock of her news. I was thinking more clearly.

'Were there any duvets or pillows in the car?' I asked. 'Any backpacks?'

'The tide . . . I don't think there was much left inside.'

'Why take bedding and clothes if he was planning to drown everyone? He could be trying to stage their deaths. Isn't that what you'd do, if you believed the authorities were out to murder you and your family?'

'Maybe.'

'It's backfired, of course. You guys weren't remotely interested in him until now.'

Rani pondered for a moment, then brought up a map of the coast on her phone. 'Topsham Cove is quite a hike from anywhere, especially at night with a six-year-old. There's moorland all around. He would have needed a vehicle. Can you think of anyone who might have picked them up, who might be sheltering them? Anyone at all?'

I was sure nobody we knew would do that. Anthony was at home in Guisborough last night, watching the prime minister. The Espinozas might be sympathetic to Scott's beliefs, but they were businesspeople at heart; I couldn't see them getting mixed up in abducting children and faking a murder–suicide.

'Unless there's someone he's met in the Truther community,' I said. 'If they lent Scott a car he could be anywhere. Maybe camping, maybe in Scotland.'

'Why Scotland?'

'His main guru is a YouTube influencer called Dr Jack. He claims to work in a Scottish hospital. They've been talking.'

Rani noted all this, and promised they'd check with car hire companies, with bus and railway stations. They would also try to trace Scott's phone. She asked for photos of him and the children. We talked about social media accounts, the possibility of his having secret funds. We took another look at the bank accounts.

I was bursting to throw myself into some kind of action—to rush straight to the coast, see our car in the surf, join in the search.

'I'd urge you to stay put,' said Rani, 'even if there wasn't a lockdown. You need to be here in case they come home. Missing people normally do.'

'You want me to hang about and do what—fold the washing? Make beds for children who may be at the bottom of the North Sea?'

'You're more use to them here than anywhere else.'

She offered to send someone to wait with me, but I refused. A minder was the last thing I wanted. She gave me her card, with a direct number to call if I needed to.

I had one more question. I didn't want to ask it.

'If they *were* in that car as the tide turned . . . if they were dragged out to sea by the currents . . . where would they fetch up?'

Rani shook her head. 'Let's not think about that yet.'

'I bet *you're* thinking about it. Where are the Coastguard searching?'

She hesitated before looking me in the eye. 'The tide was running at about six knots. It began to turn at four in the morning. Coastguard have calculated that an object caught in the outgoing tide might already have been carried up to fifteen miles.'

Fifteen miles! I blinked, breathed, did my own calculations. A fifteen-mile radius, even with knowledge of the currents, was a vast stretch of deep sea to search. It was an impossible task. If Scott and the children were carried away in that tide, they might never be found.

•

The nation was experiencing its first day in lockdown. Neighbours found new ways to reach out to one another. Celebrities had already begun sharing sourdough recipes and indoor exercise regimes. Workers-from-home moved dead pot plants and saucy knickers well away from their webcams, and asked Google what kind of lighting made them look less haggard in virtual meetings.

And me? I didn't give a toss about Covid anymore. I didn't give a toss about work either. I just wanted my children home. I'd have given anything for us all to be making sourdough and homeschooling. I came up with a mantra, repeating it ceaselessly under my breath: *He has a plan. They're safe. They're fine.*

Bethany phoned. So did my parents. They all wanted to drive straight up to Yorkshire, but I put them off.

'Wait another couple of days,' I told them. 'I know they're okay. He'll be in touch soon.'

I spent the morning combing through our cluttered office, looking for clues about old friends, new friends, anyone who might be shielding Scott. I tried his phone every half-hour. I climbed into the attic to dig out musty address books and contacted people he hadn't seen in years. They were all very surprised to hear from me. All dead ends.

Think, think. Who does he talk to?

Dr Jack was the key to all this. He seemed to have an uncanny knack when it came to manipulating my husband. A dead teenage girl with red hair, an HPV scare just as the school was rolling it out, the focus on people with chronic conditions. It felt almost personal.

Rani Kumar checked in every couple of hours with questions and updates. Searchers had motored up inlets near Topsham Cove, skirting rocks and cliffs in their search for the drowned bodies of my family. They'd used a drone along inaccessible bits of coastline and found nothing except a child's anorak that looked like Noah's, but that could have washed out of the car. Tracking Scott's phone had also drawn a blank so far. It had disappeared. No reason to assume it was underwater, Rani assured me.

It might be turned off, or the battery flat. Its last known location was near Pickering, last Thursday evening—probably when he was on his way to see us.

'No news is very definitely good news,' she said, before warning me that the police planned to release a statement to the media that afternoon—just an appeal for sightings or information. Was that okay?

I said it was, and agreed they could use the photos I'd supplied.

'Listen, though,' I said. 'If—when—you discover where they're hiding, please let me make the first approach. If Scott sees a police car, he'll panic . . . and God knows what he might do next.'

'I understand.'

'I mean it, Rani. He's the least violent person I know, but he's terrified that agents of some kind of deep state are hunting them down.'

'Okay . . .' She hesitated. 'But you don't think he's armed?'

How could I be sure of anything anymore? Scott had done things in the past twenty-four hours that I'd never have believed possible. Anyone could get hold of a firearm if they were determined enough. I'd worked with offenders who'd bought sawn-off shotguns from a bloke in a pub.

'I really don't,' I said, after a moment's thought. 'But he'll be massively stressed, pumped up with adrenaline, ready for fight or flight. If police turn up with sirens blaring, they could trigger a tragedy. Promise me that won't happen.'

'I'll pass on everything you've said.'

She gave me her personal assurance, but I wasn't remotely convinced. She couldn't make those kinds of promises, even if she had the seniority. Her shift would come to an end eventually.

I had to get to Scott first.

•

A uniformed officer, not Sergeant Kumar, read out a brief press statement on the regional news: a car had been found abandoned on the coast. There were concerns for the welfare of a father and two children aged six and thirteen. Hopes were high that they were alive and well, possibly staying with friends, but police were appealing for any information which might help to bring them home.

And there they were, suddenly, splashed across my television screen. Noah lay with his hands in the fishpond, smiling up at me. Heidi playing her guitar, hair loose and long, wearing her blue denim shirt and the butterfly choker Noah gave her for her birthday. Scott was taking off his bike helmet, one hand on the handlebars.

As the report ended, a text came in from Anthony: *Just seen Scott and the kids on the online news. You ok? You on your own? Am at my warehouse all day but can come right over, sod the sodding lockdown!*

While I was replying—*Thanks, but I'm fine for now*—my phone began to explode with a stream of shocked texts and calls. Isaac Katz, Jude from work, Chloë, Megan Espinoza. Several people from Barmoors High.

And then this one, perhaps the most welcome: *Hello Livia, sorry to use this number. I think that was your family on the news. Thinking of you. Charles Shepherd.*

I was still answering everyone when the doorbell rang. The man on the step wore a tweed jacket, a stripy scarf and a look of grave compassion.

'Sorry to trouble you, Mrs Denby. Barry Clover of the *York Press*.'

•

By mid-afternoon I'd fielded another door-knock and three phone calls from journalists, and I was losing my cool. I'd promised Rani I wouldn't talk to anyone from the media—and anyway it was torture to be trapped at home, waiting passively like a useless lummox while other people searched for my children. I had to do *something*.

Shrugging into my coat, I grabbed my car keys and, as an afterthought, shoved my Probation Service lanyard into my pocket. If I got pulled over by a panda car for breaking lockdown rules, I'd flash it. Probation must be an essential service, surely.

Gilderdale's square felt post-apocalyptic when I drove through. Just the ducks under the bridge, and one solitary person wandering past the cross. Brilliantly coloured tulips bloomed in the old horse trough, but the playground had been roped off. Only the Spar was open, its yellow lights oddly comforting. A gleam of normality.

My plan was to shoot up to Guisborough for a council of war with Anthony, since he was the closest friend Scott had nowadays. I'd called him before setting out and got no answer, but I knew he was in his warehouse. If we put our heads together we might come up with some ideas, new places to search. Scott used to reminisce about walking-and-drinking weekends spent with a bunch of other students. They dossed down somewhere near Hadrian's Wall, in a barn owned by somebody's parents. Anthony might know where it was.

They're safe. They're fine.

Google Maps easily found Anthony's business in Guisborough: *AT Fastenings Ltd, Unit 5, 17 Canal End*, and forty minutes later the upbeat tones of Google Map Lady guided me into an industrial estate on the outskirts of the town. Her pleasant calmness was reminiscent of Dr Jack's hypnotic speech-to-text, though her accent was decidedly English. *In two hundred yards, at the roundabout, take the first exit. In fifty yards, at Canal End, turn left. Your destination is on the right.*

My destination turned out to be a brick-built sprawl towards the end of a cul-de-sac. Several businesses shared the car park and entrance: transport and tech companies, an engineering consultancy. Anthony's grey Passat was the only car parked out the front, so I knew he was still here. But the lights in the lobby were off, the entrance doors very firmly locked.

'Anthony!' I yelled, banging on the glass. 'Hey, Anthony?'

No response. He probably couldn't hear me, and there were no bells or intercoms. The building wasn't designed for customers to visit. So I called his number again, tapping an anguished drumbeat on the roof of my car while it rang. *Come on, come on.* Felt like an age before he answered.

'Livia!' He was out of breath. 'Sorry, been busy getting orders together, only just heard the phone. What's happening? Any news?'

'No news. Except that I'm here. I'm standing outside your building.'

'Really? You rebel, ignoring the prime minister. Be right with you. Hold on.'

Further down the cul-de-sac, a courier van was dropping off a parcel. The driver and his passenger both wore blue medical face masks. I thought of Lawrence, the earnest young man who tried to save Nicky.

I was still waiting for Anthony to let me in when my phone's screen lit up, just a split second before it rang. Not Scott. Not Sergeant Kumar. I didn't recognise the number.

'Don't you fucking dare be a journalist,' I said aloud, as I answered the call. 'Hello?'

Silence.

But there was something about this silence that made me stand up straight, bringing my free hand to my ear to block out the whisper of the breeze.

'Hello?' I said again.

'Mum?'

I couldn't believe my ears. The relief.

'Heidi! Oh, thank God, are you—'

'Mum, this is . . . I'm sorry, I'm sorry.'

I leaned back against my car, staring up at a sky that seemed suddenly glorious.

'Where are you?' I asked. 'Are you all okay?'

'No!' It was a moan. Breathless, panicking. 'No, we're not okay.'

And just like that, relief became terror. I'd heard every nuance of Heidi's voice in every situation, all of her life. I *knew* her. I had never heard her so frightened.

'Noah's really bad, really bad, he can't breathe at all. His mouth's gone a weird colour, he's—oh my God—' The last words were strangled by sobs.

'Where are you?'

'We haven't even got his flare-up kit, and Dad won't call for an ambulance, but Dr Jack said try giving him black coffee, and cow parsley tea, and steam from a kettle to open his airways—'

'Dr Jack! Is he with you?'

'No, no. Dad's been texting him and asking what we should do, because he's a doctor, and he's texting back saying coffee and steam and things, but they aren't helping. Noah's so scared. I think he's dying, Mum. If we don't get him to hospital—'

Anthony had appeared. He saw that I was on the phone and waited, jamming the door open with a desert-booted foot.

'Heidi,' I said, 'tell me where you are.'

In the background, Scott's voice. Agitated. 'Who're you talking to?'

'I'm phoning Mum—I'm—don't you dare!' A shriek. 'Dad, give that back!'

'Put Dad on,' I said urgently. 'Where are you? Heidi?'

My only answer was a dull *pip*, and the line was dead.

With shaking fingers I navigated through to my call log, trying again and again to get Heidi back on that same number. It wouldn't connect.

'What's happening?' asked Anthony.

I didn't wait to be invited inside. This was no time for niceties. I marched up to and past him, grabbing his arm as I went.

'Quick!' I said. 'I need to use your computer. And I need your help.'

THIRTY-SEVEN

Heidi

At first, we pretended it was a holiday.

Noah was cock-a-hoop about being collected from Chloë's house by Dad and me, and twittered away like a canary as we drove out of Gilderdale.

But I was sitting in the front passenger seat and could see how jittery Dad was. He kept looking in his rear-view mirror. When a police car whizzed past the other way, he darted down a side road and through a gateway into a field. We waited for ten minutes until he was sure the coast was clear. I didn't believe the police were controlled by a New World Order who were out to get us. Then again, people in Anne Frank's world probably thought all that hate was impossible too. They wouldn't have wanted to believe it. They were normal people just like us, but gradually, gradually, they were trapped.

You never know, that's the point. You never know.

In Pickering, Dad pulled cash out of his wallet to get us fish and chips. We sat in the heather to eat them, ducking down every time we heard a car. Dad surprised me by announcing that we'd not be sleeping in a house tonight. We'd be on a boat. He hadn't told me that.

'A boat on the sea?' asked Noah.

'On the River Esk.'

'Will we have bedrooms?'

'Um . . .' Dad waggled his head. 'More like camping. All of us sleeping in one little room. But we'll be floating.'

He had a bit of shopping to do, at a supermarket and a hardware store, so it was quite late in the afternoon by the time we parked on a dead-end road on the very edge of Whitby, got our things out of the car and put on our backpacks. Dad was loaded down with bedding and lots of other luggage. Noah was getting tired and worried. He asked when would we be going home, and was Mummy coming to the boat?

Poor Mum. I felt sick every time I thought about her. She'd be ringing Chloë's doorbell any time now, and then she'd rush home to see if we're there, she'd be trying to call me and Dad. Sooner or later she'd find my daffodils and note on her pillow, which I hoped would reassure her that we were okay. She'd also find my phone. Dad had made me leave it behind in case it was bugged.

'What about *your* phone?' I'd demanded, when he asked me to abandon mine.

'Mine?' He gave a mysterious little raise of his eyebrows. 'Last seen heading for Manchester.'

'Manchester! How come?'

Turned out, he'd been cunning as a fox. He was in a fuel station when he got chatting to some boys towing a trailer full of furniture. He gave them a hand with their tarpaulin, turned his phone off and hid it among the springs of a sofa. He even waved at the lads as they drove away.

'They were tracking it,' he said. 'Their surveillance technology works even when it's turned off. So I sent them on a wild-goose chase. They're going to waste a lot of time looking for us in Manchester.'

I was in awe. 'Genius, Dad! You're like James Bond.' Then I had a thought. 'So . . . you can't listen to Nicky's message anymore?'

'I haven't listened to it for a long while. I don't need to. I can remember every word.'

I imagined his phone bouncing across the Pennines. It seemed strange that it was hidden in another bit of furniture. It felt like we'd come full circle.

●

Noah held my hand as we traipsed past allotments, across a field and a lot of scrubby woodland. The sky darkened to a lilac colour, the first stars appeared. Dad lit his head torch.

'Nearly at the river,' he said.

Our feet sank into gravel as we scrambled across a railway track. The river was just on the other side of that, though we had to crawl through a very scratchy hedge to get to it.

'Watch out,' Dad warned, his voice hushed. 'The bank's slippery along here.'

'It's really dark,' breathed Noah. I felt his grip on my hand tighten.

We made our careful way along a narrow, muddy path with the river to our left, the water pale and glinting. The bank was overgrown. I collected a lot of nettle stings on my legs. Poor Noah got tangled in the thorny arms of a bramble. He didn't fuss, though. He just kept walking. I began to wonder if we'd ever get to the boat.

But suddenly, there it was—a sailing boat, about the length of our school minibus, moored to a pair of trees. One of them was a weeping willow whose boughs arched right over onto the deck.

'Welcome to *Dixieland*!' said Dad, playing the light of his torch from one end to the other.

I could just make out the white letters of her name. 'Who does she belong to?'

'I borrowed her.'

It was a challenge to get aboard in the dark. We used a rope for balance. I hauled myself across first before Dad hoisted Noah to me, followed by all our luggage. Finally he joined us.

'And here,' he announced, opening a pair of miniature wooden doors with a flourish, 'is your temporary home.'

The doors covered a hatch with a ladder leading down into the little cabin. A built-in table had seats covered in squabs each side, making a curved V-shape. It smelled musty-fusty. Dad lifted the seats to show us lockers with supplies he'd stashed earlier—tinned and dried food, biscuits, long-life milk, water, gas bottles and a solar charger. A tiny kitchen had been set up with a gas camping stove and crockery. There was even a chemical toilet, hidden behind a sheet of canvas. Not very private. I'd rather take my chances with the nettles on the riverbank.

Dad lit a candle before getting out apples and chocolate biscuits. He seemed calmer than he had for a while. I thought he was pleased to be looking after us again.

'So remember, team,' he told us, 'stay out of sight as much as you can. No yelling, use your inside voices. We're playing a hiding game. Okay?'

'Who're we hiding from?' asked Noah.

Dad kissed the top of his head. 'Everyone. We don't know for sure who are the goodies and who are the baddies. If anyone tries to chat, call out that they mustn't come near. Tell them we're isolating on board because we've all got Covid.'

'Unclean! Unclean!' I sang, ringing an imaginary bell.

'Exactly,' said Dad. 'The Black Death.'

•

Noah was fast asleep in a duvet-and-pillows nest we'd made on the squabs. Having hatches open at each end had aired the cabin, and Dad had given Noah some of his orange preventer. He sounded wheezy to me, but Dad had a listen to his chest and said he'd heard it much worse.

That was when I realised the stupid mistake I'd made. I was horrified. 'Oh no! Oh my God, I'm such an idiot. I forgot his flare-up kit.'

Dad said that was his fault, not mine, because he never specifically asked me to pack the kit. And anyway, he should have checked we had it before leaving home.

'But Noah won't need it,' he assured me. 'He's got his preventer; that's more than enough steroids for such a little man. Steroids are bloody awful things. The only people who gain are the pharmaceutical companies.'

I was thinking that Noah gained quite a lot too. We were all very grateful for those bloody awful steroids when things went wrong. But there was no point in arguing. After all, it was me who'd forgotten the kit.

'Who lent you this boat?' I asked.

Dad looked a bit embarrassed, but eventually owned up. He said he'd taken *Dixieland* off a buoy near the marina. She was neglected, maybe even abandoned.

'So you stole her!'

He wrinkled his nose. 'Borrowed. I'll put her back later, they'll never even know. I also borrowed a rowing boat to get to her, though I attached it to the shore so they can easily pull it back in. But I've done a load of cleaning and repairs to *Dixieland*, and it's my fuel in that outboard motor—which I managed to fix. So really, I've done her owner a favour.'

'And how did you find this perfect spot? How come you knew exactly how to reach it from the car?'

'Research. Cully and I walked miles over the weekend, sussing everything out.'

His phone hummed. It was his burner phone—the twin of the grey one he'd given me. He must have shared his number with somebody else, not just me. I was surprised.

'Message from Dr Jack,' he said, reading a message. His face looked weirdly old, the wrinkles made deeper by the light of the phone. 'The government's just announced a lockdown.'

'We thought that was going to happen.'

'Yes, it was expected.' He shook his head. 'It was expected.'

He began pulling things out of his backpack. A beanie, socks, his cycling shoes.

'I've got to go somewhere for a couple of hours,' he whispered, as he pulled on the shoes. 'You're in charge. All right if I put out the candle? Pretend you're not here. Best not to let Noah up on the deck tonight, in case he falls into the river. Okay?'

'No, it's not okay. Where are you going?'

'To get rid of the car.'

'Why?'

'Because if—when—they find it parked in Whitby, they'll realise we never left. They'll start searching nearby. That mustn't happen.'

He climbed up onto the deck, and I followed.

'Can't we come with you?' I asked.

'Not this time. I've got a long cycle ride, some big hills. I'll be back soon. If you really, *really* need to reach me, use your secret phone to call mine.'

'Okay.'

'Don't call or text anyone but me. Promise?'

I promised.

'Above all,' he said, putting his hands on my shoulders, 'you mustn't phone Mum. I know you'll want to, but I'm trusting you not to, because they'll be listening. You might as well send a gigantic banner up into the sky, shouting, *WE'RE HERE, COME*

AND GET US! They'll have all their signal tracking equipment going, just waiting for you to call or text her.'

I promised again, and he hugged me.

'You're amazing,' he said. 'I'll be back before you know it.'

I watched as he jumped across onto the bank—quiet as a cat—and slipped away into the darkness. For a while I could still hear the wish-wash of his jeans as he brushed through the long grass. I fixed my gaze on the thin beam of his torch as it grew fainter and fainter until he was gone.

•

It was a whole new experience for me, to be left to babysit on a strange boat. A big responsibility.

I fetched a bottle of water and sat in the cockpit, worrying about how Mum must be feeling right now. I longed to give her a quick ring or send a text, just to let her know we were safe. My secret phone was a terrible temptation. I didn't think there'd be any baddies listening in.

But I'd promised. I wasn't going to betray Dad again.

Lights winked in the distance. Houses, other boats. I caught snatches of music across the water. Hawthorn trees in the hedge were starting to bud, white sprays glowing in the dark. I could smell dry grass, and cows, and the muddy water gently slapping against the hull. I was sure animals were living on the bank, because I kept hearing little splashes. It made me think of *The Wind in the Willows*. I felt like a part of the starlight, a part of the magic of the river.

When my eyelids began to droop, I fetched my duvet and lay on the floor of the cockpit with my legs blocking the hatch, so Noah couldn't get past me. I was dozing off when a train came rattling along the track, close enough for me to see lights through its windows. I imagined people sitting in the seats, making their journey home. That was comforting.

I was woken by a lot of rustling in the willow tree, which turned out to be Dad stashing his bike. A minute later he'd swung himself aboard. He was like a spring, bouncing on his feet, all energy and movement. Mr Bond might call it kinetic energy. Or potential. I could never remember the difference. Suyin would know.

'Did you manage to hide the car?' I asked.

'Well . . . I got rid of it.'

I didn't bother to ask what he meant. I turned over and went back to sleep.

THIRTY-EIGHT

Heidi

Noah seemed less wheezy when he woke up the next morning, though he was complaining of a sore tummy. We gave him some extra puffs of his preventer.

If I hadn't been fretting so much about Mum, I'd have been enjoying this strange holiday on the river. I loved the way sounds seemed both clear and quiet on the silky water, and dragonflies whirred around like tiny helicopters. In the distance, beyond some woods, I noticed the arches of an incredibly high bridge, which Dad told me was the Larpool Viaduct. After breakfast I sat in the cockpit, reading *Anne of Green Gables* for the fourth time, while Dad took Noah for a stroll. A tractor drove up and down a field, a train passed, a few boats puttered along the river. I don't think they even noticed our little blue rust bucket peeking out from under the willow tree.

But by lunchtime, grey-and-orange clouds were piling up like dirty laundry. Noah got tired and floppy, so he had a nap in the cabin. Dad sat beside him, reading a mouldy book he'd found on the shelf: *A Boatman's Guide to the River Esk*.

It was about three o'clock when the nightmare began. Noah dragged himself up the ladder and threw himself down on the bench beside me. He was wearing his favourite Superman T-shirt, which I'd packed for him.

'Tummy,' he moaned, and the effort of saying that one word made him cough.

'Dad,' I called, leaning into the hatch. 'Dad. Quick.'

In a nanosecond he was out of the cabin and kneeling beside Noah. He did all the usual things—listening, checking his colour and pulse.

'Might be pollen,' he said. 'The ragwort.'

I didn't care whether Noah's asthma was set off by pollen or damp from the river or by a cold—the result was just as bad either way.

'We should phone Mum,' I said. 'She'll drive straight out here with his flare-up kit.'

Dad ran a hand through his hair. 'I wish we could. But that's exactly what they want us to do. They'll be waiting like cats at a mousehole. One call to her—just one call—and they've got us.'

I glanced past him at my backpack. My secret phone was beckoning to me.

'C'mon, Captain Noah,' muttered Dad. 'Let's get you sitting up.'

He fetched cushions, arranging them so that Noah was upright. It seemed to help a bit. But my brother looked so small, so miserable, hunched over with his forehead against Dad's chest.

'Tell you what, I'll text Dr Jack,' said Dad, getting out his own burner phone. 'What's the point in having a doctor for a friend, if you never ask for advice?'

•

Two hours later, I was really getting scared.

We'd gone below. Noah was propped up on Dad's lap, his mouth and nostrils wide open as he fought for every bit of air.

'Come on, Captain,' Dad muttered, rubbing and patting his back. 'You'll soon be better.'

We'd tried everything Dr Jack suggested. More puffs of the preventer, though in our hearts we knew that was no good at all. Strong black coffee, trickled into Noah's mouth. Lots of steam from the kettle. Dr Jack even had us collecting cow parsley from the bank, making a kind of tea from the leaves and stems, which he said was a natural medicine for asthma. Noah did his best to drink it. Sometimes we had a few minutes of hope, but the improvement never lasted.

'Dad, it's time to call an ambulance,' I begged. 'It's time. Please.'

'If they pick him up in this state, he'll be dead on arrival. You might as well sign his death warrant.'

'So might you be signing it, if you don't call for help.'

Dad shook his head, said he wasn't going to deliver his son up to be murdered. But his hands were trembling. He kept blinking and fidgeting, as though he didn't know what to do with himself.

I was desperate. I had one more card left to play.

'You don't trust hospitals because of Nicky,' I said.

'Not just because of that.'

'But Nicky dying was what got you wondering, what made you start to see things differently. You had the feeling that somebody was to blame, somebody wasn't telling the truth. Right? Isn't that right? But, Dad . . . I know something you don't. Somebody *was* to blame, somebody *was* lying. But it wasn't the medical people.' I stopped to take a breath. 'It was me.'

'Heidi, no!' Dad protested. 'Of course it wasn't your fault.'

I sniffed, smudging away tears with the heels of my hands. 'I hid your phone.'

He froze, staring at me. 'You hid . . .?'

'Nicky rang at ten forty-four. Remember? I heard your phone and I saw it was him. And I was so stupid and selfish, just thinking about my bike ride. So I pushed it down the back of the armchair and covered it with a cushion. I left him to die. It was *me*.'

Dad looked as though he'd seen a ghost. Perhaps he had. I expected him to turn on me, to say he'd never forgive me. I expected him to ask how I could do something so evil. But he didn't do any of that.

'Come and have a hug,' he said. 'Come on.'

I was sobbing as I moved to sit close beside him and Noah.

He put his arm around me. 'So all this time,' he said, 'you've been sick with guilt.'

I nodded. Couldn't speak.

'And you didn't tell anyone. You've been carrying this secret all alone. Is that what the shoplifting was really about? You've taken everyone's sadness on your shoulders.'

'I *caused* everyone's sadness.'

'Oh, sweetheart. No.'

There were too many tears now. They ran into my hair, dripped off my nose. I felt his chest quavering as he hugged me.

'Listen, Heidi. I was the adult in that situation. Nicky was my responsibility. I could have insisted we find my phone, but I was looking forward to our bike ride too. He'd called just before, sounding like his usual self. We both talked to him.'

'He was so happy about my birthday card.'

'You couldn't have known that one call was important. Just one call. Nobody could have known.'

I couldn't believe I'd finally confessed. I was a total mess, sobbing until my head ached, but I felt as though I'd put down a terrible weight.

'I don't want you to blame yourself for another second,' Dad said. 'I don't blame you for one second. Mum won't. Nicky wouldn't either.'

•

The boat was rocking, ever so gently. The long cabin windows framed ripples of cloud, deep pink—*a mackerel sky*, Mum would have called it. And Noah's breathing sounded worse than I'd ever heard it, like a chorus of broken whistles.

I'd begun praying for a miracle, because my brave little brother was giving up the fight. His eyes were half closed, a drunk person's eyes. His lips were a strange, bruised colour, as if he'd been eating blueberries. With every breath his tiny rib cage heaved, his stomach sucked in, *out*, in, *out*—broken bellows, frantically working.

'Could you grab a bit more of that coffee?' Dad asked me. 'Dr Jack was right: it definitely helps to keep his airways open.'

That was when I made my decision. Telling Dad about Nicky hadn't worked, so there was only one thing left to do. I couldn't just sit here and let Noah die. While Dad was concentrating on holding the cup to his mouth—'Try again, Captain, little sips'—I slid the grey phone out of my backpack and under the waistband of my jeans. Being a shoplifter gives you all kinds of new skills.

'Not gonna use that chemical toilet,' I muttered, as I scurried up the ladder. 'Back in a minute.'

I crossed the deck in three steps and made a giant leap onto the riverbank, slipping to my knees as I landed in the mud. The leaves of the weeping willow tree sheltered me while I punched in Mum's phone number.

Please answer, Mum. Please answer, Mum.

A long, awful wait before the phone connected to the signal. A single ring. A click. And then—as I held my breath, shut my eyes—I heard the most wonderful sound in all the world.

'Don't you fucking dare be a journalist,' she said.

THIRTY-NINE

Livia

I told Anthony what Heidi had said as we ran along a featureless corridor, a succession of fire doors creaking shut behind us. The whole building was empty. No lights, no sounds.

At the far end he turned right, showing me into a storeroom not much bigger than a single garage unit. One fluorescent light. Metal shelving was half stocked with labelled boxes; a couple of parcels on a table looked ready to be couriered to their destinations. Anthony's phone lay beside them. Through an open door I glimpsed a cramped office space with a laptop and printer.

'Noah's condition sounds critical,' I gasped, battling an engulfing wave of panic. 'He might only have minutes. He's going to die if he doesn't get medical help.'

Anthony didn't seem to understand. 'Scott won't let that happen.'

'He thinks he's got no choice. He thinks if Noah goes to hospital, he'll end up on a mortuary slab like Nicky.'

'And nobody knows where they are?'

'Dr Jack. *He* knows. He's been advising Scott to give Noah black coffee, for God's sake. Fucking *coffee*! A child is dying, and that monster's still playing his games.'

Without any warning at all, I found myself enveloped in a bear hug.

'Noah's young, Livia.' I felt Anthony's murmuring breath on my ear, a touch of his mouth, the scratching of his beard. 'He'll pull through.'

Heavy arms were around me, pulling me against his body. It was all so unexpected, so invasive and vile, that for several seconds I was in a state of frozen disbelief. We were alone in an industrial warehouse while my son's life hung by a thread. I hadn't come here for comfort, and I certainly wasn't seeking an affair. In any other circumstances I'd have given him a hefty shove, if not a knee in the balls, and demanded to know what the bloody hell he thought he was doing. But I couldn't. Not now. I desperately needed his help.

'You're so kind, bless you,' I said, sliding smartly out of his embrace. Every woman knows how to do that appeasing little escape-shimmy, pretending nothing just happened. 'You're good with social media, aren't you? That's great—because I'm not. I need the use of your computer, and your expertise.'

He nodded, his glaze flickering towards the laptop in the back room. He didn't seem at all embarrassed about what he'd just done. It was as though I'd imagined the whole thing.

'What's the plan?' he asked.

'We're going to launch ourselves onto Dr Jack's platform. Hijack it. Shine a massive spotlight on him.'

'I'm not sure I get it.'

'He's a narcissist; nothing matters more to him than the adoration of his followers. They watch him constantly—*constantly*. I wrote my first ever YouTube comment the other day and the abuse began within seconds, it was like a swarm of crazed hornets. So we post all over his pages on YouTube and Twitter and Facebook and everywhere else—we get as much attention as possible. We scream and shout on those Truther forums—Reddit,

4chan—where else? Telegram? I'll do the same on my phone, we'll do it together, post after post, make as much noise as we can. Dr Jack will hear us. I guarantee it.'

'Okay. What do we say?'

'We let everyone know that a six-year-old boy is dying *right now*, and only the great Dr Jack can save him. We beg him for his expert help, we appeal to his ego. If he steps in to save Noah, he'll be a hero. If he doesn't, he'll be the coward who let a child die. Please God let him choose to be the hero.'

Anthony was running his knuckles through his beard. 'You know, the police—'

'Will get their techies to faff about with IP addresses. They'll track him down to Mexico City or somewhere. It could take days—by then Noah will be dead. And even if they find him, they can't force him to give any information. He can just fold his arms and refuse to help. We don't have time. *Noah* doesn't have time.'

As I spoke, I was herding Anthony through his open office door. It infuriated me that he seemed so slow to catch on.

'Okay, it has to be worth a try,' he said. 'There's a shared kitchen down the hall, if you'd like—'

'I don't want a sodding cup of tea, Anthony. I want to save my son's life.'

'Right.' He threw himself into a heavy wooden chair. 'Bit poky in here; how about you take a seat in the storeroom? The wi-fi password's underneath the modem out there.'

I leaned against the open door, taking in the scene. His office was just a cupboard, you couldn't swing a cat. Dingy, claustrophobic. No window. His chair was pulled up to a table only just large enough for his laptop and an in-tray. A printer balanced precariously on a shelf; plastic boxes took up much of the concrete floor.

I was still reeling from his making a pass at me, but I felt sorry for him. He talked big, but he spent his days alone in this miserable cell. From the look of the understocked shelves in the storeroom, his business wasn't the success he claimed.

He had his back to me as he rapidly closed tabs on his laptop—presumably all websites involving metal fastenings. His sweatshirt was on inside out, the label sticking up behind his neck. Funny, the things you notice when you're almost levitating with fear, when so much adrenaline is coursing through your body that you feel as though you could punch a hole right through the wall; when you can't find your children to save them, can't see your enemies to fight them. *Sweatshirt inside out. Why?*

'Any thoughts on how we word this?' I asked. 'We need to go viral. We need to hit the bullseye first time.'

The things you notice. Anthony was hunched forward in his chair, elbows on the desk, his bulk obscuring the laptop. I had the impression he was trying to hide the screen. *Bet he's been watching porn*, I thought. He never expected a visitor. His erotic preferences were none of my business, of course, but still I craned my neck to peer past him just as he closed a tab, revealing the next open one.

Google search results. But not metal fastenings. Not naked ladies either.

I had a split second. Long enough to read four words. Long enough to feel the hair standing up on the back of my neck.

Home remedies for asthma.

Scott

Heidi emerged from among the long fronds of the willow, mud on her knees, yelling with rage as I lobbed her phone far out into the Esk. It landed with a small splash, and was gone.

'What the hell, Dad? Mum's got a right to know—he's her son too.'

'Did you tell her where we are?'

'I tried, but I didn't get time.' She bashed her fists against her forehead. 'I didn't get time before you chucked my phone into the river. You *idiot*, Dad! You stupid, *stupid* dickhead!'

I wasn't angry. I understood her desperation to ring her mum—I wished Livia was here too—but it was a disaster. That one call had probably given us away. We were going to have to run.

Back in the cabin, Noah slumped over the table like an exhausted puppy.

'Hold on, mate, please hold on,' I murmured, rubbing his back.

It would be dark soon. They'd be coming for us in the night, so we must move immediately. But we had no car, and Noah couldn't possibly walk. I weighed up the odds of making a run for it downstream and out to sea, but it was much too dangerous. Our fuel was limited, I didn't trust the outboard motor and there wasn't even a full set of sails on board *Dixieland*.

Heidi was kneeling on the squab, trying her best to comfort Noah. I cursed myself, wishing for the hundredth time that I'd checked we had his emergency kit before we left home. I'd been in too much of a rush.

'What are we going to do, Dad?' Heidi asked.

'We're going to move.'

I sent another cry for help to Dr Jack: *No improvement v v worried. Hiding place compromised because Heidi called Livia. Do I risk going to a chemist and if so what can I get over the counter?*

Then I grabbed *A Boatman's Guide to the River Esk*. The book was published in far more innocent days, with charming illustrations and homely descriptions of riverside pubs, but it was all I had. It did at least include a hand-drawn chart of the river from Whitby. I began searching for another isolated mooring spot, deep enough for *Dixieland*'s keel.

I'd been smothering a rising tide of terror for days, and now it began to burst through my defences—swamping my brain, blurring my vision; my hands were shaking so much that I accidentally tore a page. Every scream-aloud nightmare was coming true. *Noah's suffocating and you're pissing about with a map? You brought him here to save him, and instead you're killing him. Do something! Think faster!* In the old days Livia or I would have been speeding towards the hospital, calling ahead for an ambulance to meet us with oxygen. Now I was scrabbling through an old book while my son struggled for every breath.

In the blindness of panic, I almost failed to notice my lifeline: the grey phone lighting up, humming as it lay on the table. *Dr Jack.*

As I read his message, everything changed.

Hi S, situation sounds urgent. Have put a call out on the Resistance network. A trusted medic will meet you at marina wharf in 40 mins. Will have adrenaline nebuliser oxygen etc.

'Thank you,' I whispered. I could have wept with relief and gratitude. Jack had been working behind the scenes for us all this time, sounding the jungle drums through the network of truth-seekers. Good people, standing up against evil.

'Great news!' I clapped my hands together as I made for the hatch. 'Heidi, hop ashore and untie us! I'm starting the motor. Dr Jack's found us a saviour.'

Livia

Anthony gave a running commentary while pretending to navigate his way into Dr Jack's social media.

'Okey-dokey . . . let's just open YouTube . . . have a look. So this guy calls himself . . . erm, Dr Jake?'

'Dr Jack.'

Home remedies for asthma.

My mind was in wild overdrive, rifling through everything I know about Anthony, everything I knew about Dr Jack. Soon after one of them appeared in our lives, so did the other. Dr Jack had popped up at the most insidious moment, reaching out to Scott when he was broken with grief and guilt. At every twist, every turn, Dr Jack was there on cue, manipulating Scott, playing with Scott. All those months I'd been battling an enemy I couldn't see. All those months I'd had the prickling sense that my enemy *could see me.*

Home remedies for asthma. Black coffee. Cow parsley.

No, no. It simply wasn't possible. I must be imagining things, joining random dots and coming up with my own conspiracy theory.

'Dr Jack . . . Dr Jack,' Anthony murmured. 'There are loads of them.'

'I think it's "Dr Jack NHS".'

I was quietly turning on the spot, looking around the cupboard-cum-office with a rising feeling of deja vu. I knew this place. I had a nightmarish, sick sense of inevitability about what I was about to see.

And there it was. The wall. That depressing shade of pale green. The Z-shaped crack in the plasterwork, running from top to bottom.

I couldn't believe it—*couldn't* believe it—and yet at the same time I knew with absolute certainty where I was. I was in Dr Jack's office. I was talking to Dr Jack.

'Does he have an icon?' asked Anthony.

I managed to answer, though my entire reality had just turned upside down.

'A cartoon doctor. He never shows himself; I've no idea what he looks like.'

That was a lie, of course. I knew exactly what he looked like. Somewhere nearby there would be a flesh-coloured mask, a stethoscope and a set of blue scrubs. I imagined Anthony peeling off his props before rushing to meet me at the entrance. He'd pulled his sweatshirt over his head in a hurry. Inside out.

'Bingo!' he crowed, nodding at the screen. 'Got him.'

Nobody knew I was here. I'd walked with this cunning manipulator into a locked and empty building on a deserted industrial estate. There wasn't a soul within earshot. A few minutes ago he'd thought nothing of grabbing hold of me, whispering intimately into my ear, while my child was starving for oxygen. He'd done those things because he could, and then he'd behaved as if nothing had happened. What else was he capable of? I noticed a key in the open door—what if he locked me in here?

My first instinct was escape. I had to get out of his lair, out of the building. *Run. Run, right now.* Make some excuse to dash out to my car, drive to a safe place and call for help.

But I couldn't run away, because Noah was dying.

Contemplating Anthony's inside-out sweatshirt, I slipped my hand into my coat pocket. It was still there. My lanyard. Charles was about my height, probably weighed less. *All you need is a belt and a lot of determination.*

'You've been a good friend to Scott,' I said. 'He didn't drop any hint about where he was going?'

'I wish!' A theatrical sigh. 'But no.'

I brought the lanyard out of my pocket. Passed one end across to my other hand, and began to wind the cord around my fists. I didn't want to use it. If this went wrong, if this man overpowered me, I stood no chance.

'He once mentioned some of you camping out in a barn when you were students. Near Hadrian's Wall, I think.'

'A barn.' Anthony drummed his fingertips on the table. 'Yes! Near Haltwhistle. The guy whose family owned that farm was our housemate. Greg . . . shit, hang on a second . . . Wilson. No, Watson. You should tell the police. Worth having a look.'

I had no choice. *I had no choice.* I didn't have the luxury of time. Dr Jack would play these games forever, and my baby's life was ebbing away. I might already be too late.

You have to catch people totally unawares.

I stepped up close, bracing my body against the back of his chair, getting ready to do the unimaginable. My heart was out of control, thudding, thumping, my breath coming too fast. But my mind was clear, as focused and certain as it had been in months. *My enemy. My invisible enemy.* I could see him at last, I could touch him, I could get my hands on him.

I gave him one last chance.

'You'd tell me where they are, if you knew?'

'Of course! Livia, you know I—'

He never finished his lie. Within a second I'd flicked my weapon over his head, across his throat, and was heaving on it with every ounce of strength I had.

The effect was immediate. Anthony writhed and rolled in his seat, clawing at the ligature, trying desperately to pull it away from his neck. A scream emerged as a ghastly rasping sound. Later, the specialist who gave evidence in court suggested it may have been in that first frenzy that I ruptured his trachea.

I didn't feel fear anymore. The rage. The *rage*. It possessed me, empowered me. For once in my life I wasn't going to count to fucking ten.

'What was it?' I snarled. 'Jealousy? Did you get off on controlling Scott?'

Charles had been right about one thing: garrotting a person doesn't take great physical prowess; it takes great determination. And there's no room for mercy. After ten seconds I slackened off enough to allow Anthony to breathe and speak.

'Talk, Dr Jack,' I hissed. 'Where are my family?'

'I'm not Dr Jack, I'm not Dr—'

I was getting into the swing of this now. As I began again he clawed, he flailed, he kicked a panicked tattoo on the bottom of the table.

'Can't breathe? Noah can't either.' I was breathless too, with the effort. 'He's choking right now, just like you. He's terrified, just like you. He's facing death. Just. Like. You.'

With each of those last three words I gave the lanyard a violent tug. Anthony's limbs paddled in a wild dance.

'Where are they?' I demanded.

He wasn't giving up easily. Too much to lose, I suppose, or perhaps he'd fallen down his own rabbit hole and believed his New World Order fantasy. Or perhaps both. He gasped that I was crazy, he had no idea what I was talking about, so I did it again. *Yank, release.* 'Where are they?' *Yank, release.* 'Where are they?' It wasn't easy or quick. It wasn't humane. It was ugly and brutal; it made me ugly and brutal. But it was him or Noah.

Towards the end, he began to weaken. I felt him slump, his body limp in the chair. I thought of Jarrod Jeffries and hoped to God I hadn't killed the man, but he revived within seconds.

'I promise you, Anthony,' I told him. 'If Noah suffocates to death, so do you.'

That's when he told me.

'Whitby,' he whispered.

'Still in Whitby! Where?'

'A boat.' He winced, trying to swallow. Blood and saliva crept from the corner of his mouth. 'Stolen boat. On the river.'

That rang true. Our family once went on a touristy cruise up the Esk. A lovely day out. Fish and chips and boating.

'Whereabouts on the river?' I asked.

'Just ... Ruswarp ... Livia, please. I'm in trouble. Can't breathe, can't swallow.'

I believed him. There was a disturbing overlay to his breathing, an inhuman, high-pitched whistle. He couldn't be play-acting that sound. I began to wonder just how much damage I'd done.

'I'll call an ambulance as soon as I know my children are safe. You've been texting Scott all day as Dr Jack—that means you've got a second phone. Where is it?'

He let out an agonised squeal as he dragged a phone from his pocket and laid it on the table. At my request he punched in the PIN: 1-2-3-4. Not hard to remember. I was going to need that phone.

He was groaning now, and weeping. The whistling sound was louder.

'I'm going to lock you in,' I told him. 'I'm going to take both your phones and turn off your modem. There's nobody else in this whole building, probably won't be for days. If I find you've lied to me again, if my family aren't where you say they are, there'll be no ambulance for you. I'll leave you to die in here. Understand?'

He managed to nod.

'Last chance,' I said. 'Are you absolutely sure you've told me the truth?'

Another nod.

I let go of the lanyard, grabbed his phone and sprinted through the door, ready to slam and lock it. But Anthony wasn't coming after me. He'd doubled up in the chair and was clutching at his throat, whistling with every breath, more blood trickling out of his mouth. I hated him, but I pitied him. For all the evil he'd done us, this was a suffering human being.

'I'll get help to you,' I promised him.

Then I closed the door and turned the key on that windowless cupboard in an empty building on an industrial estate. I turned the key on the green paint, the Z-shaped crack in the plaster. I turned the key on Dr Jack.

Scott

I sat with my arm on the tiller, watching the riverbank crawl by and cursing *Dixieland* for not being a speedboat. Every minute or so I called down the hatch: 'How's he doing? Any worse?'

It took only seconds for us to leave our mooring. Heidi understood immediately what was required, casting off from the trees and leaping back aboard in one fluid motion; you'd think she'd been a sailor all her life. Her grandfather would have been proud of her.

We had the river almost to ourselves as we motored through the gathering dusk. The nation was staying at home, as ordered. See no evil, hear no evil. A couple raised their wineglasses and waved from the deck of a moored houseboat, so I waved back. Surely these weren't spies. They were ordinary people, reaching out in extraordinary times. You'd expect the road bridge to be humming with traffic at this time on a weekday, late rush hour, but I counted only three vehicles as we passed underneath. Essential workers, presumably. Freight. No police cars.

Dr Jack sent an update. *Contact on way. Wait on wharf.*

We arrived with nightfall, early for our rendezvous. I throttled back, scanning the deserted marina while I threw out fenders. No lights in the marina office. No sign of our saviour yet either.

Heidi appeared on deck as we puttered up to the wharf. She stood waiting with the bow line in her hand, jumping ashore when we came alongside.

'They'd better get here soon,' she said fearfully, as we ran our lines around the bollards. 'Like, *now*. Noah's really bad.'

For an agonising moment we waited side by side, looking out across the darkening car park. Wavelets surged against the slipway. A rising wind rattled and clinked through the metal cables of a hundred yachts along the floating pontoons. *Rattling bones,* my father used to call that sound, using his special pirate voice. *Dead men tell no lies.*

And then Heidi tilted her head, holding up a finger. I heard it too: the whine of a car's engine, distant at first, approaching fast.

Please God, let it be them.

Headlights shot into view—revving, slewing right across the roundabout, charging into the car park to brake sharply within feet of us, the driver's door already thrown open. I lifted a hand to block the glare of the lights.

And Heidi was running, running and shouting at the top of her voice.

Livia

She hurtled into me, throwing her arms around my neck. We rocked, beyond words, clinging to one another.

Scott stood frozen in the beam of my headlights. Every instinct screamed at me to charge straight onto the boat, to get to Noah. But who knew what Scott might do next, in his panicked state? He might try to run out to sea with all of us on board, and that would be disastrous.

'How's Noah?' I shouted to him.

I'd roared out of Guisborough, treating the deserted A171 as my own private race track. I spent the journey planning how to persuade Scott to give up Noah without a fight. I had images of him producing a rifle and turning picture-postcard Whitby into something out of *Bonnie and Clyde*.

He'd never do anything like that, I told myself. *This is Scott you're talking about. He's an English teacher, not a . . .*

Not a what?

I'd just tortured and strangled a man, imprisoned him, threatened to let him die alone in a windowless cupboard. If I was capable of doing something so monstrous to save my children, why wouldn't Scott?

He came to life, whirled around and began to untie his mooring ropes. 'Who told you we were here?' he yelled. 'You're the bait! You've led them straight to us.'

'Dr Jack told me.'

That had an impact. I saw him falter.

'Dr Jack is Anthony, Scott. *Anthony is Dr Jack.*'

I heard Heidi gasp. Scott was glaring at me with something close to hatred.

'Jesus Christ, Livia, what mind-fuck games are you playing now? Who put you up to this?'

'I've just come from his warehouse. He admitted to being Jack; he told me you were on this boat. I saw where he makes his videos. He'd been googling remedies for asthma.'

'Shut up. I don't want to hear your stupid lies. Heidi, let's go. We have to leave. *Now.*'

Heidi didn't move. 'Please just get Noah, Dad,' she begged.

'See this phone?' I held it high. 'This is Anthony's "Dr Jack" phone, with which he runs his "Dr Jack" life.' I began to read texts. '*Don't blow your cover, S, stay where you are until we can get you to a safe house . . . Black coffee will open inflamed airways more effectively than steroids . . . Is there cow parsley nearby? Collect leaves and stems, make an infusion . . .* And you write: *No improvement v v worried . . .* And he replies that he's sending a trusted medic to meet you here.' I looked up at Scott. 'But by then I'm afraid you were talking to me. By then, *I* was Dr Jack.'

'Genius,' said Heidi.

Scott was breathing hard, a trapped animal. I hoped his religion was imploding. I hoped he was seeing that his hero was a fraud.

'Where's Noah?' I moved towards him, towards the boat. 'I'm taking him to hospital.'

'They'll kill him.'

'I promise I'll stay with him the whole time; I'll protect him with my life. You can come too. Please, Scott, bring him to the car. Please.'

While I was pleading, Heidi had leaped across the gap between wharf and boat. I saw her duck into the cabin. Seconds later, she was back in the hatchway.

'Dad, help!' she shrieked. 'He's hardly even conscious—I can't get him to sit up.'

Scott looked from her to me, turning in a desperate circle, both hands flat on the top of his head.

'Hurry up!' Heidi was beside herself. 'Please don't let him die.'

Her distress seemed to galvanise Scott. The whole boat tilted as he landed heavily on the deck.

By the time he reached my car Scott was in tears, a man being marched up the steps of the scaffold. But he had Noah in his arms.

•

Rani Kumar had come through for me. I would be grateful to that woman forever. I'd feared the lockdown situation might already have overwhelmed our ambulance service, but we got lucky. People were staying home; the roads were clear. The ambulance was waiting just out of sight of the marina, prepped and staffed for an asthma emergency. No lights or sirens. I noticed a police car too, parked discreetly a little distance away, in case of trouble.

The crew had obviously been primed about Scott. They spoke in extra-calm voices and stood well back as I eased Noah from his father's grasp.

Noah whimpered when he saw them, hiding his face against my chest. But he was too weak to speak, even to cry. He was losing the battle.

'They're our friends.' I hugged him close as I carried him inside. 'I promise they're our friends. I'll stay right beside you.'

I looked out at Scott and Heidi. They stood side by side, gazing into the back of the ambulance—both looking devastated, though perhaps for different reasons. Scott had promised to drive Heidi home in my car and wait with her for news. I was sure he wouldn't disappear again tonight. Not without Noah.

'Stay with him, Livia!' He shouted. 'Don't leave him alone! Don't let them—'

The doors closed. The crew sprang into action—assessing Noah, fitting a nebuliser mask over his bloodless little face, an IV line into his arm, battling to keep him breathing. Moments later we were racing out of Whitby. Still no sirens. Just the voices, the urgent flash of electric blue in the quiet night.

•

It was a horrifyingly close call. Closer than we'd ever come. I hope to God it was closer than we'll ever come again. But they saved his life, the trusted medics.

FORTY

Spring, 2020

Livia

After all we'd been through, lockdown suited me fine. I understood the loneliness and loss of others, but I welcomed it for the children and myself. It felt as though we were convalescing from a life-threatening illness that had left us traumatised, longing for peace. All that mattered was that Noah was alive, he and Heidi were safe in their home, and I had the perfect excuse to keep them close. No hum of traffic, no passing aircraft, no criss-crossing vapour trails. Even the birds seemed less wary, more curious. All nature was breathing, breathing, breathing, and so were we.

Scott wasn't coming back to us. Not physically, not mentally. He was a hero in the Truther community. Someone offered him a caravan on a site near Selby, living among like-minded people. I didn't even suggest he come home, not after what he'd put us through. I hadn't begun to forgive him. I couldn't imagine ever trusting him again.

Because of the pandemic, visits to Noah in hospital were heavily restricted, his stay kept as short as possible. Over those days Scott called me every couple of hours, desperately frightened that 'they' were going to smother his son.

'So how do you feel about Dr Jack,' I asked him, 'now you know he was Anthony all along?'

His answer came without hesitation. 'Dr Jack wasn't just one person. He was the front for a resistance group. Doctors, graphic designers, filmmakers. What a brilliant communication tool! Anthony was just one of them.'

I sank onto the sofa. What fresh hell was this?

'That's simply not true, Scott.'

'It is. Surely you don't think Anthony was capable of making those videos on his own? They were obviously the work of a team.'

'So you've forgiven him,' I said.

'He was sworn to secrecy. There are spies everywhere. All he could do was guide me to Dr Jack, to the Resistance. They'd have saved Noah, you know. They had someone on their way.'

I was shaking with fury and grief. He was choosing his truth over our marriage, over his own children.

'Aren't you going to say sorry?' I demanded furiously. 'Sorry for letting me think you'd all drowned in our car? Sorry for putting us through a living nightmare? For making Noah suffer and nearly die, for involving Heidi in your deceit?'

'I'm sorry you went through a nightmare.'

'You damned well should be! I think I'm going to be arrested for what I did to Anthony. I could end up in prison.'

'Try to understand, Livia. *Please*. I did it for you, I did it for them. I love you all more than—'

I put the phone down on him. It felt as though something was shattering inside me.

But life does go on. It does.

•

Sergeant Kumar was standing at my door again. She looked miserable. I'd been expecting such a visit for weeks, but it didn't make the moment any easier.

'Got time for a cup of tea?' I asked. 'In the garden. Socially distanced.'

When she hesitated, I smiled. 'It's okay, Rani. I know why you're here.'

She could have phoned, but she'd chosen to tell me herself. I had to make an appointment to come into the station. She explained apologetically that I was to be interviewed under caution 'in relation to an alleged serious assault upon Anthony Tait'. She suggested I bring a solicitor along. I had no choice, unless I wanted to be arrested on my front doorstep.

'Scott's not back then?' she asked, as I offered milk.

'I think that ship has sailed.'

She nodded. She wasn't surprised.

'He's in a caravan somewhere near Selby,' I said. 'Living among people who share his beliefs. All walks of life.' I rubbed my cheeks with both hands. 'He couldn't be in a worse place, could he? They'll be wearing tinfoil hats by now. You know, I honestly thought what happened in Whitby would wake him up. Like in a cartoon, when someone gets hit on the head twice, and the second blow makes them normal again. But it seems to have had the opposite effect. He's decided that Dr Jack was a front for a resistance cell, and Anthony is a martyr. He still believes the New World Order is coming and Covid's a hoax and . . . argh! It's so crazy, not even worth trying to unravel it.'

We sat in the warmth of the morning sun, our chairs set far apart. Heidi was hunkered down in the office with her laptop and a microphone, recording songs with Flynn Thomas. They hadn't seen each other in person since school closed, and the music camp had been cancelled, but that didn't stop them. They used virtual jamming sessions to write and record songs together, and posted them on TikTok. Their friendship gave me joy—so vibrant, so clever, sparking off one another's talent. They could add drumming or other instruments to their music, or make their two voices sound like an eight-part choir. Every day there seemed to be a new idea.

Noah was . . . well, I'd cheated. He wasn't homeschooling. He was watching telly.

'Anthony bloody Tait,' I muttered, as I picked up my mug. 'He nearly kills my son, and it's me who faces criminal charges.'

I knew I was in serious trouble. I'd heard on the grapevine that Anthony was found unconscious on the floor of his office with my lanyard still hanging off his neck, that he had internal injuries and needed life-saving surgery. I'd already phoned Sandra Webb, the solicitor who was with me when I got the news about Scott being suspended. She'd agreed to act for me when the time came.

'I don't suppose you've thought of anything you can charge Anthony with?' I asked Rani.

The sergeant looked disgusted. 'Only impersonating a doctor.'

'Huh. He'd be in hotter water if he failed to pay his television licence fee.'

She agreed gloomily. 'We paid him a visit to take a statement. It's as though being Dr Jack was his whole life—he's in love with his own secret persona. Hurts to admit this, but he's good at what he does. He's played this game for a long time, this social media influencing. Before Dr Jack there were others, he wouldn't say how many, but he's got an impressive suite of editing software, music, graphics, text-to-voice. He's proud of it, talks about his followers as his "flock".'

We fell silent, both cradling our mugs between our hands. I sensed that Rani wanted to ask me more about Anthony but was wary of muddying the investigation into my assault on him. I wanted to talk about him, though. I wanted her to understand.

'It used to niggle at me that he hung around so much,' I said. 'He just fetched up out of the blue, blast from the past. Next minute, he's Scott's best mate. He was here on the day Nicky died. He helped to clear out Nicky's cottage, even carried his coffin into church. He made himself indispensable when we were vulnerable. With hindsight, I can see it all . . . he used every opportunity to wind Scott up, or to gain information, to check up on his handi-work. How could I be so blind?'

'Hindsight is twenty-twenty.'

'He just seemed . . . clumsy. Helpful. A know-all, but lots of people are.' I grimaced at my own gullibility. 'I was *grateful*.'

'He's an expert con man.'

'Granted. But I'm hyper-alert to manipulation at work. Why didn't I spot it when it slithered in through my own front door?'

Rani was frowning. 'You're not suggesting he had anything to do with the death of the brother?'

'Nicky? No, I'm not suggesting that. But Anthony's nothing if not an opportunist, and that was one hell of an opportunity. He used it to the max. I'm sure he wound up the young courier driver who found Nicky, got him to tell Scott how the ambulance crew didn't seem to be trying to save him. That planted a seed.'

'Nasty.'

'Did you know the Dr Jack YouTube channel was created the day after Nicky's funeral? *The day after*. Dr Jack was tailor-made to trap Scott. Anthony had worked out exactly which buttons to press.'

'I'll check those dates.' Rani got out her notebook and scrib-bled a couple of lines.

'Doesn't stop there,' I said. 'That video about the HPV jab, the one with stock images of a red-haired girl? No coincidence that she was a Heidi look-alike. He uploaded that at half past two on the day—the actual *day*—he and Scott went for a drink. Somehow, in that pub, he found some way to manipulate Scott into watching it. And I have to live with the fact that I set it up; I asked him to drag Scott out for a pint, because I was worried. I asked him to help us.'

Rani was shaking her head in bafflement. 'Such a lot of time and effort. For fun? For power?'

'To him, power *is* fun. I think he's a narcissist: he has an insatiable need to feel cleverer than anyone else. But reading between the lines, he's always been a bit of a misfit; people haven't shared the extremely high opinion he has of himself. He *knows* he's brilliant—why don't we all see it? As Dr Jack he could be that guru, command that respect. The first time I ever met him he tried to belittle Scott. He pretended it was just friendly banter, but it wasn't. It was a power play. Scott clapped back at him and he never tried that again. Imagine: Anthony's in his forties, back in Teesside with absolutely nothing. Battered, broke, feels like a failure. I don't know what happened to his fabulous Californian life, if it ever existed. Might be another fantasy. So he looks up his nerd of an ex-flatmate, thinking he can dominate that friendship, at least—only to find that Scott's a happy man, a winner in all the ways that truly matter. Loved, respected, a pillar of the community. He's got beautiful children, a warm home, he's got—'

'You,' Rani interjected, pointing at me with her biro. 'He's got you.'

'Yes, me. Anthony couldn't believe it. He kept saying so. I reckon from then on he was looking for a chink in our armour, anything he could exploit. He set out to screw with Scott's mind. He set out to destroy us. And it looks—' I choked on my words, caught off guard by a surge of grief. I shut my eyes.

'Sorry,' said Rani. 'You okay?'

I took a moment. Breathed deep. 'It looks as though he succeeded,' I whispered.

The dominoes were still falling.

•

'Good luck, Livia,' Charles said, when I phoned him before turning myself in. 'I'm proud of you. A Probation Service lanyard! That was resourceful, I must say. You saved your little boy's life with a lanyard.'

'Any advice for me?' I was so nervous that I'd spent the morning throwing up. After all these years working in the criminal justice system, I was the one facing questions. Facing prison.

'You don't want to be taking advice from me.' I heard his chuckle. 'I'm the idiot who managed to talk his way into a life sentence.'

•

The interview room had no natural light. Sandra sat beside me. A detective inspector called Duncan Basset ran the show. We were coming towards the end of that first lockdown, all wearing face masks.

DI Basset slotted a tape into the recorder, reminded me that I was still under caution, asked me to state my name, address and date of birth. Then we were off.

To their credit, the inspector and his colleague gave me plenty of time to tell my story. I began with the morning Scott found a cheery Facebook message from his old mate: *How's life, Scotty? Got time for a pint?*

I told them about Nicky's death, Anthony's helpfulness, Dr Jack's role in the disintegration of our family. I tried to make them understand the unshakeable hold that he and other influencers so quickly gained over Scott. I described everything that happened on the day Noah nearly died. I showed them a letter from the hospital, confirming that he'd been lucky to survive. Another half-hour, and we'd have been telling a different story.

DI Basset and his sidekick knew about Noah, of course, but I could tell this letter had an impact on them. How could it not?

'It was clever, the way you tricked your husband into rushing back to Whitby marina,' the detective remarked.

I relaxed a little. He understood.

'You must have been furious when the penny dropped about Anthony Tait being Dr Jack,' added his colleague, who'd taken a back seat until now.

She combined a mumsy haircut with a shrewd gaze over her mask. The effect—on me at least—was intimidating. I felt a new sympathy for clients who made false confessions in their desperation to appease their interviewers and escape that room.

'I was blown sideways,' I said. 'And I felt vulnerable—shut in that cupboard, in that empty building, with a shapeshifter.'

'Did you give him a chance to come clean before you attacked him?'

'I gave him every chance.'

'He says not. He says he would gladly have told you where your family were hiding.'

'Bollocks. I asked him repeatedly. I'd been asking him ever since they went missing.'

DI Basset's name suited him. He really did have the sad, drooping eyes of a basset hound. When he pulled some sheets of paper from a file, I read them upside down. Anthony's statement. Some passages were highlighted. Homework had been done.

'Do you remember a conversation you had with Anthony Tait at a bonfire party on New Year's Eve?' he asked.

Auld Lang Syne. Scott bailing up half the county in the kitchen, Anthony roasting chestnuts and being Mr Nice Guy.

'I see you're nodding. You remember the conversation.' Basset read from the statement. 'Do you recall saying: "If I ever get my hands on Dr Jack, I swear I'll throttle him?"'

'I . . . yes, I think I might have said something along those lines.' It sounded pretty bad. I caught myself blinking nervously. 'It was a figure of speech. I'd been drinking. Scott was making an exhibition of himself. People were gossiping. I felt humiliated for him, for our whole family.'

'So you meant it when you said you'd throttle Dr Jack if you got the chance?'

'Not literally.'

'But you were angry when you made that threat?'

'It wasn't a threat! I never in a million years expected to meet Dr Jack. I had no idea I was talking to him right there and then. It was a throwaway remark.'

DI Basset sighed, fiddling with the elastic of his mask. 'It just seems quite a coincidence. Quite specific, isn't it? *Throttle.* Which is precisely what you did, when you finally got your hands on him.'

'Coincidences happen.'

'Not as often as you'd think.'

'Look. This wasn't about harming Anthony; I wasn't thinking about comeuppance or revenge. I was thinking about saving my child's life.'

I was echoing Charles Shepherd all those years ago, when he sat at a table like this, answering questions like this. *I didn't set out to hurt Jarrod Jeffries.* I never expected to be following in his footsteps.

The lugubrious Basset began rootling through his file again.

'Have a look at these,' he said. 'For the recording, they're photographs of the complainant's injuries.'

He brought out three large, gruesome colour photos which he told me were of Anthony's neck. Vicious ligature marks, the skin broken, wounds embedded in livid bruising—the ugly results of my brutality. In one of them, Anthony's bearded lower face was visible. He was looking extremely sorry for himself. I'd caused those horrific injuries. I was lucky not to have killed him.

'These are sickening,' I said. 'I'm appalled to know I did that. I'm not a sadist. I'm a mother, and this was my only hope.'

'Torturing a man was your only hope?'

'Yes. *Yes*. He could have just told me where they were. I kept asking and asking—all I wanted was to save Noah. As soon as he told me, I let him go. I left the keys outside the building. I asked Sergeant Kumar to send an ambulance.'

Basset straightened each of the photos with the tips of his fingers, laying them out in a grisly parade in front of me.

'Torture is banned under international law, as I'm sure you know. It's a crime against humanity. There are no circumstances in which it's condoned, not even during war. If it's okay for you to torture a man to get information, why not the army or MI6? Or the police, for that matter?'

Sandra cleared her throat. I could tell she was about to protest, so I raised a hand to stop her. I'd done my homework too. Hours of it.

'Completely different,' I said. 'That's about abuse of power, about people in positions of authority. This was immediate, it was personal, it was crucial. My six-year-old son was suffocating to death. I was acting under duress.'

'So you're saying you were acting under duress when you used a ligature with enough force to tear a man's trachea.'

Somebody knocked on the door, came in with mugs of coffee. Sandra asked if I needed to take a break. I didn't. I needed to tell my story, get out of that bloody room and home to my children. I looked at the photos one more time before pushing them back across the table.

'Have you checked with the US authorities?' I asked. 'I bet he's done this kind of thing before. He gets off on the power. To be fair, I think he might believe some of the bullshit he peddles.'

They weren't interested in anything Anthony might have got up to in America. Basset drooped over the table, exhaling heavily as he looked through Anthony's statement. Finally, he cleared his throat and asked the most bizarre, insulting question I could ever have imagined.

'Were you, um, attracted to Anthony Tait?'

'Did I fancy Anthony?' I laughed, incredulous at the suggestion. 'Categorically, one hundred percent not.'

'He says you used to flirt with him. You phoned him behind Scott's back. We've seen his call log, confirming several calls from your number. He says you confided in him, you complained to him about Scott. You invited him to your home. You turned up unannounced at his warehouse on the first day of lockdown.'

Now I really *was* furious. 'Yes—I phoned him, tried to be welcoming, because he seemed lonely and a friend to Scott. Oh, the irony of that! And we all know I went to his warehouse, but not out of . . .' I shuddered. 'I wouldn't touch Anthony Tait with a ten-foot barge pole. Have you *seen* him?'

DI Basset looked even more unhappy. 'Did the two of you embrace in the warehouse?'

'This is ridiculous.'

'Is it true?'

'Only if by "embrace", he means the creepy moment when he got handsy. The man's a compulsive liar, doing what he does best: taking a tiny bit of truth and spinning it into a massive fantasy. That "embrace" wasn't consensual on my part. He suddenly grabbed me under the pretence of being comforting. I was speechless.'

'Did you protest?'

'Of course I didn't protest. I was panicking about my dying son! I was in Anthony's warehouse, in a crisis, I needed his help, so I thought: *I mustn't hurt his feelings.* I wriggled away, pretended it wasn't A Thing. That's what women do. We shouldn't, but we do.'

I caught the sidekick's eye. I was pretty sure there was a glint in it. I was warming to her.

Basset was still reading from Anthony's statement. 'He says you instigated that physical contact as soon as the door closed behind you. You tried to kiss him, to pull him towards the table. He had the impression you were keen to have sex with him—'

'In his dreams!'

'—but he made it plain that he wasn't interested.'

'You have *got* to be kidding me.'

'He states that the real motive for your assault on him was anger at being rejected.'

'He's a fantasist.'

I wasn't laughing anymore. I was wishing I'd finished the job. I should have sawn Anthony's head right off his neck.

The DI turned to the final page of the statement. 'Mr Tait's been an invalid since this incident,' he said. 'His speech is badly affected. He never goes out, he's living with anxiety and post-traumatic stress disorder. I see you're smiling, Livia. Is there any reason why you'd be smiling when you hear these details?'

'Because he's a pathological liar. I bet he's down the pub right now, singing karaoke and leading the conga line. Or would be, if the pubs were open.'

They didn't deny it. This time, there was a definite crinkle in the scary sidekick's eyes.

DI Basset started to wind up the interview. He was noting the time, putting papers away. They'd send the file to the CPS, he said, who would decide about any charges. I'd be bailed in the meantime.

'Anything else either you or Mrs Webb would like to add or clarify before I switch off the recorder?'

The three of them waited while I gathered my thoughts. I knew a transcript of this interview would be read out in court. This was my final chance to reach forward through time, to appeal to my future jury.

'Just a question,' I said in the end. 'What would you have done, in my shoes? Are you really suggesting I should have let my son die?'

FORTY-ONE

Livia

'Attempted murder?' I echoed, when Sandra Webb phoned to give me the bad news. That could mean years in prison. Heidi might be an adult by the time I came out, Noah a teenager. Two devastated childhoods.

There were other charges on the list: causing grievous bodily harm with intent, as an alternative to attempted murder—a safety net, in case the jury weren't sure I intended to kill Anthony—and false imprisonment, since I'd locked the guy in his own office. These also meant a prison sentence, but it was the first that made my blood run cold.

The pandemic-struck wheels of justice turned slowly but inexorably. It might be many months or even years before my case came to trial, but it couldn't be escaped forever. The day would come.

I hadn't yet lost my freedom. I'd lost the career that was such a part of me, though, and I was struggling to come to terms with that. I couldn't work in the Probation Service while on bail for such serious offences. They'd no choice but to suspend me immediately, so I had resigned. I'd held on to our home by the skin of my teeth. Held on to my sanity, thanks to the kindness of family, friends and neighbours. My ex-colleague Jude was a staunch supporter; Charles Shepherd even more so. Isaac Katz put some work my way, as a research assistant in his department at Leeds University. He and his husband, Simon, had made me a welcome dinner guest at their home.

I kept my chin up in public, but the nights were grim. I lay in the dark with a lead weight in my stomach, hearing those heavy metal doors, the warders with their radios and handcuffs, smelling the sweat and despair. But you have to get out of bed in the morning, don't you, no matter what's hanging over your head? You have to live.

The silver lining of that hellish wait was that the children had time to grow older and more resilient. Noah turned seven, and then eight; Heidi would be sixteen next summer. She and Suyin Liu were still great mates, while her friendship with Flynn Thomas had turned into a pandemic romance. The pair of them set up a music studio in our office. I loved to hear them in there, playing their guitars, singing, talking, laughing. Lots of silence too, but I refused to think about what that meant. There are some things a mother doesn't want to know.

If the worst happened, my parents had offered to rent out their beloved home and move into The Forge for however long I was absent. The pandemic had finally forced my father to retire. Nobody trusted Scott with full-time care of our children, but he'd play his part too. He was still their dad. They still loved him.

'But what about you, Livia?' asked Bethany. 'How do you feel about Scott?'

'Exasperation.'

That was putting it mildly.

'He's never said sorry,' I added bitterly. 'He's never said thanks. He still thinks he was right. And I'm the one facing prison.'

I'd thought the rising Covid-19 death toll, and the non-appearance of jackbooted agents of the cabal dragging people off to concentration camps, might show Scott that the pandemic was real while the totalitarian world government was not. I was wrong. Then when his mother, poor Geraldine, succumbed to the virus—along with half the residents in her nursing home—I was *sure* he'd see the light. Wrong, wrong, wrong. Hadn't he warned me about a global euthanasia program murdering the most vulnerable? Well, here it was. Right on cue.

Throughout those long periods of lockdown, he lived among people who saw the world as he did, all talking with casual certainty about the Plandemic, the NWO, the Great Awakening. In their eyes non-believers were stupid, we were sheeple. Scott spent the pandemic fighting for freedoms that he already had.

Isaac reckoned it was all about validation and camaraderie in a time of turmoil.

'People thrive on having a cause,' he said. 'They're fighting the dark forces! They feel righteous and energised. It's addictive.'

'I'd be more sympathetic if they hadn't marked me down as public enemy number one.'

I had a starring role in the conspiracist canon. I was a secret agent of those dark forces, a cold-blooded assassin. They tried to harass me at the Probation Service—a waste of time, since I didn't work there anymore. Once they even hid in Back Lane, filming me as I came and went from the house. Heidi showed me some of the milder discussions in a Reddit thread:

— *Dr Jack predicted the NWO would silence him. Within hours he's garrotted. Coincidence? I don't think so!!*
— *Agreed. Livia Denby put out a call on YouTube before her failed assassination attempt. She was TRACKING HIM DOWN with a fake appeal for info about her children.*

— *I saw that. You know the funny part? SHE DOESN'T HAVE ANY CHILDREN!*

— *I see she's been committed for trial. Total joke. Judge is in Inner Circle. JURY ALREADY RIGGED according to my contact in the police.*

I showed these to Scott the next time he came to visit.

'Do you believe this rubbish?' I asked him. 'Do you think I'm a secret agent with a licence to kill?'

'Of course not.'

'Your mates do.'

He was still reading the thread. 'They're not all my mates. The Truther movement is vast, it's global, there's room for different ideas. I just think you're blind. You *were* an unwitting agent of the NWO when you attacked Anthony.'

'Your mates have been hanging around this house. What's next? A Molotov cocktail through the letterbox? Call them off, Scott.'

'These are good people. They'd never put children in harm's way.'

'You did,' I shot back at him. 'You put your own children in harm's way.'

Of course, when the vaccine eventually arrived and changed the game—hurrah for scientists!—Scott was one of vocal thousands who thought it the work of the devil. One night, watching the evening news, I spotted him on the fringe of a raging crowd in London, cheering as a speaker stood beside a makeshift noose, calling for 'Nuremberg 2.0' and the mass hanging of NHS staff.

I felt dirty just watching his joyous hatred. Could this fool really be the father of my children? What had happened to the clever, affectionate, laid-back man I'd adored and trusted and had chosen to share my life with? For the first time, I truly despised him. I turned the TV off sharpish, before Heidi or Noah recognised their dad.

Then I went for a long walk around the streets of Gilderdale, quietly summoning memories of our years here together. Such dreams, such possibilities, such love. All gone now. Just another failed marriage.

Bethany phoned as I was sitting on a low swing in the children's playground, gently rocking myself.

'I don't know how to tell you this,' she said.

'You mean Scott on the news, baying for the execution of people who gave their all to save us? Yep. I saw him too.'

'That's not our Scott, Livia. That's not who he is.'

'It's not who he *was*.'

'James's niece has gone down the rabbit hole too. She won't let us anywhere near her newborn baby because we're vaccinated. It's the pandemic. It's rattled everyone's cages. People have spent too much time alone; they've had too much time to think.'

'And so have I,' I said bleakly. 'I've had time to accept the fact that love doesn't conquer all.'

Dew was falling as I wandered home. Halfway across the bridge, I paused to lean over the parapet. The ducks were settling down for the night, murmuring peacefully in the dusk. They didn't feel the weight of the world.

I'd battled through the bargaining stage of grief, through the denial, some of the anger. I thought I might be reaching acceptance.

The next morning, I spoke to Sandra Webb about a divorce.

•

Since mine was such a familiar face on my home stamping ground—in regular contact with judges, lawyers, ushers, dock officers, everybody—the case was eventually transferred across to Bradford Crown Court. That was okay by me. I knew those cells at Teesside and Newcastle all too well.

Sandra instructed a barrister called Samson Gray, a heavy-set Leeds man of about sixty, who somehow managed to be simultaneously dour and upbeat.

'Interesting, this,' he announced cheerfully, when we met him before a preliminary hearing. 'I haven't found a case where duress has been raised as a defence in anything like these circumstances.'

I would find it all perfectly fascinating too, if it weren't my neck on the block.

'It's a potential defence to GBH and false imprisonment,' Samson added. 'The bad news is that it can't, in law, be a defence to attempted murder. For the life of me I don't see why not, but it can't. Never mind—it doesn't make any difference to the way we run your case. The Crown have to prove that you intended to kill Anthony when you got out your lanyard.'

'And I'm saying that his death was the *last* thing I wanted! If I'd killed him, Noah would have died too.'

'Makes sense to me. Let's hope it does to the jury.'

He ran through statements from our witnesses. One of the ambulance crew who picked us up in Whitby, doctors who treated Noah. These weren't being challenged by the Crown.

'Now. How about Scott?' Samson leaned back in his seat, peering at me.

Scott had admitted to spiriting the children away and trying to fake their deaths in the North Sea. He'd pleaded guilty in the magistrates' court to taking *Dixieland*, for which he got a community service order. But, he insisted, he did it all to save Noah from forced euthanasia, under cover of a hoax pandemic.

The prosecution weren't calling him as a witness.

'Can't say I blame them.' Samson was smiling. 'They won't want him raving about judges being in the Inner Circle. But we need someone to give evidence about what happened on *Dixieland* over those two days—the twenty-third and twenty-fourth of March. What d'you think? You know the man.'

I remembered Scott among that crowd in London, calling for
the execution of health workers, and shook my head. 'His grip
on reality is non-existent. He still doesn't believe Dr Jack was just
Anthony. He still thinks the Resistance would have saved Noah.
And he's surrounded by people who believe I'm an assassin.'

Samson slapped his palms onto his knees. 'Right. Well, there's
one other person who knows what went on aboard that boat.'

I'd known this was coming. Heidi was keen to give evidence,
and Sandra had taken a statement from her. Reading it had me
in tears.

'She's only fifteen,' I protested. 'She's been through so much.'

'I think we should call her.'

'What are my chances?' I asked, as I stood up to leave.

Samson must have heard this question a thousand times. He
considered it carefully, staring at the bound copies of law reports
on the shelves, as though the answer might leap from their pages.
Then he gave me a truthful assessment, not a brush-off.

'I reckon they'll be disturbed about this being such a sustained
attack. They'll know you weren't mucking about when you
caused those injuries. They'll think Anthony Tait is a nasty piece
of work. But that doesn't put you in the clear, because the nastier
he is, the more chance this could look like revenge on your part.
Loss of temper.'

'So . . . fifty-fifty?'

'Never safe to bet on a jury. Best bring your toothbrush. Just
in case.'

FORTY-TWO

February 2022

Livia

The dreaded first day of my trial is listed in Court One at Bradford, in front of Her Honour Judge Fazakerley QC. Almost two years have passed since I put that lanyard around Anthony's throat.

To celebrate the occasion, Yorkshire's laying on an arctic blast.

'It's grim oop north,' mutters Bethany, as she steps out of her car, straight into an icy puddle.

The law courts are housed in a modern building, a long sandstone frontage facing onto a stone-flagged plaza. Bethany and I pick our way across the car park, avoiding more puddles—in my case wondering when I'm going to throw up again, as I have twice during the ninety-minute drive. Nerves.

We've left the rest of the family at home. Heidi has to stay away from court until after she's given her evidence—which is good, because I don't want her seeing me in the dock day after day. My parents have come to keep house this week, sleeping on the lumpy futon in the office. Learning the ropes, in case they have to do it long-term.

We've just reached the plaza when Isaac Katz joins us. The psychologist is wearing a black face mask with his jeans and hoodie, hands in his pockets, head down against the cold.

'Isaac!' I clap him on the shoulder. 'Thank you for coming. I know how busy you are.'

'Least I can do! You asked my advice, and look where it got you.'

As we hurry along, I'm introducing the two of them—*Bethany, my sister; Isaac, the radicalisation guy*. She asks if he's come far, and he's explaining that he lives this side of Leeds so we're practically in his back yard. None of us are paying attention to the small crowd milling near the front of the court building, holding placards. I assume they're here for some celebrity trial. I assume this right up until the moment when someone yells my name and they rush at us in a pack. Suddenly, this crowd doesn't seem so small. Fifteen or twenty people of all shapes and sizes and ages, even babies in pushchairs have been wheeled along to jeer at the witch. The adults have one unifying quality: visceral hatred of a woman they've never met. They scream, jostle, shake their placards in our faces.

NWO EXECUTIONER
NUREMBERG 2.0
NO WHITEWASH FOR THE WHITE WITCH
FREEDOM!!!

'Bloody idiots,' Bethany gasps, once we've forced our way through and are safely inside the building, the crowd kept at bay by the security guards at the entrance. 'Morons! All because you rescued your child.'

'I'm a secret agent sent by the cabal to kill Anthony. Circles within circles, remember?'

'Total fuckwits.'

'Yep,' says Isaac. 'That's the technical term.'

•

The dominoes are falling faster and faster. They're reaching the end of their line.

Judge Fazakerley is small, brisk and intolerant of nonsense. She's heard all about the protestors outside—many of whom are now glaring at me from the public gallery—and she's not impressed. Before the jury pool arrives, she comes into court and reads the riot act. There will be no catcalls or abuse or heckling of any kind, she warns everyone in the gallery. Should anyone be harassed again, those responsible will be in contempt of court and she'll be dealing with them herself. No shouting. No placards. No gathering within a hundred yards of the building. Nothing that might intimidate witnesses or influence the jury.

'Is that understood?' she demands, and is rewarded with sullen nods.

Twenty minutes later, the jury have been sworn. Seven women, five men, in the places that will be theirs until the end of the trial. Extra seats have been added beside the jury box, so that they're spaced further apart than in pre-Covid days. Face masks are optional now, but three of the twelve are wearing them. I took mine off as I came into the dock. I'm sitting in splendid isolation with just the dock officer nearby, and it's better if they can see my face.

Samson Gray and his opposite number, Jane Randall, have set up camp in the front row, with a CPS lawyer and clerk from Sandra Webb's office behind them. Bethany, Isaac, Charles and Jude—who retired last year, finally burned out—are watching from the public gallery. My supporters are outnumbered four to one by people who think I should be hanged.

But at the last moment someone slides silently into court, easing the door shut behind him. A thin man with haunted eyes.

He's changed so much, but he's still Scott. I'm surprised at just how buoyed I am to know he's here. He takes the last spare seat.

Jane Randall is opening her case with calm efficiency, her voice almost soothing as she lays out her stall. She looks about my age, mousy hair showing from beneath her wig. Samson has assured me that she'll be fair; he says she defends as often as she prosecutes. Perhaps we might have been friends, in another life.

Anthony's first into the witness box, escorted by a minder from victim support. He needs a microphone because his larynx has been so ravaged by my lanyard. His voice sounds hoarse and rasping, barely rising above a whisper. He still has the Californian twang.

I've seen neither hide nor hair of the man since I locked him in his cupboard. I can't see him now either. Only the judge, jury and barristers can, because he's giving his evidence from behind a portable screen. Apparently the very sight of me might exacerbate the anxiety and PTSD my actions provoked—conditions so intense, so disabling, that even after two years he can barely leave his house.

'A tactical mistake on his part, I think,' Samson said, when he explained about the screen. 'Juries can spot a complainant hamming it up a mile away. Judges can too.'

I couldn't care less about the screen. If I ever clap eyes on Anthony Tait again, it will be too soon.

Jane Randall takes him through his evidence-in-chief. Yes, he croaks, he created the character of Dr Jack, but not with any malicious intent. There are thousands of influencers like him; it's just a hobby. He's been doing it for years. He never encouraged Scott to take the Denby children away from their mother or to hide on that boat. He just told the Truth. He told the Truth because he cared so much. And the Truth is—

Randall interrupts smoothly, guiding him back to the day in question, and I suppress a grim smile. The last thing she needs is for the jury to hear him ranting about eugenics and the New World Order.

Yes, he knew Scott and the children were hiding in a stolen boat on the Esk. Yes, he knew the coastguard was searching for them out at sea. But he felt the best way to support his friend was to stay in constant touch in the guise of Dr Jack.

From time to time, I steal a glance at Scott to see how he's reacting to all this. He sits transfixed, staring at the witness screen.

'Late afternoon,' Anthony whispers, 'I was at work in my warehouse. I got a call from Livia. She asked me to come down to the entrance doors and let her in.'

Jane Randall shows him a plan of the industrial units at 17 Canal End—the jury have copies in their bundle—and has him explain the layout.

'And did you let Livia in?' she asks.

'Yeah. I would have talked to her outside, but she grabbed my arm and dragged me into the building with her.' His voice fades, and he swallows painfully. 'I'm sorry, can I have another glass of water? Thank you . . . She was running along the corridor, kind of pulling me along.'

'Did you know *why* she was doing this?'

'She said she'd just heard from Heidi and believed Noah was having an asthma attack. She said she wanted my laptop, my wi-fi and my expertise to help her find them. I tried to reassure her that Scott would look after Noah.'

'And what sort of state was she in?'

'She . . . God. Sorry. My voice box . . . She didn't appear to me like someone who thought their son was dying.'

'What makes you say that?'

'She made a pass at me. In my warehouse.'

I've known this was coming, but it's a shock all the same to hear his lies.

'As soon as the door closed behind us, she threw herself at me. She had her hands everywhere—and I do mean *everywhere*. She was kissing me, trying to pull me towards the table.'

'Did she say anything while this was going on?'

'She didn't need to say anything. I knew what was on offer.' Another husky cough. 'I pushed her away, told her point-blank I wasn't interested, that Scott's an old friend. She was pissed off about that. Hell hath no fury like a woman scorned.'

Looking across at Scott, I realise that Anthony has overplayed his hand. Scott's eyebrows are raised comically high, his mouth curved in a mocking grimace. I know that expression. This is the real Scott—*my* Scott: the experienced teacher who's spent twenty years refereeing playground fights and hearing excuses of the dog-ate-my-homework variety. Back in the day, nobody could pull the wool over his eyes.

From now on, Anthony's evidence is straight out of the Dr Jack playbook: slick and scripted, truth and lies slithering all over the floor. Lots of coughing and sips of water. 'Of *course* I'd have told Livia where her family were,' he insists. 'She only had to ask.' But apparently I never gave him the chance. I tricked him into sitting down with his back to me. The next thing he knew, he was being garrotted.

'I didn't know how she was doing it, I just knew I was being hanged in my chair. Literally hanged. I thought I was a dead man. This enormous pressure, crushing my windpipe. I felt my face swelling, my eyes bulging, I got tunnel vision. The pain inside my throat was . . . I'll never forget it. I still wake up screaming most nights. I tried to get her off me, I begged for my life. But she showed no mercy. *No* mercy. She just kept choking me until . . . Sorry, I just need a second.'

'Take your time.'

'At some stage I blacked out.'

He sounds more sincere now, probably because this part of his evidence is true. From the corner of my eye, I glimpse jurors turning their heads to see how I'm reacting. I do my best to look ashamed, but I'm not. Not at all. I'm thinking about Noah's suffering at that very moment, his long hours of terror and slow suffocation. And I know I'd do it all again.

•

Samson Gray can scarcely contain his glee as he gets up to cross-examine Anthony.

'Mr Tait, help us with this. Do you have a Twitter account in the name of Dr Jack?'

'I can't remember.'

'Can't you? Do try.'

A long pause. An excruciating cough. 'I think so. I never use it. Twitter isn't my medium.'

'But Scott Denby first contacted you—contacted Dr Jack, I should say—through Twitter. That's right, isn't it?'

'I don't remember how he contacted me. It was a long time ago.'

'Don't worry!' Samson holds up a sheet of paper, closely typed. 'I've got all your messages. *DrJackNHS*. That was your Twitter handle, wasn't it?'

'If you say so.'

'You deceived Scott into thinking he was talking to a doctor, a social media influencer, when in fact he was talking to you. Why did you do that?'

'I *am* a social media influencer, and I *was* Dr Jack. I didn't tell him because I wanted to support him in waking up to the Truth. I could do that best as Dr Jack.'

'Well, let's see how you supported him,' says Samson. 'I'm going to ask you about an exchange in January 2020. That's the day Scott showed your video about the HPV vaccine to his pupils, as a result of which he lost his job.'

'I don't see how this is relevant to Livia attacking me.'

'Neither do I, Your Honour,' protests Jane Randall.

Samson isn't remotely rattled. He explains that his line of questioning goes to credibility, and the judge agrees with him.

'So, Mr Tait,' he continues, 'Scott told Dr Jack—that's you—that the HPV booster was being rolled out at his school that day, that his own daughter was to have it. And you replied: *Hi, Scott. Is there any way you can stop this? You must save lives today—even if it costs you your job.* Why did you encourage your good friend to blow up his career?'

'I was just giving the best advice I could. That vaccine isn't safe.'

'Thanks to your "best advice", that was the very last day Scott Denby ever taught in a school. By lunchtime he'd been suspended. By the following night he'd left his wife and was sleeping on your sofa.'

Step by step, Samson builds up a picture of infiltration and manipulation. No matter how Anthony tries to deflect, tries to bluster and gaslight, the barrister drags him back to plain facts. Anthony can't handle it. Pretty soon he's throwing a tantrum, firing sarcastic questions back. He forgets his ruined voice and American accent, forgets to play the vulnerable victim. By the end he's shouting about how he studied medicine—*That's not true is it, Mr Tait?*—and we are all sheep who can't see that elites are taking over the world.

Samson lets him blow his top for a time before returning to the scene in the warehouse.

'Livia Denby spent that day in terror, fearing her family had been drowned in a murder–suicide. They'd been on the news—you saw it, didn't you?'

'Okay, I saw the news.'

'And she'd just learned that Noah was showing signs of acute oxygen starvation, was on the point of collapse and death.'

'So she claimed.' Anthony sounds sulky.

'Then why did you not simply tell her where they were?'

'My loyalty was to Scott. He'd given me their location in confidence.'

Maybe it's wishful thinking, but most of the jury seem to have the measure of Anthony. Man Bun folds his arms, his lips pursed. The woman in the dove-grey hijab is staring towards the witness box with a look of pure disgust.

'You were playing a nasty game with Scott Denby,' says Samson. 'You'd been playing it ever since his brother died. You were prepared to let his son die too, rather than give up your game.'

'That's bullshit. Livia came to my warehouse because her husband and kids were out of the way, and she was obsessed with me. She attacked me because I turned her down. I'm the one who ended up in hospital, I'm the one left disabled. How come I feel like I'm the one on trial here?'

Samson's looking puzzled, rocking gently back and forth on his heels. 'I can't help but notice, Mr Tait, that your damaged voice box seems to have recovered fully, just in the past twenty minutes. How is that?'

Silence from behind the screen. Some of the jury are smiling.

Samson gravely thanks the witness, and sits down.

•

The court breaks for lunch once Anthony's evidence is over. According to the usher, he storms straight out of the building, falling into the worshipping arms of the protestors outside. Scott leaves the courtroom too, slipping away before my little gaggle of supporters has noticed him.

'Incredible,' remarks Isaac Katz, as we push our way through the swinging doors into the lobby. 'Thousands of people still follow that grifter on social media.'

'D'you think he drinks his own Kool Aid, Isaac?' asks Bethany. 'Does he believe the hogwash he's peddling about the New World Order?'

'Only for as long as it suits him.'

'His evidence was one long lie from start to finish,' says Charles. 'No gaps between the lies. He even lied about lying. The jury weren't born yesterday, though. Did you see the way they were looking at him? Like he'd crawled out from under a stone.'

'What a knob,' says Jude.

The four of them are happily engrossed in dissecting Anthony's character as they head towards the cafeteria. But I hang back. I've seen a familiar figure waiting for me in the lobby. He looks as though he needs a hug. I don't give him one.

'Hello, stranger,' I say. 'Are those your friends outside with the placards? The ones who want to hang me?'

He has the grace to look ashamed. He seems to have aged since we separated: his hairline is receding, he doesn't hold himself so straight. But the most profound change in him isn't physical. A light has gone out. I don't know how else to describe it.

'Come and join us,' I say, taking his arm.

The others have set up camp at a table behind the vending machines, keeping a low profile in case of trouble from Anthony's groupies. Bethany's already bought me a cup of coffee and a cheese sandwich.

'The prodigal son!' she cries on noticing Scott. 'Glad you could make it.'

He's met Jude before, and I introduce him to Isaac and Charles.

Isaac immediately swings into action. 'Take a seat,' he says, removing his cloth mask and pulling out a chair next to himself. 'You can share my KitKat.'

'I'll get you a cuppa,' adds Charles.

They're offering Scott a new tribe, if only a temporary one. He seems shell-shocked, sitting between my two friends with an untouched cup of tea and finger of KitKat in front of him as the rest of us swap highlights of Anthony's evidence, chortling about the moment when he forgot his croaky whisper.

Isaac glances sideways at him. 'What were your impressions of Anthony's evidence, then, Scott?' he asks casually.

'My impressions?'

'Uh-huh.'

Scott squints down at the table. He's blinking continually, like a person waking up from a drugged sleep. 'He was lying.'

'Uh-huh.' Isaac pulls the tab on his Coke. 'How so?'

Ears are flapping around the table, though we're all looking at our phones or unwrapping sandwiches, pretending not to listen. Charles catches my eye and winks.

'He just . . . he just lied.' Scott glances up at me. 'There is no way on God's earth Livia would have tried to shag him in his warehouse. No way she tried to get his kit off. Not when Heidi had just phoned her in hysterics—not when she knew Noah was in danger—actually, not at all. Never. I may believe a lot of strange things, but I know Livia, and I'll *never* believe that.'

'Thanks,' I say. 'I'm glad there's something you don't think me capable of.'

'Funny thing is, he did the same when we were students. He hit on my girlfriend then claimed it was the other way around.' Scott frowns into his tea. 'Also . . . Dr Jack was meant to be the front for a whole Resistance cell. Dr Jack wasn't meant to be just Anthony. He never mentioned that once.'

'True,' says Isaac. 'I guess he didn't know you were in court, listening to him. You were hidden from him by his screen.'

Scott picks up his finger of KitKat and dunks it in his tea. Old habits die hard. We all watch as a film of chocolate spreads across the surface.

'I'm struggling to process what this means,' he says.

Isaac shrugs. 'No rush.'

FORTY-THREE

Livia

The next day and a half bring medical and police evidence. Some is agreed and read out, but Jane Randall calls a consultant to tell the jury about Anthony's injuries. He takes us through those sickening photographs, pointing out the signs of strangulation. He talks about the likelihood of brain damage or death from obstruction of the carotid artery and jugular vein.

'These injuries were consistent with the history of strangulation involving a ligature, in this case the cord of a lanyard,' Dr Cayman says. 'Internally, Mr Tait had suffered a significant tracheal rupture, that's to say a tear in the tracheal wall, measuring just over five centimetres. It required immediate surgical repair.'

He goes into unemotional but painful detail about this tear, its exact location and what was done during the surgery. Anthony was in intensive care for four days, in hospital for ten.

'How much force would it take to cause such a rupture?' asks Jane Randall.

'Well, there are variables, but I'd say it would take considerable force. This was not a half-hearted effort.'

Samson Gray manages to elicit his agreement that the surgery was entirely successful, that he's examined Anthony more recently and can point to no physical reason for him to have problems with his voice two years on. But still, the doctor's evidence is a low point. I look down at my two hands, wondering how they found the strength.

Rani Kumar does her best for me. She fills in the background on the children's disappearance, the discovery of our car in the sea. She confirms that I phoned her at around six thirty pm on 24 March 2020, desperate for help.

'Livia Denby gave a lot of information in a very short time,' she says, 'as a result of which I understood that Noah was in a life-threatening condition and that Anthony Tait might also be. She requested an ambulance to be waiting in a concealed position near Whitby marina and assistance to be dispatched to Mr Tait's workplace at 17 Canal End, Guisborough.'

I've watched a few cross-examinations over the years. Some advocates ask ten questions where one would do. Samson Gray isn't one of them.

'It sounds as though Livia Denby went to great lengths to ensure that Anthony Tait had all the help he needed, as soon as possible,' he observes.

Rani's nodding before he's finished his sentence. Bless her.

'I'd agree with that. She was on her way to Whitby, in a state of extreme anxiety about Noah, but she repeated several times that Mr Tait's condition may also be critical. She left his keys at the entrance door. She gave detailed directions, so that first responders would find him quickly once they entered the warehouse.'

'And as a result . . .?'

'As a result, we were able to get a patrol car to his location in six minutes, and an ambulance in under twenty.'

Samson leaves a few moments for this answer to sink in, then asks, 'Was her behaviour consistent with that of someone who wanted him to die of his injuries?'

'No. Quite the opposite.'

'That's very helpful.' A charming smile as Samson sits down. 'Thank you, Sergeant Kumar.'

•

My support team are here again today, including Scott. He's quiet and awkward, but he's here. At lunchtime, Isaac Katz announces that he's walking down to the post office. He has a parcel to post for his newborn niece in Israel.

'Coming, Scott?' he asks. 'It's only five minutes away. Bit of fresh air and sunshine.'

I watch them leave by the main doors, deep in conversation. Scott's gesticulating with one hand. He looks like a normal guy. I could easily imagine he's the man I loved.

'Would you have him back?' asks Charles, who's standing beside me. 'If he saw he's been hoodwinked, if he left all the craziness behind?'

There's the question. We're not divorced yet, but we've now been separated for two years so I can serve a petition any time.

'Some things are hard to forgive,' I say.

Charles is still looking at the two men, chatting away as they cross the plaza.

'If a person's not well, and they do some strange things because of that, you wouldn't hold it against them.'

'Maybe not, but you don't have to let them back into your life.'

Charles sighs. 'True.'

'We'll always be friends. He'll always be the children's father.'

We turn towards the cafeteria, where Bethany and Jude have bagged our usual table.

'Anyway,' I remind him, 'I could be in prison by this time next week.'

'You won't be.'

'I might be.'

He pats my shoulder. 'I'll visit you. Be like old times.'

•

In the afternoon, DI Bassett and Jane Randall perform a little double act, reading an agreed version of the transcript of my police interview. The detective plays himself, the barrister plays me. The jury follow along with their own copies. It's the first time they've heard my side of the story, in my own words. I listen on tenterhooks, wondering what they're making of it.

It was a long interview. The pair run through the transcript at a brisk trot, reading clearly but with almost no expression. It's surreal to hear my words spoken by the woman whose job it is to present the case against me. I'm sure she slows down when she comes to my final question. Perhaps it's not deliberate, but I'm grateful.

Just a question. What would you have done, in my shoes? Are you really suggesting I should have let my son die?

•

Judge Fazakerley wants to canvas the views of both counsel, to ensure everyone's on the same page with the legal directions she proposes to give the jury because—as she puts it—this is 'something of a judicial minefield'.

So the jury get to leave early today, while she and the two barristers kick around concepts like intent, and duress of circumstances. Both Samson and Jane Randall have already prepared skeleton arguments. They're just three legal nerds, I realise, as I listen to them citing cases about shipwrecked sailors who claimed they had no choice but to kill and eat the cabin boy, and a man who drove while disqualified because his wife threatened suicide if he did not, and a tragic case about conjoined twins. They love this stuff. Perhaps I would too if I wasn't sitting in this dock, my stomach knotting as I imagine the children's future without me—Noah heartbroken, Heidi trying to be both mother and sister to him. She's already had to do far too much of that.

Finally the judge grants me bail overnight, and every night until she orders otherwise. The Crown has closed its case. First thing tomorrow, I'll be telling my story.

'Try to get a good night's sleep,' advises Samson Gray, who's rushing back to his chambers to meet some other defendant. 'You want to be bright-eyed and bushy-tailed in the morning.'

My chances of that would be slim, I think, but it's wonderful the capacity people have for optimism, for making the most of precious pockets of time. We have a raucous, laughter-filled evening—Mum, Dad, Bethany, Noah, Heidi and me. I'm loud and jolly and false, trying to drown out the fear. But while I'm reading to him at bedtime, Noah snuggles as close to me as he possibly can. He isn't fooled.

Once he's asleep, I slip into my bedroom to begin packing. I know what I may be allowed to keep, the things that might make life easier. Slip-on shoes—no laces. Flip-flops for the showers. Toiletries, underwear and socks. A towel, a hairbrush, scrunchies. Ear plugs. Paper, envelopes, stamps.

Heidi catches me in the act, just as I'm about to shove everything into a reusable shopping bag.

'What are you doing?' she asks.

'Doesn't hurt to be organised.'

She stands with one hand across her mouth, glaring at my grim little hoard of essentials.

'This is bullshit. You did it to save Noah's life! How can they take you away from him?'

I pick up my hairbrush from the pile, sit down on the bed, and pat the space beside me. When she sits, I begin to brush her hair.

It's as long and sumptuous as ever, coils and twists of copper all the way to her waist.

'I wish I answered when Nicky rang,' she mutters. 'I wish I could go back in time.'

'Shh, Heidi.' I keep running the brush through her hair. 'A million decisions have been made along the track. By me, by Dad, Anthony, the police, the Crown Prosecution Service, by lots of people we've never even met. A million random events have led us here, including a pandemic. It's time to forgive your thirteenth-birthday self. That little girl isn't to blame for anything at all.'

She lifts her hand to touch mine. 'Thanks, Mum.'

'I just want to be ready,' I tell her, as I untangle a knot. 'Just in case. It'll make me feel better, make me feel I've a bit of control. Will you help me? There are two things I still need: a photo album with all of us, and a book.'

'What book?'

'Any book. Whatever you think might keep me company.'

●

When I turn in that night, I find two presents on my pillow.

First an album, brimming with memories. I leaf through the first few pages: Noah and Scott making a carrot-nosed snowman in our front garden; Heidi and Noah playing in the heather; Scott and me sitting on a train, my head resting against his shoulder. Such love in our family. No wonder Anthony was jealous.

The second gift is just as precious. Heidi's copy of *Anne of Green Gables*, with her handwriting on the title page:

Dear Mum,
Green Gables is my happy place. I hope it can be yours too.
I love you more than words can say.
XXXXX Heidi XXXXX

FORTY-FOUR

Livia

Jane Randall is raring to go, leaping up like a jack-in-the-box once my evidence-in-chief is over.

'Mrs Denby,' she begins genially, 'you've told us that you never intended to kill Anthony Tait, despite putting your lanyard across his throat and yanking on it.'

I'd been over and over my own motivations a hundred times last night, in the sleepless early hours.

'I didn't intend to kill him. If he died, I lost my chance of saving Noah.'

She leaves a pause, which makes me nervous. I've stood in a witness box often before, but never to give evidence in my own defence.

'You're a very experienced probation officer.'

'That's right.'

'You've spent your adult life working in the criminal justice system.'

'Yes. More than twenty years.'

'That's a long time. Have you come across cases of fatal strangulation in that time?'

'Of course. It's depressingly familiar in domestic violence situations. Strangulation is a common cause of death where the victim's a woman, the perpetrator a man.'

She throws a mischievous glance towards the public gallery. 'And cases of garrotting, specifically? An attack from behind, on a seated victim, using a ligature? A belt, for instance?'

Ah. I should have seen this coming. I'm disconcerted, but I keep my poker face.

'Yes. Most recently in 2018, I met an offender serving a life sentence for murder. I was his supervising officer upon his release on licence. I continued to be his supervising officer during the early part of 2020.'

She's nodding. 'Charles Shepherd, who garrotted a man with a belt.'

'Yes.'

'Is that what gave you the idea, as you stood behind Anthony Tait's chair?'

Samson Gray has had enough. He's harrumphing as he hauls himself to his feet. 'Your Honour, really. I'm astonished by this line of questioning. Is my learned friend seriously suggesting that Mrs Denby used her distinguished career as a kind of training ground? If so, half the criminal bar might as well crowd into that dock.'

It's a rare, light moment. Judge Fazakerley smiles. A chuckle runs around the courtroom.

Jane Randall stands her ground. 'This goes to the question of intent. I'm trying to establish whether Mrs Denby was aware of the likely consequences of using a ligature on someone's throat.'

'You're skating on thin ice, Miss Randall,' says the judge. 'Move on.'

But the damage is done. I notice Man Bun jotting something down, and I bet it's the name Charles Shepherd. Although the jury have been warned—endlessly and sternly—that they're not to do their own research, some of them are bound to go home tonight and do a bit of googling. Then they'll begin to speculate. Better to tackle the question head on than seem to be avoiding it.

'I'm happy to answer,' I say. 'Of course I've come across cases of strangulation, including the one you mentioned. But my inter-action with Charles Shepherd had nothing to do with the details of his offence. It was all about managing his future, a man of nearly seventy being released after decades in prison. I wasn't thinking about my work when I pulled that lanyard out of my pocket. I was thinking about my dying son.'

The next hour is gruelling. We cover a lot of ground. Jane Randall asks about the amount of force I used and why I didn't let up, even after it was obvious that Anthony was seriously injured—and how long the whole thing took, and what I said to Anthony before and while I was assaulting him, and why I even went to his warehouse, after I'd been advised to stay at home. Why did I have the lanyard in my pocket in the first place—did I bring it as a weapon? She makes hay with New Year's Eve, when I vowed to throttle Dr Jack if ever I got my hands on him. She doesn't dwell on Anthony's fantasy about my wanting to screw him on his warehouse table—a wise move on her part, since even she doesn't seem to believe it.

'You didn't let on that you knew he was Dr Jack. You didn't warn him of that before you assaulted him.'

'No.'

'Why not? He was playing a silly game, and the game was up. Why not confront him with it and ask him where your family were?'

'I was certain that he wouldn't tell me. He would carry on playing that game until it was too late. And if he'd known I was on to him, he could easily have overpowered me.'

'He'd never been remotely violent towards you, had he?'

'No.'

'You'd never seen him behaving violently or aggressively in any way?'

'No.'

'So what on earth made you think he might be violent now?'

'I'd just discovered that he wasn't the person I thought. He was living a double life, he'd set out to wreck my family. I had no idea how he might react if I confronted him.'

She raises her eyebrows, glances at the jury as though to say, *Can you believe this woman?*

'A double life. You've described the moment when you worked out that Anthony Tait and Dr Jack were one and the same person.'

'That's right.'

'Which meant that Anthony had engineered all your troubles. Anthony had caused the breakdown of your marriage.'

'Partly him, yes.'

'He knew where Scott was hiding your children, but he failed to tell you, even after your car was found in the sea, even when he knew Noah was having an asthma attack.'

'That's all true.'

'And you lost your temper.'

'I was angry—but mostly I was frightened, mainly for Noah but also for myself. Nobody knew I was in that building, and Anthony had just grabbed me in a very invasive way. I felt extremely vulnerable.'

She holds out her arms. '*Extremely vulnerable!* This man who has never, to your knowledge, been violent. Why not simply leave, then? Why not go out to your car and phone the police—just as you did a few minutes later?'

'There wasn't time. There really wasn't.'

'You had Sergeant Kumar's direct number. You'd spoken to her many times that day. You knew she would answer.'

'Imagine how long it would take for her to understand the significance of Anthony's being Dr Jack, send someone to speak to him, track him down, get any information out of him. It would have taken hours. Noah had minutes.'

Jane Randall takes hold of the lapels of her gown, pulls it forward on her shoulders. She's winding up to her finale.

'The fact is, Mrs Denby, you were in a rage. You knew he wasn't going to get his comeuppance from the criminal justice system. So instead of calling the police, you doled out your own retribution.'

'This had nothing to do with retribution. I only had one shot at saving Noah, and I couldn't afford to fail.'

'You were a one-woman lynch mob.'

The jury are watching, listening, frowning. They've heard the surgeon who treated Anthony. They've seen the stomach-turning photographs of my handiwork.

'I had no choice,' I tell them.

I'm not sure they believe me.

FORTY-FIVE

Heidi

The night before giving evidence, I read my statement about ten times. Mum helps me decide what to wear. We choose my green maxi skirt and white T-shirt, with a blazer. Grandma Polly irons everything for me, including my polka-dot mask, which is the least ugly one I own.

'You look cool, calm and collected,' says Bethany, as Mum and I get into her car the next morning. 'You're not nervous?'

'Nope.'

This is a total lie. I'm doubled over with nerves. Ages ago, Sandra Webb offered me the chance to give evidence by video link. I said no, that I'd be fine. Now I'm not so sure. I feel like I'm about to take a music exam, except the consequences of cocking it up are a million times worse.

As soon as we reach the court building I have to rush to the toilets. When I come out again, Mum's gone into a room to talk to her barrister, but Dad's here. An usher shows us into Court One so I can see what it all looks like—big, modern and daunting.

'Nervous?' asks Dad.

'Nope,' I say, even though I can hardly breathe.

We sit in the lobby. People are starting to wander into our court—lawyers, police, random folk who might be anti-Mum protestors, others who might be reporters. I recognise Jude, Charles Shepherd and Isaac Katz.

Mum turns up with her barrister, Mr Gray.

'Hi, Heidi,' he says. 'I'm only allowed to introduce myself—I can't talk about your evidence at all until you're in the witness box. Are you ready?'

'Hope so.'

'Good lass. Would you like me to ask the judge if we can take off our wigs and gowns? You'd be one of the few people ever to see what Judge Fazakerley looks like without hers. Rumour has it, she was born wearing a judge's wig.'

He's trying to be jolly. It's nice of him.

'Thanks,' I say. 'But I think I'd prefer you to keep them on. I don't want my evidence to seem less important than anyone else's.'

'Fair enough.'

'You'll be great, Heidi,' says Mum, as she and Mr Gray head into court. 'Just tell the truth.'

I'm left waiting in the lobby with Dad and Bethany for company. Suyin and Flynn have both been messaging all morning, sending GIFs to cheer me up. I'm replying to them when the usher calls my name. All of a sudden, I feel sick. I'd like to sprint back to the toilet. Too late now.

How did the courtroom get so crowded? The judge up top, the clerk, the barristers, Sergeant Kumar and assorted others. The jury in two rows of six. Mum's sitting in the dock with a guard beside her. She's wearing simple clothes: black trousers and a jersey, her hair scraped into a plait.

I feel dozens of pairs of eyes on me as I walk into the witness box, taking off my mask. I tell the usher I want to affirm, not swear on the Bible. My voice sounds breathy and babyish when I read out the words on the card.

Mr Gray starts by asking easy questions about my family. It's a good warm-up; it helps me to calm down. Then I have to tell the *Dixieland* story, beginning with Dad giving me the secret burner phone. Eventually we reach the afternoon of the second day, when we realised Noah was having a major flare-up. 'Normally we'd be giving him his reliever inhaler and either calling an ambulance or driving him straight to hospital.'

'Why did you not do either of those things this time?'

'Because Dad was sure they'd murder Noah. I suggested we at least phone Mum and ask her to drive out to Whitby with the flare-up kit I'd forgotten to pack.'

'And did he agree to that?'

'No! He reckoned evil people were tracking her phone, that as soon as we called her they'd come and get us and'—I shrugged—'kill us all. Make us disappear.'

'Kill you all.' Mr Gray looks rather sad. 'Did you believe that, Heidi?'

'Not really.'

'And how was your dad, at this time?'

'He was beside himself. He tried to hide it, but he's got this thing he does when he's anxious where he can't stop fidgeting. He texted Dr Jack to ask for medical advice, and Dr Jack started sending all these suggestions. Things like getting Noah to sip strong black coffee. He even had us making tea from cow parsley. Apparently coffee and cow parsley were going to open Noah's airways.'

I don't even try to keep the anger out of my voice, though I know Dad's sitting in the courtroom listening to all this. Good! It's time for him to shut up and listen. It's time he faced up to what he did to Noah and me. I love my dad, but I can't forgive him for not being the adult on that boat. In fact, as I've grown older, I've understood more just how shitty and crazy it all was. Mum's going to divorce him, and I don't blame her.

'Now, it's no secret,' says Mr Gray, 'that "Dr Jack" was in fact Anthony Tait. But at the time all this was going on, who did you believe him to be?'

'Dr Jack? Just some influencer. I'd watched some of his videos, so at one time I thought he might really be a doctor. But when he started sending these stupid ideas about coffee and cow parsley and using the preventer inhaler—which is hopeless, you need the reliever—I knew for sure he wasn't a doctor. A real doctor would have said, *For God's sake, get that child to a hospital*. I kept pleading with Dad to call an ambulance.'

'What did he say, when you pleaded with him?'

'He said we might as well sign Noah's death warrant. I told him we were signing it anyway.'

I risk a quick look at the jury. Every one of them is staring at me. I recognise some of them from Mum's descriptions. There's the guy with a little goatee beard, hair in a bun. The Dancer, with her blue glasses. The kind-looking woman in a hijab. And in the back row, second from the right, the grumpy guy Mum calls Mr Darcy: beetling eyebrows, always frowning.

'What was your dad doing all this time?' asks Mr Gray.

'Panicking. Just panicking. Texting Dr Jack again and again. Taking Noah's pulse. Making more black coffee, more cow parsley water, trying to make Noah drink them. Putting the kettle near him so he could breathe in the steam. But none of it was working. And the worst thing was that Noah was so scared . . .' I feel a sob coming. 'I don't even believe in God but I was praying. I love Noah so much and I knew he was going to . . .'

I lose it before I get to the word 'die'. The usher fills up my water glass, offers tissues from a box.

The judge looks sympathetic. 'Would you like to take a short break, Heidi?'

'Thanks. I'd rather go on. Sorry.'

I take a deep breath.

'By this time it was getting on for evening. I don't know exactly what time, but there was pink in the sky so . . . maybe about six? Noah had been fighting for hours and he was giving up, he was exhausted. He'd gone floppy and his skin looked strange.'

'Strange?' asks Mr Gray.

I close my eyes, trying to remember those horrific moments. 'Grey, but almost see-through. I knew that meant he wasn't getting enough oxygen. I was'—I swallow, open my eyes—'I was literally watching him die.'

Such a silence. All those people, and not a single movement.

'My dad was letting my brother die.' I'd never said it aloud. 'And all because of a stupid fairytale he'd heard on the internet. I couldn't let that happen.'

'What did you do?'

'I said I was going to the toilet, then I jumped onto the river-bank and phoned Mum.'

'Did she answer?'

'Yes! Straight away.'

'What did you say to her?'

'I told her about Noah. I made a stupid mistake, though— I should've started by letting her know where we were. I was in a state, and I thought I'd have time to tell her.'

'But you didn't get time?'

'No. Dad heard me talking to her and came flying off the boat. He thought secret agents would be listening in on the call, so he grabbed the phone out of my hand and threw it into the river.'

'How did you react to that?'

'I was screaming at him. Calling Mum was my last hope, just hearing her voice meant so much. But Noah needed us so we went back below, and Dad started looking in an old map book.'

'A map book?' Mr Gray glanced at the jury as though he couldn't believe his ears.

'He was searching for a new hiding place, because they'd be coming for us now. I was holding Noah in my arms and comforting him as best I could. I was dreading the moment when he died, which I was sure would be soon. But then Dad looked at his phone and jumped up and said that Dr Jack had come through for him. We were to go to the marina, and a doctor would meet us there.'

'How did that feel?'

'Like a miracle. Dad steered, I stayed down below with Noah. I kept telling him to hold on, keep fighting, keep breathing.'

Normally I try not to think about these details. I can't block out the memory of how scared I was, though—that's with me all the time, as clear as if it were yesterday. I remember how Noah's breathing got quieter, but not in a good way, and how his body felt both taut and lifeless.

'We got to the marina—it was pretty dark by then—and a car came screaming off the road like a racing driver was at the wheel. Dad and I were in the headlights, so it took a second for me to see who it was.'

'And who was it?'

I look over at her, sitting in the dock, and smile. 'It was Mum.'

Then I'm off again. Tears streaming down my face. Lucky I've got the tissues.

'She had an ambulance waiting around the corner. So it was a miracle, after all.'

'Did you go too?'

'No. I stayed with Dad. The police had a word with him, and then he drove me home. I remember us watching the blue ambulance lights disappearing up the road. We were both in pieces; we thought we'd never Noah again.'

'But you did see him again!'

'We did.'

'How's he doing?'

'He's eight now, and cheeky as ever.' I hold up both hands, with my fingers crossed. 'I hope he never comes that close again.'

Mr Gray gives me a little bow. 'Thank you, Heidi.'

The other barrister is half standing, shaking her head. 'I've no questions.'

I didn't expect my evidence to be over so suddenly. I've not quite finished.

'Could I just say something else?' I ask the judge, and she nods.

'Thanks. Okay.' I do another inhale-exhale. I mustn't mess this up. 'I know what asthma flare-ups look like—I've seen lots of them. I've always known how to spot the first signs, how to use reliever medicines and when it's time to get Noah to a hospital. And I'm telling you that he was dying on that boat. He was six years old, and Anthony Tait was letting him suffer, letting him die. His own *dad* was letting him die.'

I swing around in the witness box, searching for Dad. He's hunched over with a hand covering his face.

'You were, Dad!' I tell him. 'I know it was because of all your beliefs and fears. I know you love Noah. But the fact is, you were going to let him die. He'd be dead and buried now, if it wasn't for Mum.'

I don't wait to see his reaction. I turn back to Mr Gray, to the jury.

'My brother is only alive today because of what Mum did. That's a fact. You should be pinning a medal on her, not threatening to throw her in prison.'

I've no more to say. I'm done. The judge is thanking me, saying I can leave. As I stumble out, I hear Mr Gray telling her that I was his last witness.

'That's the case for the defence,' he says.

I just hope I was good enough.

•

It's a relief to have got it over with, but I feel dizzy and weak when I leave the courtroom. I think it's the adrenaline wearing off. I keep thinking of things I forgot to say. I flop into a quiet seat in a corner of the lobby and start texting Flynn to let him know I've survived.

All of a sudden, the doors to Court One bang open and Dad barges out. As soon as he spots me he rushes over and sits next to me, throwing his arms around me. He looks as though he's been crying.

'Did I do okay?' I ask.

'You're worth a million of me,' he says. 'I owe you everything. I'm so sorry . . . I'm so sorry.'

He's holding on to me as though he's drowning. And I think perhaps he is.

FORTY-SIX

Livia

Towards the end of her closing speech, Jane Randall tackles the elephant in the room.

'Anthony Tait . . .' She pauses, peering at the jury. 'Now, you may have mixed feelings about him. You may have been disturbed by his inventing the character of Dr Jack and deceiving the Denby family for so long—Scott in particular. You may be shocked that he did nothing to help Noah, aside from googling home remedies for asthma. You may feel that he wasn't completely honest with you about aspects of his own behaviour. But you do not have to like him. He, along with every other witness who ever stands in that box, deserves to have his evidence evaluated fairly.'

Some of the twelve are looking cynical, I think. I *hope*. The Dancer pointedly raises her eyebrows. Man Bun seems to be suppressing a smirk.

Jane Randall moves on. 'You cannot find Livia Denby guilty of attempted murder unless you are sure that she intended to kill him. You'll hear directions from Her Honour about exactly what "intended" means in this context, but really, it is common sense. You've heard from Dr Cayman about the considerable force it must have taken to inflict those injuries. In his words: *This was not a half-hearted effort.* You heard Livia Denby's admission that as an experienced probation officer she was no stranger to the reality of deaths by strangulation. You can be sure that when she crept up behind Anthony Tait, flicked her lanyard across his throat, pulled it hard enough to rupture his trachea and—despite his struggles— held it there until he passed out, she knew exactly what she was doing. You can be sure that she intended to kill him.'

They're bound to convict me. Hell, *I'd* convict me. I can still feel the madness, the exhilarating rush of hatred and power as I yanked on that lanyard. *For once in my life I'm not going to count to fucking ten.*

As her coup de grâce, Jane Randall gets the jury to take another look at those high-resolution photos of Anthony's ravaged throat.

'Remember what Livia Denby said at that New Year's Eve party—perhaps the very last words she uttered in 2019? *If I ever get my hands on Dr Jack, I swear I'll throttle him.*'

The barrister eyes the jury, making a *gotcha* face.

'Well. She *did* get her hands on Dr Jack—and she kept her promise.'

The Dancer, who has been polishing her blue glasses as she listens, nods and takes a note.

●

Samson Gray stands up, thinks for a long moment. When he begins to speak, his tone is reflective, intimate, as though they're all chatting by the fireside in a country pub.

'What an extraordinary story we have heard these past days. We all remember the very first day of lockdown, don't we? We've all got our pandemic memories. But on the tranquil waters of the River Esk near Whitby, and in an industrial estate in Guisborough, a near-tragedy was playing out. What are we to make of all we've seen and heard?'

Samson is a storyteller. Over the next half-hour he takes the jury by the hand and leads them through the evidence, showing them precisely how they can acquit me on each count. Towards the end, he begins to draw it all together.

'You've seen Anthony Tait, aka Dr Jack: six foot tall and a big physical presence, broad, heavy. Also deeply dishonest, deeply manipulative, a man who plays dangerous games. He set out to destroy the Denby family, people who thought he was their friend. You've seen for yourselves that he flies into a temper when challenged. You've seen the petite Livia Denby, who found herself alone with him—alone in that small room, in a deserted industrial building—at the very moment when she discovered his true identity. He claims that she tried to seduce him in his warehouse—this devoted mother, who'd just learned that her six-year-old son was close to death. He claims that she assaulted him because he turned her down.' Samson shakes his head with a weary smile. 'Oh dear. If you believe that, members of the jury, you will believe anything.'

The jury don't smile back. Mr Darcy's looking thunderous. I don't think he likes me at all.

'Miss Randall says you can be sure that Livia Denby intended to kill Anthony Tait. Well, let's think about that. She had every opportunity to finish the job—by his own account, he was at one stage unconscious, incapacitated. But far from killing him, she went to great lengths to make sure he survived. Within seconds of leaving his warehouse she was on the phone to Sergeant Kumar, arranging an ambulance. She left keys and gave directions for his rescuers. All of this, while she herself was speeding to Whitby to save Noah. Are these the actions of someone who intended to kill him? No. The *last* thing Livia Denby wanted, when she put that lanyard to his throat, was the death of Anthony Tait. As she told you: if he died in that chair, Noah would die too. She would never find her family in time.'

He ends with Heidi's evidence, touching lightly on the most unbearable parts. He quotes her last words:

'*My brother is only alive today because of what Mum did. That's a fact. You should be pinning a medal on her, not threatening to throw her in prison.*'

Samson pauses, stands for a moment as though he's lost in thought, doing that rocking-back-and-forth-on-his-heels thing.

'You might think Heidi deserves a medal herself. And she was absolutely right: Noah is alive today because of what his mum did. Livia Denby had one chance to save her son. Just one chance. It was dangerous, it was difficult; but she took that chance, and she saved Noah's life. She had no choice.'

FORTY-SEVEN

'If they so much as look at you,' Charles assures me, 'you're in with a chance. If they look right at you and smile, they're definitely going to let you off. I've got a good feeling about this.'

He and I are back in the court cafeteria, loading a plastic tray with the condemned woman's last cup of tea. The judge's summing-up took most of yesterday afternoon—meticulous directions on all the relevant law, a recap of each witness. She gave the jury a series of printed questions; a kind of flow chart, guiding them down alternative pathways towards verdicts, depending on what they make of the evidence.

Finally, first thing this morning, she sent them out to begin considering their verdict.

I feel as though I'm floating outside my body. I can't focus. Last night, after we'd read together, I lay down beside Noah and cuddled him, told him how much I loved him. Then I went for a long walk with Heidi. We talked about her future, about what A-levels she might choose. She said she loved Flynn, but in the autumn he'd be leaving for university. 'And long-distance doesn't work, so we'll have to decide what to do.'

'You'll be okay,' I said, taking her arm as we strolled along. I didn't want to let go, not ever, ever, *ever*. 'Whatever happens tomorrow, don't let it derail you.'

At three o'clock this morning I wrote a long list of things Mum and Dad need to know if they're to be left in charge. I took off my wedding and engagement rings, my watch and earrings, the two bangles I always wore—gifts from Scott, when Heidi and Noah were born. Mum cried when she understood why I was giving them into her safekeeping.

'And what if the jury refuse point-blank to look at me?' I ask Charles now.

'Well . . .' He waggles his head. 'Some people reckon if a jury won't meet your eye, you're going down the pan.'

'Some of them can't seem to *stop* looking at me. I reckon they're expecting to see horns and a tail.'

We head for our favoured table behind the vending machines. The others are already there: Bethany, Heidi, Scott and Isaac Katz. Jude's husband—Bill, with the emphysema—has Covid. She's isolating at home with him, waiting for my news.

Samson Gray has other cases today, in other courtrooms. He's warned me to prepare for a long, nerve-shredding wait. The jury has a lot to think about, none of it straightforward. There might be no verdict for a couple of days, and he wouldn't expect a majority direction until Monday at the very earliest. Heidi pulls her chair close and leans against me, gripping my arm, as the awful minutes pass.

Scott, Isaac and Charles are chatting like old friends. Scott couldn't be in better company. Isaac's trying to persuade him to move up to Leeds, on the basis that he won't want to live in a caravan forever.

'My sister's looking for a lodger. Shall I call her? She runs a language school, she might be able to line up a bit of teaching work for you.'

We're jumping every time we hear an announcement over the tannoy, especially when Court One is mentioned—which happens constantly because Judge Fazakerley has a busy list while my jury are out. At one o'clock she sends a message that she'll take no verdict before two.

More cups of tea. More hours crawling by. The cafeteria staff are packing up, the court building begins to empty. At three forty-five, Samson joins our anxious huddle. He's removed his wig and gown, but still wears the white bands and stick-up collar.

'Doesn't look like we'll be getting a verdict today,' he says, then freezes, holding up a finger. We all listen to the announcement over the tannoy.

'The jury in Court One have reached a verdict, and are returning to court.'

•

'Would the foreperson please stand?'

The Dancer gets to her feet. Of course it's her.

My own legs are rubber, my knees literally knocking together. There's no air in my lungs. I grab at the rail of the dock, clinging on for dear life.

Heidi and Scott sit pressed together, clutching one another's hands. Heidi's face is ashen. I catch her eye and force a smile. I'm trying to let her know that I'll be okay. Whatever happens now, I'll be okay. She has her life to live.

The clerk faces The Dancer. 'Has the jury reached verdicts upon which you are all agreed?'

'We have.'

If they won't meet your eye, you're going down the pan.

Samson's promised to come and see me down in the cells. I've asked him not to apply for bail while I wait to be sentenced; I don't want to say goodbye to the family again. I have my shopping bag of essentials at my feet. It all seemed to happen so suddenly in the end. Just that tannoy announcement, and we were hurrying back into court. I barely had time to hug Heidi before the dock officer opened his gate, let me in, and then locked it behind me.

Three security guards have been deployed in case of trouble. Two of them are positioned at the back of the room, near where I sit in the dock. It's me they're protecting. Anthony's supporters glare balefully from the public gallery. One of them draws his finger across his throat as he stares at me.

'On count one,' begins the clerk, 'attempted murder, do you find the defendant guilty or not guilty?'

Time stops. The last domino has been nudged. It hangs suspended, quavering, still undecided.

The Dancer flicks an almost imperceptible glance towards the dock, just long enough to meet my gaze. For the first time, I notice that her eyes perfectly match the frames of her glasses.

Then—just a tug at the corner of those vivid blue eyes—she smiles, and my life begins again.

•

To call the reaction pandemonium would be an understatement.

Not guilty on all three counts. You can see the weight lifting off the jurors' shoulders. Gasps and shouts from the public gallery— of pure rage, of pure joy. Several protestors hurl obscenities as they storm out, deliberately banging the doors. My supporters are on their feet, throwing their arms around one another. Heidi's jumping up and down. And Scott—Scott's whole face is alight. I've not seen him smile like that since we lost Nicky.

The burly security guards stand with legs akimbo, making it clear that pitch invasions won't end well. At a word from the judge, the dock officer, grinning from ear to ear, opens the gate to free me.

I can't move fast enough. Only a few steps, just into the well of the court, but it feels like another world.

If this were television drama, Judge Fazakerley would be banging a gavel. Instead, she uses sheer force of personality, insisting on *absolute* quiet before thanking the jury for their service, for the care they've given a difficult case.

As the twelve file towards their exit, I mouth my own thanks. The Dancer smiles again. The woman in the hijab dips her head, Man Bun gives a discreet thumbs-up. Mr Darcy astonishes me by waving exuberantly. One or two seem more grudging, perhaps remembering the raw ligature marks on Anthony's neck, perhaps suspecting—correctly—that it took pure rage for me to do that to another human being.

These randomly chosen strangers have held my life in their hands. I'll be grateful forever.

•

Once the judge has gone, I hurry over to Samson—he's packing up his laptop, chatting with Jane Randall. She nods cordially to me as she leaves.

'Congratulations, Livia!' Samson cries, throwing his wig into the air and catching it. 'I never doubted our jury for a second.'

'Thank you. Thank you.' I'm shaking his hand too vigorously, as if I'm drunk. He doesn't seem to mind.

While Samson heads off to the robing room, the security guards guide my euphoric little group out of the building through a back entrance to avoid the crowd of angry protestors waiting outside. Rani Kumar tags along, escorting us all the way to the car park. Her shift ended long ago, but she stayed for us.

The cloud cover has broken into wispy trails, leaving a washed sky. The light is thin and sharp and glorious. I'm still carrying my prison-ready bag, but I'm floating, floating. My head isn't just light, it's a helium-filled balloon. Tomorrow a reaction will set in, real-life problems will have to be faced. I have no idea whether I'll go back to my old career, or start something new—I haven't dared to look beyond this verdict. Right now, my feet aren't touching the ground.

As we walk, I text Jude with the good news. Bethany's calling Mum and Dad, while Isaac phones Simon. Heidi sends several beaming selfies to Flynn.

'Who're you calling, Charles?' I ask, seeing him with his phone to his ear.

'Carol at the cafe. She's been demanding daily updates.' He skips across a puddle like a child. 'Hi, love! Not guilty on all three! Yes, it's fantastic, she's over the moon.'

Scott's the odd man out. He doesn't contact anybody. I suppose his friends will be outraged. NO WHITEWASH FOR THE WHITE WITCH.

As I float along, I realise Rani Kumar has fallen into step beside me.

'Bit of news just in, Livia,' she says quietly. 'Anthony Tait got off a plane at Los Angeles airport this morning, and was promptly arrested.'

I stop dead in my tracks. Perhaps the whole day's been a dream—any minute now, I'm going to wake up and find myself facing prison all over again.

'Anthony's been arrested? For what?'

'Fraud.' We begin to walk again. 'Anthony is Dr Jack. Anthony is also . . . drumroll please . . . Father Gabriel Murphy. A Catholic priest, who appeared on the US conspiracist scene in April 2020. And unlike Dr Jack, who was in it for power, Father Gabriel was keen on fundraising.'

'How did he do that?'

'By scamming American pensioners. Loads of elderly people were isolated in the early Covid days, spending too much time alone and online, which meant they were more easily cheated out of their savings. The wolves moved in. Anthony Tait was one of them. Always the opportunist! He's been raking in donations to a little band of heroes called "Gabriel's Army". Father Gabriel is a former Navy SEAL turned priest. He leads this team, rescuing trafficked children kept as sex slaves in crypts under churches in Californian cities. It's all a lie, obviously. Most of those churches don't even have crypts.'

'For heaven's sake!' I smack my forehead with my palm. 'And no army, of course?'

'Nope. Just Anthony. A keyboard warrior, sitting on a sofa in Guisborough. But I'll say this for the guy: he's versatile. They reckon he made tens of thousands of dollars. Bought a flasher car, holidays, got a nicer flat. Shame he didn't put his talents to better use.'

So tonight I am free, while Dr Jack is not. I'm sure Anthony will find a way to spin his arrest as the work of dark forces, of totalitarian tyranny. This new martyrdom will probably gain him followers, not lose them. But he isn't my problem anymore. He's not going to live rent-free in my head.

'I can't thank you enough, Rani,' I say. 'For everything. Especially for that ambulance waiting for us in Whitby.'

People reel and stagger when they step off rollercoaster rides. Adrenaline levels have been high for so long, and the fear has lifted so suddenly. Nobody's quite ready to leave. For a while we stand around debriefing, freezing cold but happily bewildered in the slanting rays of the setting winter sun, our dancing shadows stretching far across the potholed asphalt of the car park, making us into giants.

But at last we part company. Rani's heading home. Charles has a lift back to Middlesbrough. Bethany and Heidi have piled into Bethany's car, turning on the engine to defrost their feet. Isaac is taking Scott to have a look at his sister's place in Leeds.

'Strike while the iron's hot,' Isaac mutters, when I thank him. 'There's a long way to go, but he's made a start. Such a nice guy.'

As Isaac begins to walk away towards the station, Scott hangs back to speak to me.

'I don't know where to begin . . .' he says.

'It's okay.'

'No! No, it's not okay. I feel like there are cracks opening up under my feet, cracks in my reality. I might fall through. I don't know what I believe now. I don't know which way up anything goes, or who can be trusted, or whether there's a plan, or whether everything is random chaos, which is terrifying, but maybe not quite so terrifying as . . .' He shoves his hands into the pockets of his donkey jacket. 'But I know I owe Noah's life to you.'

I slide my arms around him, and feel his tight around me. We stand in the evening light, clinging to each other.

'I'm so sorry,' he whispers. 'I feel such impossible shame.'

It's too late for us. I think he knows that.

•

The night is clear, The Forge dimly lit. It looks just the same as it always did, when I arrived home from work on winter evenings. I can almost imagine that nothing has changed.

If, if, if.

If I could go back in time, would I?

It is exactly ten forty-four on Heidi's thirteenth birthday. Our family are frozen in our various places around the house, the garage, the garden. Two bright-eyed blackbirds pause their hopping and pecking on the lawn. Nicky's phoning, crying out for help, but nobody is answering him.

If, if, if.

And then Noah and my parents erupt through the front door on a foaming wave of relief. Mum and Dad are crying, laughing, *Thank God you're home, Livia, thank God you're home, ooh I could kiss every one of that jury!*

Stars gleam in the indigo depths of the sky. I can make out Orion with Gemini, the twins, on his shoulder. I tilt my head to gaze up at them, while Dad opens a bottle of bubbles and the fizz erupts over the top, and Mum shrieks with laughter, and Heidi is singing as she runs for glasses.

It's a nice idea, though, isn't it? That there's some kind of guidance up there. That it isn't just random chaos.

A celestial road map?

Any kind of road map.

'Just good old humanity, doing what it does,' I say aloud. 'Making a hell of a mess. No road map. No evil master plan.'

Noah can't contain himself. He sets off at top speed, whooping, arms out like an aeroplane as he pelts around and around the pond. I'm entranced by his galloping feet, his flying mop of hair, the mischief in his smile. He has his whole life ahead of him.

It's enough. This is enough.

Acknowledgements

I used to share Livia's commute across the glorious North York Moors. For years, I appeared in those same courts, visited those cells, talked to probation officers much like her. Feels like yesterday. But it *wasn't* yesterday; memories fade, the courts and the law have evolved. So, when it comes to the trial scenes in this story, I owe affectionate thanks to my sister Sarah—aka HHJ Sarah Whitehouse KC—for embracing the plot and being wonderfully enthusiastic and helpful, even from 12,000 miles away. An Old Bailey judge has better things to do than field endless random WhatsApp questions from feckless younger sisters who dump perfectly good careers and run away to the Antipodes—but I got speedy, considered answers every time. She knows her stuff; all inaccuracies, howlers and dramatic liberties taken are my own.

I'm also indebted to Sue Wilkes, for her generous and invaluable help with all my questions about the minutiae of life as a probation officer in North Yorkshire. Once again, all inaccuracies are mine.

I researched and wrote during a post-truth era, in a rapidly changing social landscape, constantly aware that one person's conspiracy theory is another's truth. I can't list the addling throng of websites, forums, blogs, articles, books and platforms I visited, or the generous people who shared their personal stories with me, but I'm grateful to them all. I recommend the work of Marianna Spring, the BBC's disinformation correspondent, especially her podcast *Marianna in Conspiracyland,* and Gabriel Gatehouse's superb podcast *The Coming Storm,* also from the BBC.

Thank you to Tim, and to George, Sam and Cora—my family—who held me by the ankles while I lowered myself into the rabbit hole for two years. To my sister Julia: for unicorn emojis and cheerleading during some of the worst essay crises I've ever had. Espresso Loco in Central Hawke's Bay: your coffee and smiles saved my sanity, time after time. And to Abi Collins: thank you, my dear friend, for bringing Whitby to life.

This book owes its existence to a host of dedicated people. Thank you to Annette Barlow and the team at Allen & Unwin for making the whole thing happen yet again; to Angela Handley for adeptly steering the process and caring about the details; Ali Lavau, who transformed that second draft; Christa Munns for painstaking proofreading; and Clare Drysdale and Kate Ballard in London, whose advice and encouragement on the journey made all the difference.

At David Higham Associates: my heartfelt thanks to Jane Gregory, who got *Home Truths* underway before retiring. Jane, I still feel the privilege and magic of your taking me on, eight books ago. Thanks to Veronique Baxter for such a seamless transition, and to Stephanie Glencross for priceless editorial insight and support.

Home Truths is dedicated to my eldest sister, Hetta Norman. Henrietta. She was once a vibrant young woman with everything going for her—until that May evening in 1984, just before her twenty-eighth birthday, when an accident on her Vespa left her with catastrophic head injuries. Her life was irrevocably shattered in that moment, and so was she. Yet she still had her courage, and soldiered on as the decades passed.

Hetta died on 17 March 2022, after a short illness. Like so many people during the pandemic years, I said goodbye through Facebook Messenger. I don't imagine they'll ever read this, but—unlike Scott, in the story—I thank the ambulance crew and all at St George's Hospital in Tooting who cared for Hetta with skill and compassion. By then I'd already written a detailed synopsis for *Home Truths*, including Nicky's life and death. Any echoes between real life and fiction are purely coincidental.

Hetta's dog, Sebbie, was her constant companion; the slightly eccentric lady and her little black dog a familiar sight on Tooting Common. Perhaps Sebbie wasn't the best behaved of chaps, but he loved her, and she him. He survived her by only a few weeks. I think she'd be pleased to share her dedication with him.